"Selena!"

She couldn't  breathe. But it sou *no . . . no.* She had to be dreaming.

But then suddenly, he was there. *Impossible.* But he was. Somehow, pulling and beating at the monsters that crowded around her. Tearing through them to get to her. *Oh, God, Theo.*

She couldn't think what this would mean, now. Not now. Later.

"Selena," he shouted, as he found her with his eyes from outside the ring. *"Come on!"*

He swung something large and heavy—a massive branch—and it crashed into the skull of one of the *gangas.*

"No!" she shouted at Theo. "Stop!"

Tears stung her eyes, but her battered body wouldn't move . . . she couldn't breathe but she had to stop him before he killed any more of them. "No, please," she cried, trying to make her voice work, even as she grabbed the hand of a creature close to her.

The surge bolted through her, and this time it brought her gasping to her knees. "Go, Theo," she cried when she caught her breath. "Let me do this!"

"I'm not leaving you," he shouted back, and whaled again at the zombies.

Romances by Joss Ware

NIGHT BETRAYED
ABANDON THE NIGHT
EMBRACE THE NIGHT ETERNAL
BEYOND THE NIGHT

Night Betrayed

JOSS WARE

AVON

An Imprint of HarperCollinsPublishers

AVON BOOKS
An Imprint of HarperCollins*Publishers*
10 East 53rd Street
New York, New York 10022-5299

Copyright © 2011 by Joss Ware
ISBN 978-0-06-201863-2
www.avonromance.com

First Avon Books paperback printing: February 2011

Avon Trademark Reg. U.S. Pat. Off. and in Other Countries, Marca Registrada, Hecho en U.S.A.
HarperCollins® is a registered trademark of HarperCollins Publishers.

Printed in the U.S.A.

10 9 8 7 6 5 4 3 2 1

For hospice workers everywhere:
Thank you for your beautiful compassion and care,
as you help our loved ones to find death with dignity.

And for my ninety-three-year-old, superhero grandfather,
Frank Zeits:
If anyone could survive the Change, it would be you.

ACKNOWLEDGMENTS

I always have so many people to thank for their support and energy with each book, and the list continues to grow. I consider myself blessed to have them using their talents and time to help me—including the team at Avon: Erika Tsang, Amanda Bergeron, Pam Jaffee, Christine Maddalena, and everyone else who works behind the scenes to make the Envy books so fantastic. Thank you for your time and energy on my behalf.

I owe a big thanks to Gaylene Murphy, who was the one who suggested a cougar for Theo, and who was definitely right! Thanks, too, to you, Nancy, Jean, and everyone else at NBPR for all of your hard work and dedication for the Envy books.

Special thanks to Mike Wiley, a literal Pinball Wizard, who took me on a tour of his workshop and let me gawk over all of the pinball machines and video games of my youth. And also for his great solution to the zombie problem!

Big hugs and kisses to Robyn Carr, for being there every time I need you.

I can't thank Jeaniene Frost, Nalini Singh, Lara Adrian, and Kathryn Smith enough for being such avid supporters of the Envy books. You ladies are so talented and so busy that I'm humbled by your time and effort toward reading and recommending these books. Thank you!

Also to Kelly Young, for being such an amazingly bright spot in my life . . . and also being there whenever I need someone to lay it all out for me.

Of course, I wouldn't be where I am without the love of Tammy and Holli, who are unfailing and unwavering in their support for my work, and who are so very talented in their own right. Hugs to both of you!

Thanks to Erin Wolfe for being an early reader of Theo's story (and for the line about Electric Man); also to Danita and Jen, Beth, Shae, Donna L., Darlene, Jeannie, Kate and Kayla, and Paula R. for your enthusiasm and support. Thanks to Alex and Becca Wyeth for helping me get into the head of a ten-year-old girl.

And, as always and without fail, so much love to my husband and children for their understanding and acceptance that sometimes Mom gets a little stressed and disorganized, and makes you talk about plots at dinnertime, doesn't do laundry, and insists on carry-out instead of cooking . . . I love you all!

They called her the miracle baby.

There might have been others who were born during the devastating events that annihilated most of the earth in June 2010, but she was the one of legend.

She was born in a concrete-block garage in the midst of raving earthquakes and horrific storms. Three days later, her mother simply passed away, as did nearly all of the other survivors. They had thought they'd made it through the worst. But even after the sun finally rose on a silent world, frosting it with a hopeful, golden glow, they learned the destruction wasn't over.

People dropped to their feet, dead, by the hundreds. Thousands. For no apparent reason.

Yet the pretty baby girl stubbornly lived through it all.

And with the miracle of her birth and survival came a burden and a blessing.

PROLOGUE

When they brought him to Selena, he was already breathing the death rattle.

"Pigment found him covered by a pile of brush," Sam told her. "Sniffed him right out like he was a little rabbit. He doesn't look too good, but . . . I thought at least you could make him more comfortable. Help him along."

She looked at Sam, looked at his young, sad eyes and sighed inwardly. She might be used to the constant face of death, to the "helping along," but he shouldn't be. The brittleness that seemed to settle over her lately felt sharper. *What kind of life am I giving my son?*

"Well, thanks to Pigment," she said, concentrating on a gentle smile. "I hope Tim gave him a treat."

"He's going to give him a rib bone right now, but we wanted to bring him to you first."

"He was alone?" she asked, thinking about the man's family. Surely they'd come along and find him. They'd want to be with him.

Sam nodded. "No one else around. Looked like someone either buried him, thinking he was dead, or hid him. We looked," he added with an earnest gaze.

"All right, then. Thanks, guys," she said, her gratitude encompassing the two other seventeen-year-old boys. "I'll do what I can to make it easier for him."

Selena turned to the man who lay sprawled on one of

the beds, having been deposited there gently yet, with
the enthusiasm of three teenagers, awkwardly. The familiar gray haze of death shimmered around him, but
the afternoon sun pouring through the window sent
waves of lavender filtering through it. What should
have been dull motes of dust sparkled silver and purple
in the light.

She frowned and stared, stepping closer, drawing
her fingers gently through the mist, disturbing the glit-
tery dust. Selena hadn't seen it do that before . . . and
she'd been seeing the death cloud, as she called it, for
as long as she could remember.

Yet she never found the gray miasma frightening;
rather, it was like a cloud enveloping and then cloaking
the body—as if to soften passage into the next world.
While it often sparkled, she had never ever seen it man-
ifest in hues other than gray to blue.

A quick glance around the room told her that everything else remained the same: Jules lay in the corner section, his breathing shallow and quick—rattling faintly
but not as deeply as this new arrival. The haze around
this forty-eight-year-old-man had morphed from gray
to blue, indicating that he'd be gone soon. Most likely
within the next hours. Jules's heavenly guides, visible
only to her and him, of course, sat vigil nearby, waiting
for him to relinquish his last hold on life. One of them
was Jules's daughter, who'd died three years ago in this
very space. His wife, who was still living, had left an
hour ago to tend to their cows and was expected back
soon.

On the other side of the room, cloistered by a blanket
screening off her section, Maryanna's breathing was
nearly silent. The gray vapor around the young woman
wavered, but rose tall and strong, readying itself to

buffer her during the change. Her husband rested next to her, exhausted and ashen-skinned, waiting for the inevitable. She looked more peaceful than he did as he held her small, blue-veined hand in his large one.

Selena's heart squeezed and the edge of emptiness poked her. She pushed it away—for now. She had Sam. And Vonnie. And even Frank.

Later, she would grieve for all of them. But now, she had work to do.

Turning, she checked on little Clara, the sole survivor of a zombie attack in her settlement two years ago. She'd survived that horror only to succumb to a different one. The tumor that distended her belly made her look as if she had an extra pillow under her blankets. She was bathed in the same gentle mist as Maryanna and Jules. And her death cloud had blued as well, though she was conscious, her eyes open and watching Selena from across the room.

"Are you in pain?" Selena asked. "Can I get you some water? A little puff?"

Where the hell is Jen? She should have been back by now. I've got to see if there's any hope for this guy.

But she already knew there wasn't. Once the gray haze came, that was the beginning of the inevitable. Maybe fifty years ago before the Change, when everything was different, there might have been hope.

"No," Clara replied. "I'm just looking at him. His cloud is so pretty. All the sparkles."

Selena smiled at the simplicity and accuracy of the eight-year-old. She wasn't surprised that the girl could see the death cloud. After decades of experience, nothing about the dying surprised her anymore. They were the only ones who really understood.

And, yes indeed, the new arrival *was* pretty—all

covered in faint sparkling lavender and silvery gray. But what did it mean?

She turned her full attention to him. Sam and his friends had tried to be gentle, but they weren't used to carrying and moving the deadweight of a full-grown man, especially one as solid and muscled as this one; and he'd been deposited clumsily, half on his side.

Blood stained his shirt, dried and crusted in places, yet damp and oozing directly over his chest. Already, it colored the blanket beneath him, seeping into an irregularly-shaped spot. One arm, bared by a sleeveless shirt and streaked with blood and grime, had a long red dragon tattooed on it.

Selena glanced at it but didn't have time to look closely because she needed to call Cath, over in Yellow Mountain, to determine if there was anything to be done for him. Usually by the time the sick got to Selena, Cath had already seen them and done what she could.

His breathing shifted, the rattle deepening, sounding like his lungs were filling with fluid. It could be blood or edema, and that meant nothing good. Selena looked at his face, which appeared to be drawn with pain and fatigue. He couldn't be more than thirty.

Young pup.

And a handsome one at that, with shiny black hair cropped short and falling every which way in ragged spikes. Long sideburns framed a face with high cheekbones, and there was more than a bit of Asian in his eyes and skin tone. Full lips, smashed into an almost-pucker as he lay on his side. Nice, rounded muscles on his arms and beneath the hiked-up leg of his jeans.

If I were twenty years younger . . . Oh. And if he weren't dying . . .

Smiling wryly to herself—because, after all if she didn't have a sense of humor in a life like this, she'd be even more screwed up than she was—Selena washed her hands with the lemon-infused soap and reached for his uppermost hip, ready to shift him onto his back. At the last minute, she decided to remove his shirt first. At least she could clean him up, see the injury, and put him in a fresh tunic.

Something fresh in which to die.

She frowned. Humor was all good and well, but lately her thoughts had trailed into unpleasantness more often than not. She needed a change. Or at least some way to find relief and ease from the sadness of her work.

As she removed the grimy, sodden clothing, she saw that he had another dragon tattoo curling down his muscular back. This one was blue, and its single visible eye sparkled down near his hip.

Sparkled?

Selena knelt next to him to get a closer look, unable to help noticing the beginning curve of his butt just below his sagging jeans. Hmm. It was more like a glint than a sparkle. *What in the crazy world* is *that?*

Gingerly, she reached to touch it with her finger.

A fiery, painful jolt shot through her, and she jerked her hand away. "What the hell!"

Selena stared down at him, listening to the ragged, guttural breathing that portended no good and went inexorably on and on. She could see the shine of something metal right there, as if it were embedded in his skin.

Or as if his skin was merely a covering *over* something metal.

Was he some kind of Klingon? A robot?

An Elite?

Heart pounding, she sat back on her haunches, still crouched next to the bed. Could that explain the odd-colored sparkles in his death cloud?

She'd never had an Elite brought to her here—which was no surprise, since, *duh*, Elites were immortal because of the crystals embedded in their bodies. They didn't die, so they didn't need the Death Lady.

But . . . this guy had metal under his skin. Maybe he wasn't even a man after all.

But then why did he have the death cloud? The haze?

He felt warm, he *felt* human. He breathed. He obviously bled. His heart tried to pump, but it was weak and erratic. He was definitely a man.

"Use the crystal."

Selena stiffened so sharply she nearly lost her balance, catching herself with a palm on the rug. She turned. "What did you say?"

Clara had somehow shifted to sit up in her bed. Her eyes in their youthful face were full of wisdom and clarity. "They told me to tell you to use your crystal."

Heart pounding, Selena rose slowly to her feet. No one knew about the crystal except Vonnie. "Who?"

Clara smiled and made a sharp, jerky gesture to the corner near her bed—where her guides, or angels as she preferred to call them, usually appeared. They weren't there, or at least weren't visible to Selena at that moment. "You know," the girl told her. Her smile grew broader, almost beatific. The blue cloud billowed.

Then, suddenly, the light in her eyes faded as if a dense fog slid in front of the sun. A pang of fear stabbed Selena in the gut and she ran.

She got to Clara's side in time to touch her hand. "Clara." *No, oh no.*

It was hard enough watching life ease from the eyes of any person, but it was the most difficult with children. Yet, they were always so brave, so clear-eyed about it. The death haze had deepened; and as she sat there next to the little girl, feeling herself pulled into Clara's blue cloud, she could see Clara's parents in the fog, waiting to help her, and her aunt as well, their images wavering in the distance. Her throat dry, Selena closed her hands over each of the girl's smaller ones and felt warmth ease from Clara's fingers.

At least she would be with her parents now.

As the life slipped away and Clara's muscles relaxed, waves of her memories came to Selena. Images, visions, feelings; in short, jerky vignettes and dreamlike moments flooded into her mind, prickling like a million pin-needles as she absorbed them. She fought back tears and accepted them. This part of her calling was the most intimate, the most difficult . . . and yet, the most beautiful.

At last, the little girl's hands went soft and limp. Her breathing stopped. Her little heart rested.

The blue haze disintegrated.

And Selena closed the young, wise eyes with two gentle thumbs, then wiped her own.

She didn't know how long she sat there, looking down at the serene little face with its wispy hair brushed back from the temples, doing her private grieving, her prayers and memorials, but suddenly a gasp from the corner pulled her out of her silence.

Selena was up and away from the small body in a flash, but by then it was too late. The dragon man gave a violent shudder, his eyes closed as if in pain, and a last desperate breath. And then . . . nothing.

She bent, tucking her ear to his chest. Silence. No

heartbeat. No faint heave from the lungs. The haze disintegrated, leaving nothing but a few last sparkling dust motes in the air.

He was dead.

And she didn't know who he was or where he belonged.

Chapter 1

"What the hell do you mean, you *lost* Theo?" Lou Waxnicki heard his own voice rise and crack, not with age but with fear and disbelief. He looked up at the massive man looming over him. For once, Fence didn't have that devil-may-care glint in his eyes.

In fact, the guy looked downright miserable, and the misery had nothing to do with the streaked blood dried on his coffee-colored face or the way he cradled his left arm. Lou saw the red and swelling flesh on his chin and arms and knew it would turn purple and green with bruising by the next day. He'd been in some hellacious fight, but the real misery was in his eyes, bloodshot and dull with pain.

"And Quent? Where the hell is he?" Lou demanded, but in a marginally lower voice. "Did he find his father?"

Theo was Lou's twin brother, and Theo and Fence had insisted on going with Quent on his suicidal mission—to find Quent's father, one of the leaders of the immortal Elite.

Sage rose from her computer chair and placed her cool hands on Lou's shoulders, a thumb brushing the edge of his gray ponytail. "What happened?" she asked, squeezing gently in a silent suggestion of patience. Her fingers, strong from working on keyboards day after day, were firm and sure.

And how frail he felt, even to himself, under those

slim fingers. How old and frail. Both he and Theo were seventy-eight years old, but through a crazy twist of fate, Theo had been affected physically so that he'd hardly aged in the last fifty years. He still looked the same as he had when the cataclysmic events of the Change had occurred, leaving Lou to appear more like his grandfather than his twin.

"We were captured by one of the bounty hunters and Theo was shot. Bad. In the chest," Fence said, looking at Lou steadily. "The only hope was to get him back here to see if Elliott could save—uh, fix—him 'cause there wasn't anything else to be done. Quent went on to find Fielding while I brought Theo back here to Envy. He was bad off, and I was goin' so fast when I—"

A little tone from the computer in the corner had Lou and Sage both glancing over. The chime played the first few bars of the *Mission Impossible* theme—one of Theo's little jokes since he knew how much his twin hated the Tom Cruise movie—but even from where he sat, Lou could see that the email wasn't from Theo. It was an automated update from one of the thirty network access points that had been secretly installed around a fifty-mile radius of Envy.

His sharp peal of hope ebbed.

"Long story short, I had to put Theo down and hide him." Fence had continued as if nothing had interrupted the conversation—but then, he probably wasn't as attuned as Lou and Sage were to every single sound made by the dozen PCs and Macs. "I was fixing to come back for him right away, but then I did a number through the floor of the building. Banged my head pretty good. When I woke up, I had to climb my ass out of there, and when I got back to where I left him, Theo was gone."

"No clue where he went?"

"He sure as shit didn't get up and walk away, Lou. And it wasn't an animal that got him, or a zombie, 'cause they'd have left evidence." Fence's temper, which, truthfully, seemed more aimed at himself than Lou, appeared to abate as he smoothed a hand over his bald head. "I looked everywhere but couldn't find hide nor hair of him. He disappeared good."

"But he was shot," Lou said, taking care with his words. Because the reality was starting to sink in. "He wouldn't last long without medical treatment."

"No." Fence's voice was a barely audible whisper. "I can't see him making it without Elliott's help."

Which was the big guy's way of saying he was dead. Theo was dead.

No.

Theo was indestructible. He had more lives than a cat.

No.

Lou pulled to his feet, feeling every seventy-eight-year-old joint creak in protest. Some days he felt as young as his brother looked—which was to say, thirty-ish. But on a day like today, he felt older than God.

"I'll get Jade and Elliott," Sage said, already starting toward the exit of their secret subterranean computer room. "Simon will want to go too, and Wyatt . . . to look for Theo." She glanced at Fence.

He nodded, his dark face weary but his eyes sharp. "Yeah. It's a day trip from here."

"I'm coming this time," Lou said, his voice flat. "I'm not staying back here again."

Sage opened her mouth to argue, but Lou wasn't about to listen to her. "I'm fucking going. End of story."

And then he closed his eyes for a moment and felt.

Reached out for that tangible thread that connected him and Theo, that same thread that had told him his twin had survived the Change too. The thread that had drawn him closer and closer to his brother until he'd found him.

For the first time, he felt nothing. The thread was broken.

Lou opened his eyes and realized that he was alone.

Use the crystal.

Selena gazed down at the man, beautiful even in death with his smooth, faintly sheened olive skin and thick dark lashes.

It's too late.

Yet, something compelled her to move toward the small chest in the corner where she dozed while on watch during the night. She'd put the crystal in there this morning, which was unusual, since she usually kept it safely in her room.

She opened the latch and dug out the small jagged piece of pale rose-colored stone. It felt warm to the touch; and for a moment, Selena indulged anger and guilt. If she'd moved faster, not needed to attend to Clara, would it have made a difference for him?

Use the crystal.

But how? Even if it wasn't too late, what could she have done with it? It wasn't used to heal people.

The translucent stone, which was about the size of her thumb, had dark red veins deep inside. Selena looked down at it, and the gem seemed to grow warmer as she stared. *Because my hand's closed around it, of course.*

Or not.

She'd had it for as long as she could remember. According to Vonnie, when Selena was found, the crystal had been wedged inside her swaddling blankets, beneath her arm. By accident or design, no one knew. For years, Selena had kept it tucked away in her personal effects, having convinced herself that it belonged to Lena, the name she'd given to the woman who'd given birth to her during the Change. Whether it was or wasn't, she didn't know. But she *did* know that there had always been a small pink mark under her arm about the size of that stone.

When she was eighteen, she'd discovered its power and purpose. There were days when she wished she hadn't—when she wondered . . . *Why me?*

Selena glanced automatically toward the window, checked the sun's position, and a shiver prickled over her. Night would come soon.She forced herself to turn from the window, smoothing her thumb over the crystal. Despite its power, she didn't see how it could help in this situation. He was a man, not a zombie.

Gripping the red-veined stone, Selena returned to the dragon man's bed. He still lay half on his side, having shifted during his last moments of life. One leg, sturdy and powerful-looking, lay sprawled half over the other one, bared by the hiked-up leg of his jeans.

As before, Selena's attention was caught by the fierce blue dragon curling down his sleek back, ending in the glint of its eye.

A little prickle zipped up her arm from the hand that held the rose stone. Almost like a spark. Or a really sharp nudge.

She gasped, not from pain or even surprise, but from realization. Understanding . . . *Oh—*

Huh . . . Really?

Wetting her lips, chewing on the lower one nervously, she adjusted her grip on the stone and settled it against the dragon's eye. Closed her eyes. And prayed.

A fiery shock jolted her eyes open just in time for her to see the man arch, recoil and snap once like a whip, and then collapse back onto the bed. She stared: at the crystal she still held; at the smooth-skinned, *heaving* chest that was now fully visible; and up along his tense, corded throat to his parted lips and higher.

He opened his eyes.

"Bang," said Selena. "And holy shit."

Theo's brain was filled with mush, like the gray, gloppy oatmeal his mom used to make him and Lou eat for breakfast in the winter. The only way it had been palatable had been when they drowned it in brown sugar, dried cherries, and lots of milk.

He looked around the room, trying to remember how he'd come to be here. Or even where he was. The place was unfamiliar, with light-colored sheets of fabric hanging from the ceiling as if to cordon off a private space for his bed. The window next to him indicated it was early in the morning or getting toward night. A floral-scented breeze filtered through.

The low murmur of voices told him he wasn't alone, but because of the privacy, he couldn't see anyone. *Is this some sort of hospital? An old house that had been made into a hospital?* Pretty damn big house, from what he could tell. Ceilings were high and the window next to him was tall and wide. He tried to sit up to look outside and see if the exterior looked familiar, but he was too weak and his head spun.

So Theo focused on what he knew, closing his eyes

in concentration. Memory flashes blitzed through his mind: riding on horseback in the cool, green forest with Quent and Fence . . . the confrontation with the bounty hunter named Seattle, and the unexpected fire flooding his chest and beyond. He'd been shot.

Then . . . sluggishness and swirling gray behind his eyes. A soft voice, light hands, fleeting memories of daylight and nighttime, of something warm and liquid trickling between his lips.

Sage.

He drew her face, her brilliant, fiery red hair and clear aqua eyes into his memory like a comforting blanket. He had books for her in his pack, didn't he?

Theo opened his eyes, staring at a small crack in the ceiling as he concentrated . . . and then another wave of memory flooded him, followed by a crash of pain. Dull and heavy, it settled in his belly.

Sage had chosen Simon.

Right.

Theo squeezed his eyes closed, turning his head to the side as if to avoid the knowledge. That was why he'd been so eager to go with Quent and Fence on the mission. To get away from Envy, away from Sage and Simon and the intimate glances between them. And the passing touches, so casual and easy. And, most of all, the underlying glow of happiness on her face.

He became aware, suddenly, that he wasn't alone. Something shifted in the air and the change brought a flowery scent with it. Theo opened his eyes and found a woman standing near the edge of the bed, looking down at him.

He couldn't really consider her old, because she was probably younger than he was, although he didn't look any older than thirty. He guessed her to be about sixty, based on the delicate lines crisscrossing her cheeks and the bit of sag in her jawline. A young sixty, but still, eighteen years younger than he was in actual years.

And such long, long years they had been, these last fifty. Living in a world that had been fairly razed to the ground and slowly rebuilt.

The woman, who was soft and rounded with age, had heavy dark hair liberally streaked with white that curled in a crazy mop around her face and jaw. Her green-brown eyes danced with energy and her mouth formed what seemed like a perpetual smile. She was holding a cluster of silvery green leaves in one hand and a mug with a spoon sticking out of it in the other. "You're awake," she said, stating the obvious, then turned away to call to someone in the distance. "He's awake again!" The spoon clanked.

Then, as if she hadn't just split his eardrums, she drew up a chair, pulling it close and settling on it with enthusiasm. The spoon clattered in the mug again as she shifted even closer. "You've been in and out of consciousness for the last three days. But this is the clearest I've seen your eyes, so maybe you'll stay awake for a bit, hm?"

Theo wasn't ready to try his voice yet, so he nodded once. The smell coming from whatever was in that mug made his stomach convulse. He was damned hungry and he hoped it was for him.

To his disappointment, she put the mug on the table next to him and gestured with the bundle of pungent leaves. They were oblong and slender, with a pebbled texture and smelled a bit musty, almost skunky. "We weren't sure what you wanted with these," she said, waving them in front of him. "Do you want us to make tea or put them in that—it's broth," she said, jerking her thumb at the cup. "Or do you just eat them? Like a salad?"

Theo stared at her, trying to make sense of her words. But he couldn't, so he had to try his voice—which, it turned out, worked pretty well. "What is it?"

The woman settled back in her chair, surprised. "Why, it's sage. You've been asking for it, haven't you? Took us a few days to find it, but . . ."

Theo had already turned away; and if it was possible for a sick man to flush, he was doing it. *Oh, Jesus.* "Could I just have the broth," was all he said. "I'm hungry."

"Of course," she told him, and to his relief, she set the cluster of leaves down on the table.

He'd had three good spoonfuls of the most delicious broth he'd ever tasted when another woman appeared from behind the curtainlike walls. Though he was more interested in the soup than this new arrival, Theo's first impression of her was one of peaceful energy.

Which seemed like an oxymoron, but he was going by half-formed first impressions in a still gloppy-gray brain. Other things filtered through the mush: the fact that she was younger than the first woman, with long, thick dark brown hair; more spare in build, not quite as boisterous and energetic . . . but capable. *Capable, peaceful, serene.*

She came up to the bed and stood next to it, staring down as if she'd never seen him before. And maybe she hadn't; how the hell would he know. "You're really alive," she said. Wonder in her voice. "How do you feel?"

"Hungry," he said, opening his mouth enough for the spoon to slip in. Suddenly, he felt odd lying there with two women gazing down at him, being spoon-fed like he was a baby.

"I'll take over," she said, turning to the older woman. "Thanks, Vonnie."

Vonnie stood with the same alacrity with which she'd sat, bumping against the bed as she moved out of the way to make room for the newer arrival. "I'll go check on Maryanna."

"She seems to be in pain. Maybe you could burn a little for her? She's not ready to go yet." Her voice sounded a little taut, but how would Theo know what her voice normally sounded like? "And Sam's complaining about being hungry."

"So what else is new?" Vonnie said, bustling from the sheet-enclosed carrel. She gave a little laugh and a toss of her hand as she passed by the outside of the area, making the fabric billow a bit. "I'll handle it. Take your time, Selena."

Selena had lifted a spoonful of broth, but Theo, feeling ridiculous and also a bit like an insect pinned to a corkboard from the way she was looking at him, hauled himself into a more upright position. "I can feed myself. Thank you."

She handed him the mug and spoon without comment and watched silently as he ignored the spoon and sipped from the mug.

"You died three days ago," she said after a moment.

Theo's head hurt, and so, suddenly, did his chest. His everywhere. *Surreal.* That was all he could think. This was surreal. Sitting in a place where he didn't know anyone, having no idea how he got there, being nursed by a woman named Selena, being told he died. Three days ago.

With a fucking bunch of *sage* sitting on the table next to him.

He wasn't sure whether to laugh or cry.

"Am I dead now?" was the only thing he could think of to say. He could be in heaven. Or wherever you went before you went there—because, God knew, he wasn't perfect. He certainly wasn't in hell. Because that had been back in Envy, watching Sage and Simon.

Selena shook her head. "No. I brought you back to life."

Theo slammed the mug back too hard and choked on a healthy gulp of broth. Being brought back to life was an impossibility in this world. It might have happened before the Change, back before June of 2010, when there were shock treatments and defibrillators and emergency rooms . . . but not here.

Although . . . didn't Lou claim he'd resurrected him when he found him in the subterranean chamber during the Change? He'd made jokes about bringing Theo back to life by waking him from what had been a comalike sleep.

Theo swallowed. "How did you do that?" he asked, keeping his voice as nonchalant as hers had been.

"I'm not sure," she replied, and her eyes crinkled a bit at the corners. A little smile, a bit rueful and even bemused, it created a few more delicate lines near the corners of her mouth. Not dimples, not wrinkles . . . but life lines. He realized suddenly that she could be in her forties, even.

"It was a sort of miracle," she continued. "A definite miracle. It's never happened before. But you were definitely dead. For a good . . . five, ten minutes."

Theo found he didn't really like that idea after all. He hadn't actually died last time, had he? He closed his eyes, then opened them again—and noticed that her eyes, focused on him, were a light, rich brown. The color of caramel or brandy.

"Maybe you want to tell me your name so I don't have to call you Miracle Man? Or Dragon Guy?"

"Theo."

"Well, welcome back to the living, Theo," Selena said. She shifted in her seat and Theo revised his guess at her age. Definitely no older than forty. Not with a golden body that tight and curvy. Maybe even early thirties. *Look at those arms.*

"How do you feel? Besides hungry?" she asked.

"Tired and sore," he replied, pulling himself up a bit more. "Fuzzy-headed. Where am I, by the way?"

She'd picked up that damned bunch of sage and was smoothing her fingers over the long oval leaves. "Near Yellow Mountain."

Yellow Mountain. It rang a distant bell, but the gloppiness prevented him from focusing. "I'm from Envy. Do you know where that is?"

Selena shrugged and flapped a hand. "That way? I've had people come from all over, Envy included. I don't ask the details; it's enough that they're here."

Theo smelled something, and it distracted him for a moment. A familiar smell, sweet and unmistakable, wafting in the air. He sniffed again, just to be sure. "Is that marijuana?"

She nodded, taking the empty mug from him. "Yes. Would you like some?" She smiled, then added, "I meant, would you like some more soup? Unless you're in pain, and then I'll have Vonnie bring the bong over when she's done with Maryanna. It seems to help her; and if there's anything I can do to make things easier, I will."

All righty, then. It wasn't as if pot was illegal anymore. The laws in this world were fairly nonexistent, especially outside of Envy, which was the largest known settlement of humans.

"I'm not in pain. But I could eat some more."

And then all of a sudden, the murkiness slipped away enough for him to realize who she was. "*You're* the Death Lady."

A little humorless smile twitched her lips, and she nodded. "Yes, that's what they call me."

He'd heard of her, this woman who spent her life sitting with people as they died, caring for and helping them. Like a post-Change hospice, he guessed. And since there weren't any real doctors and certainly no hospitals, let alone drugs or surgeries, Theo knew just how busy she must be. And how important her role was. He'd heard about her back in Envy, and on his missions beyond those safe walls as he tried to add members to the secret Resistance movement and set up network access points to build their version of the post-Change Internet.

"How the hell did you ever—" he started, then realized his tone made him sound like an ass, so he amended, softening his voice. "How did you get started doing this?"

Selena put the mug down and settled in her chair, folding her arms under the breasts that filled out her T-shirt quite nicely. "Most of my patients—I guess you'd call them that—don't talk much, and certainly don't ask me such pointed questions. But then again, everyone else who's ever come to me has left this world and crossed over to the other. So I guess you're just different all around."

"So, yeah. Since you brought me back to life, you've only yourself to blame. You coulda let things alone, you know." He cracked a rueful smile.

She looked at him thoughtfully. "I sure could have," she replied, nodding as if some great mystery were revealed in his eyes. "But I was told how to save you, so I did."

"You were told to save me. Dare I ask by whom? And how?"

Selena rose and picked up the mug, the spoon clinking once more. "You can ask, but I think I'll keep that to myself. I'll get you more soup, and if you're really nice, I'll tell you how I got to be named after a female wizard."

With that, she turned and walked out of the area before he had a good chance to really check her out.

Nothing surprised him more than the vague disappointment that he hadn't.

Guess I'm not dead yet.

Selena scooped up the broth, which had been made from peppers, carrots, and onions, roasted then simmered in water and wine and flavored with celery, parsley, and garlic. It smelled delicious and set her mouth to watering. And Theo had certainly enjoyed the soup if the way he slurped it down was any indication.

But being brought back to life . . . not so much.

Not a bit of gratitude.

He didn't come out and *say* it, but she sensed it. There was some reluctance to return to this world, this plane.

There were some who fought death, and some who went easily—it depended upon whether they had unfinished business here or not. But this one . . . this dragon man . . . he'd done neither. He just seemed ready. Tired.

Why did you tell me to save him? She looked around, reflexively up toward the ceiling, even though the guides usually sat or stood at eye level. As if there'd be an answer. She'd been asking why for forty years, and she'd never had a clear one yet.

But occasionally, the guide she'd come to think of as her own guardian angel would appear. Not giving answers to why, of course . . . just guidance. Just as she had the first time she had experienced the death cloud—or at least the first time she remembered doing so.

Selena was five years old, sitting next to an old woman out in a field and making daisy chains while Vonnie picked raspberries with the old woman's daughter. The old woman seemed dry as an old stick, ready to blow away in the breeze, shriveled into herself in peaceful silence. Her eyes were watery but bright, and she spoke very little, but mostly not at all. Her hair was white, with a bit of gray threading through it.

Selena remembered chattering on and on to the old woman when the blond-haired woman who often came to help her and Vonnie appeared, sitting on the grass. At that time, she thought little of the fact that the mysterious Wayren often materialized like a puff of air; it was just the way she came and went. As Selena had come to learn since, children were much more accepting of the presence of guides and angels than their older counterparts.

"Watch," Wayren had told her, her pale blond hair shining in the sun. She always seemed to have a happy glow around her, but that day it seemed to grow larger and larger . . . and eventually encompassed the elderly woman.

Selena saw the glittering in the sunlight, the little sparkles around the woman. Silver and gray, and then bluish, spinning, whirling, spiraling up.

"It's pretty," she said.

Wayren nodded. "No one can see it but you. It's a gift. But more than that, it's a responsibility. Now . . . hold her hand, for she'll need you to help her. She's about to leave us."

Selena didn't understand how the woman was going to leave if she held her hand, but she did as her guide said. Grasping fragile, skinny fingers, she looked into the elderly woman's gray-brown eyes.

The flurry of glittering gray and blue fog grew larger and she knew something was going to happen. "Hold on to my hand," Selena said, not knowing what prompted those words. "I'll be here."

And so it had happened. Selena hadn't been frightened, or even particularly sad. She gained those attributes as she grew older and began to understand what it meant to the people left behind.

It took her longer to realize what Wayren had meant about it being a responsibility—that it was something she must employ, must use to help people find their way from life into death. She helped ease their discomforts—pains physical and, more importantly, emotional and spiritual.

But the greatest part of her calling she didn't learn until she was much older, when she discovered the power of the crystal and what she had to do with it.

Giving herself a little mental shake, and coming back to the present, Selena gathered up Theo's refilled mug and a clean spoon. After a moment of thought, she added a hunk of bread studded with sunflower seeds to a small plate. He looked hungry enough. As she passed by the window, she couldn't ignore that the sun had lowered to rest on the horizon, an infinite expanse away.

Darkness in a few hours. Night seemed to come so much more quickly lately. Too quickly.

She'd have to go out into it too. Find whatever zombies she could—or have them find her. Selena looked into the distance, toward the purple-gray jut of the mountains, the dull green of forest, and the boxy shapes of ruined buildings studding the space between. *So peaceful. Now.*

But soon . . .

I could stay in tonight.

The temptation seized her, tightened like a vise on her throat. *Just one night.*

She could sit with her patients, she could even exchange jokingly rude comments with miraculous Theo, watch him gulp down more soup. Maybe even see if he'd give her a decent game of chess since no one else could; or if he'd try and figure out how to fix the old DVD player that had finally ground to a halt.

Staring at the long shadows, and at the same time watching for the hulking movements of the zombies, Selena's shoulders tightened. She felt as if her muscles would snap at the slightest movement.

She knew she couldn't save them all. Of course she couldn't save them all. Just as she couldn't ease every dying person into the next plane.

She could stay in.

But I wouldn't, dammit.

She would't.

Because it was her gift. And her responsibility.

CHAPTER 2

When Theo battled through the dreams and dragged his eyes open, it was dark. But this time, he didn't need a moment to recall where he was.

"Ruuu-uuuthhhh. Ruthhhhhh."

The distant, mournful cries of the zombie-like *gangas* filtered through the silence, and at first he thought they'd followed him from out of his dreams. The window next to Theo was open; a fresh night breeze streamed over his clammy skin. Damp and sticky he was, from the memories of death and destruction, as vivid and horrifying now as they had been in reality fifty years ago . . . and over all the years since. He closed his eyes, trying to banish the remnants of the nightmares that clung like stubborn moss. They wouldn't release him.

They didn't come every night, not anymore. But often enough that he had to drag himself free, and that the nights he didn't, he awoke grateful for a full sleep.

"Ruuuuuuuthhhh."

The hair on his body rose when he realized the groaning monsters were the real ones, out there somewhere in the night.

Still prone, he stared out the window, able to see only the black sky twinkling with stars. In the distance, he could make out a few awkward shadows with orange eyes, lurching and lost, beyond the other side of the safe wall enclosing the area. Zombie-like *gangas*, searching for a man named Remington Truth.

And somewhere out there, beyond, miles away, was Envy. And Sage.

With Simon.

Theo's mouth twisted, flattened, in the dark where there was no one to witness his weakness. His heart hurt. Emptied. *Why not me?*

And what now? It would be a long time until he could bear seeing her with someone else.

From beyond the gently wafting blanket walls, Theo heard soft muttering, likely a fellow patient, followed by the rustle of bedding. Someone murmured back, low and soothing, and he wondered if it was the Death Lady crooning to one of her charges. *What exactly did she do besides hold their hands and offer them pot?*

What a depressing job. Watching people die. His mouth flattened again.

He'd seen enough suffering and death in his lifetime; more than most people of his generation would have ever expected. And he had so often relived the tragedies in dreams and memories that he couldn't imagine *choosing* to face them every single day.

And yet . . . that woman, the Death Lady, had a peaceful, accepting aura about her.

Other than her offering of a replenishment of his broth, along with a hunk of thick, dark bread, Selena hadn't made another appearance—at least not in Theo's carrel. But her friend, the older, plumper woman whose name was Vonnie, had come by several times before night fell and the lights were turned off. She'd helped him wash up and get comfortable, all the while chattering on about . . . well, everything. To his mind, she seemed much too light and enthusiastic to be hanging around dying people all the time—knowing there was nothing that could be done for them but watch them in pain and weakness.

Within Vonnie's nonstop prattle, she made a point of saying more than once that never before had one of Selena's patients recovered as Theo had, which led him to his own snarly, grumpy thoughts: *So why change her track record now?*

And who the hell had seen fit to resurrect me from the dead—a second time? Wasn't once enough?

Theo sighed and stared at the ceiling. Okay, so here he was again: should have been dead; brought back to life— *For what? And why me?*

Hell, he'd asked these questions for the last fifty years, and hadn't gotten an answer yet. He'd been searching for the reason he'd been transformed—or not—and the purpose. He'd been going through life since then, watching and waiting for some great event to explain it all.

But nothing. Just days and days and years and years of trying to get beyond the horror of losing everything he'd ever known, except for Lou.

Lou.

Dammit.

His twin was probably worried beyond sick. And Theo had hardly given him a thought, being dead and all.

Though it wasn't as if he hadn't squeaked by death before. Lou said Theo had more lives than a cat, and that had been even before the Change. And since then . . . well, only a month ago, he'd been trapped by *gangas* in an old shopping mall with Elliott. And that was only the most recent brush he'd had with the Grim Reaper—other than this one.

He really had tried to curb his recklessness, his yen for adventure, in hopes that he and Sage would get together. She was quiet and studious and shy, and he hadn't wanted to intimidate or worry her. But that had obviously not mattered—because Simon was a man with a past of violence and death.

Now, in darkness cut only by the wisp of moonlight and a distant glow beyond the cloth dividers, Theo pulled himself upright with sharp, frustrated movements. Easier to do now anyway, when he couldn't see the room spinning quite so well. Head pounding. *Ugh*.

He had to contact his brother. His feet touched the floor, identifying some sort of bumpy, soft covering. He shifted off the edge of the bed . . . and had to grab at the table to keep himself from crashing to the floor as his knees buckled.

Guess I was only mostly dead. The reference to the old movie made him smile in spite of himself, and he imagined Lou responding, *Have fun storming the castle!*

Seated on the edge of the bed, once again stable, Theo closed his eyes and extended a tentative thought, searching for Lou in his subconscious or whatever it was that connected the two of them so closely.

That was why Lou hadn't ever stopped searching for Theo after the Change. They'd both been in Vegas together, working on that high-level computer security project for Casino Venuto. They liked to tell people they did stuff like in *Ocean's Eleven* or *Ocean's Thirteen* (never *Ocean's Twelve*, because that movie sucked).

After all hell broke loose, Lou claimed he knew Theo was still alive. What he didn't know at first was that Theo was buried, three levels below ground in a computer safe-room under Venuto. Theo had not only survived the Change, but he'd been physically altered.

After the Change, Theo's body was almost frozen in time; he hadn't aged for decades . . . or, at least, had aged but very, very slowly. His nails and stubble hardly grew at all for the first thirty years; and the day he'd found his first gray hair—long after Lou had gone white—was a time of celebration for Theo. But this wasn't the extent of the changes to his body that had occurred in the computer safe-room, deep below the surface of Vegas. Something else had happened during the cataclysmic events, when everything in the room of mainframes and computers and wires had exploded and shifted and sizzled into darkness . . .

When Theo woke up, he'd found his body battered, bruised, and lacerated. And, in the lower part of his back, a wound that took too long to heal. It wasn't until weeks after Lou had dragged him from beneath the ground that Theo realized a small integrated circuit had become embedded there in the soft flesh at the back of his hip. And it wasn't until weeks later that Theo realized this little IC could send a surge of energy through his body at will.

He was, in short—*Holy shock-me-Batman, let me light your fire!*—a superhero: Theo the Energizer.

Now, miles away from the place he'd considered home for fifty years, that connection was still there with Lou. Theo reached out, felt that little sizzle of awareness . . . and just as it connected, he drew in a deep breath . . . felt his brother . . . and that wave of familiarity. *Hey.*

Theo! The response was immediate, and Theo felt a wave of guilt for not remembering to contact him sooner.

I'm here. I'm fine. Tired. Safe. His reply wasn't so

much sent in words but in sensations and feelings. They understood and read each other thus.

Thank God! Worried, damn you!

Theo nodded to himself. *Sorry. More later.*

Hands closed tightly over his knees, he stared into the dark and allowed the connection to sever. He wasn't ready for more, yet. Nothing more than that brief *Yo, I'm here and safe.* That, at least, would keep his brother from coming to look for him. Bringing Simon.

He needed . . . time. Time to figure out what he was. Who he was.

And why in the hell he'd been resurrected, so to speak, for a second time.

"Ruuuuuthhhhhhh."

The groans pulled his attention back to the world outside.

Holding on to the bed and then the table, he leaned toward the window, then braced himself as he thrust his head through its opening. The cool breeze, tinged with the foul scent of rotting *ganga* flesh, brushed over him.

The flicker of orange lights, always in pairs, caught his attention. They might be coming closer, but the zombies were far beyond the wall that had been erected around this . . . building. *A large house? Maybe some sort of apartment building?* Theo hadn't seen enough to be able to tell exactly what it was, and now it was too dark.

But whatever it was, he and the other occupants of the structure were safe from the *gangas*. They couldn't climb, so there was no way they could get over the walls. And even if they were smart enough to find an entrance, they'd never be able to figure out how to open a gate or door.

Stupid, slow, and single-minded, the zombies never-theless were tall and strong—and a threat to everyone. They fed on human flesh, tearing into it and leaving nothing behind but piles of bone and tendons. The only way to destroy them was to smash their brain; though they were afraid of fire and light, they were impervi-ous to it, to falling, or to bullets or even knives. Bottle bombs had become the defense weapon of choice for humans, knowing that the explosion would destroy many at one time.

The darkness wasn't spinning any longer, and Theo pulled carefully to his feet. Still holding the edge of the table, his fingers brushing the wilted sage leaves, he paused to get his bearings.

Moved by curiosity as well as the mundane desire to relieve himself, Theo eased toward the entrance to his corner of the hospice. The fact that he remained upright emboldened him further, and he walked with more confidence beyond the dividing wall.

There he found that he was in a sort of corridor that was made up of more sheets. Dark spaces between the colorless fabric walls indicated other "rooms" or spaces for patients, and Theo paused to determine which way might take him to a lavatory. Or at least something more interesting than billowing blankets hung from a high ceiling.

A noise in the distance caught his attention. It wasn't the muffled voice he'd heard earlier, nor did it sound like someone soothing another in pain.

It sounded like . . . *urgency.* That was the only thing he could think of to describe the dull noise, quick and short, followed by the low snap of a voice. And another in sharp response.

Despite his weakened state, Theo moved quite

rapidly down the hall toward the sounds. A thump and bump reached his ears as he walked through an entrance—an actual entrance in the building not one constructed of blankets or sheets—and found himself in another room. Beyond it, he saw the gleam of metal counters; and farther on, a sink. *A kitchen.* So he was in a dining room, perhaps, and there ahead was a kitchen.

A huge one, he saw when he got closer, with a large island in the center and gleaming countertops stretching for miles. The voices, low and staccato with need, came from a dark corner somewhere in there. He paused when he heard one of them say, "Shush. You'll wake—"

"I don't care," replied another low one, this with anger spiking it. "You've got to stop doing this. My *saints.* Look at you." The volume rose, sharp with fear, and Theo recognized Vonnie's voice. No longer sounding enthusiastic or sunny.

"I didn't finish. I've got to—"

"No. You're not."

He peered around the corner and saw two figures struggling in the corner. Not with each other; that was immediately clear in the dim light from over the kitchen sink. No. The larger, cushier one had her arm around the slighter one and was moving awkwardly toward the island counter. The fall of sleek dark hair identified Selena as the one staggering in a steadying embrace.

Something gleamed on the front of her clothing. Something dark and shiny. *Wet.*

"What happened?" Theo said. He couldn't call what he did *bursting* into the room, but he moved pretty quickly considering that he'd been dead three days ago.

Both faces lifted to look at him, a pale circle and a

shadowed oval marred by dark streaks. Shock widened two sets of eyes. A slash of light bounced over unbound hair and a face tight with pain.

"What are you doing out of bed?" Vonnie said, looking as if she'd been caught with her hand in some cookie jar. "Go back now."

Theo suspected that Selena would have looked furious if she hadn't been moving so slowly due to the *blood* that shone and glistened on her shirt and face. She opened her mouth to say something, but whatever it was turned into a gasp as her companion clumsily bumped her into the edge of the counter.

Theo was there in a heartbeat, shoving Vonnie out of the way and sliding Selena's arm around his shoulder. Despite her agitated attempts at protest—which included a feeble shove at him and a muttered, "Go back to bed"—he easily got her to a chair in the corner of the kitchen. It was only then that he realized the room was tilting a bit and that his knees threatened to give way again, but there was no chance in hell he was going to let them go right now.

"What the hell happened to you?" he asked, clutching the counter as an overhead light came on.

"I'm fine," Selena said with a definite glare as she sagged in the chair. "You shouldn't—be out of—bed." The hitch in her voice told him that she was struggling to keep her breath steady.

Once relieved of her awkward burden and turning on the light, Vonnie had metamorphosed into calm efficiency. Water splashed in the sink and cupboard doors thumped and banged as she, presumably, searched for first aid supplies.

But from what Theo could see, Selena needed more than simple first aid. "Where are you hurt?" he asked, plucking at her shirt with one hand while steadying himself against the counter with his other.

He realized it was testament to her weakness that she allowed him to yank at her shirt after trying so hard to push him away only moments before. In fact, she tilted her head back, eyes shuttering, and leaned against the wall behind her. And let him have his way, so to speak.

Theo hadn't undressed a woman in more than a year, but there was nothing about this moment of tearing (literally) the blood-soaked shirt from her body that he found erotic. Beneath the tatters of the thin cotton, he found gashes in her left shoulder, nearly to the top of her breast. He also noted that she wore surprisingly interesting lingerie, a rarity in this world—lacy pink shells, one of which was now dark with her blood.

Ganga slashes. Deep and ragged.

"Out of my way," Vonnie said, barreling over. Theo complied and she snatched in a horrified gasp when she saw the four bloody slashes. "My God," she breathed. "Selena. You've got to stop. *You've got to stop.*"

The other woman hissed—a warning, or was it the pain? And rolled her head from side to side in a quick jerk of negation. But that didn't keep Theo from asking, "Doing what?"

What the hell was so important that she had to go out of the walls at night? Alone? Even Theo, who'd done his share of ballsy and crazy things over the years, rarely took such a chance.

"I'm going to have to send for Cath this time," Vonnie said, her voice unsteady as she stared at the gashes without making any move to touch them. A cloth dripping with steaming water dangled in her hand.

"*No.*"

"Who's Cath?" Theo asked, maneuvering Vonnie

out of the way so he could examine the wound. He'd seen and treated more than a few *ganga* marks in the last fifty years—and those people were the lucky ones.

These gashes were deep but not life threatening, that he could tell—unless they got infected, which was a real possibility, considering where those filthy, flesh-tearing hands had been. She'd need stitches probably. "What do you have to put on them?" he asked, taking the warm cloth from Vonnie's hand. "Any alcohol?"

"Cath's the closest thing we have to a doctor," Vonnie told him, coming back to life as Theo began to gently dab at the gashes. "Here. We have this balm to put on it. I'll get bandages." She set a lidless jar on the counter next to them and bustled away.

"Yeah," Selena said, her voice tight, her face raised back to the ceiling after her emphatic negation a moment earlier. Other than that, she seemed unmoved as Theo shifted a pink bra strap out of the way. "Cath gets to save the ones who can be saved. I get to watch the rest die."

The bra strap hung, useless, halfway down a toned arm that curved with sleek, feminine muscle. Theo noticed . . . then moved on from the fact, and also noticed that one of the lacy pink shells now gapped away from a nice handful of breast. "*Ganga* nails are probably going to cause an infection," he said, wishing that Elliott could be here. "You need to be stitched up. Have you got anything to clean it with, Vonnie?"

His voice was calm, if not peremptory, but the thing that scared the shit out of him was the fact that she'd been that close to a *ganga*. Close enough that she could have just as easily been torn to shreds and devoured. "What the *hell* were you doing out there?"

Selena pressed her lips together, but if she meant to glare at him, she didn't succeed. Her face, grimy and blood-streaked, seemed to have gray undertones, although it was hard to tell for certain in the faulty light. She had long thick lashes that fanned over her cheeks; and her straight hair was plastered to her chin and temples. As he brushed it out of the way, exposing slender shoulders and an elegant neck, he noticed a long thin cord around her throat disappearing in a deep vee beneath her arm, as if something weighting it down had fallen to the side.

She must have realized he noticed it—maybe his fingers had pulled on the lanyard, tightening it against her skin—and she sat upright suddenly, clapping one hand over her half-bared breasts as the other gripped and slid down along the cord. "You should be in bed," Selena told him.

A fierceness blazed in her eyes as she stared him down. Ferocity and determination.

"I'm in a lot better shape than you are," he said. Much as he wanted to, he didn't allow his gaze to travel along that cord to see what she was trying to hide. That would give her too much satisfaction.

"*I* wasn't dead three days ago."

"No, but you could have been tonight. How the hell did you get away from them?" He looked at her. The peace and serenity he'd admired earlier was gone. She was bedraggled and clearly exhausted; in pain and yet in control—and for a minute, her look reminded him of Sarah Michelle Gellar in *Buffy*: defiant, and yet weary. *World*-weary.

But Selena wasn't a vampire slayer. Or a zombie slayer, for that matter.

Yet, the fact remained . . . she had obviously been in close proximity to one. And had escaped with little more than a few scratches. *How?*

Just then, Vonnie bustled back into the room (he hadn't even noticed she'd left). "Here," she said, setting a heavy bottle on the counter. "Vodka."

Before Theo could snatch it up and pour the antiseptic over the seeping gashes, Selena said, "Can you take over here now, Vonnie? He needs to get back in bed." She steadied her breathing and continued. "I'm not sure what he was doing out of it in the first place."

"Looking for the john," he said flatly. Pain had tightened her features once again and the faint little grunt at the end of her sentence told him she wasn't feeling any better.

It wasn't worth arguing any longer. Clearly Vonnie had regained her competence, and Theo saw no reason to waste any more time here. The sooner he left, the sooner Selena would get cleaned up and taken care of.

He wasn't needed, nor should it be his concern. In a day or two, maybe sooner, he'd be leaving this place.

"Stitches," he suggested firmly, turning away and realizing that his knees had strengthened considerably during the last thirty minutes. At the same time, however, that shadowy warning hovered at the edge of his vision. Bed might not be a bad idea.

"I'll take care of it," Vonnie said, her voice just as firm as Selena's. "Now back to your bed. The bathroom is on the way. The hall on the right."

Theo cast one more glance at Selena. Her gaze met his—that determination and defiance sitting there, thicker than a brick wall.

The thing that niggled at him, though, was what the hell was she hiding behind that wall?

* * *

When Theo opened his eyes again, sunlight blazed through the window. He sat up without difficulty this time, shaking off the remnants of dreams with his copper-haired Sage, some orange-eyed *gangas* . . . and the curve of a blood-slashed shoulder.

He wasn't certain which image left him the most unsettled.

A crash in the distance, followed by an annoyed bellow, drew Theo's attention to the area beyond what he'd come to think of as his own hospital room.

"Goddamn zombies!" came a gruff exclamation. Whomever it was slammed a door and stomped across a nearby floor in what sounded like heavy boots. "Don't know what the hell I have to do . . ." His voice trailed off into something unintelligible, but clearly annoyed as he clanged and banged and thudded. "Damn things!"

Fascinated, the way he might have been by a mountain lion toying with its prey, Theo slid his feet to the floor, cocking his ear to listen. Then he was off the bed and out of the room, following the sounds and padding on bare feet back to the kitchen to find an elderly man sorting energetically through the contents of a pantry.

Elderly he might be, the man appeared to have excellent hearing—or maybe just a sixth sense for being crept up on—for he turned just as Theo walked in on what he'd thought were silent feet.

"Who the hell are you?" the man asked, turning from the pantry and skewering Theo with sharp gray eyes. He wore olive green workpants and a matching shirt that strained over a rounded tummy, although he wasn't by any means fat. Short white hair bristled all over his head as if to match his personality, and

rolled-up sleeves exposed surprisingly muscular fore-
arms. "You one of Selena's friends?"

"I'm Theo," he replied, and realized with a start that
this man was probably at least a decade or even two
older than he and Lou. There weren't many people who
could claim that.

The man had already dismissed him, turning back
to the pantry and muttering in a gruff, nasally tone,
"Nobody tells me any damn thing around here. Damn
good thing I don't care."

Something bounced out of the closet and tumbled
to the floor, eliciting another round of cursing from
the man. Before Theo could move to offer assistance,
Vonnie stalked into the room.

"What are you looking for, Frank?" she asked,
standing there with her hands on her hips in that age-
old way of feminine annoyance.

"Eh?"

"What are you looking for?" Vonnie repeated in a
louder voice.

"A goddamn pair of pliers," he replied. "Don't need
to shout, dammit. Have to fix the damned fence around
the—"

"They're right here," Vonnie said, interrupting him
as she yanked a drawer open.

Theo didn't miss the meaningful look she gave
Frank—a tight-lipped glare that meant for him to
shut up.

He either didn't notice or didn't care, for he continued his tirade. "Goddamn zombies always have to
tramp through my ca—"

The pair of pliers clattered onto the counter. "Frank,"
Vonnie said loudly, "did you eat breakfast?"

"I didn't have no breakfast but my damned coffee,

as usual," he growled, snatching up the tool. "Nobody around here to cook when I got up. Everyone sleeping the damn morning away. Damn day's half over already."

Theo had edged farther into the kitchen by now, at once fascinated by the bundle of energy in drab olive and curious about what Vonnie was trying to hide from him. She glanced at him warily, but before she could speak, Theo asked, "How's Selena?"

"What the hell's wrong with Selena?" Frank demanded, pausing for the first time. Was the guy deaf or not? Theo couldn't figure it out.

"She's fine," Vonnie replied, looking as if she were walking a tightrope.

"I don't know why the hell she's got to mess with those goddamn zombies," the old man said. But instead of a complaint it sounded more like worried affection. "Leave them be."

Theo tried not to look interested, certain that the moment he did, Vonnie would put the kibosh on any further information from Frank. And he realized suddenly that he was more than a little interested in what the hell was going on here.

He watched as Frank jammed an old baseball cap on his head and snatched up a rifle that had been leaning in the corner. Pliers in hand, he stalked out of the kitchen with the faintest hitch in his step, but at a pace that would leave most people half his age in the dust. Theo had to squelch the urge to follow him.

"So you got her stitched up?" Theo asked, sliding onto a stool at the kitchen counter as Vonnie busied herself at the sink.

For a moment, a blast from the past settled over him and he felt a long-submerged wave of nostalgia. He was catapulted back to his mom's sunny lemon-and-lime kitchen.

He and Lou sat at the counter and Mom made them oatmeal or eggs or whatever for breakfast in the morning before school. Dad would come streaking in to grab a cup of coffee on his way out the door to the hospital, where he managed the lab. He'd cuff them each affectionately on the back of the head as he passed by. Their older sister was already at work, so they didn't have to fight her for the bathroom.

When they got older and visited home from college, Mom made them sit there and talk to her while she cooked dinner, refusing to let them have their laptops or iPhones open. Anyone who dared even think about accessing a keyboard would be served cold liver and onions, she'd threaten. Or lima beans with some awful healthy grain called quinoa—a threat she actually carried out once. And after they turned legal, she even offered beer or wine as an incentive for getting information about what was new in their lives.

"I only find out what's going on when I check your Facebook page," she'd complain good-naturedly. "Can't even call your mother and tell me you got a new job, but you can post it for all and sundry to read?"

The memory of his mother—a PhD in English lit—using such phrases while wielding a wooden spoon coated with spaghetti sauce brought a breathtaking pang of grief to Theo.

Mom and Dad, and their older sister from Dad's first marriage, had perished during the Change, at least as far as he and Lou knew. Since the catastrophic events had wiped out ninety-eight percent of the human population—as well as actually changing the continental makeup of the earth—there was no reason to think otherwise.

"Are you hungry?"

Reality swooped in over him, jerking Theo back to the year 2060, where he looked as if he were no more than thirty years old, even though he'd been alive for almost eighty.

"I could eat," Theo said, looking at Vonnie. He suddenly realized how starved he was. Maybe that hollow feeling in his stomach was because he was hungry. Maybe not. "Something more than soup, if that's all right."

Vonnie beamed at him. "Eggs and sausage sound good?"

Theo liked the sound of that, and as he watched her mound scrambled eggs onto a plate, he realized she hadn't responded to his earlier question about Selena. But rather than call her on it, he decided to take a different tact.

The eggs were like ambrosia: light and fluffy, salted just right. And the sausage wasn't in casings but fried up like ground beef. He didn't think he'd ever tasted anything so good. Vonnie poured him a cup of hot tea—something Theo hadn't been a big fan of in the past, but he found that by adding a bit of honey, he almost enjoyed it despite its woodsy aftertaste.

"This is really good. Do you do all the cooking around here?" he asked, figuring that while food might be the way to his heart, admiration of mothering skills was often the way to a woman's heart. Especially one like Vonnie.

"As much as I can," she said, bumping her round hip against the counter as she reached for something.

The kitchen, it seemed, couldn't be a quiet place when she was there. Pots clanged, silverware clashed, things fell on the floor and bounced into the sink—she was the epitome of "haste makes waste" . . . but in a delightful sort of way.

Theo watched her drop a towel twice, then lunge too fast to grab an apple in the bowl across the counter, knocking over the salt on the way. "Oops," she said, picking up a pinch of salt and tossing it over her shoulder, then continuing with her work.

He was more than amused; he felt so much at home, it hurt. Right in the center of his gut. "How many people do you have to cook for?" he asked, glancing longingly at the bowl of uncracked eggs.

She must have seen his look, for Vonnie snatched up a trio and cracked them into a different bowl, then whirled to get a pitcher of milk. "It depends. There's me and Selena, of course, and Frank—who you just met; he eats like a horse—and Selena's son, Sam, and his friends Tim and Tyler, and Andrew, when they're around. Sometimes there're family members of the people Selena's seeing to. They don't usually eat much, but sometimes. It's Tim's dog Pigment that found you, you know."

So Selena had a son. Did she also have a Mr. Selena? And how did he feel about being married to the Death Lady? If so, why the hell wasn't he lecturing her about tangling with the gangas?

"Do you grow all your own food, or is there a place to trade nearby? . . . I'm from Envy," he added, "and we have most everything there." *Except chocolate.*

Though Theo had traveled around quite a bit in his work for the Resistance, he'd never been near Yellow Mountain. He wasn't even certain where it was.

"Frank keeps chickens, cows, and a goat; and he's got a big garden out there. Sam, Tyler, and Tim help him with it. And Selena said you were from Envy. Mmm, that's a long way away," Vonnie said. "How did you get all the way up here?"

"Hell, if I know," Theo said. "The last I remember, I was about a day and a half from Envy, near the ocean, and the next thing, I wake up here. Where is *here*?"

"*Here*," she said, slapping two scoopfuls of eggs down on his plate, "is about ten miles from the ocean. And there's a settlement up yonder between Lake Isabella and the shoreline called Yellow Mountain. They've got lots of things to trade there. That's where Jennifer and Tyler and the other kids live. Only five miles away."

Theo wasn't certain where Lake Isabella was, or whether it had existed before the Change. It did sound vaguely familiar, though; so when he got back to Envy, he'd try and find it on the cobbled-together version of the Internet he and Lou had put together. They'd used caches from as many computers, mainframes, and servers as they could find over the decades to create a semi-working version of the Web on their own private little network. There were countless holes and 404 page errors, but it was better than nothing.

The satellites that he and Lou—mostly Theo, a point which he never resisted reminding his twin—had managed to hack into after the Change had failed decades ago. What data they'd managed to collect about the state of the earth after all of the cataclysmic events (not pretty) was more than twenty years old and had certainly altered since then. But there were clearly significant changes: most of California had disappeared, and the ocean's shore now cut into what had once been

Vegas. The entire West Coast line was violently different than the map they'd grown up with.

And the East Coast? Even worse. Europe, Africa,
Asia . . . all a mess.

And then there was that new continent that seemed
to have erupted or somehow formed in the Pacific
Ocean. It was about the size of Texas.

Just then, Selena walked in. Her eyes scanned the
room, caught on him and continued to Vonnie as she
made her way over to snatch up an orange. "You look
like you're doing all right," she said, and eyed him as
she jammed her thumb into the thick skin and peeled
the fruit.

The smell of orange filled the air, citrusy and fresh,
as Theo gave her the once-over. Her shiny dark-brown
hair was pulled up into a messy sort of bundle at the
back of her head, a couple of thick strands straggling
down the nape of her neck. Her eyes seemed a bit soft,
as if she were tired or worried, but the rest of her face
wasn't drawn or tight with tension. She seemed to be
moving all right, considering the wounds he'd seen last
night. Whether by accident or design, she was wearing a shirt that covered every part of her torso, so he
couldn't tell what the gashes looked like now. But Theo
trusted that Vonnie had done a good job taking care of
a woman she clearly had great affection for.

"You too," he replied and tugged his eyes from the
apple-sized breasts hinted at in the vee of the simple
linen tunic she wore. His gaze skittered away and over
the lean sweep of thighs in jeans that had seen better
days—hell, they had to be fifty years old, because no
one made Levi's anymore—and down to the surprise
of bare feet.

She had slender, golden feet that matched the rest

of her skin—the color of honey—with elegant arches, slender toes, and red toenails.

Red toenails?

Theo looked again. He hadn't seen a woman with painted toenails for fifty years. He pulled his attention away from the anachronism and found Selena watching him. But she didn't make any comment about the fact that he'd been staring at her toes. Maybe she thought he was looking at the floor.

"Thought I saw a spider," Theo said, then wondered why he'd bothered. "There on the floor." His mouth seemed to be working all on its own.

Selena squeaked and stiffened, doing a little dance, and said, "Did you? Don't kill it!"

Hiding a smile, Theo replied, "No, I was mistaken."

"Good," she said briskly, all in control again. He had to fight even harder to control the smile at her lightning-quick change. "I don't like spiders, but there's no need to kill them. Just put 'em outside."

Vonnie spoke up: "That's not all you're going to eat."

"That's all I need," Selena said, gesturing with the peeled orange that now had three sections taken out of it. "Gotta go check on some things."

And before either of them could say anything else, she streaked from the kitchen in the same direction that Theo had come from.

"That girl," Vonnie said, shaking her head, "doesn't eat enough to feed a bird."

"She doesn't look like she's wasting away," Theo commented, wishing again that he could see how her rear filled out those jeans. But the tunic was too long and she'd zipped away before he had the chance to try.

And it occurred to him that he was surprised that he was actually *interested* in trying.

It had been a long time since he'd been interested in the shape of any woman besides a shy, curvy redhead with the freckle on her lip. Theo's stomach tightened as he pushed the thought away.

It was over. Done. She hadn't wanted him.

"No, Selena's not wasting away," the older woman said. "But she's very picky. Won't eat much of anything. No meat, hardly any cheese or milk. Just vegetables and fruit. Nuts and seeds. Like a little bird. Always been that way."

That probably explained her tight, slender body. Theo shrugged mentally, wondering how they'd come to be talking about Selena's eating habits. "What about Sam's father?"

Vonnie looked sharply at him, acknowledging his curiosity. "He's not in the picture anymore. Good riddance, if you ask me."

Well, that was good. He guessed. "How long have you known Selena?"

"Since she was a tiny baby," Vonnie replied. "I found her. In the middle of it all."

Those words settled over Theo like a cool blanket. "In the middle of . . . ?"

For the first time since he'd come into the room, she actually stopped, positioning herself there in front of him at the counter. "In the middle of the Change. She could only have been a couple days old. It was a miracle that she survived. A little tiny mite with a head of dark hair, hardly bigger than a kitten. She was completely alone."

A wave of thoughts assaulted him like a wave of video missiles, but one zoomed to the front of his mind and sat there: *Holy shit. Selena's* fifty*? No effing way!*

Vonnie had gone back to her efficient if not overly enthusiastic ways by the time Theo formed a reasonable comment. "You were a child yourself." It was true. She couldn't be more than sixty, at the outside.

She tossed him a beaming smile. "How nice of you to say, Theo. I was eleven years old. And somehow . . . well, somehow we muddled through. We managed to live. I found diapers and figured out how to open bottles of formula. We lived in an old Wal— An old store. It really was a miracle, when you think about it. I had a little bit of a guiding spirit to help. I called her my guardian angel."

Just then, the bang of the rear door being whipped open, followed by a vehement round of cussing, heralded the reappearance of Frank.

"What's wrong now?" asked Vonnie with that same tone of annoyed affection Theo's mom used to have when his father came in from the garage—or from whatever home improvement project he was working on—in a similar mood.

"Damned electric fence around the vegetables is shorted out again or something," Frank grumbled. "Came in to find something to fix it with."

Theo was standing up before he quite realized it— that had been happening quite a bit since he'd awakened from this most recent death: his body taking over for him, his mouth saying things he hadn't planned on saying. Maybe something else had happened when Selena had brought him back to life. "I might be able to help," he said.

Frank cast him a sidewise look laced with suspicion. "Well, come on," he snapped. "Ain't got all day. Let's take a look at it."

For some reason, Theo felt the same rush of satisfaction he'd had when he got hired for his first job, at age fifteen, pushing shopping carts at the grocery store.

Outside, Theo followed the elderly man, who walked faster and with more surety than most people he knew. They'd exited from the back door of the kitchen and were walking across a large expanse of grass.

This was the first look Theo had of the place, and he found himself trying to figure out what it had been before the Change. The building from which they'd just emerged was a large house; not quite a mansion, but a good-sized single-family residence built in a hacienda style.

The house was made of stucco, which was probably why it was still standing, and its architecture had a southwestern feel to it: long, low, three or four stories high like a hacienda, with deep eaves to help keep the sun from blasting through the windows.

Right away Theo noticed a large fence running in front of the house and off into the distance. Made of brick, and stretching as far as he could see up and around the curve of the yard, it stood perhaps ten feet tall. Broken and crumbling in places, the barrier had nevertheless been maintained enough to keep the *gangas* out.

He wondered how the ones that had attacked Selena had gotten in . . . or whether she'd gone out; if there was a vulnerable place out of sight, among the trees and bushes that grew on the parklike grounds. A wrought iron gate still hung in place at what had clearly been the entrance to . . . whatever this was. *A large ranch? An estate of some sort?*

And what was that peeking up over the trees? *A Ferris wheel?*

Mystified, Theo paused, stared, trying to see if his eyes were deceiving him. It sure as hell looked like one.

"Well, come on," ordered Frank, breaking into his thoughts. "Time's wastin'."

"What is this place?" Theo asked, hustling to keep up with the elderly man. They walked around the back of the house, passing what had once been a five-car garage.

Behind that, he saw a barn where a slew of fenced-in chickens ran around and two cows nibbled on grass. And then he saw the garden.

Garden was an understatement. "You've got one heck of a green thumb," Theo said, looking at about ten rows of corn in various stages of growth and a variety of other plants that he wasn't certain he could identify. *Tomatoes and peppers, for sure. Are those carrots with the bushy tops? And the viny things on the ground might be cucumbers. Or pumpkins.*

There had to be about two-acres worth of produce growing there. And all was enclosed by a cobbled-together fence that looked as piecemeal as the new Internet he and Lou had built. The fence had wires of different thicknesses and lengths, wooden and plastic posts, and a few concrete ones as well. Even an old car on its side in one place.

"Wow," Theo said. "You take care of all this yourself?"

Frank looked at him, frowning. "Don't get smart, young man. It used to be bigger, but I can't keep up with it like I used to. Damn kids're always running off to Yellow Mountain or over to the ruins when I want'm to help."

Theo thought about trying to explain what he meant, but the old man shuffled off at top speed, grumbling about teenagers never changing. He followed him to the corner of the fence where the fuse box had been installed.

"Keeps shorting out on me," Frank said, jabbing at it with a large-knuckled hand. "Can't see the wires like I used to either, dammit. Sun's too bright."

Theo crouched next to the fuse box and examined the wiring. Although his forte was with integrated circuits and motherboards, he'd cut his electronic teeth, so to speak, on everything from the electric garage door opener to the family can opener to his mother's sewing machine. That hadn't gone over well when he was nine, but since Mom really didn't use it all that often, she got over it.

He and Lou used to have races to see who could rebuild something faster, or even better. They eventually graduated to computer electronics by the time they were in middle school, much to their parents' relief. He didn't think they'd ever known about the hacking contests he and Lou had had, though. Or the time Theo had rewired and souped up an old riding lawn mower's engine. He'd crashed it into a ditch when he'd tried to jump it over a lit gas grill.

"Who did this?" Theo asked, admiring the neat, organized—if not simple—work that included solar panels arranged to generate the electric charge. Someone knew what they were doing but from the looks of it, years or even a decade had passed since the original job.

"No one else could figure it out, so I fixed it up," Frank said with a defensive note in his voice. "Used to be a mechanic."

"Wow," Theo said again. Seemed like this man could do just about anything. "Do you have wire cutters? I think I see the problem." And he could understand why Frank couldn't fix it; the kinked wire was down in the corner, difficult for Theo to see.

Frank handed him the tool without any further comment; and while Theo worked, the old man walked through a swinging gate and began to weed a row of some faintly familiar plant. Its smell wafted on the warm air and Theo recognized the fresh scent of cilantro.

"Got it," he said with a grunt of satisfaction. "Watch out—I'm going to try it." Theo flipped the switch and heard the faint hum of power, then watched as Frank tested out the fence.

A sharp sizzle sounded, followed by a faint smoky smell, and the old man actually cracked a smile. "Damn good charge there, young man. Stronger than before. Don't know how you did it, but good job."

Theo, of course, didn't mention that he had the ability to create his own electric charge, thanks to the embedded IC in the back of his hip. It exhausted him to channel and use the electric surge, so it was a skill best saved for compelling situations. Like being trapped in a mall by a few dozen *gangas* and using the power to turn on a tanning bed as a barrier. He smiled to himself. They certainly had gotten his juices flowing, to so speak.

"So what is this place?" Theo asked again, walking into the garden and crouching in the row opposite Frank. *Strawberries. Red and juicy and sweet, warmed by the sun.* He picked one and popped it into his mouth.

"What the hell you talking about?" Frank asked, squinting in the light despite his cap.

"I mean this house and yard . . . what was it before the Change? It looks like some big ranch. Is that a

Ferris wheel over there?" Theo was suddenly touched with the urge to explore the grounds. A frigging Ferris wheel, for pity's sake. There'd been a roller coaster in Envy—the one that had been part of New York-New York in Vegas, but it had been destroyed during the Change.

Frank had already weeded half the line of cilantro, and Theo was still working on the stubborn plants littering the strawberry row. Hell, this man put him to shame. He was a freaking machine. "What?" Frank called, barely looking up.

Theo repeated his question, moving closer to the old man. He glanced over his shoulder, back at the house. The main gate seemed to have letters on it; and from his perspective—he was seeing them backward—half of them were missing. But he could make out a prominent *B* and perhaps a *P*, or maybe an *R*.

"Big damn ranch belonged to a famous guy, back before. More goddamn space than he knew what to do with; had to have an amusement park put in like that damn guy with the glove. Jackson."

Theo frowned, something niggling in the back of his mind. "Do you remember the guy's name?"

Frank looked up at him, annoyance creasing his face. "Of course I remember his damn name. I used to work for him. Took care of all the vehicles here. What the hell is that on your arm?"

Theo looked down and saw that Frank was glaring at the red dragon on his wrist and arm. "A tattoo," he replied, not sure what else to say as it was pretty obvious what it was. He didn't mention that her name was Scarlett.

Nor did he mention the other one, on his back. About three years after the Change, he'd had one of his fellow survivors—a woman whose body was clothed in tat-toos—create the blue dragon whose eye was the little metal chip. Scarlett, who curled along his arm and around his right wrist, had been done when he was in college, and it seemed only fitting that he have match-ing ink to commemorate the change in his body and the superpower it brought him. Lou had made a smartass comment about him also getting a big *E* tattooed on his chest instead—and walked around calling him Electric Man for months.

"Brad Blizek," Frank grunted, and turned to shuffle off toward the tomato plants.

Theo nearly fell back on his ass. Brad Blizek? This was *Brad Blizek*'s place? He fairly leapt to his feet, turning to look full at the house and then around him, turning in a slow circle.

Brad Blizek had been the Steve Jobs of Theo and Lou's generation. In fact, Jobs had mentored the man when he was younger and interned with him at Apple. But then Blizek had gone on to work with video-game guru John Carmack, and then went on to create his own games company, UniZek, which was the first to introduce ray tracing into video games.

Independently wealthy by the age of thirty, Blizek was a self-proclaimed geek who not only attended every comics or sci-fi convention he could, but also even held his own—on his private ranch and retreat in southern Utah called, ironically, Blizek Beach. Be-cause, of course, there was no beach in sight. Only low green and purple mountains.

Which was where, which *had* to be where, Theo now stood. Weeding strawberries.

Holy crap.

He looked back at the house. Was it possible some of

Blizek's computers and systems were still here? Possibly workable? His mouth fairly salivated at the thought.

"Well, hi there."

Theo turned to find a young woman standing behind him. He rose to his feet, noticing long, tanned legs in very short shorts and a white button-down shirt that strained over a pair of great breasts. Light brown hair brushed her shoulders and curled in thick waves behind her ears.

"Hi, yourself," he replied, unable to help scanning over her again. *Wow.* They sure grew them hot here at Blizek Beach. Wonder Woman or Xena in the flesh: all curves, all the time.

"You're new around here," she said, and they both laughed. Hers was light and airy. "I'm Jen."

"Theo," he said, and glanced down to look at her feet. She wore sandals and some sexy bracelet around her ankle. Jen looked to be in her mid-twenties, which technically put her about fifty years younger than Theo. But who was counting? She certainly wasn't. Not the way she was looking at him.

"Where did you come from?" Jen asked, bending over to pick a strawberry.

Theo wasn't sure if it was on purpose or not, but she bent away from him and he got a very nice view of her round behind; perhaps a little too much of a view to be strictly proper because those shorts were really short. He held back a smile. Not that he was complaining.

After all . . .

It hit him then, like the proverbial ton of bricks: he could look; he could appreciate and flirt. He could do a hell of a lot more than that now, couldn't he?—and without feeling guilty as if he were betraying Sage.

Because she hadn't chosen him. And there was no chance of them ever being together.

Not that there'd ever been anything to betray. At least, as far as she was concerned. But he'd been—hell, he supposed he still was—in love with her. And when that happened, there was no one else.

But now he was free to consider—and appreciate—other opportunities.

With that thought settling firmly in his mind, even as he tried to ignore the empty scraping in his chest, Theo tested out a warm smile on Jen. "I'm from Envy, and I'm not quite sure how I got here. I just know Sam brought me to Selena."

Jen's eyes traveled over him and back up. "Well, you don't look too sick to me." She smiled and . . . *Sheesh, was that a little flicker of tongue over her top lip?* Just enough to get his attention, but not enough to be crude. "You look just fine. To me."

Theo met her eyes just long enough to let her know he read her loud and clear, then pulled his gaze away. It still felt odd, but he'd get over it. In fact, maybe this was exactly what he needed. A little diversion.

Then her eyes widened in horror and she clapped a hand to her mouth. "Oh. Oh no. Are you . . . do you know one of Selena's patients?" She looked as if she'd just walked into a pile of something messy. "Like . . . is someone you know dying?"

"No," Theo replied, trying to hide a smile. "I don't know anyone here."

She frowned, and he didn't think it was wholly because of the sun in her eyes. "So you were here to see Selena? Or Cath? I mean. You don't look like you're dying. Are you? I mean . . ." She gave up and sort of shrugged. "People only see Selena when they're dying."

For some reason, Theo didn't want to say that he'd just been brought back to life. Might put a damper on things if the girl thought he'd been dead. Unless she was into those vampire books that had been all the rage back before, and undeadness didn't bother her. The ones in which the guy looked about her age but was really a hundred and twenty years old.

Kinda like him.

"I'm perfectly healthy," he replied.

"You sure look like it," she said, perhaps unaware that she'd just made the same observation moments earlier. "That's a bang-ass tattoo on your arm."

Theo smiled back and let a little heat into his gaze. It felt good. It had been a long while since he'd done that. "Her name is Scarlett. I've got a blue one on my back I call Rhett."

Jen looked at him blankly.

"You gonna stand around all day, or you gonna do your job?"

Theo and Jen turned to see Frank standing there, holding a clump of weeds dripping dirt from their roots.

"Oh, right," Jen said, and adjusted the hem of her shirt by pulling it down tighter over her breasts. "I better go see if Selena needs me today? Maybe I'll see you later tonight? In Yellow Mountain? For the story-telling?"

That was three question marks too many, but who was counting? Although he didn't know what she was talking about, he figured there was nothing else to do. "Probably will," he replied. She gave Theo a melting smile as she skirted away, walking toward the house.

"Spends more time lookin' in the damned mirror or scavenging for clothes," Frank grumbled, "or talking, than doing anything else."

"She lives around here?" Theo asked, bending dutifully to the strawberries. A basket had appeared on the ground next to him, ostensibly from Frank, and he began to pick the ripest berries.

"In Yellow Mountain. 'Bout five miles down the hill," replied the old man. "Supposed to relieve Selena, but spends more of her damn time talking to Sam and Tim than working. And when she's around, they don't do nothing either."

Theo hid a smile. Sounded just about normal for young people with raging hormones. He hadn't met Sam or Tim, but he figured he'd need to make a point of doing so—if for no other reason than because if they hadn't found him, he'd still be dead.

He paused for a moment and thought of Lou. *Damn.* And as he sat there, in the hot sun, red stains from the berries on his fingers, he opened his mind once again to his brother.

CHAPTER 3

Lou was working in the subterranean computer lab when a familiar sizzle of awareness zipped over his shoulders. His hands stilled over the keyboard.

Theo! he thought, and opened his mind. *You there?*

Yeah.

Lou's fingers collapsed onto the keys, creating a jumble of letters. Relief blitzed through him. *Are you okay?*

He didn't know for certain whether Theo could actually understand those specific thoughts, but he tried anyway. On his end, it was more of a *feeling* that communicated whatever they were trying to say to each other. But it had been more than a day since he'd had that brief connect from his brother, and Lou wasn't certain if he'd imagined it or not. So to have that *feeling* again was a great relief.

I'm safe.

That came through loud and clear. *Solid.*

Lou opened his eyes and was mortified to find that they were damp and stinging. He wasn't ready to lose his brother, not quite yet. *Thank God, he's still here.*

Good, Lou sent back vehemently. He waited, wondering if Theo had anything else to say. Ever since the whole thing with Sage had gone down, Theo had been a little more reticent and quiet. And snappish. But although there had been silence from his twin, now the connection was open and Lou took comfort in the familiar bond—simply the awareness that he was still there.

Lou looked at the computer screen on which he'd been writing a new program to analyze numerical information they'd obtained from a journal stolen from the Strangers, who were also called the Elite. The jumble of letters and numbers was, ironically, comforting to him, despite the fact that he hadn't figured out the significance of the sequences.

Now he could concentrate. Now he'd be able to set his mind to the task that he'd merely been using as an escape from fear that he was once again alone.

Elsie had died a little more than a year after the Change, trying to have their baby in a world without Pitocin, without epidurals, without emergency C-sections. A little flutter of her presence brushed over the back of his neck, beneath the silver-gray ponytail.

Where are you? he asked Theo.

You won't believe me.

Where?

I'm at Brad Blizek's ranch.

Lou's eyes widened. *Holy shit.*

He could almost hear Theo's chuckle. *I have to look around. More later.*

Report back ASAP with deets. I'm expecting Tony Stark's lab, you know.

Me too. Later.

Brad Blizek's ranch. *Sweet.* Would there be anything left of his office? With that tantalizing thought, Lou returned his attention to the computer screen, deciding then and there that if it was even half as amazing as he imagined, he was going there too. No matter what Theo said.

* * *

"What's up with that new guy Theo?" Jen asked as she passed Selena in the hallway from the kitchen.

"What do you mean?" Selena replied. The front of her shoulder hurt where the *gangas* had torn into her, and there was a deep abrasion on her lower back that she'd made certain Vonnie hadn't seen.

"Well, he's not dying. And he doesn't know anyone here," Jen replied, seemingly unaware of Selena's tone. "Why is he here? Do you know him? Is he staying?"

Good question. Selena shrugged and then winced at the sharp twinge. "I don't know if he's staying, but he's perfectly healthy as far as I can tell."

"He sure is," Jen said with relish. "Did you see that red dragon on his arm? *Bang.*"

Selena resisted the urge to mention the even more *bang* dragon on Theo's back, and merely shrugged again—this time, more gingerly. Jen had been leading Sam on a merry chase for a while—poor sixteen-year-old Sammy was too young for the cute, if not easily distracted, twenty-three-year-old, but since she worked a lot with Selena, the proximity had contributed to what Vonnie called a big, fat Orange Crush.

Obviously, Jen had found another, more appropriate outlet for her flirtations, if the way she peered out the window toward Frank's garden was any indication. Selena had seen Theo walk out with the elderly man some time earlier, and could pretty much assume that Frank had put him to work. Jen must have met him as she walked through the area from her home, halfway between here and the settlement of Yellow Mountain.

Selena wondered if Theo had gotten hot enough in the sun to take off his shirt yet, and the thought made her pause in surprise. Not the idea itself, but the fact that she'd *thought* it. Selena certainly admired a wixy male body when she happened to see one, but normally those sorts of thoughts didn't just crop up in her mind out of the blue. She was over fifty years old, for creep's sake, and her days of passion were long behind her. Besides, having a man in her life would be too dangerous.

Aside from that, she had other things to deal with. Things that generally put a damper on anything like passion or sex.

What guy wanted to sleep with a woman who got up close and personal to zombies in order to save their souls?

"What?" asked Jen.

"Nothing," she replied. "I just forgot something I wanted to check on. How's Maryanna doing?"

But as Jen rattled on about the young woman, Selena couldn't quite keep her attention from the window. She wondered what his skin tone, already a rich olive color, would look like when it tanned. And she knew how sleek and muscular his back was, how it curved into square shoulders and round biceps.

"Remember?"

With a start, Selena looked at Jen. "Uh," she began.

"You promised," the younger girl reminded her. "Vonnie will be busted if you shove it off again. And my Mom and Dad are going to stay here so you can go."

Right. Vonnie was doing her monthly storytelling gig in Yellow Mountain tonight. Everyone from the surrounding areas—about a hundred people—attended the pig roast and entertainment without fail, partly because Vonnie painted amazing pictures with her words, and partly because it was a social activity that brought them all together and gave them a rest from the daily work.

"Yes, yes, I'll be there." She smiled, but it was a little forced.

It wasn't that she didn't want to go or to socialize, but she had to be careful about that sort of thing. She'd learned her lesson back in Sivs. And again in Cross-roads. She couldn't let anyone too close, because once they found out what she did, it could get ugly.

Which was why Selena never thought of herself as alone—for she had Sam and Vonnie and Frank—but she *was* lonely. She didn't have a partner. Someone whom she neither had to take care of, nor who tried to mother her to death. Just . . . an equal. Someone to listen. To talk to. To laugh with. And . . . other things.

Someone who didn't *need* anything from her.

But maybe tonight . . . maybe she'd just have fun. Drink a little wine. Relax a little.

Maybe she'd even drink a lot of wine. For some reason, her gaze wandered back to the window. She knew what would happen if she drank a lot of wine. It had been a long time . . . she searched back in her mind . . . *Three years? Four?*

No, good grief—Six! Six years, because it had been Sam's tenth birthday party, the last time she'd let herself relax. Have a good time.

No wonder she was a little tense.

And so . . . maybe tonight. A night where she could just do . . . what *she* wanted.

Selena couldn't help glancing toward the window again. Would it be so bad to flirt a bit with a guy younger than her? Especially one who looked like Theo? Plus he wasn't from here; surely he wouldn't be around much longer anyway.

"I'm going to ask Theo if he wants to go," Jen was saying. "He can sit with us."

Selena pulled her attention away, her light thoughts deflated. *Right*. He'd fit in perfectly with the group of friends that Jen normally interacted with. Young, vibrant, and filled with energy.

She turned away. It had been a while since she'd felt like that.

Young. Vibrant. Filled with the joy of life.

Since he'd gotten the news that this was Brad Blizek's place, several things had occurred to Theo. Aside of the realization that there could be some awesome plans or even prototypes of some of Blizek's unmanufactured brain children (which he fairly salivated at the thought of getting his hands on), he had to believe there would be a state-of-the-art NASA-like technology setup somewhere.

Maybe even still viable.

So, as soon as he finished helping Frank with a variety of chores in the yard, he asked about it. And was rewarded by the old man trudging him up two flights of steps to what he said they called the arcade.

Theo was conscious of holding his breath when he entered the space, and it took long moments before he expelled it.

Holy gearhead's wet dream, Batman.

It was like the Bat Cave meets Tony Stark's lab meets NASA.

The space was long and open, running the entire length of the ranch. Tinted transom windows kept the glare of the sun from messing with computer or video screens. The left half looked like something from an old '80s movie: it was lined with old arcade video games—Pac-Man, Centipede, Galaga—along with some from Theo's generation, as well as pinball machines. But on the right, the large room was a fantasy. Massive computer touch screens built into the walls, clear acrylic countertops and keyboards, a clear glass electronic whiteboard, and projector screens and webcams. Theo saw a data glove and headgear for AI work. He could hardly form words to thank Frank—for he'd learned that the man had kept the space clean, dry, and powered up.

And yet . . . the stairway to the arcade was kept boarded up and inaccessible.

"Keeps the damned snoot outta here," Frank said, eyeing Theo sharply.

"The snoot?"

"Bounty hunters. They take this stuff. Take anyone who's got it too. No one knows it's here, so you shut your goddamn can about it to anyone."

And that was all Frank would say on the subject . . . but Theo didn't care. He just wanted to get to work. He didn't even spend much time wondering why Frank trusted him enough to give him access to the secret room.

The first thing he did was set up an access point, or NAP, to link into the Internet that he and Lou had been trying to create. Despite the fact that Envy, which of course was the cornerstone of the network, might be as far as a hundred miles away, Theo figured he could find the equipment here to build a receiver strong enough to tap into it. Aside of that, he, Lou, Sage, and Jade had spent the last two or three years setting up NAPs in a roughly fifty mile radius around Envy, and hopefully there would be one close enough that he could link into.

It took him only a few hours to rig an NAP, and he

sent off an actual message back to Lou, who would be in the Resistance's Command Center, hidden two stories below the ground of New York-New York. Later, he might even be able to send him webcam pictures of the place. Lou would be fucking insane to get here, get his hands on this stuff.

By the time he finished that and sent off a message to Lou, Sam was calling up the stairs that it was time to leave for Yellow Mountain. And, mindful of Frank's warning that the place must be kept secret, Theo had no choice but to leave the Bat Cave before everyone came looking for him.

"Once upon a time there was a magical place with castles and princesses, and a little, winding river. A bright red-and-yellow train trundled along on a track that surrounded the land, stopping at three different stations. There was a busy place called Main Street, filled with families and couples walking along. Shops lined a street where people could buy ice cream or chocolates or wonderful sandwiches called hot dogs . . ."

As Vonnie's sure, easy voice lulled the audience, Theo found himself alternately sliding into the story and watching everyone and everything around him. And fantasizing about getting his fingers back on those sleek, dust-free touch screens.

The audience sat on an expanse of grass, safely inside the walls of the settlement of Yellow Mountain, with a fervent fire blazing in a stone-lined pit in the center of the group. He estimated about eighty people of all ages had either settled on the lawn on blankets or on portable chairs similar to those he'd taken to picnics or sporting events fifty years ago, except these chairs had seats made from curtain remnants and supports

from broken pieces of wood or reformed plastic. A few
dogs settled near their masters and mistresses, and off
to the left, a man had just put his guitar aside.

The fire gave off a bit too much heat for a warm July
evening, so there was a ring of empty grass around it.
The sun was just sitting on the horizon, and its disap-
pearance would plunge the world into dangerous darkness in an hour or two. In the air lingered the remnants
of barbeque smoke; and behind the crowd, the carcass
from the roasted pig still hung on its spit. A few yards
away were the scattered buildings that made up the settlement, the largest of which was an old McDonald's.

"Hot dogs weren't made from puppy dogs, of course!
Who would want to eat a sweet little puppy?" Vonnie
said with a little laugh after one of the girls squealed
in horror and clutched her own dog closer. "They were
meats, long and skinny, these hot dogs," she explained
to a group of youngsters who sat in the front row and
gazed up at her with wide eyes. "And you'd put them
in a special long bread called a bun, which sort of
hugged them. They tasted *sooooo* good, especially
with ketchup on them. Princesses loved to eat them,
and there were lots of little shops in this magical world
where you could buy them or other tasty things called
corn dogs."

A little pang flipped inside Theo's belly. Every so
often that happened—a sharp reminder of what he'd
lived through, what it had been like *before*. How many
hot dogs had he had by the time he was the age of those
kids there—eight, maybe nine or so? And none of them
would have seen or tasted one in this world.

Not that the lack of processed food was anything to
be upset about.

"And there was something called *cotton candy*,"

Vonnie went on, her own eyes growing wide and a big smile rounding her cheeks. Her voice dropped into a tantalizing whisper as she bent forward to the young audience. Theo smiled. Here, for the first time, her enthusiasm was channeled into something more deliberate, more controlled than when she was in the kitchen or caring for Selena's patients.

Selena.

Theo shifted his attention to the so-called Death Lady, who was sitting on a small rise of ground above and behind Vonnie. It put her in his vision without him having to move to look at Selena. He could sneak peeks without even turning his head. *Convenient.*

And interesting that I should care.

He turned that thought over in his mind for few moments, considering.

Something bumped Theo gently in the ribs and the warmth of a body sliding next to him pulled him back to his grassy seat. Jen had walked away from their little group a few moments before the story began, and now she'd returned to take her place between Theo and another young woman.

Jen's long bare leg slid along his calf as she settled on the grass next to him. Bare toes, ringless and painted pale pink, burrowed into the cool green blades. She carried the scent of some flower that he couldn't identify and didn't really care to—he just knew it was a nice, girly smell. Then she giggled and whispered something to her girlfriend, bumping her arm against Scarlett as she did so.

About two hours before, Theo and Jen, along with Sam and Frank, had ridden in a horse-drawn wagon to Yellow Mountain. They'd arrived early enough for dinner and to join a collection of about twenty young people. Theo assumed he fit right in, at least visually, with the twenty-somethings, two of whom were pregnant and all of whom were looking forward to tonight's social activities. Several bottles of wine and beer had passed around while they ate, and now all had the makings of a good, warm buzz.

Life was pretty good, considering the fact that he'd been dead days ago.

"Cotton candy was like pink or blue clouds," Vonnie was saying, spreading her hands to demonstrate. "And it melted in the princess's mouth, so sweet and sticky! In the hot sun, it colored their fingers so that they turned pink and blue, and when she gave her mama a kiss, she left a sticky blue lip-print on her cheek."

Jen whispered something about her hair to the friend next to her, smoothing her hand along its blondish brown length. She lifted it in a bunch, twisting it high at the crown of her head, then draping it over her shoulder as she laughed softly. Then she leaned back to say something to the young man behind her, something about his "bang" jeans, which were torn over one knee and stitched with bold black at the hems. A little bit of knot work hung from the edges of the tear in the denim.

She bumped against Theo again; and, whether by accident or design, she managed to slide her arm along him too. Her long hair, now loose, cascaded over her shoulder and gleamed in the sunlight as it slithered briefly over Theo's arm.

Subtle, she is not.

But she was young and lithe and she smelled good. She might be able to make him forget about Sage.

In fact, Jen reminded him more than a little of Sage, although Jen wasn't as quiet as the redhead. Perhaps it was her young age that did it. He noticed the same youth and ingenuity in Jen's eyes, the free smiles and laughter that came easily. The giggles, the talk about clothes and hair . . . Simple things.

While the things that were on his mind were always so much bigger and broader.

"And so, the princess climbed into a large teacup," Vonnie said, lifting a palm-sized china cup and saucer that had somehow remained intact through the violence that had ravaged the earth. "It looked much like this, but it was *wayyyy* larger. In fact, it was so big, six people could fit inside it! It was pink with red swirling designs painted on the outside."

"Was it made of glass?" piped up a tiny voice. "Or plastic?"

Vonnie pursed her lips, pretending to think, and then she looked at the cup in her hand and leaned forward to respond. "It was made of something *magic*," she said. Then she lifted her face to look around the entire crowd, and repeated: *"Magic."*

"What did the magic do?"

"It made the cup fly, around and around and around . . . so fast that the princess giggled and laughed. The wind brushed her face and tickled it, and tossed her hair. And inside her tummy she felt it curl and flutter like a thousand butterflies were inside!"

Jen shivered next to Theo—or at least, she hugged herself and rubbed her arms, whispering *brrr*. Hiding a smile, Theo shifted so that she could tuck under his arm, and he thought about how smooth her skin was, and how pretty she was when she smiled.

And how young. So, so young. So young that wisdom and experience had yet to cloud her gaze and imprint her skin. Gay and carefree, enjoying life.

While he felt old and used.

Theo looked over at Selena again. Alone, sitting high above and away from everyone else with her arms clasped loosely around bent knees. Despite the fact that he was in the midst of people, even hugging a lovely young woman, he felt just as separate as Selena seemed to be.

And, it struck him at that moment, he'd felt this way for a long time. Longer than he'd realized. For decades: distant, separated, outcast. Despite the awesomeness of his superpower, despite the fact that he looked like a young, buff athlete at the top of his game, he was separated. Because of it.

Distant even from Lou in many ways, despite their brotherly connection. For at least Lou looked like who he was: an old man. At least people understood who Lou was merely by looking at him.

That was not true for Theo. His whole person was a lie.

And although he and Lou were close, connected so intimately, they were still so very separate. Alone.

The sun had begun to dip into the horizon, which flattened its curving bottom and sent pink and gold beams of light shooting through distant trees. He noticed the rosy-bronze nimbus touching one side of Selena's hair, for she sat perpendicular to the horizon. Half of her face would soon be shadowed as the other half of her head captured the last rays of sunlight.

The woman who'd saved his life.

No, the woman who'd brought him back to life. Literally. It still blew his mind.

How long had she been living while people died around her? How long had she lived a life filled with the pain and anguish of others . . . and why did she separate herself from the living? How did she go on when she saw death every day and still be fresh and upbeat and optimistic? He wanted to know more. He wanted to know the secrets of this woman, who looked nothing like who she really was.

Just like himself.

Something unfurled inside him, like a little shudder of awareness. A soft, slow understanding that settled into a question that would not be dislodged: *But who am I?*

As if feeling his attention on her, Selena glanced in Theo's direction. Perhaps their eyes me; perhaps she merely skimmed her gaze over him. Regardless, she stood, easily, suddenly, looking away from him and the audience.

Not so very tall, but deliberate and curvy in those lean blue jeans and loose tunic. With long, thick dark-brown hair that was now sun-tipped with pink and bronze. And even from here, he could see bare feet.

"When the princess climbed out of the teacup, she found herself in a world of bright-colored houses. Blue and yellow, pink-shuttered and green-roofed houses. Everything was a splash of color, as if it had been painted with the happiest rainbow. And the houses were sweet, big and bright cottages with heart shapes cut from the shutters and plate-sized poppies and daisies springing up along the walkway. Everything was bigger than life, and so happy that the princess couldn't help but smile as she walked along the street."

Theo's attention was drawn to Vonnie and something tickled the back of his mind. *Why does this sound familiar? What story is she telling?*

"There was a place where she could play, with a little airplane that swooped through the air on a track so she didn't need to be scared. It soared and dipped and whizzed around, through a happy red barn and back out into the sunshine. The princess sat in the front seat behind the blue propeller and looked down at large, bright rows of corn as she flew above them."

Jen leaned away to whisper something to a friend, and Theo saw them pass something between them. A twine bracelet with beads, followed by the bottle of wine. Jen drank and with sparkling, laughing eyes, offered it to Theo with a little huff of vintage-scented breath.

He drank, too, and by the time he lowered the bottle to pass it on, he saw that Selena had disappeared from her spot on the hill. And that the sun had sunk more than halfway. Shadows were lengthening. He had more than a mild attack of disappointment that he wasn't going to get back to Blizek Beach tonight; he'd had visions of spending all night in the arcade, playing Bruce Wayne.

But there could be other benefits to hanging around here in Yellow Mountain tonight. A quick scan around the makeshift arena told him that Selena was gone from there as well, and his interest sharpened.

Out to hunt zombies again? Sneaking off into the coming night while everyone else was occupied? Crafty woman. Crazy, crafty woman.

While part of him could understand the exhilaration of doing dangerous things, the biggest part knew she must be crazy.

Theo tried to extricate himself from Jen and stood.

When the young woman looked up at him and made as if to rise, he gave her a little "stay-put" gesture with his hand. "Be right back," he said, leaning down to whisper so as not to interrupt the story.

"The princess walked on"—Vonnie's voice followed Theo as he walked off—"past the bright-colored cottages where the famous mice lived and soon came to a new part of the land. It was called the Magic Kingdom. And there she would ride on a *flying* elephant. And she would meet another princess—a mermaid with red hair."

Theo paused to look back over his shoulder, comprehension dawning. That was why the story had seemed so familiar. The princess was visiting Disney World.

As the story continued, Theo carefully picked his way through the seated people. It reminded him of the outdoor rock concerts he'd attended when he was no longer a poor college student, where half of the audience spread out on the grassy hills beyond the stage and arena. They'd lay out blankets and drink beer and the sweet smell of pot would weave in and out of Coldplay or Kings of Leon and the summer breezes.

He scanned the fringes of the crowd, looking for a standing silhouette that was edging off into the growing darkness. The cluster of little houses around the McDonald's—some of them had been trailers, or a gas station, and a couple seemed to have been constructed from remnants of buildings—was enclosed by a wall built of old cars, pieces of billboard or rooftop, and other large remains from the devastation.

Theo focused his attention on the wall, looking for the crazy woman, the Death Lady, who apparently was trying to get herself killed by leaving safety when the day ended. The *gangas* would be out, with their glowing orange eyes and murderous claws, as soon as the sun slept.

Vonnie's story had become absorbed by the distance and the rustle of a breeze through trees and bushes so that it was little more than a rising and falling murmur.

When he thought about the monsters beyond the walls, waiting for someone like Selena to walk into their hands, he wished he'd brought the makings for a bottle bomb. But the knapsack he'd left Envy with was long gone, and he hadn't had the time or resources to think about replacing it.

Idiot.

Theo walked more quickly, feeling an unusual urgency he didn't understand. Where had she gone?

"Looking for the john again?"

He stopped and fairly spun around. "Selena," he said. Her hair gleamed, rich and thick and dark. He wondered if it was as soft as it looked. He wondered when she slept, being up all night and with her patients all day . . . and how she would look, tousled freshly from sleep.

"It's over there," she said, pointing . . . in the direction from which she appeared to have come. "The Tendys' house, with the blue shutters." Next to the overgrown McDonald's parking lot.

"I wasn't—" He stopped and reengaged his brain. "Where are you going?"

Well, damn. That came out wrong too.

And when her full lips pursed, he realized she thought so too. "I think I'm old enough not to need looking after," she replied.

The slanted-eye glance that accompanied the low hitch to her voice was almost flirtatious and he smiled back.

She looked up at him for a moment, her lips half curved. She had a wide mouth that looked as if it would be amazing to kiss—full and mobile and dark red.

Speaking of red . . . "Your toes," he said, yanking his eyes away from her mouth. "They're . . . painted. Red." *Gee-sus, Theo. Engage your brain. Could you sound any more ridiculous?*

"I didn't think guys noticed things like that," she said, still smiling a little. It was written all over her face: fascination, contemplation . . . tinged with a little bit of horror.

He hoped the *fascination* would win out over the horror—whatever it was—because he realized he was definitely wanting to kiss her. "Well, they're bright red. Kind of hard to miss. Where did you get nail polish?" he asked.

The fascination, contemplation, and horror dissolved into confusion and surprise. "Nail polish?"

It just dawned on Theo: no one had had nail polish for fifty years, at least the kind you bought from the drugstore in a little bottle. Maybe they called it something different. "Nail paint?"

Her brows had drawn together, and now they eased. "I know what nail polish is. I just haven't heard anyone use that term . . . in a long time."

Yeah . . . forget the nail polish then. So where were we? "What were you saying about needing to be looked after?" he asked with a grin. Then he stepped closer and reached to touch the swath of hair brushing the front of her shoulder.

Fascination was back in her eyes, and he took advantage, sliding his hand around to the back of her shoulder and drawing her closer. Remembering her *ganga* slashes, he was careful in his movements.

The corners of her eyes crinkled a bit. "I don't think I—*ah*."

He'd covered her mouth with his, and caught the little

huff of surprise just as their lips met. As kisses went, it was an easy one, a tentative *Am-I-really-doing-this* sort of kiss. And when she tasted good, *really* good, of heat and sweetness and wine, he stepped in closer for another, deeper sample.

Now, both of her shoulders were under his gentle hands, her hair, silky and warm, trapped beneath his fingers, her mouth parting just enough so their lips fit together. She made a soft little noise against his lips, a little *mmm*, which sent a surprise flash of response shuttling through his body. *Whoa.*

He sunk into her a bit deeper, taking more—still a gentleman, but one now with serious intent.

And then, she pulled gently away. Her hand had ended up on his chest, and he liked the feel of that solid warmth there, leeching through his thin T-shirt. That was, in fact, about the only thing he was aware of—besides the throbbing of his well-kissed lips and other very attentive parts of his body that were demanding more of the same.

"Well," she said, a little breathless. "Not bad for a guy who was dead three days ago." And she smiled, a free, sexy smile that did almost the same thing to his insides as red-painted toenails and ankle bracelets.

"At least you didn't say it was 'nice,'" Theo said, remembering Sage's reaction the first time he'd worked up the nerve to kiss her. That had been the first warning that it was going to be bad.

Selena smoothed her hand over his shirt as if to straighten away a wrinkle, and all thoughts of Sage scattered as his skin leapt and prickled beneath her touch. *Sage who?*

"Nice?" Selena replied. "That's not the word that

comes to mind." Her eyes narrowed as her smile became a little flat. That tinge of horror was back in her face. "You're a damn good kisser—for a youngster," she said, and before he could reengage his brain from where it had gone to mush, she turned away.

He could have gone after her, but he was still a little shaken by how much that kiss had . . . well, shaken him. And not only that. He'd only taken a single step when, suddenly, there was Jen, coming from around the corner of one of the houses.

Talk about a youngster.

Selena made herself move with casual slowness even though her knees were weak and her mind was reeling.

It was the wine. She told herself it *had* to be the wine, the half a bottle she'd drunk with dinner, that had made one simple kiss go *right* to her head. *Holy cats.* She'd practically drooled all over him. Thank God, it was getting dark so no one—let alone Theo—would see the embarrassed flush on her cheeks.

Of course, she could explain that too. Didn't everyone get flushed from drinking red wine?

But the wobble in her knees and the fluttering in her belly as she walked away from him . . . not so easy to explain away. Definitely not so easy to disregard the heat that had swarmed her as she leaned into that solid, *young so* young *so* hard and muscular . . . body.

What the hell was he doing, kissing a woman old enough to be his mother?

Then the rush of embarrassment got worse when she realized exactly what must have happened. Why, he'd felt compelled to kiss her. The kid probably figured he owed her.

It was a pity kiss*!*

Oh God, oh God. I need a drink. Her face was burning and her stomach tight with shame. She felt ill.

Selena looked around for Frank—he'd probably know where she could find another glass of wine. Or even something stronger.

She was no better than Jen. No . . . worse. Jen was only six years older than Sam, and hopefully she hadn't kissed either of them . . . and Theo had to be at least twenty years younger than Selena.

Oh no! she wailed inside her head.

She'd seen how cozy Theo had been with the young woman, all cuddled up there on the blankets. *Oh my God, I am such a busted idiot.*

As if he'd look twice at Selena when he had slim, young, gorgeous Jennifer hanging on him.

Could she feel any worse? Any more embarrassed? Yeah, she could. If anyone else had seen her throwing herself at a young man. *What if Sam hears about it? Oh, geeeez!*

Was there a chance that no one had seen them? A decent chance, she thought, focusing on that problem instead of what she was going to say and how she was going to act the next time she saw Theo. *Oh God.*

They'd been away from the audience, and a few clumps of bushes squatted between them and the little grassy area where everyone was sitting. It was growing dark, there were more shadows, and no one was probably paying any attention to them because Vonnie had them in the palm of her hand with her story. And the angle at which they'd been standing to one of the houses would also have blocked a direct view.

Selena felt a little bit easier once she realized that. Sure, it was going to be horrible to see Theo tomorrow, but she could get through that. She'd had a lot worse things to handle in her lifetime.

And aside from that, now that he was feeling well, there was no reason for him to stay around Yellow Mountain anyway. He'd be leaving soon. Maybe even tomorrow.

Hopefully tomorrow.

Ah, there was Frank, walking along more quickly than a ninety-three-year-old man had the right to. He always came to the storytelling nights, but rarely sat and listened for more than fifteen minutes at a time. There were too many other things to do, he said— torches to light when it got dark, the pig to roast and clean up, the fire to keep going, and so on. And he was one of the few—probably the only person—who left Yellow Mountain's walls when it was all over. *Hell,* he'd say, *when it's my time to go, it's my goddamn time.*

"Frank," she said, moving toward him. "Got anything to drink?"

He paused in his energetic stride. "Does a dog shit in the damned grass?" he said gruffly. "'Course I've got some beer." He peered at her with his sharp eyes, glinting clearly in the lowering light. "You look like you could use one." He started off, then turned and said, "Are you coming? I ain't got all damned night. Gotta get those damn torches lit 'round there so no one falls and breaks a goddamned leg. People don't think around here, leave every damn thing to me."

Hiding a smile, Selena followed him off. As she did so, she glanced back toward where she'd left Theo standing. He was still there, not looking after her, thank goodness. But that was because Jen was there, standing very close, right up against him, looking up into his face.

As Jen reached up to touch his cheek and Theo bent his head toward hers, Selena turned away.

Well, thank goodness that's settled. They make a much better picture than the two of us did.

And that little squiggle of jealousy grinding into her belly? Well, she just would have to ignore that.

Just then, a loud shout echoed through the air. Filled with terror and shock, a woman's voice broke into the lull of story time. "She's gone! I can't find her anywhere!"

A little prickle ran over the back of Selena's shoulders as she heard the rumble of responses from others in bits and pieces: "Are you sure?" "Maybe she's in the yard." "Or the barn." "Maybe she fell asleep."

"No, no. I've looked everywhere!" The stress in Myra Tendy's voice became hysteria. "She was talking about the river today. She wanted to go swimming."

The prickling down her spine became stronger and Selena automatically looked toward the protective walls. Her fingers touched the thumb-sized crystal that hung low on its cord beneath her tunic shirt. If the little Tendy girl— What was her name? Hannah? . . . If she somehow sneaked out of the walls, this was going to be bad.

Her heart pounding, her palms dampening, Selena moved closer to the north side of the wall. She was aware that the audience had broken up and people were forming search groups. Maybe the zombies weren't out yet tonight, hadn't come close enough to see or smell the little girl. Maybe she wouldn't have to deal with it.

Maybe she'd be lucky this time.

So far, Selena hadn't heard any of their guttural moans, their desperate calls of *ruuuu-uuthhh* or *arreeyyyy-aaaane*. She peered through the glass window of an old truck that had been used as a monstrous brick in the protective wall. The glass was dirty and crusted with mildew, but Selena scratched it away and looked into the dingy night beyond the settlement.

The orange, glowing eyes of the zombies were bright enough that she'd be able to see them even through the dirt, if they were out there. The river was on the south side, the far side from where she was. But Selena knew that the *gangas* would come from the northwest, from the direction of the ocean.

All the while, behind her, she heard the shouts, the calm voices of the organizers, the freaked-out voice of Myra Tendy being calmed.

And she hoped that she wouldn't have to go out there tonight and risk exposure.

This was the core of her life: the delicate balancing of hatred and disgust for the flesh-eating, mutilating zombies, with the knowledge that every one of them who died a violent death, without her help, were never truly free.

"Hey."

The voice right behind her had Selena whirling around. It was Theo.

Great. Just what I need now.

Yet, her heart gave a little jump at the sight of him. He stood there, the fingertips of one hand shoved into a front jeans pocket, with a tight expression on his face. His jet-black hair gleamed in the light as if it was wet; and his high, elegant cheekbones caught the iffy light like a magnet.

"You aren't going to try to sneak out there through that car window are you?" he said in a flat, funny voice. He looked as uncomfortable as she felt.

And so the weirdness begins. "No," she said. *Not yet, anyway.*

"Good," he said. "Because after last night, that would be a stupid thing to do. Go out by yourself. And you're not a stupid woman."

Wanna bet? Selena bit back the words before they could slip out. She'd said enough tonight.

"I don't know who you think you are—some misguided Buffy or Eowyn or something—but you can't go out there alone," he said. "You don't even have anything to protect yourself with." His eyes clearly skimmed over her from head to toe.

Somehow she didn't mind the comparison to Eowyn. That woman was kick-ass, and she didn't even have superpowers. Kind of like Selena herself. "What a laugh. A kid like you telling me what to do."

His jaw moved, shadows shifting over his face in Frank's torchlight. "I'm not as young as you think I am," he said. His voice was still flat and calm.

Selena smothered a snort. "You don't look a day over thirty," she said. "And you aren't my father."

"Damn straight," he said. Her stomach flipped and her mouth went dry.

Before she could respond, she heard it. Faint, in the distance, but unmistakable: *"Ruuu-uuuthhhh."*

Damn.

Her palms went damp and her fingers cold. Selena turned away from the wall. If she was going to have a chance to intercept the zombies, she had to do it now. Quickly, before the rest of the search parties got beyond the walls with their sticks and bottle bombs and all the other weapons. *Got to go.*

"Jennifer's looking for you," she said. "Over there." She pointed east, over and beyond Theo's shoulder toward the milling clusters of people—and when he automatically looked away, she darted. Slipped into the shadows.

"Selena!" he shouted, and she glanced back to see him looking at the wall of cars and garage doors and old roofs, as if she'd somehow discovered a way to slide inside.

Good. Let him look for her while she found another way out.

The search parties had begun to leave the protection of the walls by the time Selena located one of the smaller entrances. Her crystal on its long leather thong hadn't begun to glow yet, but its temperature had started to rise. She felt its warmth against the hollow at the base of her breastbone. Not precisely a comforting feeling but a familiar one, nevertheless. A peek down at it confirmed that it wasn't burning . . . *Thank goodness*.

The zombie moans had grown louder, and by listening intently, Selena confirmed that they were coming from the northernmost direction. Fortunately, it was on the opposite side of Yellow Mountain from the river's swimming area, which was where the search parties would head first, then likely split into east and westerly directions.

But the fact that Hannah Tendy had dark hair, and that the *gangas* had been programmed to kidnap blond people (and do what they wished, which was to maul and feed on their flesh), gave Selena little hope that if the little girl was out there, things would end well.

And she didn't really want to be the one rushing out to ease the zombies into the afterlife in the wake of something like that.

The small north-side gate opened easily to a set of

steps that led to the ground below. *Gangas* couldn't climb stairs, so all but the main entrance to Yellow Mountain were accessed thus.

Selena was just about to pull open the grate when a familiar voice came out of the darkness. "Selena, don't."

"Vonnie," she said, turning to her best friend, her mother, her savior. "You know I have to."

The older woman's arm came down to block her from the gate, strong and solid. "Not tonight. Just . . . not tonight. There's nothing you can do."

"Yes, there is. I can't let them—"

"Have you forgotten Crossroads? They might see you."

Selena's voice rose and her throat burned. "Of course I haven't forgotten—"

"Then leave it. Tonight. Just leave it. You're still injured from last night; and if anyone sees you, Selena . . . if anyone sees you—it's a little girl. A child. They won't understand and they won't care." Vonnie's voice cracked with emotion.

"I know the zombies are horrific, but they don't know what they're doing," she replied. Her words were taut and the crystal was much warmer now against her skin, even through the small thick pouch that hid its glow beneath her shirt. "They're trapped."

"You can't save them all," Vonnie told her. "Selena. You can't save them all."

"But I can save some of them. And I have to save as many as I can." She looked at Vonnie, blinking back tears. "I'm the only one."

She loved Vonnie, she owed her *everything*, but the older woman would never understand. She couldn't see the terror in the zombies' eyes, she didn't feel their desperation. She didn't watch their human lives pass through their memory, and into Selena's, as she set them free.

She didn't know that a human soul and mind was trapped for decades inside each hulking, flesh-starving body.

Vonnie wasn't dragged out of *her* sleep by nightmares.

"I'm the only one. That's why I have to go. Please, don't make it any harder than it is."

Her vision blurry, her stomach in knots, Selena ducked under Vonnie's arm and pushed at the gate. She heard the last low cry of her name, and had to ignore it. Blinking rapidly, she heard the grate closed behind her.

Darkness surrounded Selena as she hurried down the stairs. In the distance, she saw orange lights shifting about with jerky motions, in pairs. The groans were laced with desperation as the *gangas* called for *ruuuuuuthhhhh*: searching, always searching for a man named Remington Truth.

Given that Selena absorbed all of their human memories, these creatures who had been just as alive as she and Vonnie before somehow being turned into such horrifying beings, she still didn't know much about their purpose. She did know that the zombies were programmed to walk the earth looking for the silver-haired man who had been one of the Strangers, a member of the Elite. And when they weren't carrying off light-haired humans as candidates, they were tearing into dark-haired ones with their filthy claws and rotting teeth. That was how they fed. How they lived.

If one could call what they did *living*.

Selena's throat burned. It was difficult enough to guide the souls and ease the pain of normal humans as they passed on, but to take on the pain and anguish of these other horrifying, cannibalistic ones . . . it was often too much. The battle between her horror for what they did and her need to save them—because she believed they weren't in control of their urges—was a nightmare.

Yet, Selena couldn't stop. She knew that every one she saved meant one less soul would be trapped in limbo—or somewhere worse—forever. Even one soul saved was worth the danger, worth being ostracized for, worth the constant internal battle she fought.

Selena blinked away the tears. Now was not the time to be distracted. They might be damaged creatures, deranged and mindless, but they were lethal in their desperation.

The terrain in front of her was clear and open, purposely, so that any approach could be seen from the walls. But less than a hundred yards out, trees and the buckled concrete of roads from days past made the ground uneven and provided shadows in which to hide. The overgrown remnants of an occasional building made low, unnatural humps in the land, tall grass shooting up and filling in amid the rubble.

Selena gripped her crystal, pulling it out from beneath her tunic and letting it hang free. She wasn't ready yet to slip off its protective covering, and allow the rose-colored stone to glow in the night. Not until she got closer to a band of zombies.

By counting the lights of their orange eyes, which looked like staggering fireflies from her vantage point, she guessed that there were fewer than a dozen tonight. She'd dealt with more, but any number over five was frightening and chancy.

The familiar fear clogged her throat and her hands had gone clammy. Selena was suddenly acutely aware of the breeze that had been so refreshing earlier, but now felt like an icy blast. The last bit of warmth from the wine that had made her so loose had disappeared, leaving her taut and edgy and her heart pounding.

No matter how many times she did this, no matter how important it was, how critical . . . Selena still felt the fear. As if to remind her of the dangers, the wounds on her chest tightened and ached. And a gash along her back that had healed long ago, twinged.

But she went on.

Now she could smell them in the air—the musty, death smell of old flesh and the putrid rot of their breath. Like swamp and garbage that had been sitting in the sun, baking, for days.

But this was nothing. When they got closer, she'd hardly be able to breathe for the stench.

Selena's hands were cold and clammy and she automatically curled one around the crystal. It was hot now, like a stone that had been tucked amid the ashes of a fire and then withdrawn. The thick pouch protected her from the heat, but she'd soon remove it so that the rosy glow could beam through the night.

She stopped in a shadow about three hundred yards from the wall, and even farther from the troop of *gangas*. The blossoms from the small cluster of apple trees had already dropped their petals and tiny buds had begun to form. The crushed and rusted form of a car sat a few feet away, and what looked like an old sign leaned against it. It was too dark to read the faded letters, but she knew there was a large fancy *R* on it.

The creatures were somehow taller than the humans from which they'd come—taller and broader and thicker, as if their original bodies had been stretched and stuffed to make them larger, causing their skin and skeletons to protest the mistreatment and begin to tear and protrude.

Selena counted eight zombies. *Too many.*

She shuddered and swallowed. Time to move closer.

From behind her, then, suddenly in the night, came a loud clanging sound.

Selena froze and turned, her heart skipping a beat. A great beam of white light shot into the air from behind the walls, accompanying the ringing bell.

That was the signal. They'd found the girl Hannah.

Selena felt a wave of relief so strong that she nearly doubled over, her fingers brushing the rough bark of a tree next to her. They'd found her. She was safe.

An answering light shone into the dark sky in the west, and then another, to the south. The search parties: acknowledging the message and confirming their locations. Far from where Selena was in the north.

The searchers were coming back, and Selena could—

Her thoughts were interrupted when she heard the sound of hoofbeats.

He was riding across the expanse of field, clearly outlined by the slice of moon and the glow from the torch he held high over his head.

Selena watched as he galloped madly toward the cluster of zombies, the fire blazing a stream in the dark blue night above him.

She realized in an instant what he was about to do, and she had to move.

Dashing out of the trees into the open, the crystal swaying and bouncing against her, Selena shouted and waved her arms. She was exposing herself and him as well, but her biggest concern was to stop him before he tore into the zombies and tossed the blazing fire onto them.

At the sound of her shouts, he looked over. In an instant, he wheeled the horse expertly, front hooves flailing briefly against the sky. Then suddenly they were barreling down toward her.

Upright and steady in the saddle, he held the horse's mane in one hand and the fiery torch in the other, looking like some primitive warrior. As one, they leapt over a small crevice in the ground and then over a pile of old tires. He barely shifted in his seat, his hair gleaming from the flames above.

It wasn't until they came closer that she actually saw his features, but somehow she'd already known it was Theo, even from a distance. She'd never seen anyone ride a horse like that, except on a DVD. And even then, she'd been warned by Vonnie and Frank that nothing on DVDs was real, or ever had been.

The mustang stampeded up toward her without slowing, and Selena realized he wasn't going to stop. She started to dart out of the way, but the next thing she knew, the large, pounding animal was upon her. The ground shook and the hoofbeats filled her ears.

What the hell—

They tore past her, hardly slowing. A hand swept down and curled behind her and under her arm, lifting her quickly and fluidly into the air without straining the gashes on her chest. Selena found herself jolted onto the muscular, undulating back of the horse in an unstable sidesaddle position. Instinctively, she grabbed the dark mane in front of her with both hands as she tried to settle her heart and stomach—as well as her rear end—into place. Out of breath, startled and angry, at first she couldn't speak.

Then she was terrified.

As the shock eased, she became aware of the flickering light above them from the torch he still held, and the strong band of an arm that curved from behind her to a clump of mane above her two-handed death-grip. And the very young, very hard thighs that veed and jolted *right* behind her. And the solid torso she'd bumped back against when she got settled in her seat.

"You *busted* idiot!" she managed to gasp, realizing that he must only have been holding on to the horse with his *legs* when he reached down to grab her up. "You might have killed both of us!"

"What the hell did you think you were doing?" he shouted back, the wind whipping his words behind them.

She realized they had made a wide turn and were barreling back toward the cluster of zombies in the distance. "No!" she shouted back at him, twisting in the half-embrace and nearly falling backward off the side of the galloping horse. She gasped and clutched harder. "Go back to the walls!"

The crystal on the long cord bounced and jounced against her stomach, heavy and hot but still covered by its heavy pouch. She bent forward to try and subdue it because there was *no flipping way* she was going to let go of that mane. Especially since her ass was shifting and bouncing like a popcorn kernel in hot grease.

"I've got to take care of them first," he replied in a determined voice by her ear. "Got to find that girl."

"No," she shouted, chancing to turn once again in her seat. She nearly clipped his chin with her temple, and he gave her a quick downward glance. "They found her! Go back, Theo!"

"They found her?" The tension eased a bit from his torso, but still they shot toward the zombies, his bracing arm solid as before.

The crystal was getting warmer and the heat seeped into her belly where she'd bent over to cup it close, and she worried that the temperature might bother the horse. And the zombies, few as there were, would soon sense it, if she didn't get Theo to turn around. "Please! Go back! It's too dangerous!"

He eased up on the horse at that moment and she felt him shift away to look down at her. "Are you hurt? Are you all right?"

"Take me back. Please," she said, avoiding the question but clearly leading him to believe that she was hurt. "They found her. It's not worth it."

Her teeth were chattering now; somehow, her body was supporting her in the misleading of Theo. Selena gripped the mane more tightly and felt his legs shift as he eased up on the horse. The creature responded, slowing and turning to head back to the settlement. The mustang was by no means walking or even trotting; they were still going along at a gallop—but at least it wasn't at breakneck speed.

Which was good . . . and bad. Because now she was even more acutely, insanely aware of the details of her surroundings: the warmth leeching into her back; the bare, muscled arm next to hers; the lap into which she'd been positioned; and the clean, masculine scent of Vonnie's soap mixed with fire smoke, wine, and Theo.

At that moment, she wasn't certain which was a bigger threat to her sanity: his proximity or the orange-eyed zombies stumbling away in the distance.

She had a bad feeling it wasn't the zombies.

CHAPTER 4

Theo hadn't felt this exhilarated in a long time.

The brush of thick, sweet-smelling hair from the woman in front of him, combined with the anger vibrating from her, only made him feel even more alive.

Not that it had been the smartest thing he'd ever done—barreling up to her and swooping down like Viggo Mortenson in *Hidalgo* to scoop her up—but what a rush when she'd landed perfectly in front of him. Reckless, yeah, but when hadn't he been a little crazy?

And it had been a while since he'd let loose like this. He'd fucking missed the rush.

Theo grinned in the dark, still holding the torch in one hand and getting a mouthful of thick hair because of the way he had to lean forward. She was pissed, but she'd get over it when he reminded her how dangerous it had been for her to be out by herself. But, hell, what a crazy-brave thing for her to do . . . stupid but brave.

Not unlike me.

The wall of the settlement, and its main gate, loomed ahead, and he found the doors spreading wide to allow them entrance.

Selena slid to the ground the moment he slowed the mustang to a walk, and before he even dismounted, she'd disappeared. *Again*. Theo wasn't able to follow her immediately, for their arrival had drawn a cluster of people around them—including Jen.

"You were amazing," she said, rushing up to him, her hand already clinging to his arm as he slid off the horse. "I saw you out there; I was watching over the walls. *So* bang."

An unfamiliar flare of impatience washed through him, but he resisted the urge to dislodge her grip. Instead, he looked at Patrick Dilecki, who'd coordinated the search parties and remained in the settlement as a point of contact. "You found the girl?" Theo asked.

"Yes, she's safe. She'd fallen asleep under her bed." He sounded grim and tired as he laid his hand on the horse's neck. The mustang belonged to Dilecki, and he'd been the one to offer it to Theo when he explained that Selena had gone out by herself.

Theo wasn't certain whether to be relieved or annoyed. He supposed Hannah's mother was feeling the same way, so he merely settled on relieved. Yet, the urge to get back out there, to destroy those zombies before they could hurt anyone else, spiked through him. They'd been lucky this time, but he'd been a witness to many other events when the outcome hadn't been so rosy.

His adrenaline rush hadn't faded. And the memory of the carnage he'd seen over the years spurred in him the desire to go back out beyond the walls and finish the job he'd begun. Those damn, blockheaded zombies would be waiting for their next opportunity.

"What were you going to do?" asked Jen. "With that torch?"

Her eyes shone as she looked up at him, and once again Theo was struck by how young she looked . . . and by how she hadn't mentioned Selena at all.

Speaking of which. He needed to have words with that crazy woman. What the hell did she think she was doing, going out there by herself, with no protection, no weapons but whatever that pendant she was hiding around her neck?

"I was going to throw it at them," he told Jen absently as he scanned the shadows. Surely Selena had to be around here somewhere; she wouldn't be sneaking out again . . . *Would she?*

"The torch?" she asked.

Pulled back to the moment by her urgent hand, Theo looked down at Jen. "Yes," he said, trying to keep the impatience from his voice. "I was going to throw the torch at them. They're afraid of fire."

"Where are you going?" she asked, a bit of petulance in her tone.

It was the same sort of petulance that had caused him to give in and kiss her awhile ago, just after that exchange—that kiss—with Selena. Still annoyed by her calling him a youngster in that condescending tone, he'd given Selena the mental flip-off when she walked away—as if the kiss had never happened.

Probably what surprised and annoyed him the most then was the way his fucking knees had gone weak. And his brain had collapsed. Because if his brain would have been working properly, he would have yanked Selena back for more . . . instead of succumbing to a different pair of puckered lips and an easy assuagement of his ego.

Hell, after what had happened with Sage—who'd called his kiss "nice"—and Selena—who'd pretty much done the same, though not in so many words—Theo couldn't be blamed for feeling a little petulant himself. His ego had been more than bruised. "I have to take care of something," he told Jen now. "I'll catch up with you later."

He didn't hear what she said as he slipped away, his eyes paring through the milling crowd. The festive mood had obviously deteriorated since the girl had gone missing, and despite the happy ending, it was tainted by the false alarm.

Theo passed a group of the twenty-somethings he'd been hanging out with all evening—Jen's friends—and realized they weren't all *that* young. They merely *seemed* young to him. Hell, at age twenty-eight, he and Lou had been raking in the bucks because of their techno-geek brilliance. They'd had the CEOs of two Fortune 500 companies afraid to turn off their Black-Berrys without asking them first. They'd had the owner of one of Vegas's biggest casinos turning the entire electronics systems over to them and their consulting firm for a security upgrade. They'd been workaholics on track to retire by the time they were forty-five, figuring they'd have a chance to live and travel and maybe even marry by then.

It probably would have happened, too, if all hell hadn't broken loose. If the men and women in the elite Cult of Atlantis hadn't decided that immortality was worth the destruction of the rest of the earth and civilization.

And so, as Theo walked past the group and they offered him a beer, he took it. He nodded and smiled and wished to hell that he remembered what it was like to be so young and to have had such an uneventful life. It would, he thought, be heaven not to have those nightmares that still woke him in a cold sweat.

Gangas sucked, but they were nothing compared to what he and Lou and the rest of the survivors had lived through for the first twenty years after the Change.

* * *

He was halfway through the beer when he found Selena.

Rather, when she found him.

It wasn't exactly how he'd planned for the meeting to go.

"What the hell did you think you were doing?" she said, walking right up to him. She bristled like the way Lou used to wear his hair—straight up spiky all over.

"I might ask you the same question," he responded, removing the beer bottle from his mouth. He'd been in the middle of a drink. "Sneaking out without any protection or any weapon except that thing around your neck."

That surprised her, for she grabbed at her belly where he suspected the object hung, beneath her tunic. But that didn't keep her from flaring back at him. "What I do is none of your business. You're not my father or my son—or anyone in between. You have nothing to do with me and you couldn't even begin to understand the things I've been through in this life. Your busted stunt out there could have gotten either one of us killed."

"I was trying to save your life," he shot back wryly. "Paybacks, you know?" Theo shifted on his feet. "Did I hurt you?" he asked, thinking mainly of the *ganga* slashes.

"Other than to give me a damned heart attack, no. But I don't need any help from you," Selena replied. Her voice had calmed, as if she realized it had risen too loudly, but they were in the edge of a shadow from one of the small houses, beneath an apple tree. "I knew what I was doing. I'm a long damn way from being a child."

He had to agree with that.

And from the look in her eyes, she was pretty damn pissed at being treated like one. "I'm old enough to be your mother," Selena was saying. "So back the hell off and go hang out with your friends. You can give orders to Jennifer all you want. She'd probably appreciate it. Just don't go riding around and doing stupid stunts like that."

He smothered a smile. He'd never heard *that* lecture before. Not that it ever made a difference.

Theo felt some of his annoyance drain away. He was getting it now. "That's not what you were saying a while ago, over there. I believe your exact words were something like 'not bad for a guy who was dead three days ago.'"

That flustered the hell out of her. Her eyelids fluttered and she stepped back.

Theo pressed his advantage, all of a sudden feeling very much in control. That fascination he'd seen earlier in her face, and the flash of horror, had given way to worry.

The kind of worry that made him want to cuddle her up and tell her it was all going to be okay—except that he'd realized *he* was the cause of the worry. And that, in his mind, wasn't an altogether bad thing.

"Maybe we ought to test it out again and then you can compare the way I kiss to a guy who's *never* been dead." He stepped closer and suddenly his own veins were singing. His skin leapt and prickled and he looked down at her mouth . . .

. . . which had sort of puckered and crinkled, and then a little tip of tongue slipped out nervously, and that little flicker nearly had him dropping to his knees.

"Don't," she said, and put out a hand to stop him. It touched his chest.

Now, Theo had been taught very well that when a woman said *no* or *don't* or *stop*, that was what a guy did. Even if her eyes said *yes*. Even if the *zing* of attraction between them was practically visible. So, much as he wanted to, he didn't move any closer. But he looked down at her and caught her gaze with his—a bit difficult, in the faulty light, but he did manage to do so.

"Aw, come on, Selena," he said coaxingly. "I'm just a kid. What do you have to fear from me?" He grinned when her lips twitched and he noticed that her breathing had shifted into something more sketchy. A little disrupted.

"Nothing," she managed.

"Then why don't you teach me a thing or two? Show me how it's done?" he asked, his voice low and mellow; his eyes focused on hers.

Her fingers convulsed on his chest and he reached up to close a hand over them. "You're crazy," she managed to say. He could tell what a task it was for her to force those words out.

"What do you expect from a guy who was dead three days ago?" He leaned in, trapping her hand against his chest, and was rewarded by her eyes widening and her breathing shifting. "I might be crazy, but I still want to kiss you"—she opened her mouth to speak, but he continued—" . . . among other things."

Her eyes fluttered and her body shivered. Taking that as a good sign, he leaned in.

She met his mouth with hers, lush and warm. Their lips shifted and molded, their tongues danced and slid, and he gathered Selena closer. His body jolted alive and hot as he tasted her—the warm sleekness of her mouth—and as she gave a little sigh against his lips.

Good. Really . . . fucking . . . good was about all his brain could process, because it was all hot and needy and alive. *More . . .*

But before he could get in deeper, get her gathered up against him and get down to business, she shifted back a bit. Pulling her mouth away from his reluctant one, she pressed both hands flat onto his chest. He was certain she could feel the racing of his heart.

"You could have killed us, doing that whole *Kate & Leopold* thing." The lecture tone was back in her voice, albeit unsteadily.

"That what?" He literally had to shift his brain back into play and he eased away—fully, painfully aware of how close the swell of her breasts were to the back of his hand where he held hers pinned gently to his chest.

"The horse thing," she replied a little more steadily. "Riding up and yanking me onto the horse without stopping."

"That wasn't a yank, that was a scoop. Or even a sweep," he said, his mouth sliding into a smile. Now they were getting somewhere. "*Kate & Leopold*?"

She gave an exasperated sigh. "It's on a DVD."

"I figured that. A chick flick, with a name like that. But I was thinking more like *Hidalgo*," he replied. "When I saw it in my head. The whole sweeping-scooping sort of thing."

"I don't remember it in *Hidalgo*," she replied, looking as if she was considering it. "But maybe."

"Okay, then, *Robin Hood*."

She shook her head, a twitch of a smile on her lips. "I don't think so."

"*Prince of Thieves*, with Kevin Costner?" he replied, shifting to brush a lock of hair back from her shoulder. It was warm and heavy, and she smelled fresh and alluring. His heart was still pounding and he couldn't quite pull his attention from her pretty kissed-and-crinkled mouth. "I'm pretty sure it happened in that movie. Just like that."

She shrugged and the back of his hand burned from the brush of her breasts. "Maybe, but I wasn't paying any attention to Kevin what's-his-name. I was more interested in Alan Rickman."

"Alan Rickman? Geez, you and every other female I've ever known have had a thing for that guy." He was chuckling, breathing easier now, and her eyes had lit with humor. He was fully aware of her warmth, her curves, the alluring, feminine smell that clung to her skin and hair . . . He was already thinking about sliding his hands under her loose tunic to cup those breasts she'd been bumping against him . . . not to mention the round curve of her ass. His mouth dried, thinking about sliding against her, skin to skin—

But then Selena stepped back, her hands leaving his chest, breaking his hold on her. "Theo," she said, all business back in her voice, the laughing dying from her eyes. "You're too young to be messing around with someone like me."

Man, this woman can change like quicksilver. He tried to readjust, to rein in his heated thoughts, but she was continuing her motherly lecture before he could respond.

"I realize I put you in an awkward position earlier," she was saying, easing away with her hand, palm out as if to keep him at arm's length. "And I really appreciate that you played along. But I don't need a pity kiss. And, really—continuing on this way would just embarrass both of us. You don't owe me anything. I would have saved anyone's life if the opportunity arose, so you don't need to feel like you have to make it up to me."

At last Theo was catching up. *Pity kiss?* But, by

then, she was finished; and with a last little shove of her hand in the air toward him, as if to say *Stay there*, she ended on, "And I know you're going to be leaving soon, so thanks. And good night." She turned and flitted off.

Again.

Her speech settled in his mind. *A pity kiss?*

So she thought *he* thought he owed her for saving his life? For resurrecting him? And she was worried about him being embarrassed because she was too old?

He started laughing. *If she only knew.*

Theo could have gone after her but didn't. Instead, he smiled to himself in the dull light. This could be fun, keeping this little secret awhile. Because, clearly, she was attracted to him—and it was her fear that he was downgrading himself.

Nothing, he realized with a start, could be further from the truth. Because it wasn't Jennifer to whom he'd gone back for more.

And was he leaving soon?

Between Brad Blizek's workroom and Selena? . . . Not a freaking chance.

Theo got a ride back from Yellow Mountain with Frank—who was up at dawn. After putting in a few hours at the behest of the elderly slave driver, he accrued enough goodwill with Frank that he allowed Theo to go off and work in the arcade.

"Why'd you show it to me," Theo asked as he wiped the sweat off his forehead, "if it's such a secret?"

Frank looked at him with old gray eyes and said, "I been around a long damn time. Too goddamn long. Don't know when I'm going to go. Someone's got to take care of that goddamn equipment. Someone's got to use it."

Theo grinned. "And you figured I'm the one?"

The old man's face turned grumpy. "I'm ninety-three years old. I ain't stupid. You're not like everyone else."

Theo decided to take it as a compliment, and escaped to the arcade. He couldn't wait to get deeper into the systems, down below the layers of security. *Or, hell, just to play with some of the games.*

After all, this was Brad Blizek's place. His computer, his LAN . . . all his stuff. He looked around, touched the acrylic keyboard and brought the system to life.

What could he find in here? What mysteries or information or even— *Wait!*

Wait . . . Theo went cold and his fingers paused over the keyboard. He was already shaking his head. *No, no way; absolutely not. Not Brad Blizek.*

There was no way a guy like him would be a member of the Cult of Atlantis.

But . . . yet . . . he would be a prime candidate to be offered "admission" to the most elite of the elite. To the group made up of the *uber*-rich, the even more powerful, the people who had everything they ever could dream of having . . . except the one thing they couldn't get in this world.

Immortality.

His fingers were already flying over the keyboard, searching, digging, drilling down through LINUX and the hidden folders and manipulating the passwords that he'd already hacked through to find whatever there was to find.

He wished to hell Lou was here to help him.

Recently, Simon Japp had learned from an old acquaintance who'd been a member of the Cult of Atlantis, and was now one of the crystaled Elite, that the price of admission to the club had been $50 million.

Pocket change to someone like Brad Blizek. And besides his money, there was his electronics expertise. His company. His factories. His *mind*.

Just like Stark Industries, it would have been so easy to use UniZek as a cover for research, development, and creation of whatever it was that the Cult used to cause an island to erupt from the middle of the Pacific Ocean, bringing with it the tsunamis, earthquakes, and other catastrophes that shifted the earth on its axis and destroyed the world fifty years ago.

His stomach swishing and tense, Theo dug deeper. He swore and pounded on the keys, forcing them to do his bidding, cranking, and culling until he finally broke the impenetrable firewall.

Theo's exultation at hacking through Brad Blizek's security system collapsed when he saw the image on the screen before him: the circular drawing of a traditional labyrinth. It was topped with a swastika, and around the edges were the scrolling lines symbolizing oceanic waves.

The sign of the Cult of Atlantis.

Holy shit.

Theo erupted from his chair and turned away to pace. Brad Blizek. Attached to the Cult. The people who'd destroyed the world. He felt sick.

Hell, he and Lou had both idolized Brad—not only for the man's ingenuity and creativity, but for who he was. They'd watched the young man's rise, noticed with delight that he supported the same political figures they had. He'd donated millions to Haiti when the massive earthquake struck in 2009. He'd given scholarships and outfitted several inner-city schools with computers.

But he'd also paid $50 million to join a cult that

destroyed the world, just so he could wear a little crystal that made him immortal. Theo felt ill.

He turned away from the large wall screens, settled in front of a laptop-sized machine, and logged into his email. Lou was going to be just as devastated about the news.

Remy figured the best place to hide from the Elites and their bounty hunters was right in plain sight. Smack in the midst of them.

Not that any of them knew that she was the granddaughter and namesake of the infamous Remington Truth; she doubted any of them even knew her grandfather was long dead—but she hadn't lived in careful anonymity for fifteen years by being stupid about it. And, she supposed, even if they figured out who she was, they couldn't know what she possessed.

Her fingers moved, as they often did on their own, to the small orange crystal she had nestled in her navel. *Guard it with your life. You'll know what to do with it when it's time*, her grandfather had said. So she kept it there, in an intricately wrought silver setting that completely enclosed the crystal. It was held in place by four piercings through her belly button, two at the top and one on each side. Sometimes the stone grew warm, even hot. But she never removed it.

If it hadn't been for that group of men and one redhaired woman who'd shown up at her home in Redlo and tricked her into telling them her name, she would still be living there, making pottery, and being content with her beloved Dantès.

As if he read her mind, Dantès lifted his snout from where it rested on his massive paws and looked up at her, cocking his head. *Baroo?* he seemed to say, in that way dogs do—*What is it?*

She reached over to scratch him between his two huge triangular ears, relieved beyond measure that he was back with her. She'd lost him for a time when she fled Redlo, and had only recently been reunited with her protector and companion.

Remy frowned. That had been another unpleasant occurrence, despite the fact that she had regained Dantès. Who could have predicted that the same jerk who pissed her off so badly she lodged a bullet in the wall above his shoulder back in Redlo—just to make a point—would have been taking care of Dantès in Envy? He had tried to keep her from leaving, and Dantès hadn't been any help because he thought the guy was a friend. The jerk had refused to give her his name, so she had taken to calling him Dick. As in Mr. Head.

And in order to escape, she'd tossed a snake at him.

"Something funny?"

Remy, who was sitting on the floor on an old cushion that might have once been blue and most certainly had, at some point, been the nest of a rodent, looked up at her partner. The life of a bounty hunter was a transient one, filled with unfamiliar, and questionably sanitary sleeping accommodations and a variety of other inconveniences. But Ian Marck was one of the advantages.

She didn't give him much, just a bit of a smile. "Just thinking of an amusing occurrence."

Ian was a rugged-looking man, probably close to forty, with a wide, square jaw and dark blue eyes. He had a broad forehead and cut cheekbones, with a long, straight nose and dirty blond hair. Harshness and violence oozed from him, ruining what otherwise would have been very good looks. He had a sort of lethal proficiency, as if he'd do whatever he had to do without giving it a second thought. Remy knew that was true. She'd seen him kill a man with his bare hands. Just a quick twist of the neck in an ugly direction, without a change of expression or shift in his breath.

After that, he'd dropped the man and walked away. Cold and hard as a diamond.

Remy didn't trust Ian anymore than she trusted anyone else—maybe even less, because he was infamous in his own right. His father, Raul, had been a much-feared bounty hunter who worked for the uppermost echelon of the Elite—one of the Triumvirate—until he was killed.

There were those who said that Ian was smarter, more violent, and more ruthless than his father had been—but that, unlike Raul, Ian wasn't greedy. He had no price—not even his own life. Which made him a man without a weakness.

The most dangerous sort.

In the last month or so, Remy had seen and experienced absolutely nothing that refuted that belief.

She changed the subject. "We're meeting up with Seattle and Garrett tomorrow?"

Ian's face twisted with revulsion. "Yes." His eyes scanned her, raising little prickles on her skin. "Seattle's already heard about you from Lacey, so expect a lot of attention from him. She may not like that you're with me, but she'll still rub Seattle's face in anything that gives her an advantage."

Bounty hunters worked for the Elite, searching for whoever might be considered a threat to their power and domination over the rest of humanity. Right now, the bounty hunters were not only looking for Remington Truth, one of the original members of the Cult of Atlantis, but also an escaped member of their own—a woman named Marley Huvane.

These rogue hunters and their partners generally had allegiance to no more than one Elite at a time. It was a sense of pride and display of power for the immortals. And if a bounty hunter was loyal and successful at whatever task was set out, then he or she could be rewarded by being crystaled as well. Someone like that wouldn't be considered an Elite—for that designation was only for those who'd been part of the Evolution fifty years ago—but for many, the immortality was enough.

Lacey was neither a bounty hunter nor an Elite, but she was crystaled. And, according to Ian, she had a love-hate, competitive relationship with Seattle, who aspired to being crystaled so that he could be her equal.

"And we're meeting up with them, why?" Remy stood and gathered up the simple bowl and spoon she'd used for breakfast. Ian appreciated that she was a far better cook than he, and had gladly given over that task to her since they'd become so called partners.

He'd fairly blackmailed her into that arrangement when she walked into Madonna's one day, unaware that the bar was a gathering place for bounty hunters and crystaled immortals. He claimed it was for her protection, which Remy found ridiculous since she was always accompanied by Dantès. But Ian had pointed out that the dog wasn't impervious to bullets, and had given Remy little choice.

But being in the midst of the bounty hunters and their ilk gave her a better hiding place than she could have concocted herself. So she agreed.

"They want a good, strong showing at Yellow Mountain—a little settlement north of here. We're doing a raid, going in to clean it up next week. For some reason, Seattle is a bit spooked by some woman there who can foretell someone's death."

Remy smiled again and took up his bowl. "Maybe he's afraid she'll foretell his demise."

"If that were the case," Ian replied, lounging back against the wall and watching her with those cold eyes, "I'd be first in line to find out. Seattle is a stupid, violent, and reckless bastard."

"Whereas you are simply a violent and reckless bastard," she said mildly, bending to give Dantès the bowls. He liked to make certain every bit of stew was gone before she washed them up.

"It's the only way to be," he said.

His words made her blood chill because she knew he wasn't being amusing, and she tried to ignore the way the back of her neck prickled. She didn't trust him, and she wasn't afraid of him . . . not really. Aside of the fact that he'd never made any threat toward her, there was Dantès, who watched him like a lion waiting for its prey. The dog didn't trust him either.

But he was a hot, demanding kisser. And he had a strong, lanky body with golden skin marred by lots of scars.

They weren't lovers, but Remy suspected it was only a matter of time until that happened. Between the proximity, the lack of privacy, and the fact that they had, in fact, shared more than one session of deep, rough kisses, she knew it wouldn't be long. One of those sessions had ended when she jammed her elbow into his belly and then her foot onto his instep, twisting away to make an escape from Ian and his father.

Not that she hadn't enjoyed the kiss—or the ones that had tangled their tongues before—but the opportunity had arisen and she'd taken it. And it was shortly after that that she'd been reunited with Dantès and met up with "Dick," and then only a week later that she'd come upon Ian again at Madonna's.

Her relationship with him was indescribable and illogical: they were neither friends nor lovers, nor were they enemies. They neither trusted nor liked the other . . . and yet they remained together.

One thing Remy knew: he hated the fact that he had kissed her. It was as if he'd been forced into it, and now reviled himself for doing so. Whether it was because he had shown weakness or some other emotion, she wasn't certain. She only knew what she read in his eyes.

He watched her, not with the heat Remy was used to seeing in a man's gaze, but with cold calculation.

She stayed with him because it was the best camouflage and the safest place to be.

She wondered, not for the first time, just what he wanted from her.

Selena didn't realize Theo had returned from Yellow Mountain even earlier than she had, and she found herself glancing out the window, wondering if he would even come back at all. But about two hours after she finished checking on all of her patients, she saw him walking toward the house, deep in conversation with Frank. He was wiping sweat off his brow, and he looked as if he'd been working for some time.

So apparently, he hadn't stayed in Yellow Mountain this morning to be with Jen. Why did that make her feel so warm and hopeful? She bit her lip, realizing she was smiling. Despite him scaring the crap out of her with his stunt on horseback, she'd enjoyed being with him. They'd joked, they'd smiled, she'd found herself relaxing a bit. She felt comfortable around him in a way that she hadn't been with anyone for a long time.

When her patient groaned, Selena turned her attention guiltily back to Maryanna. The woman's death cloud sparkled softly in the morning sun. Bluish gray glitter, like shiny dust motes, curling and swirling, told her that the young woman's time was near. Maryanna's guides waited patiently, watching as their charge sighed and shuddered in what was no longer sleep but the ease of life into death.

Maryanna hung on between life and death for longer than Selena expected, the pregnant cloud coiling delicately in the corner of her room as the guides hovered silently. The young woman, who'd been breathing with rough desperation, opened her eyes and looked at Selena, lucid and calm.

"I'm going soon," she said, her voice low and halting. "I'll see my brother again and it's going to be all right."

Selena nodded and reached to cover her patient's hand. Preparing. "Whatever separated you on this plane will no longer matter, I think, after."

Maryanna's smile looked to be one of peace, despite what Selena knew: she must be feeling searing pain from the infection that had wormed into her body, culling every bit of energy and leaving her little more than skin and bone. "He's waiting for me too. Thank you for listening to me all these days."

Selena returned her smile and curled her fingers tighter over weakening ones. "That's what I'm here to do. I learn from each of you, all those who come to me."

So very true. Every soul that she'd ushered into whatever came beyond this life had touched her or taught her in some way—and not only through their inherited memories. They taught her forgiveness and grace, peace and even humor. Often, humor.

And then there were the zombies . . . the ones with whom she could only communicate at the moment of their release. Those were the ones that haunted her.

"Are you in great pain?" she asked, seeing the flash of an uncontained grimace. There was so little she could do . . . but she would try.

The woman's lips thinned and the peace from her smile ebbed. "It's nearly over. I . . . I can manage."

The guides had moved now, and Selena saw them reaching out their hands for Maryanna. Between them, and behind, was a young man waiting. The one person Maryanna needed to see before she could let go . . . and so she did.

The glaze of discomfort left her expression, and was replaced by a beatific one when she slid out of her body and into their arms. As she died, the slam of memories barreled into Selena, prickling and rushing through her in flashed images.

When Maryanna was gone, Selena did as she always did. She spent quiet moments in prayer, remembering some of the images that had flashed through her mind at the moment of death, as a sort of private memorial.

Sometimes, that was nearly as difficult as the moment of actual death, seeing those times of happiness and joy. But the angry or frightened ones were the most difficult. Their sadness and grief.

It was as if she lived every emotion from a person over and over. But she did it in memory of the person who died. Then she wrapped the body in lemon-scented cloth. It would be given to the family if there was one, or taken to Yellow Mountain for cremation if not.

Selena looked down at Maryanna and wished that it was always this easy. This painless. This peaceful, ushering a soul into the after.

Her stomach tightened and she glanced outside. She'd been eighteen when she learned of her other responsibility. Of the power of the rose crystal.

She'd been outside the walls one night, returning to her home, when she became lost and couldn't find her way. She was in the forest, lost and without light, and she pulled the crystal from her pocket because she knew sometimes it lit up.

Tonight it was glowing, and offered some illumination to help her find her way.

When she heard the moans from the orange-eyed creatures, Selena knew she didn't have a chance of returning home. The trees were too tall for her to climb and there was nowhere else to hide from them.

She sat on the ground and prayed that it would be quick, holding the crystal, wondering if she'd see her own death cloud. She heard a voice in her mind that said, *Be brave. All will be well.*

She tried to heed the advice, for she knew it was her guardian angel. But when two of the zombies came to her, she tried to fight them back, terrified and screaming.

Suddenly, she realized they wanted only to touch her crystal. They didn't tear into her, didn't try to carry her off.

They groped and grabbed at her crystal, and deep inside her Selena heard the voice again: *Help them. They need your help.*

And when she opened her eyes—which had closed

in fear—she saw the blond-haired Wayren standing there, watching and nodding.

As with the others that she helped, Selena didn't wholly understand how or what was expected of her. But she knew peace when she saw it; and as she allowed the creatures to touch her, she saw it fill their eyes.

And when she looked at Wayren, she saw the woman nodding. *This is your gift. Use it to help them.*

And so, for more than thirty years, she had.

Some time later, Selena padded into the kitchen and found Vonnie in there, stirring something that smelled incredible. As usual.

Filled with a combination of love even as apprehension weighted her, she bundled the woman into a big hug. "You're the most amazing person I've ever known," she said, then smiled down at her.

Vonnie patted her on the cheek. "The feeling's mutual, honey," she said. "But what prompted you to say that?"

"Just the fact that it's true. And because you feed me. What are you cooking?"

"Roasted mangos and potatoes with stewed chicken," Vonnie said, removing a dripping spoon from the pot to the counter. She left a trail behind and swiped a quick rag over it. "And, for you, tomatoes and peppers and corn with quinoa. Lots of garlic and cilantro." She knew Selena couldn't eat anything that had a face, and always went out of her way to make meatless food for her.

"Thank you. Sounds delicious. Make sure to save me some of the mangos." She reached into a bowl of newly picked almonds, most likely shelled by Frank. Three years ago, they'd almost lost their last almond tree, but Frank had babied it through a pest-infested drought just as he had their other special plants.

Selena cast a guilty look out toward the ruff of tall trees and thick bushes in the back third of the grounds. They were lucky the snoot hadn't ever found their way past Frank's camouflage. Part of the reason they didn't get that far was that their leader, Seattle, was half terrified, half fascinated by the Death Lady—a fact that she exploited whenever she could.

"I'm sorry about Maryanna," Vonnie said.

Selena nodded and shrugged. She was too, but there was little to say. It was a fact of life.

Another *Why?* for which she had no answer.

She glanced toward the window. The sun seemed to have moved much too quickly all of a sudden. It was still high . . . but now on its downward slope. She'd have to go out tonight.

"How about going to find Theo and letting him know there's something to eat?" Vonnie said casually. "That man eats more than Sammy and Tyler combined!"

"He's back from Yellow Mountain?" Selena asked, just as casually.

Vonnie shot her a look laced with skepticism, a little smile twitching her lips. "He's up at the arcade, I think."

What does Theo want with all those old things in the arcade? And who gave him permission to go there?

Vonnie answered before she could ask. "Well, it's Frank. He's taken a bit of a shine to the kid, and said he could go up there."

Kid. Right. He's a kid.

Selena had to keep reminding herself of that.

The house they lived in and where Selena cared for her patients was generous—a mansion, said Vonnie; a hacienda, argued Frank—but they used very little of the area for living. And since there weren't many people who wanted to share space with constantly dying people, it was only Frank, Vonnie, Selena, and Sam who actually lived in the long four-story building.

What they called the arcade took up the entire third floor of the house; the doors that led there had been sealed off by Frank years ago so that no one—especially the snoot—knew it existed. Selena had seen arcades on DVDs, and Vonnie had apparently been to them before the Change—but the one here was much larger and more interesting than anything she'd ever seen, if one considered rows and shelves and counters of dust-ridden machines that no longer worked *interesting*. She hadn't been up here for more than five years, she guessed, and only briefly with Frank.

When she opened the door, which Frank had fixed to look as if it was boarded up but really wasn't, at first she didn't see Theo anywhere.

"Theo?" Selena called, hearing a soft whirr from one of the far corners. She realized belatedly that she should have put on shoes before coming up to this dusty, abandoned place.

No answer. She walked toward the whirring sound and became aware of a quiet clicking and a rattle—he was definitely there. She found him then, around a corner with the window behind him open and stirring the air and dust.

He didn't look up as she approached; he was staring at the screen of a computer. His lips were moving and his brows furrowed as his hands moved like lightning over a keyboard, clicking the keys, stabbing them with emphasis, then suddenly, "Fuck you, asswipe fucker, you know you're fucked if you don't fucking do what I fucking say!" . . . and then he was back attacking the keys with his fingers as if his life depended on it.

"My, what a sweet-talker you are," Selena said,

moving closer, fascinated by the intensity on his face. His eyes were so focused, his hair standing up in all sorts of loops and spikes like the feathers of a ruffled bird.

He whipped around to look at her, hands settling on the keys. The surprise in his expression was fleeting, but indicated that he truly hadn't heard her approach. His face seemed strained, a little tight, as if something was bothering him.

"If she would behave and do what I wanted her to, I wouldn't have to get tough on her," he said, his expression softening. "Females can be very temperamental." Humor warmed his eyes. And warmed her. "I'm glad to see you. I needed a break."

Selena walked closer, her attention drawn to that writhing red dragon on his arm, and up along the swell of his biceps to a solid, curving shoulder. *Not exactly a kid . . .* She blocked the rest of the thought from her mind.

No more pity kisses. That was going to be her new mantra.

Selena regrouped. "We females certainly can be temperamental if the situation warrants it," she replied, turning her attention resolutely to the screen. It was lit up with all sorts of characters—lines and lines of them. She'd never seen a computer in real life, working like this. Only on DVDs, and then what was on the screen looked a lot different—almost DVD-like. This looked much less exciting.

Nevertheless, her skin prickled with worry; it was dangerous. *He shouldn't be here.*

"Yes, especially when they disappear without warning," he commented, holding her gaze now with his dark one. "Last night . . . did it occur to you that I might be a little concerned for your safety when you went off outside the walls?"

"Does it occur to you that I'm a grown woman and well able to take care of myself?" she replied very mildly. She didn't want or need to argue with him about this again. He seemed to be looking at her feet, or the floor. She hoped he didn't see another spider—or something worse—but she wasn't going to ask, as the likelihood of that was higher than she preferred.

Then all at once, she realized the significance of what she'd somehow ignored, and her brain refocused. "You really know how to work these?" She waved her hand to encompass the machines in the room.

"Yes." He glanced up at her.

"How?" she asked. A little shaft of prickles rushed over her body as the memory washed through her mind. *His* memory. Sitting in front of a screen like this one—but much smaller than the ones that took up the walls. *Very at home there.*

"I've been working on them for longer than you can imagine. I'm kind of a genius with computers and electronics." The flicker of a smile returned to his lips and eyes. "My twin brother and I both are."

"There are two of you?" The horrified words slipped out before she realized it. Then she laughed a little at the delighted expression on his face. "You must have turned your mother's hair white by the time you were ten."

"Somehow Lou doesn't come across as reckless as people seem to think I am."

"You don't think you're reckless?" she asked incredulously.

"I'm still alive, aren't I?" he replied. Then he raised his gaze and their eyes locked. "Thanks to you," he added, his voice pitching lower.

Her throat dried and all she could remember was being pulled up against his solid, very *un*childlike body last night. She was suddenly very aware of the fact that they were alone. Again. And he was looking at her in a certain way.

No more pity kisses.

"Last night was definitely not a pity kiss," he said. "Selena."

"Did I say that out loud?" she said, then clamped her mouth closed. "Yes," he replied, that smile playing about his lips. He stood now, shoving the wheeled chair away behind him. He seemed taller than she remembered. And broader. And whatever annoyance he might have had about her disappearing back in Yellow Mountain seemed also to have evaporated. "I have to tell you," Theo said, standing there in front of her, "I can't stop thinking about you."

He shook his head, folding his arms over his torso, continuing conversationally—as if they were talking about the weather and he didn't quite understand why it was raining when the sun had been shining all day. "I find I'm fascinated by you, about what you're sneaking out for at night, what you're wearing around your neck that you don't want anyone to see . . . what it's like being the Death Lady and holding the hands of people dying, and how you do it every day without fail." He nodded, his eyes holding hers. "How you got to be so strong, and why you do what you do. And other things, like the fact that you don't eat very much and that you like to run in the morning—Vonnie told me that—and how you both ended up here, with Frank. And where in the hell you got red toenail polish."

Selena realized her mouth had dropped open slightly—not enough that she was slack-jawed but, rather, sort of relaxed in surprise. "Um," she said, trying to tamp down the warmth that was flushing through her. She was all trembly all of a sudden and her stomach was all aflutter. *Good grief.*

And then . . . *He's fricking serious. He really wants to know about me.* Both delight and terror rushed through her.

"And about Sam's father, and whether he's still around and why he isn't," Theo continued. "Whether it was your decision or his or what. And," he stepped closer to her, "how I'm going to make it clear to you that I don't give pity kisses. Not even for women who bring me back to life." His hands landed gently on her shoulders and she felt his shoe bump against her bare toes.

"How many of them do you have?" she managed to say, realizing belatedly that her hands had risen and settled flat onto his broad, warm chest. *Wow. Solid as a brick wall.*

"How many of what?"

"Women who bring you back to life."

"Only one." He started to lean in, then stopped and pulled back. Selena released the breath she'd been holding, startled out of the warmth he'd lulled her into. "Make that two."

"What?" she asked, her voice rising—partly in surprise and partly to hide her disappointment. "You've been brought back to life before?"

His lips curved and one of his hands shifted to flick a heavy lock of hair off her shoulder, then slid along its length. "Well, technically, yes. When I was a baby, the umbilical cord was wrapped around my neck and I came out blue everywhere, limp as a wet noodle. Heart stopped and everything. There was a nurse who did

CPR—she breathed inside my mouth—and brought me back to life."

"A *nurse*?"

"But don't worry," he added quickly, "I don't remember the incident at all. So for all intents and purposes," he said, slipping his hand around the back of her neck, lifting her hair, cupping her skull, "you're the only woman who brought me back to life. And this is most definitely not a pity kiss."

She met him halfway as his lips moved to add, " . . . at least on my end."

Selena's laugh was smothered by his mouth. She closed her eyes as their lips met, softly at first and then hungrily. He held her head with strong fingers as the kiss turned deep and sleek. Beneath her own palms, the planes of his chest shifted and his heart bumped fiercely.

He didn't feel like a kid to her, not now, not with this demand and confidence, not with the solid muscle and strength against her. Her body had turned warm and liquid, awakening from a dormancy due to neglect. Selena stopped questioning, stopped resisting, and when his hands moved down along her back, following the line of her torso, she eased into him, molding her body into his.

Why not? Why not enjoy this? It's been too long.

He's so young!

And he'll be leaving any day now. No problem.

He makes me laugh.

Theo gave a soft little groan and shifted, pushing her back against something solid, holding her there so their bodies lined up, imprinting every curve and every rise into the other. If she had any lingering doubt about pity kisses, it was effectively erased at that point. His desire was blatant, and the gentle, insistent pressure as their hips ground together had her pressing just as hard back into him.

"Geeezz . . . uzz," he muttered, disentangling their mouths and burying his face into the hair by her ear. "Selena . . ." He breathed roughly, nipping and sucking along the line of her neck so that she twitched and shuddered against him.

She murmured her pleasure, sliding her hands under his shirt, feeling the flat slabs of his pecs and skimming over the tight nipples, aware of the faint trembling beneath her fingers, deep in his muscles. He was warm and sleek and her world had turned hot and bold . . . so much that she hardly realized when he pulled back, tugging her with him.

The next thing she knew, he pulled her onto his lap, her toes bumping the base of the chair as she straddled him. Theo grinned briefly up at her, but his mouth was tight and his eyes hot as he slipped his hands beneath her loose shirt. She resisted instinctively when he tried to lift it—*No, no, not in the light!*—and he seemed to get the message, instead moving to her spine.

As her bra loosened and sagged, Selena arched toward him, half aware of the hot sun streaming through the window on her behind and the way his hands moved around to cover her breasts. *Ahhh*. His thumbs were firm and his palms warm as he lifted, pressed, stroked.

Now she had her hands on his shoulders for stability, her eyes closed, allowing the pleasure to grow and roll, unfurling from belly to chest to between her legs, where she pressed against him. His hair was warm and soft, thick beneath her fingers . . . his shoulders wide and square.

Theo moved beneath her as he bent and pulled the

vee of her tunic to the side, finding one of her nipples and covering it with his warm, sleek mouth.

Selena jolted at the spike of sensation, then gasped as it didn't stop, didn't relent . . . but became a long, slick tug, a sensual dance of tongue and lips sucking, swirling, stroking. The hot shaft of pleasure arced through her, from her belly down south. She shifted on his lap, her fingers digging into his shoulders, heat and pressure building and throbbing between them.

Suddenly, he released her with a soft groan, leaving her nipple wet and throbbing, chafing back beneath her tunic. Pulling her up against him, his arms bundling her close, he slammed his mouth over hers once more. The kiss burned, deep and fierce, as his hands shifted down to her hips and jerked her close, into him, settling her legs wide against him. She felt the throbbing settle between them, his erection hard and waiting, she herself full and wet, the seams of their jeans meeting and intensifying the sensation.

And then, once again, he was shifting her, and once again, she moved at his direction—hazy, full, aroused—her legs coming together, sliding to one side of him. Before she knew it, he'd jammed his fingers down beneath the loosened fly of her jeans, down beneath the hot cotton of her panties, and into the sleek warmth that pulsed there.

They both groaned and sighed at the same time, and Selena's eyes flew open when he first touched her. She nearly jolted off his lap, but he held her steady, safely, his fingers so long and easy, sliding and stroking where she was full and ready.

Oh God . . . She held on to him, lifted her hips as her jeans opened wider, feeling the stream of hot sun blasting through the window over her head and shoulders. His fingers . . . a wide, determined plane, curling and slipping, coaxing smoothly and evenly, as his own breath hitched and roughened against her ear.

"Yes," he whispered into her skin. "That's . . . it."

As she released herself, sliding wholly, into the pleasure, it took a moment before the sound registered in the depths of her lust-fogged mind. But then, all of a sudden, she heard it.

"Mom?"

CHAPTER 5

It took a moment before Theo heard it.

"Mom?"

And then another second before it registered.

Selena, who had been a soft, sensual bundle in his arms, stiffened—and her eyes flew open just as Theo realized the "mom" was the woman on his lap. The woman whose pants his hand was down, whose flushed face and swollen lips were a breath away from him, whose tight, unfettered nipples thrust through the light fabric of her shirt.

Holy crap.

He grabbed Selena's arm to steady her wild escape as she scrambled off him, and managed to keep her from stumbling into a heap against the wall. His brain wasn't functioning at optimal levels quite yet; his breathing was still irregular; and his jeans, full of a massive hard-on that, only moments before, had been anticipating a happy ending. He stood and jammed his hands in his pockets to make the necessary adjustments for both comfort and obscurity.

"Mom? Are you up here?"

"Yes," Selena called back. She was standing by the window, just done buttoning her jeans. Her voice was unbelievably calm and steady. For someone who'd been writhing and moaning on his lap only moments earlier, she sure looked in control. Hardly ruffled at all, except for the sheen of damp on her full lips, and hair that looked as if she'd just rolled out of bed. *And . . . oh, crap . . .* the outline of one nipple poking damply through the thin tunic.

Sam and one of his other friends—*Tim? Tyler? Tom?*—suddenly appeared, walking across the long room. Theo gave a moment of thanks that he and Selena had been tucked behind a computer station in a corner not immediately visible from the door.

"Nana Vonnie wanted me to tell you there is lunch," Sam said. He glanced around the room, but his attention settled on Theo, and then Selena—who, thank God, had adjusted her tunic—and then back to Theo, who tried to ignore the suspicion in the teenager's eyes—after all, he couldn't have seen anything.

But when the look of shock, followed by revulsion, blanched over Sam's face, Theo realized the kid must have sensed something. He hoped like hell it wasn't the musky smell of sex that clung to Theo's fingers, permeating *his* consciousness, at least.

"Thanks, honey," Selena said, looking perfectly at ease, in spite of . . . *Crap*—Now Selena's loose bra was clearly showing through the deep vee of her tunic. "I'm getting hungry, too," she replied, "but when I came up to let Theo know, we got talking about all the things in here."

"Yeah," Sam replied, flat disbelief in his voice.

He was a handsome kid, with dark blond hair and hazel eyes. Well over six feet, but still had lots of filling out to do. Probably sixteen or so, maybe seventeen. Just getting into manhood, still trying to figure out what to do with all those hormones he'd been dealing with for the last few years. And the last thing he probably wanted in his mind was the image of his mother screwing around with some guy who was not his father.

Or with any guy.

Theo managed a smile and attempted to divert their interest. "Those are pinball machines over there," he said, gesturing to a row of the dusty machines. *The Lord of the Rings* version was one of his favorites, and just about one of the best pinball machines ever made. He'd enjoy it just as much as Sam and Tom—Tyler?—would. "I might be able to get one of them working again, if you want."

"No," Selena said sharply, just as interest lit Sam and Tyler's—Tim's?—face. "We don't need to get involved with those things. Too dangerous."

Theo saw the disappointment on the boys' faces. *More dangerous than sneaking out at night alone?*

"Maybe he could at least look at the DVD player. The one that's broken? He might be able to fix it?"

"Maybe," she said. Selena didn't acknowledge Theo any further except to give him a warning glare as she started out of the room. The other boy whose name Theo was certain began with a *T* started after her, but Sam didn't. He caught Theo's eyes and positioned himself in front of him—not overtly threatening, but just enough that it was clear he meant to talk to him.

Theo had to give the kid credit. A lot of it. Despite the fact that Sam was a bit taller than he was, he was more slender and certainly not as solid as Theo.

"Look"—Sam said in a voice that sounded just a little breathless. He glanced over his shoulder to make sure his mom was gone—"I don't know what's going on with you. Last night you were all over Jennifer, and now you're . . . uh . . . well, if you're messing with my mom, well, I'm not going to be too happy about that."

His Adam's apple bobbed a bit too much and Theo saw him folding his arms together over his chest as if to keep himself steady.

Theo nodded and held the young man's eyes. Figuring honesty—without a lot of unnecessary details—was best, he kept his face serious and said, "I can see how you'd be upset. But I'm not into Jennifer, okay? That wasn't gonna work. As for your mom . . . well, she's pretty amazing" —he barely caught himself from saying *hot*— "and I'm not sure what's going to happen. But I promise you that whatever happens, I'll treat her with care and respect. Okay?"

Sam's nervousness seemed to have eased a bit, but he wasn't ready to give in. "You're not from around here, and you're not staying. I don't want you getting her all happy or relying on you, and then up and leaving one day. You know?"

Theo blinked. *Yeah. I'm not from here.* But at the same time, the thought of leaving, even only after four days (which somehow seemed like a lifetime), was foreign and unpleasant. "I'm not planning on leaving any time soon, Sam," he said. "Like it or not. And as I said, your mom is an amazing" —*smart, sexy, fascinating, strong*— "woman and I always treat women with respect."

Sam was still looking at him, his head inclined slightly, and at last he gave a short nod of acknowledgment. "All right." Then he glanced around furtively, and looked back at Theo. "And I'd really like to learn about these things," he said, gesturing to the room. "Will you show me?"

Theo opened his mouth to agree, then stopped. Selena understood the same danger Frank had mentioned, but that was precisely the reason for the Resistance that he

and Lou were building. Technology was powerful, and
that was why the Elite wanted to suppress any knowledge or use of it. But until he had a chance to talk to
Selena, he'd better resist the knee-jerk reaction to cir-
cumvent her wishes. "I'll talk to your mom," was all he
said. "Now, let's go find something to eat."

The meal, though delicious, was excruciating.

Selena avoided his eyes so studiously that Theo figured she'd gone back to the whole ridiculous "I don't
want pity kisses" stance, which annoyed him no little
bit and made his disappointment at their interruption
even more acute. Sam's attention shifted back and forth
between them as if waiting for any sign of misbehav-
ior. Vonnie, on the other hand, seemed to be watching
both of them with barely concealed amusement. Frank
couldn't hear (or, more likely, pretended he couldn't),
so everything spoken at the table had to be shouted the
first time if they didn't want to have to repeat themselves.

And to top it all off, somehow Jennifer had arrived
just in time for lunch, and although Theo barely managed to keep from sitting next to her, she'd positioned
herself across the table from him. Between the long,
hot looks she sent Theo, the constant references to last
night's horsemanship and the bang ink on his arm—
not to mention the fact that Sam was hardly able to
keep his eyes from straying to the way Jen filled out
her tight white tank top—Theo felt as if he were in the
midst of an episode of some family sitcom.

It didn't help that he could hardly keep his own attention from Selena, especially now that he knew how
she tasted, smelled, and felt all loose and aroused.

Sure, Jen was younger, very attractive, and certainly

more overtly interested than Selena—plus she didn't
have a teenaged son—but Theo had no desire in picking up anything with her. It was Selena who'd captured
his attention. She was easy to talk to, she was quick-
witted, and she was a person who spent her life trying
to make a difference in the world—*besides* trying to
get herself killed hunting zombies. But even then, she
was trying to make a difference in this fucked-up place.
Just as he was.

He definitely intended to pick things up where they'd
left off. And the one time he managed to catch her eye
during the meal, he made his intentions blatantly clear.
Her cheeks flushed and she turned away.

As he'd been trained by his mother, Theo helped
clear the dishes after lunch, stacking them by size
and type. Even though it had been a long time since
he'd been in a kitchen and served a meal like this, old
habits—and training—died hard.

But he kept his eye on Selena, who also made trips
to the sink from the cozy round table in a space that
was much too big to be called a breakfast *nook*; and
the minute she headed for the door, he followed. Just
outside the kitchen, she turned down a hall toward the
back of the house.

"Hey," he said, managing to snag her arm.

Selena looked up at him, lips slightly parted, cheeks
flushing, and her thick hair a wild mess over her shoulders. It took everything he had not to pull her up against
him for a kiss. Instead, he merely said, "That was dis-
appointing."

"It was?" she replied, a little smile playing over her
lips. "I was thinking I got the good end of the deal."

Ah. Relief swarmed him. She wasn't going back to the
pity-kisses game. "Not quite as good as I'd intended."

He let his smile fill with promise. "I was thinking we might want to pick up where we left off. Very soon."

Her lips curved more, sending a shot of lust down through him. "That sounds like a really good idea. Maybe somewhere a little more comfortable?"

He moved then, with a quick glance to make certain no one had followed them, and eased her up against the wall, hands on her slender shoulders. "And a little more private." He slid into her space, covering her lips with his . . . not in a raucous, lust-inducing kiss, but one of promise and anticipation. "My place isn't very private," he murmured against her mouth.

"Mine is," she said, pressing her hips against his.

"I accept," he said, slipping his tongue in to tangle with hers. "Tonight, then."

"Mm . . . hmmm. . . . tonight," she murmured, her hands resting on his chest, her breasts pressing into him. Then she pulled away. "No, wait . . . not tonight," she said.

"What?" He pulled back now, too, but kept his hand playing with the ends of her hair. "Why not? After the kid's in bed—"

"No, no, not tonight," she repeated. Her face had changed from the soft, desire-filled one to something else. Something . . . reserved. Taut. Then she smiled again. "I don't want to wait that long."

Oh, really? Much as he liked that thought—and agreed with it—Theo wasn't born yesterday. Definitely not yesterday. "Then when?"

"After dinner. Follow my cue," she said, and her hands moved over his shoulders, back up into the hair at the nape of his neck and she pulled him down for a long, thorough kiss.

When she pulled away, Theo was breathing heavily

and was trying to remember exactly why he couldn't drag her into a deserted corner *right this damn minute*.

"Until then . . ." she said, easing away. Promise burned in her eyes.

"I'll try to manage," he replied jokingly. "But after that . . ."

She smiled hotter. "Just wait. We older women . . . we're worth the wait." And with that sultry curve to her lips, she slipped away.

Holy shit.

Theo turned and went back out, in the opposite direction, and nearly ran into Jennifer.

"Hey," he said, trying to unclog his brain. And for the life of him, he couldn't think of anything to say that couldn't be interpreted as interest in her.

But Jen was looking at him, her eyes narrowed and a shocked expression on her face. "You and Selena?" she said, disbelief rising in her voice. "You've got to be kidding me. Do you know how old she is? Way too old for you."

Fleeting thoughts about scorned women zipped through his mind and Theo forced a smile. "Believe it or not, I'm a lot older than I look."

Jennifer looked at him, her lips flattened in disdain. "She's old enough to be your mother. That's just . . . *busted*. Totally rank."

"Uh . . . well," Theo said, struggling valiantly to find something to say that couldn't be construed as offensive to said scorned woman.

"And what about last night?" she demanded. "You were all over me!" Her arms crossed under her breasts, lifting and jolting them, which did nothing to help the situation because his gaze dropped there automatically. Because he was a guy. *Shit.* He shifted his eyes away.

Theo's brain just wouldn't work and he couldn't think of anything to say except, "I'm sorry if I gave you the wrong impression last night." He forbore to point out that she had hung on him; she had thrown herself into his arms; and yeah, he'd kissed her . . . but only after she'd blatantly offered.

"Whatever," Jennifer said, and spun around. She flounced away, her sun-streaked hair bouncing with annoyance.

Theo let out a sigh of relief. At least now she knew there was nothing on his end.

Now all he had to do was wait until after dinner to get his hands back on Selena.

And in the meantime, figure out what the hell she was planning tonight.

Lou adjusted the weight of his pack and gave one last glance behind him.

He could barely make out the tops of the buildings that remained on the Las Vegas Strip—or as it had been in 2010. From where he stood, in a sludgy puddle of water between two tall vacant buildings, two miles behind him, he caught sight of the rooftop of New York-New York. The bastion of civilization in this world.

I must be fucking crazy.

Lou looked back at New York-New York, where, far beneath the towers, Sage was likely just settling into place at one of the banks of computers. She wouldn't realize he was gone until lunchtime . . . or later.

Yep. I've crossed the line. Definitely crazy.

He lifted his burning torch and a rat slinked into the shadows. The walls of Envy, built from old cars, billboards, semi-trailers, airplane wings, and whatever large pieces of rubble they could find, had been constructed fifty years ago to protect the residents from *gangas* and wild animals. Now they loomed above him as Lou started through the intricate secret tunnel through cars, culverts, and boxcars that led to the outside.

Moments later, he stood on the grass on the other side and snuffed his torch. He placed it against the wall next to one of the broken lights from a Bellagio billboard. It would be there on his return.

If he returned.

I'll return. I haven't lived this long by being stupid.

He wasn't even certain of the last time he was outside the walls. And that was part of what had prompted him to leave now. Theo needed his help. He had to be sitting on a fucking gold mine of information about the Cult of Atlantis—not to mention other goodies that might be found at Brad Blizek's—and while Theo was a hell of a gearhead, Lou was the better hacker. And . . . he was tired of being confined, of being treated like a decrepit old man. He was old, but he wasn't by any stretch decrepit.

Besides all that, he wouldn't—*couldn't*—believe that Brad Blizek had been in the Cult of Atlantis.

He was fully aware of the dangers. A little more than a month ago, Vaughn Rogan, the mayor of Envy and Lou's friend, had nearly died from a lion attack. For, not only did zombies lurk, but tigers, lions, wolves, feral cats, and even elephants lived in the former Nevadan desert. Now the terrain was lush and green, overgrown and practically tropical at times.

Part of the shift of the earth after all of the cataclysmic events.

"You're a long damn way from your gadgets, old man."

Lou nearly shot into the air. He whirled to see Zoë emerging from behind a crushed and overturned mail truck. The red-and-blue insignia was faded to gray.

"What the fuck?" he demanded, a hand clapped to his chest. It was going to be hours before he settled his seventy-eight-year-old heart. "Are you trying to give me a heart attack?"

She had her quiver of arrows slung over a slender shoulder, and her short dark hair was winging every which way. Her look was withering. "If you didn't hear me, then that's even more damn cause for worry. I made enough fucking noise to bring the zombies out of their day sleep. How the hell do you think you're going to get where-the-fuck-ever you're going without getting ambushed?"

He stood up straighter and adjusted his pack. "No one's going to ambush me but you. I've been living in this crazy world longer than you have. I've taken precautions." He looked into the distance, into the direction he sensed that Theo was. "I'm traveling during the day and holing up at night where the zombies can't get me. I'm going to be just fine."

"Let me guess. You didn't tell anyone, that's why you had to sneak out the back-ass secret entrance."

"They would've argued with me. Don't even think about trying to stop me." He glared.

Zoë smiled and leaned back against a tree. "You obviously don't know me well enough, Lou. I'd be the last damned person to try and stop you. Even Quent knows better than to try and keep me penned up behind those fucking walls."

Lou relaxed. "Good. That way I won't have to hurt you."

Their eyes met and they both laughed. Zoë was a

crusty wench, but he liked her. It was hard not to, once you saw through her facade.

"You going after Theo?" she asked.

"Yep. He found some things I need to see. Computers and other stuff."

"How the hell you going to find him?"

He shrugged. "It's this twin thing. I can sort of sense him . . . I'm just going to follow that. I'm taking one of the Humvees."

"They're going to have a fucking zombie cow back there, you know."

"Half of Envy already thinks I'm crazy." His talk of the Strangers and their desire to control the remains of the human race, not to mention the abductions and massacres related to the zombies, had long been dismissed as the ravings of a senile old man.

"That's a damn true statement," Zoë said. "Fucking good thing we know you aren't."

"True." Since no one paid attention to him, that made it easier for them to build the secret Resistance.

"Well, I'd go with you, but you'd just slow me the hell down," Zoë told him, but there was worry in her eyes. "Remember to keep your hair covered, old man. Those ass-crap zombies like blondes."

Lou chuckled. "Silver is a far cry from blond, but they sure as hell can't tell the difference. Tell Sage I'll be all right. She likes to worry."

"She's not the only one," Zoë grumbled, glancing back toward Envy. "Quent is going to be one volcanic pimple on my ass." She frowned, frustration emanating from her.

"You mean he isn't already?" The arguments between Zoë and Quent had become legendary for their vociferousness, volume, and frequency. Of course, everyone knew that those battles were most often followed by very exuberant make-ups in their room afterward. And sometimes in the stairwells, as Lou knew from personal experience.

He was still trying to decide if he was embarrassed or delighted by that bit of a free show.

Zoë's face darkened. "Hell, yeah. He couldn't be a bigger pain, always trying to butt in on my hunts, telling me how to do it. Him and that fancy-ass bomb of his. But it's going to get worse." She flattened her lips, considering. "Hell, I might have four months . . . *if* I find something loose to wear, dammit."

It dawned. "You're pregnant?" Then he started chuckling. The very thought . . . it was amusing and horrifying all at once.

"Shhhh!" she snapped, as if the trees could hear. "Don't say it so loud or he'll be locking me up tomorrow. It'll be the last damn time he lets me out on my own." She'd planted her hands on her hips. "Maybe I should go with you . . . I could come back after this is all the hell over. Then I wouldn't have him breathing down my damn neck all the fucking time."

Lou was laughing out loud now. *Zoë, with a baby?* He could only imagine. She'd probably strap the poor thing on her chest in a little pouch and take it hunting for zombies. "I don't think so. I take it he doesn't know?"

Her almond-shaped eyes grew wide. "What the hell? Do you think I'm fucking crazy? The minute he finds out, I won't see a damn arrow for nine months. Or longer." She moaned. "He's going to go flipping crazy on me."

"You—uh—don't seem too happy about it," Lou ventured.

"Well, yeah. It's kind of unexpected, for fuck's sake."

His heart sank a little. He and Elsie . . . they'd been on their way to being parents, but everything went wrong when she tried to deliver. It was more than forty-nine years ago, but he still mourned them both. If he'd just had one of them . . .

"I mean, what the hell am I going to do—as a mom? I don't know shit about nurturing and all that crap. But I think Quent . . . he's going to be a hella good daddy," Zoë said. And the smile on her face was just soft enough, just sheepish enough, to let him know that she was going to be okay with it. Once she got used to the idea.

"Congratulations," Lou said. "And . . . stick near Envy. In case anything goes wrong. So Elliott can take care of things."

Zoë huffed an exasperated puff of air up into her bangs. "Don't you get started on me too. You've got places to go. What the hell are you waiting for?"

Lou saluted her and adjusted his pack. "Nothing."

When he got back to the arcade late in the afternoon, Theo logged into his email to check on Lou's reaction to what he'd learned about Brad Blizek and found three new messages. All from Sage. None from Lou.

And the first header from Sage was: *Lou's GONE!*

Followed by: *WHERE ARE YOU?*

And: *LOU IS MISSING!!!!!!*

Theo's heart dropped to his knees. He couldn't get the first message opened quickly enough.

Where are you? So relieved to hear from you. Have you heard from Lou? He's missing. He left a note that he was going to find you. Is he with you?

The next message was a little less calm: *Are you*

in contact with Lou? Where are you? Are you safe? Please respond. I'm waiting!

And the final one was practically shouting, which, if one knew Sage, was something one knew didn't happen often—despite her fiery hair. *DON'T SEND A MES-SAGE AND THEN NOT CHECK YOUR EMAIL FOR HOURS WHEN YOU KNOW I AM SITTING HERE ALL THE TIME, THEO! What the hell is going on? We're worried about you and Lou. I NEED TO HEAR FROM YOU. PLEASE.*

Ooops.

And *shit.*

Theo concentrated. *Lou? You there?*

Waiting. Waiting.

Lou?

Meanwhile, he typed: *Sage, sorry. Dont have much access. Lou not w me. Will lyk asap. Am fine.*

He sent the message then got up and walked over to the window, as if that might make the connection better. *Lou.* He tried again.

Just then, he heard the soft *ding* of the message program on the computer and, at the same time, felt the sensation of a mental response: *What the fuck?* The meaning, if not the actual wording, of Lou's grumbly message came through loud and clear.

Where are you? Theo asked him.

He opened the email message—which was of course from Sage again. *Finally!! Glad you're okay. Where are you? I'm worried about Lou. Zoë said she met him leaving Envy. He said he was going to look for you. Haven't you been in touch with him through your mental-thingy?*

Lou stirred in response. *On my way to find you.*

Idiot. Theo sent back an affectionate reaction to him,

and then began typing to Sage: *Am talking to Lou now thru mental-thingy :) He is OK. Dont worry. More ltr.*

Theo messaged back to Lou: *Are you safe?*

Dude. The heartfelt reply came through loud and clear.

Theo grinned in the light of the monitor and sent a message back. *I'm coming to find you.* Lou was southwest; he could feel the direction from which their connection was coming.

No! Not necessary.

The sensation and emotion in that response was vehement and unambiguous. Theo mulled on that for a minute, holding back his automatic, protective reaction. They might be twins, but it was certainly as if Lou was the grandfather and he was the younger man—at least physically. Lou was seventy-eight years old, and looked and moved that way. Theo did not like the idea of him out there alone.

Theo. Stay there. Am coming to you. Another very strong message. *Help with Blizek.*

But . . . Lou was by far the smartest man Theo had ever known—not that he'd ever fully admit that to his brother. Theo still couldn't get Lou to admit that Torvalds—not Jobs—was the greatest genius who'd ever existed. Lou had lived in this new world as long as Theo had; in fact, he'd actually lived *through* the Change while Theo was unconscious in the subterranean chamber until he was found, days later.

Okay, he sent back in response to Lou. At least he knew he could always check on him. *Network?* he asked. He couldn't imagine Lou leaving Envy without a microcomputer or some way to tap into the network. Maybe he'd even planned to set up NAPs along the way too.

Later. Driving. Roads are for shit.

Theo smiled and let the connection lapse. He hoped he wasn't making a mistake, leaving Lou on his own. But he was right: he needed his help here. And he was a grown man, for God's sake.

Despite the fact that the Resistance movement was Lou's life and breath, and that he worked long hours with Theo (and Sage) to develop the network, to rebuild a very incomplete, but growing, Internet, and to begin to pull contacts together, he had no other life. Little pleasure and no adventure. Sure, Theo was known as the reckless one—but that was just because he was so overt about it.

It had, after all, been Lou who'd rewired the fire alarms to go off during midterms their junior year of high school. And who'd tried to make a sort of snowboard/ski jump off the top of their house in Seattle. (It was on the side of a small hill, which made it a logical attempt . . . or so they argued when confronted by their parents.)

Most of the people in Envy thought the old man was crazy, with his talk of conspiracies and repression—either that, or, more likely, people simply didn't *want* to believe what he claimed could be true. Or, even more likely, there were just plain fearful of what would happen if they confronted the truth.

Theo had seen that sort of ignorance, fear, and apathy over and over. He'd also seen the effects of propaganda from powerful entities—such as had happened in Hitler's Germany, as well as with twenty-first century North Korea before the Change. People could believe and buy into the most illogical, incorrect things if their minds were manipulated and their information restricted. The Strangers had their ways of doing both.

So Lou and the others kept their theories and knowledge to themselves as they quietly built their network of computers, and also of contacts embedded in various settlements around Envy.

Theo resolved to make communication with his brother regularly until he arrived. If he was in a truck, he guessed it couldn't be more than a few days.

In the meantime, he had tonight—after dinner—to look forward to.

Thus, to say Theo was disappointed, when he sat down for dinner to find the table missing Selena, was an understatement. But . . . yeah. She wasn't there, and although he, Sam, Frank, Tim (Tom?), and Vonnie all took their seats, there wasn't even a place set for her. Yet the fact that Jennifer, who obviously ate with them as often as she assisted Selena, was also absent didn't bother him in the least.

"Selena's with a patient," Vonnie explained, as if she'd read his mind. She set down a large dish with her customary verve, and the long-handled spoon became unbalanced and tipped out onto the table. "Two new ones today, plus Robert's been holding on and Selena thinks he's almost ready to go now too."

Theo nodded and resisted the temptation to glance back down the hall toward what he'd come to think of as the hospice ward. Instead, he dug into the soup, spooning up quarter-sized carrot slices as he inhaled the delicious smell of roasted peppers.

"That probably happens a lot," he said.

"Yeah," Sam replied. His expression, although not as cool as it had been earlier, wasn't what one would consider warm either. "All the time. We're all used to it." Same with his tone of voice.

Theo figured holding the hand of a dying person

might put a bit of a damper on any amorous thoughts Selena might have had anyway. *Probably just as well.* There were other things he could be doing until the time was right . . . not that that meant he wouldn't try and catch up with her later. *Definitely.*

But until then, he could easily occupy his time. "She's going to be busy for a while," Vonnie said, looking at Theo.

He got the message. But at the time, he didn't realize it was going to be three days before he actually saw Selena again.

He did realize, though—with a start late on that third day—that he was feeling settled here at Blizek Beach. Working in the arcade, helping Frank with his garden and the animals and out on the grounds of the estate, he'd found some other things to occupy his time and thoughts.

He was comfortable. And even happy. And that was despite the fact that he couldn't wait to back that hot piece of Selena into a dark corner somewhere . . . if he could ever get her alone.

"So . . . ," Vonnie said as Theo brought a stack of dishes over to her after dinner one night. "How long you planning on sticking around here?"

The evening loomed ahead. Theo was getting a little restless, ready for companionship from someone he could talk to. He'd heard that one of Selena's new patients had passed away, but that Robert was still clinging to life, against all odds. He wondered if she'd be able to get away. Surely she needed a break. Frank had commandeered Sam and his friend (whose name Theo had finally confirmed was neither Tim nor Tom nor even Tyler—but Andrew) to help with some work in the garden.

Theo grinned at Vonnie. "Just until I clear the table. I'll let you handle the scrubbing and rinsing. I don't want to ruin my hands."

She laughed and bumped him cheerfully with her round hip as he dropped off the dishes. "You know that's not what I meant. And at least you'll clear the table without me having to ask, unlike Sammy-boy. If Frank doesn't snag him quick enough, he disappears and heads down to the river to fish or over to Yellow Mountain to hang out with his friends. He might even do his homework, but it's never top of the list."

"Sounds like a typical teenager to me," Theo said. "But he seems like a responsible kid, anyway."

"He is, more than some. Misses having a dad around, though. Frank . . . well, he's a good man, a *very* good man. But he's too busy with all his projects to give him much time, and too durned deaf to hear half the things anyone says." The dishes clashed and clattered merrily in the sink.

Theo turned back to the table. *Holy crap. She wasn't hinting—was she?—about how long I'm going to stay and how badly Sam needs a father. Was she?*

After all, he'd only been here a week. And besides that, the kid didn't seem terribly pleased with the idea of Theo being around. And why would Vonnie even *think* of him and Selena hooking up? Everyone else seemed to think that the age difference—such as it was—was some sort of cardinal sin.

"What happened to Sam's dad?" Theo asked, figuring since she'd brought it up . . .

He didn't miss Vonnie's secretive smile. Holy Jewish Mother, she *was* matchmaking. How the hell should he take that?

"He and Selena had a disagreement and there was

a big tragedy involved. She left—we all left; me, her, and Sammy-boy—and eventually ended up here. Was about seven, eight, maybe ten years ago now," Vonnie said, her little nose wrinkling up. "We met Frank and he invited us to stay here."

"A disagreement?" Theo asked.

Now Vonnie stopped all of her exuberant ablutions and looked at him. "He didn't understand her and he didn't trust her, when it all came down to it."

Down to what?

"He was a damn fool," Vonnie said, clanging and clinking at the sink again.

"Who was?"

Theo's stomach did a pleasant little flip at the sound of Selena's voice. She walked into the kitchen, giving him the briefest of glances—cool, so casual—and scooped up a handful of almonds.

"Brandon," replied Vonnie, a definite sneer in her voice.

Selena's expression tightened. "Didn't you always teach me not to tell tales?"

Vonnie snorted, but instead of replying, she offered Selena a plate already filled with food. "Eat something and don't lecture me. How's Robert?"

"Doing all right. He's not ready to go yet . . . maybe tomorrow or the next day. Stubborn guy. I expect Frank will be like that when it's his time too." She glanced toward the window, where the sun was low to the horizon, and nibbled on a piece of red pepper. Her hair, which had been pinned up, was sagging and hanging in sexy little strands around her face and neck. She was wearing jeans and, instead of a loose tunic, a short shirt that showed the curve of her ass and was buttoned down the front.

Hmmm . . . easy access. And his skin was already prickling with expectation.

Theo dried his hands on a towel and caught Selena's eyes. "I'm sorry to hear that," he said, referring to the dying man and trying to keep his thoughts on the matter at hand . . . not on the way that one button between her breasts was straining a bit more than the others. He'd be happy to relieve its pain. "Is he in a lot of discomfort?"

Selena drank some water from the cup Vonnie handed her, and met his gaze briefly over its rim. "He says he's not," she said as she lowered the glass, "but he is." Her lips tightened a bit and she shrugged in acceptance. "The marijuana helps sometimes, and the tea, but it can't eliminate all of the pain."

"That must make it even harder for you, knowing there's not much you can do."

She nodded. "I wish I had some of the medicine and treatments they had . . . before. Or at least, more information about how they alleviated pain then. It might help."

I might be able to help you with that. Either me or Elliott. Theo folded the towel and set it on the counter. "I'm going to go back up to the arcade. There are some things I want to check out up there." He took care not to look at Selena—both for his own sake, and Vonnie's as well.

"Where's Frank?" Selena asked as Theo paused to get a drink of water.

"He went out to work in the garden, same as he always does," Vonnie replied.

"Sammy go with him?"

"Yes. He didn't get away fast enough."

"Darn," Selena said. "I wanted him to help me move that big shelf for the supply room."

"I'm sure Theo would help you," Vonnie said in a very smooth voice. "Wouldn't you, Theo?"

And that was how it happened.

"You didn't fool her in the least," Theo said to Selena as he followed her down the hall. His heart was suddenly racing, and his belly had become embarrassingly filled with fluttering butterflies. He felt like a middle-schooler going to his first dance.

She tossed back a smile at him that did nothing to calm the upheaval in his stomach. "I know. But it made me feel better."

He felt odd, following a woman to . . . well, he assumed, her bedroom. But he wasn't quite certain. Maybe she did need help moving a big shelf. *Probably not.*

But it was a little strange to him, knowing that this was all planned. That they were *going* to have sex. *Could it be any less spontaneous? Could it be any more awkward, for a first time? Any less . . . special?*

And why was he making such a big deal about it? It was going to be good, no matter how it went.

They started up a flight of stairs near the far end of the large house, and Theo couldn't resist asking, "Your supply room is on the second floor? Not very convenient, is it?"

Selena curled her fingers on the top of the banister, stepped up, and turned to give him a hot smile as she went around the corner. "I have a feeling you'll find it very convenient."

Oh, yes. A dart of lust shot through him, and he vaulted up the last few steps with a little jump, landing next to her. "If you're sure . . ."

"I'm su—"

But Theo'd decided he was through with waiting, and he had her in his arms before she could finish her sentence. He found her mouth easily, covering it with his as he edged them away from the stairs. Instinct from living in a deteriorating world for fifty years had him shifting from the railing at the top of the landing, and instead pulling her up against his chest as he leaned against the wall.

Steadying himself, so that he could put all his energy and effort into tasting and enjoying her, he smoothed his hands up over her delicate shoulder blades, crossing them to stabilize her as he deepened the kiss.

Selena had at first stiffened in surprise. But now she melted against him, pressing Theo into the wall and received his kiss, drawing his tongue and lips into her mouth as if she wanted to devour him. Theo lost himself for a moment, just drinking in her smell, the soft, welcome lines of her body, the way he tilted back, stable, against the wall, holding her against him. Everything became hot and sleek as their kiss eased into serious business.

His hand found her ass, sweeping over that sweet round curve as he slipped his knee between her legs. "I've missed you," he said. "Where have you been?"

"I really do," she said, shifting back a bit, clamping her teeth around his lower lip and tugging at it, "have something heavy . . . for you to move."

Theo closed his eyes against the niggling pleasure-pain at his lip, the muscles beneath his skin shivering with want. She released him and then swiped her tongue in a little apologetic dance over his throbbing lip.

"Want to make me work for it, do you?" he murmured, slipping his fingers between them to give relief to that straining button on her blouse. And then the one below it.

"Oh, yes," she replied, pressing down onto the knee he'd slipped between her legs. "I wanted to get you all hot and sweaty first."

Another button. And then another. He slid his hands beneath the opening of her shirt, taking care of the still tender *ganga* slashes on the front of her shoulder. For a moment, he paused and looked down at them, a stab of anger and something like fear shooting through him. "Selena," he whispered, imagining those awful, evil nails scoring her smooth, tanned skin . . . and some-how, her getting away from such a threat. *Miraculous.*

How? And why would she risk it again? At least he knew she hadn't gone out the last few nights. He'd been watching.

As if reading his mind and looking for a way to detour it, she shifted, her hand cruising down between them to cover the raging hard-on straining the buttons of his shorts. The confident weight of her hand, cup-ping him, sliding over the center of his desire, drove all other thoughts from his mind. He couldn't hold back a groan as she found the length of him through the fabric, up and along, back and forth, as he filled his hands with her bra-clad breasts.

"About that heavy thing . . . you needed me to move," he muttered. "Can I do that later?"

She laughed against him and then slipped away, quickly and suddenly. "Come on," she said, her eyes hot and her full mouth curved with promise and humor. "You can show me what you've got."

He liked the sound of that.

Theo followed as she darted down the hallway past

what had likely been bedrooms and guest suites when Brad Blizek lived here. Her shirt flapped open behind her, and her sagging hair was now drooping even further. And her slender feet . . . bare and quick beneath her jeans.

It occurred to him then, as the heat of the moment ebbed temporarily, that her neck and throat had been devoid of the long cord that she'd been trying to hide before. He didn't remember feeling or seeing it the other day either, but he'd only had his hands up her shirt instead of it being open . . .

Selena slipped into a room halfway down the hall and Theo followed her, closing the door behind him. He wasn't sure what he expected, but it wasn't this: a very cozy, very inviting room that was clearly a woman's boudoir. A bed piled high with pillows of all shapes and sizes, in shades of green and blue. A swath of some light, shimmery material hanging from the ceiling, draped half over the bed—which, by the way, was at least a queen, maybe a king. *Hot damn.* Heavy bedposts marked each corner, and it was covered with a thick quilt or blanket. And a plush rug made from scraps of material tied and woven together covered the scarred wooden floor. A long triangle of gold from the lowering sun cut the room, shining through a westerly window.

"Wow," he said, moving toward her. "Not what I expected." His heart was pounding. He couldn't wait to get her on that lush bed, covering her equally lush body with his . . . preferably with nothing between them.

She put up her hands as if to stop him, and they landed right on the planes of his chest. "I'm not sure whether I should be offended or charmed by that comment."

"Charmed," he said, capturing her mouth again,

sliding his hand under her open shirt. "Definitely charmed." *Oh, yes.*

"This is Vonnie's room," she said, pulling away with a quick little pirouette. Tossing a heavy-lidded, catlike smile over her shoulder, she added, "I don't think she'd like it if we messed up her bed."

Theo stopped. "You're joking, right?"

"No, not at all," she said, and gestured to a large . . . bookshelf. "I was hoping you'd help me move this down to the supply room."

"Down the stairs?" he asked, all amorous thoughts fleeing. It wasn't that he couldn't do it; it was that this whole event was taking a much different turn than he'd anticipated.

"Well, yes. Because, if it doesn't get moved down there, Vonnie will want to know why, since that's why we sneaked off together." Her eyes narrowed in delight at his obvious consternation.

"I wouldn't call that sneaking off . . ."

But she continued. "I realized that if I'm going to mess around with a man half my age, I might as well take advantage of all the benefits—which include not only having you do a little heavy lifting, but also *seeing* all those muscles in action."

The way she said that . . . *all those muscles in action* . . . in that low, throaty voice . . . made his knees go weak. *Damn.* Was this how it was? A little fluttering of the eyelashes, a little flattery, and a guy was no longer master of his own mind? Not that he was complaining . . . because pretty soon, her knees were going to be jelly too. He grinned.

"Shall I take off my shirt, then?" he asked, half serious, half joking. "Wouldn't want you to miss the show."

"I thought you'd never ask," she replied. And crossed her arms, waiting.

Theo hesitated only a minute and then yanked his stretched-out T-shirt up and over his head, then tossed it to her. She caught it neatly and he had a moment of pure delight when he felt her attention, her eyes, score over him. "Shall I turn around?" he asked mockingly.

But he knew that, for a self-professed geek, he was ripped enough for any woman to look twice. That was something that had happened since the Change, when he found himself doing a lot more demanding physical activity than in 2010.

"I'm just noticing," she said in a decidedly husky voice, "that your wound is gone. Hardly even a scar."

He looked down at his torso, smoothing his fingers over where the wound would have been. She was right. There was nothing there. "That's wild," he said. "It's only been a week."

"Wild? Impossible is more like it," she replied, reaching to touch him. Her fingers skated lightly over his chest and he felt the prickling swarm his body, scattering to every nerve ending. The edge of her shirt hem and its cool buttons brushed his bare skin. He drew in a steadying breath, feeling her fingers press more heavily as his chest rose.

"If you want me to move that bookshelf," he said, using every ounce of control to step back, "you'd best let me get on it. Or we're going to be messing up that bed, Vonnie or not."

Selena stepped closer, back into his space. "A little impatient, are we, young man?" Her fingers settled onto his shoulders and she looked up at him. Her lips curved mockingly. "You see, that's one advantage of age. We older folk know how to enjoy anticipation. We have more patience. We can—"

With a little annoyed growl, he yanked up a handful of her shirt and dragged her against him, his mouth cutting her off. She chuckled beneath his kiss, then slid away to nibble on his jaw.

"Work before pleasure," she said, trailing her tongue sassily around the inside of his ear.

"My mother used to have a word for people like you," he said, stepping back. "Hellion. That's what you are. A hellion."

"What's wrong, little boy? Can't keep up with an old girl like me?"

He paused from where he'd turned to lift the bookshelf. "Just wait, Selena. Just *wait*."

The bookshelf was heavy, but mostly awkward; and he had no trouble carrying it down the nice, wide staircase to the supply room—which did turn out to be on the first floor, and much more convenient. He realized she'd been teasing him all along, and he found himself alternately laughing and mentally shaking his head about Selena.

How could a woman who lived with the dying every day, who looked death in the eye, have such an off-beat, silly sense of humor at times?

Maybe she had to, in order to face the ugliness and sorrow she had to contend with.

But now . . . he fully intended to give her something else to focus on.

Theo turned to her. "Now that the work's done . . ."

CHAPTER 6

"What about some pleasure?"

Selena's belly dropped as Theo closed the supply room door behind him, leaning against it as if nothing would move him. As their eyes met, a wash of heat and anticipation rushed through her and *darn* if her knees felt as if they'd give way. *Darn*.

She'd hardly been able to keep her eyes from his broad-shouldered torso . . . shirtless and sleek, his olive skin devoid of hair and without an extra bulge or crease anywhere. He was more beautiful than she remembered from the day she'd revived him. Obviously, life agreed with him.

She wasn't sure whom to thank for this gift, but Selena was not one to question miracles. She'd seen her share of—and lack of—them enough in her life.

"My place is a little more private," she reminded him. He looked as if he were stalking her . . . watching, waiting for her next move. Uncertain, wary, but in an anticipatory way.

"No more detours?" he asked.

She shook her head, unable to talk. Her mouth was dry, her heart was racing.

When was the last time she'd had sex? Longer than she liked to admit.

When was the last time she'd had sex with a guy like him? *Never.*

"No, this way," she managed to say as he turned to open the door. "My room connects."

"That's convenient," he said in a voice that could only be described as a purr. And closed the door. "*Very* convenient."

Selena led him through the back of the supply room to a small exit in the rear, where stairs led up to her bedroom, which was on the other end of the hall from Sam, and about halfway from Vonnie's room. She'd decided about six years ago that she'd rather Vonnie hear what was going on in her room—not that anything ever did—than her son.

And vice versa.

No sooner did they move into the room than Theo was there, right there, his mouth on hers, his hands pulling the shirt from her shoulders. She began to shrug out of it, then realized that there was too much daylight and he'd see all her stretch marks and bulges—a crime next to his young body—and tried to pull it back over to cover her.

"We'll have none of that," he murmured, firmly removing her hands and sliding the cotton from her shoulders, taking care not to scrape her wounds. "You've been ogling me . . . now it's my turn."

Before she could reply, he had her bra undone and eased it down along her arms, leaving her breasts bare in the warm sun that shone through the window. Then he gathered her back up against him, torso to torso . . . her curves pressing up against his solid muscle, warm skin to warm skin, the tenderness from her *ganga* marks hardly noticeable. His arm locked around her back as he played with her mouth, his lips sliding over hers, fitting them sweetly together and then exploring with his tongue.

She kissed him back, closing her eyes when the heat flooded her, their long kiss turning sleek and languorous.

Theo directed them smoothly to her bed, which she'd actually made this afternoon in anticipation of the possibility of messing it up tonight. It wasn't quite as inviting as Vonnie's, with all the pillows and the thick blankets—

And then she stopped thinking about anything but the large, warm hands covering her bare breasts as she settled back down onto the bed. He had found her nipples, which now hardened into sensitive little tips, and he used his thumb to brush over one of them back and forth, back and forth and around and around, until those little shooting pleasure-darts became long, strong tugs down deep below her belly . . . where she was already swelling and throbbing, waiting for him.

Theo was on the bed next to her, one hand trailing over her breast, the other propping him up on the mattress next to her as he bent to kiss along her chin and jaw, and over to the side of her neck.

"You've got a hell of a body," he said, low and rough into her ear. "I can't wait to see all of it."

His hand left her breast and eased down over her belly, down beneath the waist of her jeans and to where his fingers threaded gently into the sensitive hair there. Gently, he made little circles with his fingers, tight beneath her panties, and let their very tips skim over the top of her labia . . . teasing, promising, making her shift her hips in a little impatient jiggle. *Yesss.*

Her eyes closed, and when she felt his warm, moist lips close over her breast, Selena jerked and gave a soft little cry. He chuckled, warm and close, over her nipple, then drew it long and hard into his mouth, sending another battery of those shooting pleasure-darts to her belly and below.

Suddenly, his fingers slipped lower, down into where she was hot and wet, finding her pulsing little core. She stiffened, jolted at the sudden surprise slides . . . and then with one little stroke, like the flick of a switch, his magic fingers set her shuddering and exploding into a big, hot orgasm.

"Oh," she managed when she caught her breath, still feeling the delicious little heat licks spreading through her thighs and belly. Selena smiled as he shifted to kiss her, feeling better than she had in forever.

"The best is yet to come," he murmured, as if reading her mind.

"I'm counting on it," she replied, and, still loose and tingly, reached for the button of his shorts.

He wasn't shy about helping her; and in moments, she had her hands full of a very happy, very hot and thick Theo. He let his head rest back and his eyes close as she gave him a few strokes for good measure, slow and easy . . . and then tight and fast, tighter and faster, until his lips flattened to white and she felt his body gather up, ready to go over. And then, she eased up, slowing and watching the change on his face.

His eyes popped open, his expression filled with chagrin. "That was almost too easy," he said in a tight voice. He covered her hand with his, slowing her lazy strokes even further.

"We wouldn't want that, would we?" she asked, leaning over to kiss him with a deep thrust of tongue.

"How about we get on the same playing field, so to speak?" Theo said, removing her hand from where she still grasped him, and getting down to business with her jeans.

Selena didn't have time to worry about stretch marks or the wobbliness of her thighs, because he was fast and smooth. One minute, she was still packaged up, tight and swollen and hot in her jeans and panties, and the next, she was bare on the bed . . . with a solid, warm body lining up next to hers.

His knee slid between hers, riding up gently to pressure her core as he gathered her close, kissing her sleekly on the mouth. The prod of his erection against her belly gave her a little shiver of anticipation, and when he slipped a hand down to cup her breast, caressing and stroking lightly over her nipple, she arched into him, burying her face in his silky throat, feeling the ramrodding of his heart.

This is good. This is really *good.*

Selena felt the matching throb between her legs with every draw of his lips over her nipple, the tease of his knee up into her, the damp of skin plastered against skin, salty and warm . . . his smell, masculine and fresh . . .

She was done with the foreplay. With a dangerous little nip at his collarbone, Selena pulled away, planting her hands on his chest and shoving him back down when he would have risen to follow.

"Age before beauty," she said, straddling him quickly.

For some reason, he found this wildly amusing, but his face lost all humor when she slipped him perfectly inside her and slid right down. *Oh.*

They both just froze for a minute, reveling in the beauty of the sensation. Selena tightened her muscles around him and his eyes, half-hooded, rolled back, flew open again. She smiled and did it again and then shifted in her position, enough that he could feel it . . . but that she could *really* feel it.

Just a little rocking motion. Pleasure rippled through her.

"Selena," he said in a voice that sounded thin as a strained thread. "Are you trying to kill me . . . again?"

Her hands settled firmly on his pectoral muscles, she leaned forward and caught up his mouth for a good kiss. Rose then lowered her hips, and then he grasped them, held her in position, high and steady, as he slammed up and then eased down . . . then again, hard and fast and intense.

The orgasm caught her by surprise and she gasped as she pulled her face up and away from Theo, the waves rolling through her as she shuddered around him, her elbows weak and threatening to collapse. He thrust up once more and then yanked her down onto him as he gave a last heartfelt groan that sounded like her name.

She felt him explode inside her, felt the undulating of their bodies meld as she collapsed on him, hot and breathless and glorious.

Glorious.

She didn't move for a long time, her head resting on his chest, feeling the air rush in and out, lifting and lowering, the thud of his heart. The warmth of skin, of man, of comfort. His arm slid around her, his fingers stroking up and down her spine as if to say he was feeling the same way.

Then she ruined it.

She opened her eyes, and her gaze fell on the window. And she saw the low sun sending brilliant orange-red rays into the sky.

Night was coming.

Theo uncurled his toes and rebooted his brain. *That . . . was . . .*

He had no words to describe it, even to himself . . . so he didn't even try. Instead, he held Selena, his face full of her hair; her warm, smooth skin burning into his. She felt so damn good.

This first round of lovemaking . . . well, it hadn't been his best. He'd been a little quicker on the trigger than he liked, but at least he'd made sure she was taken care of. There would be a second round, and a third . . . and, he hoped, a multitude more. As soon as he recovered.

Then his eyes flew open. *Son of a bitch.*

He wondered if this was a good time to bring up the fact that they'd done nothing for contraception. He fucking knew better than that. He'd even been prepared, as much as one could be nowadays. Especially in a world where the more babies being made, the better to recreate the human race. But that wasn't reason enough to be sloppy. But then again . . . *What* were *the chances?*

Before he could speak, she shifted and rolled off him, her arm sliding along his torso, her fingers giving him a little pat of what he interpreted as thanks as they trailed away and now she lay next to him. The open window brought a welcome shift of air over his warm, damp skin.

"Um," Theo said, manning up. "Crap, Selena . . . I didn't plan that very well."

Her lips curved, but she didn't turn. "Dare I ask what you mean, or is it going to get me in trouble?"

Poor choice of words. He plowed on. "I didn't—we didn't—well, there's the chance you could get pregnant."

She'd been lying there next to him, looking up at the ceiling, just as he had been. Now she rolled to face him and their noses were too close. Selena shifted back a bit, and her golden, wide-lipped face came into better focus.

"There's a chance, yes," she said with a little laugh. "But not only am I past my prime in that way, I'm also old enough to know when I'm most likely to conceive . . . and right now, I'm not." She smiled, and reached over to brush her finger over his lips. "So I planned for both of us."

She was so beautiful it made his breath catch— Beautiful physically, and in her confidence and . . . something else . . . wisdom. As if nothing surprised her. As if she'd seen it all, experienced it all . . . and could drag herself through it. And still have a sense of humor.

This was, he thought again, a woman who's *lived*. Interesting. Compassionate. Confident.

Something loosened inside him as he looked at the delicate lines at the corners of her eyes and in the paper-thin skin beneath them, the little grooves cupping the corners of her mouth, the curve of her cheekbones and slender nose. He noticed for the first time the faintest brush of freckles over her skin. Her lips were wide and full and her thick, heavy hair tumbled over her face and neck.

She glanced behind him, toward the window, and he saw the change in her expression. Subtle, but noticeable. She looked back at him.

"What is it?" he asked.

She smiled. "Not a thing," she said. Then she reached for him, for the beginning of a hard-on that had already started to respond to her again, and added, "Not a thing that we can't take care of."

She was lying.

But he pushed the thought away and pulled her close for a kiss. He'd put it out of her mind, whatever it was. He'd keep her so busy that she'd forget whatever it was that called her out into the night. He wasn't leaving this bed, this room, her side, until they'd both become unmoving, sated piles of jelly-bones and damp skin.

Theo opened his eyes to discover darkness. A thin shot of moonlight rippled through the window, sketching the lines of the bed, the rumpled clothing and bedcovers.

He sat up with a start when he realized the bed was empty but for himself. Selena's bed. Empty.

Fuck.

The last thing he remembered was her murmuring something . . . slipping away as he lulled into a satiated sleep . . . *What had she said? And how the hell, after the last couple of hours, did she have the* energy *to even move?*

"*I have to check on Robert.*"

That was what she'd said. She was going down to check on her patient.

Theo got out of bed, his heart pounding harder, a sick feeling heavy in his belly. Judging from the darkness, that had been a long time ago. Too long ago.

He scrambled around, unaware of where a light was—*Hell, we hadn't needed it*—and unwilling to take the time to look for one as he scooped-up wads of clothing, sifting through to find his shorts.

Another glance toward the window, and the sick feeling increased. She wouldn't be that foolish. She still had *wounds* on her . . . crusted gashes that he'd gently kissed and taken great care of during their lovemaking.

He paused, listened . . . and then he heard it, in the distance. The sound made his blood chill and he ran out of the room on bare feet.

"Ruuu-uuuthhhhhh."

He knew it. He simply *knew* that she wasn't with Robert, that she wasn't with any other patient or Sam or anyone. That she had gone out.

The house was quiet. Of course it was. She only sneaked out when everyone was asleep. *Dammit.*

Theo paused in the kitchen to try and find a weapon—something, anything—that he could use. A bottle of beer on the counter—probably Frank's. It was half full (maybe not Frank's; he never seemed to have any left over), but he snatched it up, followed by one of Vonnie's towels, and wondered if beer had enough alcohol in it to make a Molotov cocktail.

Matches. . . . and something else . . . A knife? A gun?. . .

They wouldn't have guns. Only the Strangers had guns. And a few members of the Resistance. *What else?*

Despite the fact that his thoughts whirled and babbled, Theo moved quickly, smoothly, and with purpose. Those times in the kitchen with Vonnie, watching her, had somehow imprinted on his memory, and he found the things he needed: a handful of homemade matches, even the whiskey that Vonnie had used on Selena's wounds a few nights ago.

That would make a nice bottle bomb.

Then he was out the back door of the kitchen. It had probably taken him less than five minutes from the bedroom to the outside, but it felt like forever. He'd remembered to button his shorts, but he didn't have a shirt or any foot coverings—a disadvantage that became clear when he stepped on a really sharp rock.

He paused, listening, as his foot throbbed and he shoved his makeshift weapons in the pockets of his shorts. The zombie moans had grown louder, more insistent. Theo's heart raced as he followed the sounds, running toward the wall that protected the Blizek estate.

All he could think as he ran, as he found himself at the wall but with no exit in sight, and thus had no choice but to climb up the crumbling brick wall with his bare fingers—all he could think was that Selena wasn't blond.

They wouldn't take her away as they did with blondes; they would slash into her. Tear into her skin and devour her . . . flesh, muscle, organs, brain. His throat closed and he pushed the fear away.

A clear mind. Strength and a steady mind.

He made it to the top of the wall somehow—it was a blur, the running and jumping, and digging his fingers into the mortar and pulling himself up with a desperate strength. At the top, he looked out and saw them yards away, in the shadow of a group of trees . . . the glowing orange eyes, bobbing and jolting in unsteady pairs in a cluster, a gang of them. A murderous gang. Less than a dozen, but deadly nevertheless.

Where is Selena?

He didn't see her. His heart raced, his breathing hitched, and he leapt down from the wall, landing on heavy feet but able to steadily keep his balance and the bottles in his pockets. Beer and whiskey sloshed over his shorts as he ran on quiet feet, using trees and bushes and a pile of rubble for cover.

Is she out here? Am I wrong?

But he knew she was out here, somewhere . . . either hunting zombies in some misguided, Buffy-wannabe way, or doing something else that put her beyond the walls during the most dangerous part of the day. He looked around and saw nothing but the monsters, and he moved closer, relieved that he was upwind.

That, at least, would keep him from being scented and noticed for a little longer. The zombies moved, staggering and stumbling . . . not toward him, nor even toward the walls of the estate, but rather speedily for *gangas*, and toward the east.

He wanted to shout for Selena, to see if she was out there somewhere, but he dared not.

The *gangas* were still making their desperate moaning cries for Remington Truth . . . but something changed. The groans seemed to become higher in pitch, more tense . . . more something. Something eerie. Something that raised the hair on the back of his neck.

Their desperation reverberated in the night.

This was different than anything Theo had ever seen. The monsters seemed to be being drawn somewhere . . . away. As if being called. If it was possible to feel more uneasy than he already did, he felt it.

Is there a Stranger out there, calling the zombies to him? Bounty hunters like Seattle, or Ian Marck, had a purple crystal that seemed to call and control the zombies.

Theo stilled, crouching behind a tree, and watched.

Where were they going?

Then something caught his eye . . . a glow. A small rosy light, emerging from behind a pile of old cars, not far from the *gangas*. Or maybe from within the old vehicles.

It bobbed and swung, . . . as if it were . . . *on a cord, around someone's neck.*

Theo went cold. He yanked one of the bottles from his shorts and began to jam the corner of the towel down into its neck as he started toward her.

Her silhouette became clear as she stepped away from the pile of junkers, the pink glow illuminating the lower part of her face. The zombies were fairly running toward her now, their hands outstretched, their cries high and wild and horrifying.

Theo ran, fueled by his own desperation. If he could get a bomb off before they got too close . . . but they were fast. My God, faster than he'd ever seen the monsters move—lurching and staggering, hands grasping in the air, crooked fingers outlined by the sliver of moon and stars.

He caught a glimpse of Selena's face, taut and empty, limned with the pink glow. She didn't move as they surged around her. She *didn't move.*

Theo cried out in fury and desperation as he fumbled for a match, even knowing it was too late for a bomb.

The monsters slashed and clawed as they swarmed closer, descending on her like ravenous wolves.

"Selenaaa!" he cried as she disappeared into the mob.

CHAPTER 7

Selena wanted to close her eyes as the monsters surged in around her, grasping, clawing, desperate.

So desperate.

But she didn't. She willed herself to remain still, steady, strong; not to give in to the fear and pain. Every time, it seemed to get more difficult . . . every time they seemed to be more violent, more desperate.

As they swarmed, the stench from the creatures seemed to sink into every one of her pores, to clog her nostrils and make her eyes water . . . and then there was the sagging, rotting, gray flesh brushing against her like thick, dry snakeskin. Flesh that had once been tight and smooth, white, black, olive, mahogany . . . and every shade in between.

The eyes were burning orange, but empty inside . . . until they saw the crystal.

She held it steady in front of her. Its rosy-red glow illuminated only a small circle around them, but they seemed to sense it from a great distance. And it burned. As if it were on fire.

One of the zombies cried out in a long, low wail that sounded nothing like *ruu-uuuthhhh* but was more like *meeeeee-noowwwww*. And she—it was a female— swiped toward Selena with her awkward, lethal paw.

Trembling and shuddering, Selena closed her fingers around the female's thick, wrinkling wrist and covered the hot crystal with her other hand. Immediately, the shock bolted through her, deep and ugly, dark and strong—and she gasped at the pain, at the blinding surge.

The female cried out and their eyes met. And in that moment, Selena saw her humanity. The flash of her soul . . . being released from the jail of a body that had contained and controlled her for half a century. For as long as Selena had been alive.

Her orange eye-glow burst bright, and then was extinguished. And the female buckled to her knees, crashing to the ground. Dead. And free at last.

Tears prickling her eyes, Selena had no time to recover, for there was another zombie there, reaching for her, and another, and too many of them, clawing, grasping, tearing in a frenzied bid for what they knew was safety and freedom.

Like beggars, like a mad crowd, like feral animals, they surged and groped, staggering into each other, pushing and bumping. She did it again: closed her fingers around sagging flesh and allowed herself to be the conduit for the crystal's power, accepting the breathtaking bolt of pain and anguish, the flash of memories, and freeing the human inside.

And again.

A searing pain over her shoulder burned when a desperate monster reached for her, and another bumped into her, jolting her, and the aches mingled with the white-hot shock and the abhorrent stench and the closeness. She couldn't breathe, could hardly think. The world spun and closed in, became dark and then rosy light, and was filled with snatches of memories, of humanity. *Keep going. You can. One more—*

"Selena!"

She thought she was dreaming the sound of her name. Another monster grabbed at her and she took his hand, looked into his eyes, and released his soul. The shock battered her again and her knees buckled, but the closeness of the mob kept her from falling to the ground.

"Selena!"

Something bright slashed through the air, arcing overhead. And then there was an explosion, just beyond them, causing the zombies to rear back—and then to surge even closer, even more reckless now, pummeling her with their awkward bodies, even more lethal with their nails.

"Selena!"

She couldn't focus, could hardly move or breathe. But it sounded like Theo. *Theo. Oh, God, no . . . no.* She had to be dreaming.

But then suddenly, he was there. *Impossible.* But he was. Somehow, pulling and beating at the monsters that crowded around her. Tearing through them to get to her. *Oh, God, Theo.*

She couldn't think what this would mean, now. Not now. Later.

"Selena," he shouted, as he found her with his eyes from outside the ring. *"Come on!"*

He swung something large and heavy—a massive branch—and it crashed into the skull of one of the *gangas*. Selena cried out in horror as bone crunched and the creature staggered back, collapsing onto the ground. Dead.

But still trapped.

"No!" she shouted at Theo. "Stop!"

Tears stung her eyes, her battered body wouldn't move . . . she couldn't breathe but she had to stop him before he killed any more of them. "No, please," she cried, trying to make her voice work, even as she grabbed the hand of a creature close to her.

The surge bolted through her, and this time it brought her gasping to her knees. But she held the gaze of the old man until the orange glow went out and he was freed.

"Go, Theo," she cried when she caught her breath. "Let me do this!"

"I'm not leaving you," he shouted back, and whaled again at the zombies. Another one fell when he caught it at the back of its knees, but its brain was intact. Still safe.

"Please!" she pleaded. "Theo, *stop!*"

She touched another of the trapped humans, the red-veined crystal burning into her hand as she stared into the female's eyes, wondering why there still seemed to be so many of them. *So many.*

Never ending.

Selena dimly realized that Theo seemed to have gone. He'd listened to her. *Thank God.*

And then she looked up to find him there, again, somehow pulling through the mad mob, yanking back the creatures trying to get to her.

"Don't hurt them!" she screamed, trying to make him understand. "Don't . . . hurt . . . them!"

She was sobbing now, her face wet; and through the tears, she met his stark, horrified eyes in the rosy glow. The next thing she knew, he was there, somehow, with her, next to her.

He didn't speak. He just closed his arms around her and enveloped her from behind, pulling her up against his solid body.

"I'm here," was all he said. "I'm not leaving until this is done."

* * *

Theo held on to Selena as the zombies fought through to them, slamming against him, pummeling her in their need to get to her. *What is this?*

He held on to Selena, protecting her from the slashing nails, holding her upright as she battled whatever it was that compelled her to be here. He wasn't certain what was going on; he dared not think about it right now.

Instead, he focused on breathing without inhaling the wall of putrid stench, on holding himself steady and keeping Selena upright; on easing them back, to bring the whole mob of monsters with them so he could protect their rear with the nearest car. This circle of madness, of wailing cries and greedy hands, of empty glowing eyes paralyzed him.

They had to get out of here. He had to fight through them . . . and then he realized what a fool he'd been. He *had* a way to drive them off.

His power surge. His "let me charge you up, baby!" His fucking after-the-Change superpower. Something he'd never used in hand-to-hand combat with a bunch of *gangas* . . . because he'd never had to. He'd never been trapped in a mob of them. He'd never gotten this damn close.

Theo closed his eyes as a renewed wave of zombie weight surged into Selena, sending him staggering as he fought to hold her up. She was sagging even more in his arms. How much longer could she last? Why wouldn't she let him get her out of here?

There weren't that many left—*Four of them. No, five.*

The rest of them seemed to be dead.

He had to concentrate now; he could fight them

off with a shock—stun them for a moment, get away
. . . *Don't hurt them!* Selena had cried.

He'd fucking hurt them, all right, if he had to get her
out of here safely. She was putty in his hands, and not
in a good way.

Theo grabbed at the arm of the nearest monster,
touching the dry, wrinkling, peeling flesh of the creature. Pieces of skin shifted beneath his hand, separating
like dried mud and exposing layers beneath, sending a
new blast of rank odor into his face. He closed his eyes,
focusing, gathering the power that rested somewhere
within him . . . that germinated from the little integrated circuit embedded in his back . . . ready to send
a shock into this creature, to send him staggering away
. . . for at least a moment of relief.

The mob of five beat and pushed and cried, flailing
and staggering, and Theo concentrated, blocking them
out, pulled his power from the depths, waited for the
little tingling surge . . .

And nothing happened.

Nothing happened.

His eyes flew open and he released the zombie, staring at his hand even as he swung up and out with his
other elbow to keep one of the others from falling into
them. *Nothing?*

Stunned, Theo tried to ignore this new development
in the interest of saving their asses. He couldn't spare
the thought or time to consider the reasons now.

Selena hung in his arms, her face tilted up, her lips
flat and grim. Even in the low light, he could see the
gray of her skin. Her breathing was rapid and shallow;
he could feel her torso move. But her eyes were open
and she held on to that crystal around her neck as she
reached for another monster.

She can't last much longer.

He held on to her, trying to drag her closer to the cars behind them. The zombies couldn't climb . . . maybe they could find refuge there.

But it was slow going, and she kept seizing the monsters one by one—and he realized she wasn't going to stop until she was finished. He watched her, held her, felt the jolt through her body when she touched the creatures. He felt her weakening, heard the little gasp that came after.

And at last . . . the final zombie buckled to the ground. And all was silent but for Theo's rasping breathing.

For a moment, she didn't move. Just stayed there in his arms, shuddering, dragging in breaths.

"Selena," he said finally, turning her to face him. Shock and confusion made his mind dart in infinite directions, unable to settle on one train of thought or question. Something trickled down his bare back— blood, maybe sweat—and her face was streaked with tears, grimy with dirt and scrapes from the mob.

She drew in a deep breath and pulled away from him. The fact that she wasn't looking at him didn't bode well, but Theo was still too horrified and stunned at the experience that he couldn't formulate a question. As he watched, she lifted the glowing crystal on its long leather cord and slipped a little pouch over it. The glow disappeared and she tucked it down her shirt.

"I have to burn them," she said in a voice weary and taut. "I can't leave them . . . like this."

"Sit down, dammit," Theo said, a wave of fury turning him cold. Numbness spread through his body. "Just sit down for God's sake, Selena. You can hardly stand up. Jesus. I'll take care of it."

"Thank you," she whispered, and sank down on the warped, rusted hood of a car.

Theo worked off some of his anger and confusion by dragging the twelve zombie bodies into a pile some distance away. By the time he was finished, he was breathing roughly—but not from physical exertion.

No, it was nothing to move the horrible bodies into a makeshift funeral pyre.

It was what lay ahead: the murderous anger burning inside him, the confusion, the questions and answers. The reality that would come with tomorrow.

That was what burned and curdled inside him, and left him with a hollow heart.

He lit the second bottle bomb and tossed it onto the pile of corpses. As the explosion lit the night, he turned to Selena.

"Let's go," was all he said.

CHAPTER 8

Selena awoke the next morning to a blast of sunshine streaming through her window.

She opened her eyes with no problem, but when she tried to move, her body protested. Pain, aches, throbbing—everywhere. But that was nothing compared to the dark memories, the remnants of that night's terror.

She blinked, pushing them away with relative ease, and looked outside. By the height of the sun, she knew it was late in the morning.

She lay there for a moment, digging around the wisps of nightmares and benign dreams and trying to retrieve the memories. Her own memories.

Theo had brought her back after. He'd insisted on carrying her, and she wasn't a fool. She let him. He'd helped her clean up, put salve on her old wounds that had reopened and on the new ones that, fortunately, weren't as bad, thanks to the protective shirt she'd worn. He'd made her drink something, eat something, drink something else, and then he tucked her into bed.

All the time, speaking very little except to give her orders.

And then had, obviously, left.

Something unpleasant scraped deep inside her, but she ignored it. The shock and disbelief, even betrayal, had been all over Theo's face. In his eyes.

Even anger was there.

Just as it had been with Brandon.

But, she told herself, forcing her body to cooperate and pull upright, the whole situation with Theo was worlds different than with Brandon. The only comparison was that both had included great sex.

Although calling last night "great sex" would be an understatement. Her lips actually moved in a smile, and a little flutter awakened in her belly at the memory. But she didn't have enough energy to appreciate it any more than that.

Someone knocked on her door, and her attention whipped toward it. "Come in," she called, dread filling her heart. *Theo? What am I going to say to him?*

A sandy brown head poked around the entrance. "Mom . . . how are you feeling?"

What did Theo tell Sam? "I'm . . . fine," she said carefully. Wondering how bad her face looked.

Her son came in, looking so much like Brandon— except for the mouth—that she stilled in surprise. She hadn't noticed how much he'd come to resemble his father. He was carrying a tray with food and drink on it, and a vase with a flower. A *flower*. "Mom. Theo said you got hurt last night and that you needed rest."

Oh my God. How could he? "What else did he say?" She tried not to sound panicked or accusatory. Then in a desperate attempt for diversion, she gestured to the daisy. "Nice flower. Was that your idea or Vonnie's?"

Sam's expression of worry vanished, replaced by one of indignation. "It was mine! Geeesh."

"Thanks, love." She took the tray and saw that it had Vonnie's fingerprints all over it—except for the touch of the flower, of course. Tea with lemon and honey, a bowl of cut pears, a dish of almonds, crusty bread and butter, and a neatly folded yellow napkin.

"Theo said you were going down to check on Robert last night and you fell in the dark. Down the stairs. *Mom!* You have to be more careful!" Sam no longer channeled his father, but now was taking on the characteristics of Vonnie.

She'd lifted the cup of tea so as to have a moment to think, unsure of what he was going to say. Now she lowered it, relief and appreciation rushing through her. "I know. It was stupid of me." She raised the tea to sip again. "How is Robert? Do you know?"

"Vonnie's with him. She said to tell you he's doing okay." Sam sat on the edge of the bed and looked at her.

Selena's heart sank. He had that look on his face . . . the same look he'd had when he asked her what had happened to his father. And why the bounty hunter Seattle looked at her the way he did.

"Mom," he said firmly. "This Theo guy . . . he's a little . . . different."

Selena nibbled on a wedge of pear. "Different how?"

Sam shrugged and looked away, then back at her. "He offered to show us about those things in the arcade. I want to learn."

The relief she felt because he didn't seem to be aware of the depths of their relationship was swiftly usurped by unadulterated fear. "*No.* Absolutely not." She drew in a deep breath, squelching a different kind of panic. "Sam, it's too dangerous. They're too dangerous. There's no reason to get involved with those things— they're from another world. Another time."

"But Mom, he knows all about 'em. I saw him working on them . . . He's like . . . magic. Like on the DVDs. It's so cool." His voice rose, half pleading, half in admiration.

"No. Stay away from them. And from him. This is a

direct order from your mother, Sam. And besides . . . he's not going to be here much longer. Now that he's healed and healthy, he'll go back to Envy or wherever he's from." *Thank God. And the sooner the better.*

Sam's face twisted with frustration and belligerence. "Mom, that's—"

"Sam." Her voice whipped out with more sharpness than was probably necessary. But it had the effect of silencing him—for now.

"Whatever," he said, sullen.

"Sam," she said, remorse soft inside her. "I love you. That's why."

His features eased a bit. "I know. But I still think it's busted." He stood. "I have to go help Frank before he pukes a 'phant." He bent to kiss her on the cheek, and she lifted her sore arm to hug him. "Rest awhile. Okay, Mom?"

"I will."

But that wasn't likely. She had things to do. Patients to attend to. And—her heart squeezed—Theo to handle.

How *was* she going to handle him? She needed to get rid of him. Get him away from here, away from Yellow Mountain and back to Envy, where he could forget about this whole thing.

Not only that, but he was too young for her. It was ridiculous to want or expect anything more than a little fling. She'd heard Jennifer's horrified conversation with Theo the other day. The girl hadn't attempted to hide the shock in her voice. *"She's old enough to be your mother. That's just . . . busted! Totally rank."*

Jennifer was right.

As if conjured up, the expected knock came on the door at that moment, followed by Theo's ink-black head poking around the door. "I just saw Sam and he said you were awake," he explained without preamble.

His slanted eyes seemed more deep set than before, with shadows beneath them. His hair was wet, as if he'd just showered; and what she could see of his olive skin carried a damp sheen. Selena's mouth dried as she noticed the outline of muscle beneath the dark shirt that clung to his chest and shoulders.

"Yeah," she said. Selena eyed him, trying to read his expression. But it was inscrutable. So she dove right in. "I've been expecting you. A visit from you."

"I'm sure you have," he replied mildly, closing the door behind him.

"Thank you for . . . everything." Her voice roughened and she blinked.

Last night . . . she couldn't think about it. It had been the worst. It had been so close, and she'd feared for her life like never before. If he hadn't been there—if he hadn't brought her back and taken care of things . . . and told Sammy and Vonnie lies—

"What does Vonnie know about your night time activites?" he asked, sitting on a chair next to the bed.

Not *on* the bed. Not on the same bed they'd done a thorough job of destroying last night. She was acutely aware of that. *Good. Keep your distance. Let's make this as easy as possible.*

If it were one of the old romantic DVDs, they'd both be dancing politely around what needed to be said— but both would have the same goal: to end it without hurting anyone. Without awkwardness.

Here's hoping it works the same way now.

"Vonnie . . . not much really; she doesn't know *all* of it."

"Well, what the hell part does she know?" His voice tightened, got a little louder. "The part about you going out alone at night without a weapon? Or the part about the damned monsters mobbing you half to death? Or does she know about the way you have to touch them and—what?—kill them? Tame them? What the *hell* was going on out there?"

He clamped his lips shut and shoved a hand through his hair, making it spike all over. And glared at her. "You know, there's a helluva lot safer way to get rid of them besides shaking their damned hands."

Selena's heart was pounding. How could he understand? No one else did, not with *ganga* attacks year after year. All he and others saw were murderous, flesh-eating creatures; everyone except Vonnie, and even she didn't really comprehend it. She didn't understand what Selena had to do.

Why?

"Theo," she said, forcing herself to smile, "last night was . . . well, I wish you hadn't seen it. It's terrifying and incomprehensible, and it's probably best if you just forget about it. It's not going to happen again, and everything worked out all right. In the end. Thank you."

Now his face darkened and, for a minute, she was almost afraid. "What the hell kind of fool do you think I am?" he said from behind a tight jaw.

"I don't think you're a fool, Theo," she said soothingly, trying to hide her desperation. This was not going to go well. "But it's really nothing you need be concerned about." She moistened her lips. "Look, Theo, there's no reason for you to stick around here now that you're healthy—heck, you don't even have a wound. You're going to head back to Envy or wherever and get back to your regular life. And please . . . just *please* . . . forget about this. It's nothing."

He stood abruptly, his motions jerky. Instead of leaving the room, as she'd expected, he paced. Across, back and forth, with heavy, furious steps, his hand curling into a fist and his other swiping through his hair. And then he sat back down and glared at her again.

"Cut the crap, Selena. I know you'd like to relegate me to being your young studly boy toy and send me on my way after you've had a little fun, but I don't believe it for one goddamn minute. I'm not a child—in fact, I'm far from it—and I've seen and experienced things you have no idea about."

"I heard the conversation you had with Jennifer," she began.

"Yeah? Then you must have heard me tell her I wasn't interested in her. And I don't care what she thinks. There are things about me that *you* don't know either." He calmed a little. "You keep hinting that I'll be leaving soon. *What?* Do you expect me to slink off with my tail between my legs after having been involved with an older woman? As if I'm ashamed of it? Have I given you any indication that that's my intent?"

Selena shrugged, trying not to wince—*God, I'm so sore*. "There's nothing for you here. And what about Sage?"

"Sage?" She might have found the shock on his face amusing if the conversation hadn't been so intense. "Huh. I haven't even thought about her in . . . wow. Quite a while. But what do you know about her?"

"That you love her, for one," Selena said, realizing how difficult it was to force the words out. And to accept the concept that there was another woman in

his life. "You were raving about her when you were
. . . well, when you first got here." She wasn't about to
mention at this point that she'd caught one of his memories during his resurrection—an image of a beautiful,
young redheaded woman.

"Loved. Definitely past tense. Besides, she's with
someone else," he said quietly.

"I'm sorry."

He shrugged. And try as she might, she didn't see
any real grief in his face. "She's happy, so I'm happy
too." Then he shifted, and his eyes grew flinty. "So now
that we've discussed my romantic past, how about your
turn? Is this what happened with Brandon? He found
out about you and—what?—tried to help and got hurt
or killed? Forbid you from doing it? He got all angry at
you for *risking your life*? I can't say I blame the guy, if
that's the case."

Selena didn't think she'd ever felt so out of balance
and outnegotiated. He was quick. Too quick and insistent. "Leave Brandon out of this. It's a totally different
situation."

"What? How the hell am I going to understand you
and help you if you won't fucking *talk* to me?"

Understand me? . . . If only. Selena drew a calming
breath. *Here we go.* "I don't talk to anyone, Theo. It's
no one's business, no one's burden but *mine*. And I'm
going to keep it that way."

Theo didn't slam the door when he left Selena's room,
but he wanted to.

Instead, he went outside to work off some steam by
helping Frank and Sam rebuild a weak area of the protective wall. And then, when he was good and hot and
sweaty—and still angry as hell—he took a long, hard

swim upstream in the nearby river. Half of the anger that fueled him was directed toward Selena, but the other half was with Brad Blizek. Theo had discovered more layers of security, which made him realize he'd only made it through a false gate. He had to start over again and try to get in through the back door.

After his swim, because he knew he would be no good company to anyone but a machine with a keyboard, Theo went back up to the arcade and forced himself to face yet other problem.

At first, he'd assumed last night's failure to produce the power surge was simply due to pressure and lack of concentration while in the midst of a zombie mob. Not exactly comforting, but understandable.

But the first thing he'd done this morning, after slipping away from Selena's side once the sun was up (to make sure she didn't do anything insane like sneak outside again; and yes, he fully believed she was capable of such a thing) was to test it out.

And . . . *nada*. Zip, zero, zilch.

And . . . that was also when he'd taken a good look in the mirror and noticed not only a healthy dose of stubble . . . but a white hair.

For a guy of seventy-eight, stubble and a white hair would be no cause for alarm. But since, in the last fifty years, Theo had barely had to shave once a week, and hadn't grown more than a few white hairs, it was a bit of an eye-opener.

Had he not only lost his superpower, but was he also doing a Dorian Gray?

The thought of his age suddenly catching up to him was not a happy one, because how the hell was he going to protect Selena the next time she decided to do something suicidal if he was a doddering old man?

What would she think if she found out the truth? Would she run in the opposite direction—not because he was too young for her, but because he was nearly three decades *older* than she?

He'd thought it would be a little amusing to keep the truth from her for a while. He'd let her think he was really a young stud and watch her make all of her excuses for being involved with him. And then he'd tell her the truth, once she realized he cared about her regardless of how old either of them were—or looked. But now, he was more than a little worried that instead of being able to give her everything she wanted in bed, he'd be looking for the extinct little blue pills called Viagra.

Theo took out his frustration and fear on the keyboard, letting his fingers fly over the keys with ease, letting himself sink into that familiar pleasure. There was something soothing about coding. Hacking too. There, it all had to work out. It all had to fit.

Everything in its place. Every answer logical and perfect.

Unlike life, dammit.

After a while, he took a break and started flipping through some of Blizek's files, using the transparent electronic whiteboard to bring up some of his game prototypes. Sometimes, clearing the mind and rerouting it to come back at a problem from a different direction helped.

Aside from that, looking at screencaps and concept images for new video games from the master was pure pleasure. Seeing how the man's mind worked, from concept to prototype to even the coding, was fascinating.

He was looking at the files for Jolliah's Castle, which looked like some sort of sweet adventure game when Theo was jolted out of his zone to see Vonnie standing there, holding a tray in her hands. *Damn.* He blinked, trying to pull himself out of the zone.

"I thought I might find you up here," she said.

"Oh. Wow," he replied, pulling his attention reluctantly from the board, as if awakening from a deep sleep. *Connectus interruptus.*

He would realize later what a shock it was that Vonnie—the haste-makes-waste Vonnie—had made it all the way into the room and over to his corner without bumping into or dropping anything. In fact, she sounded a bit out of breath—probably from climbing three flights of stairs—but her curly salt-and-pepper hair was smoothed back in place and her round cheeks were only a bit pink. He thought she looked adorable, in a comfortable sort of way.

"You missed lunch, and I thought you might be hungry." She set the tray down on the table, moving a bunch of circuits and cords he'd laid out . . . just the way he wanted them.

Now, they were all jumbled up.

Theo smiled at her anyway. "Thank you. It smells good."

It did. And he was hungry. A chicken sandwich on that brown, sunflower-seed-studded bread with tomato slices and soft, fresh cheese oozing out the sides. A ripe pear cut into wedges. Raw carrots and some iced tea. His mouth began to water, and he looked at her again. "Thank you."

Vonnie was peering at the three monitors he had on, all of them lined up in a row, each with their own keyboard. "I remember some of that," she said, gesturing vaguely to one of the screens. "It's long before your time, but we used to have something called Facebook, where you played a game and built a farm. And YouTube. Where you could watch movies—you know, DVDs—right on the computer."

Her voice trailed off and she looked at him. Suddenly, there was a sharpness in her eyes that hadn't been there before. "So, are you going to tell me what really happened last night?"

Working on a mouthful of sandwich, Theo blinked and kept chewing. The way to a man's heart—or in this case, confidence—was definitely through his stomach. Talk about a bait and switch. "I figure," he said after he swallowed, "you can probably make a good guess."

They looked at each other for a moment, neither of them willing to give in. Then he caved and took another bite of sandwich.

Vonnie just glared at him, all traces of mother hen gone and replaced by the principal tapping her foot, waiting for an answer about who had rewired the fire alarms to go off at precisely the beginning of English midterms. Amazing how a woman could quick-change like that. Frightening, really. Theo's mom had been like that. And so was Selena.

"What happened with Brandon?" he asked stubbornly. "At least give me that."

"Were you with her out there? At least give me that," she parroted right back at him. And lifted a pert nose to look down at him just a bit.

"Yes. I was with her."

Vonnie's shoulders seemed to deflate. "Thank God. She refuses to let me go with her; and I sleep so heavily, I never hear her leave. I only find out after the fact . . . when it's time to patch her up."

Theo filed away that information for future reference—the part about Vonnie sleeping heavily. In the room only two doors down from Selena's. "She didn't let me go with her," he clarified. "I followed her out there."

He popped a wedge of pear into his mouth. "Is that what happened with Brandon? He found out about her? Then what? He tried to make her stop? Can't say I blame the guy not wanting the mother of his child to be torn apart by zombies."

Vonnie's pretty face grew soft and sad. "It wasn't that simple. And I don't know if I should tell you what happened—"

"I think you'd better," he replied flatly. "I saw her out there. I don't want that to happen again. And she . . . well, I get the impression that she wants me to forget about it and leave it alone. And leave here. Is that what Brandon did? He left her?"

"No, oh no. She left him. We all did. Me and her and Sam. We had to." Vonnie blinked rapidly and stared out the window for a moment. "She tried to explain to them—to everyone—what she was doing. They didn't really understand, but at least she got them to listen."

"Who are you talking about? In Yellow Mountain?"

"No, oh no," she replied. "This was before we came here to Yellow Mountain. We were at Sivs. Over south of here, more than a week's travel time." Like Selena, she flapped her hand in a generic direction that wasn't even close to south. "It took her a long time, but she finally told him—Brandon—what she was doing. That her way was better and kinder to the zombies. He didn't want to believe her, and he didn't want her to get hurt. He did love her . . . he just didn't understand her."

Vonnie jabbed her finger toward the last bite of his sandwich. "Like, she won't eat any meat or anything from a creature that's been killed. It's her way. And that was one thing he never accepted. He'd try to get her to eat a piece of chicken or a bit of fish now and then. Once he tried to trick her into it by slipping a bit of meat in a stew she was eating. When she found out, she was sick afterward. Really sick. So now she won't eat anything unless I cook it."

"I can see that." Theo was only half following Vonnie's rambling explanation, but it was interesting nevertheless. Sounded like Brandon was a real asshole. He wasn't too sad about that. "What happened at Sivs?"

"Brandon found out about what she was doing and tried to stop her from doing it. But she wasn't going to let that happen. She can't *not* do it, she told me. It'd be like her not helping the people dying. She can't ignore it. Even though it's hard."

"How long has she been the Death Lady?"

Vonnie glanced toward the rest of the room, as if to make sure no one was approaching. "She saw her first death cloud when she was five. But she didn't know what it was. She didn't realize what she was doing until she was older."

"Death cloud?"

Vonnie looked uncomfortable. "It's really not my place to tell you, Theo. But . . . it's what she sees when someone's going to die. She guards her secrets well; and if she wants you to know more than that, she'll tell you. But the last person she told was Brandon, and that didn't turn out so well. Brandon and the people at Sivs."

Theo struggled to control his frustration. "What happened at Sivs?"

"Everyone hates the zombies. They're terrified of

them. Everyone's lost someone to a zombie. Someone they know."

"Yeah. For sure. That's why the earth needs to be rid of them. They're the only creatures on this earth that don't have a reason for being. They're evil." Theo glanced outside, checking the position of the sun. "Abnormal, not a part of the circle of life. Cannibalistic monsters."

Vonnie bit her lip. "Selena has a different perspective."

"She kills them—it can't be *that* different of a perspective. And she does it in an inefficient, dangerous way. Why the hell doesn't she use arrows or a bomb or fire or something?"

"Because that's not her way. It's more humane, she says, the way she does it. She has to rescue them. Selena can't bear to see the destruction of life. She won't let Frank set mouse traps unless they're cages and the mice can be set free outside."

Theo shook his head, frustrated and confused. "What zombies do isn't living. It's . . . I don't know what, but it's not *living*. It's evil. They eat anyone or anything; and what they don't eat, they destroy just for the hell of it. It's a damn good thing they're dumb as rocks or we'd have ceased to exist on this earth." He'd made his way through the carrots and now lifted the iced tea to drink. *Ahh. Just the perfect amount of sweet.*

Vonnie's lips pursed. "Well, you're sounding like Brandon a bit now. But somehow, she convinced him to see her side of it; and when he made a big fuss about her going out at night, they came up with an idea. If the rest of the town would help, they could corral all the zombies and then Selena could do her thing in relative safety."

"Sort of like putting a group of wild dogs down one by one after you cage them?" Theo asked. "Still not very efficient, but at least it would be safer for her."

"Selena convinced them to try it and they built a corral. And they managed to do it—to trick a bunch of the zombies to go in there one night. Locked them in and everything was fine. She took care of a few every night, carefully."

"Until . . . Aw, crap. Let me guess. They got loose!"

She nodded. "It was ugly. Horrifying. They were trapped *inside* the walls with the rest of us, and they got out. By the time we realized what was happening, it was too late. The zombies were crazed and frightened and wild—and hungry—and they attacked. Selena tried to stop them, tried to help, but by then it was too late. The damage was done. Children, the elderly, even some of the young, strong men who'd been building a solar-powered vehicle were all destroyed. The death count was nearly half of the population of the settlement."

Theo felt sick. He didn't really need to hear more; he could imagine it. "What did they do?"

"Well, of course, everyone blamed Selena. As if she'd caused it herself, as if she'd forced those zombies to come out and attack everyone. And Brandon couldn't even look at her. He wouldn't listen to her. And she . . . well, of course she took it all on herself. All of it. She needed him and he couldn't give her what she needed." Vonnie glanced at him sidewise and Theo felt the pointedness of her glare. "And so, we left. They would never forgive her. She couldn't go anywhere without being spat on or pushed or ignored or . . . whatever. It was ugly.

"They called her a zombie lover. And it wasn't a

compliment," Vonnie said, seemingly following Theo's thoughts along its silent path. "Then they started wondering whether what she was doing out there with them wasn't really killing them, but somehow hypnotizing them and training them to do her bidding. We had to leave."

By now, Theo was feeling ill himself. What a horrible story. He could understand both sides, both perspectives of what had happened. It was the same sort of thing that had happened after 9/11—too many people blamed every Muslim for what had been done by a dozen radical ones.

It was human nature: to find a scapegoat, to place blame on someone when something tragic happened.

It wasn't always right, nor was it the best aspect of humanity, but it was a common reaction.

But he still didn't have any greater admiration for Brandon.

"But that's not the last of it," Vonnie said. "We moved on and stayed at a place called Crossroads for a while; maybe a year or so. Of course after that last experience, Selena wasn't willing to trust anyone about her mission. She was still helping dying people find their way to wherever their afterlife was, but she wouldn't ignore her need to help the zombies. So this time, she didn't tell anyone what she was doing. But, then, people started to see her. Out, in the dark, beyond the walls at night with the zombies. It appeared to them that she was helping or training them, or something.

"Since there'd recently been a rash of zombie attacks against three teenagers, the people of Crossroads became incensed at the thought of someone *helping* or protecting the zombies. They started calling her horrible things and shunning her, and it escalated there too. Then a young woman was attacked one night beyond the walls, and killed, and that was the end of that. They blamed Selena's 'zombie loving' for attracting the monsters, and an angry group from the settlement came and tried to take her away and lock her up. We left instead."

Jesus. No wonder Selena didn't want to talk about it. No wonder she didn't feel as if she could trust anyone. He understood, but it still bothered him that she wouldn't trust *him*.

"So we came here. Actually, we met Frank and he brought us here. That's why we don't live in Yellow Mountain, and why she doesn't go there very often. The less people know about her, the happier she is. To them, she's just the Death Lady. Not a zombie lover."

Theo was nodding, but his stomach churned. The stories reminded him of the Salem witch trials—innocent people tainted and judged, even murdered, because of a bunch of superstitious people.

Yet he still didn't understand why Selena was so intent on making the deaths of zombies so comfortable. Why she risked her life to help them—as if they were her pets that had somehow gone feral.

It reminded him of one of their neighbors when he and Lou were growing up. Mrs. Cloud had had a rottweiler that had attacked and killed another neighbor's cat.

Theo and Lou had played with the rott many times, and had even seen it be around a cat without showing any aggressive behavior. But this one time, something must have happened to provoke it, and the dog had attacked. The courts had ordered the dog to be put down; and although Lou and Theo had protested and picketed and wrote letters (this was before Twitter and Facebook groups) for the life of the dog, the decision had prevailed.

The cat owner celebrated at the dog's death, but Mrs. Cloud and the others who'd known Butch grieved.

"And Brandon? What about Sam?"

Vonnie shrugged. "Selena sure as hell wasn't going to leave him in Sivs with Brandon. And he cared more about his standing in the settlement than about his family. It wasn't a tough decision."

Theo nodded. That cleared a few things up. "Thanks," he said, "for telling me about that."

Vonnie looked at him. "Now I want something from you."

Back into mother mode. Theo nodded again.

"How long are you planning to stick around here?"

"Here, up here?" Theo gestured to the room.

She frowned at him and actually tapped her foot in rapid succession.

"Oh, here? . . . around Yellow Mountain?" He tried out the grin that always had worked on his own mom, and was rewarded with a twitch of her lips. "I don't know. I can tell you that, right now, I don't have any reason to leave. And . . . I feel like I have a lot of reasons to stay."

Vonnie looked at him, then snatched up the tray. She gave a brief, sharp nod. "All right, then, young man"— she looked at the computers, and then at him—"I don't know what you're doing up here, and I'm not going to ask. Just be careful with those. They've caused a lot of grief."

"Thanks, Vonnie," he said as she walked out of the room.

Then he turned back to the touch screen computer

and stared at it. *They've caused a lot of grief, but they hold secrets. They must.*

"What the fuck is your secret, Blizek? Did you join them? Did you help to destroy the damned world?" Theo demanded, staring at the large screen. "Are you living somewhere with a damned crystal in your skin?"

Frustrated, he began to wing his fingers around on the screen, pointing, spreading, pinching, and he watched windows open and open and open inside and on top of each other. He left the area of prototype games, and stopped trying to dig into the deepest layers of security.

Instead, he went to photos and emails and videos. He looked at simple documents and some basic coding.

And then he saw it. His whole body went cold and still.

IF THE WORLD ENDS.mov

A video.

Not even very well hidden; in fact, he'd have found it sooner if he hadn't been digging for what he thought was the good stuff.

His heart pounding, Theo clicked on it and suddenly a video opened, filling the touch screen, and there was Brad Blizek. On the wall, just like the Wizard of Oz.

He spoke to the camera, quickly, in a low voice. Urgency written all over his homely face.

"If you're seeing this, then the worst has come to pass. I'm dead, for they won't let me live once they realize that I'm not really part of them. I'm not with them. They're going to destroy the world."

At this point, Theo gave an audible sigh of relief—and in the video, Brad glanced behind and hunched his shoulders as if expecting to be interrupted at any time.

"I'll talk as long as I can, give you as much as I

can, but when I hear them, I'm going to close this. It's coded to automatically upload to news outlets, You-Tube and back to my own LAN."

He flinched, his face tightening, and then spoke even more quickly and softly. Theo could see that his hand was positioned on the desk in front of the webcam he was using, as if ready to click a mouse at a moment's notice.

"I found out about them years ago. They wanted me to join and I pretended to do so. For fifty million. The cost was nothing, so I gave it to them because I wanted to know what they were doing. While developing hardware and software for them, I've also carefully hacked into their systems. It's hard because it needs to leave no trace of my presence; and even though I'm brilliant, they're watching me. I'm working with truth to begin to collect data, to try and find a way to stop this. They're so strong and so far-reaching that any attempts to publicize will result in it being squelched, not to mention my death. So I'm trying to find a way to use their—"

Another sound was audible enough to be heard on the webcam, and his eyes grew wide and he leaned closer to the computer, whispering loudly now. *"It's them. It's the Cult of Atlantis. They're fucking raising the island of Atlantis and it's going to wobble the world. They're doing—"*

He glanced behind him and the screen went blank.

"Holy mother-fucking shit." Theo stared at the screen for a long time before the hair on his arms relaxed. Then he played it again. And again. And again. His heart had gone up into his throat and he stared at the screen.

If he'd seen it fifty years ago, he'd have thought it was a joke.

But now he knew three things: He and Lou had been right in their theories. Brad Blizek had been a good guy all along. And Brad Blizek was definitely dead.

CHAPTER 9

Robert didn't pass on to the afterlife until late the following morning, a whole twenty-four hours after Selena had told Theo she didn't talk to anyone about her secrets, and almost ten days after Theo had been resurrected.

Despite her abused body, she had been busy in the last day. A bit slower, but busy. She'd kept herself that way on purpose.

Whether by accident or design, she hadn't spoken to Theo since he left her bedroom with a very sharp, telling click of the door closing behind him. She hadn't even seen him, except from a distance through the window when she caught sight of him walking back from what looked like a swim: dripping wet, bare torso gleaming in the sun, every muscle and curve perfect on his dark skin, the red dragon shifting in the daylight. Her mouth had gone dry and her belly filled with butterflies, and she turned resolutely away.

The thing that made her stomach unsettled wasn't so much the look of his body, but the thought of how much she missed him. Just . . . missed him. She sensed he might never be comfortable around her again, after what he'd seen last night.

Surprisingly, since the horrible events, Selena hadn't been the recipient of an anticipated lecture from Vonnie about her nocturnal activities. In fact, everyone seemed to be particularly kind and quiet around her.

She wondered why. She wondered, uneasily, why it felt as if the calm before the storm.

However, the most disturbing occurrence happened on the third day after she awoke in her bedroom. Theo was absent again for the evening meal, and Selena wasn't certain whether she should be relieved that he seemed to be avoiding her—possibly even preparing to leave, as she'd suggested—or whether to allow just a bit of sadness to seep into her mind. She certainly felt a little lost, but tried to talk herself out of it.

It had only been *one* night.

But she missed him.

Yet Theo's absence at yet another meal wasn't what concerned her. It was the way Sam was looking at Jennifer, and how Jennifer was overtly flirting back with him. *Thank God Frank's deaf,* Selena thought after one particularly obvious double entendre.

It got worse, when, feeling the deep need to go for a head-clearing walk after dinner, she came out of the house and was walking down one of the stone paths when she came around a corner and found Sam and Jennifer in a passionate embrace.

They were under a small arbor covered with vines, out of sight from the house. And Jennifer's shirt was up, baring a sleek, naked back.

Selena froze and then made a lot of rustling in the bushes. Sam's head popped out from behind Jennifer's and he met his mother's eyes. His eyes widened for a moment and then she saw him actually draw a deep breath.

"Hi, Sam," Selena said, managing to keep her voice steady, but inside her mind was screaming and scrambling: *What are you doing? She's almost ten years older than you. Well, maybe only seven. But you're too young for her!*

The two young people had eased apart, but Sam's arm remained slung possessively and protectively around Jennifer's waist. His face was flushed and his lips full and damp, and he had an unsurprisingly glazed expression. Jennifer, on the other hand, took her time in adjusting her T-shirt over braless breasts—and the look she sent Selena was not a warm one. Nor was it embarrassed.

It was *gotcha.*

And all at once, Selena understood. A chill of anger and disappointment rushed over her. "Sam, Frank was looking for you," she lied without remorse.

"Mom," he said with admirable firmness, taking responsibility for his actions. "I didn't mean for you to find out this way." He gave the girl a little hug-nudge and Selena noticed with a sick feeling in her belly that he looked so young next to her.

Not allowing even a glance of recognition to Jennifer, Selena focused on her son. Her innocent, just-barely-a-man, seventeen-year-old son who'd had an Orange Crush on Jennifer since he was fifteen. "I know," she replied. "Maybe next time you'll pick a more private place." It was important that she didn't allow her anger with Jennifer to show. "Can you imagine what Frank or Vonnie would have said if they found you?"

He glanced at Jennifer and gave her such a sweet, sappy smile that a new wave of nausea licked through Selena. "We just thought it would be a nice walk after dinner . . . and, well, you know," he said. There was pride in his expression and in his voice. *Look who* I *have. Look who wants* me.

Selena swallowed hard and managed to nod. *She's going to eat you alive.* She would have a heart-to-heart with him later. Now she just had to get past this without tearing out the eyes of the woman who was using her son—and without letting him think she didn't approve of the relationship.

"I think I left my sweater over there," Jennifer said in a smooth voice. "I'm going to go get it. Okay, hon?" The girl still had that cat-swallowed-a-canary look about her. "I'll be right back."

Selena remained resolute in keeping her thoughts to herself; and she could only pray that the daggers she felt weren't shooting out of her eyes as the girl walked off along the path.

"I am sorry you found out about it this way, Mom," Sam said.

"How long has this been going on?" she managed to ask.

"Only in the last couple days. I know you probably think things are going too quickly"—*Hell-fucking, yes!*—"but she's really bang. And she's so mature, you know?"—*Yes, I know!*— "So, anyway, I'm going to walk her back to her horse before it gets too close to dark," he said. "Unless you don't mind if she stays here tonight?"

Selena nearly swallowed her tongue and wasn't successful in keeping her attention from Jennifer as she reappeared on the pathway. "I don't think that's a good idea," was all Selena managed to say. *Don't get her pregnant. Please don't get her pregnant!* It was almost a blasphemous thought, but she didn't care.

Sam seemed to take that with grace. Perhaps he figured he'd already pushed things enough with his mother. "Okay, Mom. But I think we're going to need to talk about this soon."

"I think that's a very good idea," Selena said. "I'll see you back inside in a little while."

Numb, furious, and not just a little bit nauseated, she walked off . . . casually at first, and then with greater speed as the fury propelled her. *That little bitch.*

She was not going to stand by and let her son get used and hurt just because Jennifer wanted to make a point. The girl hadn't ever looked twice at Sam before now. And it wasn't as if there weren't several single men her age living in Yellow Mountain.

Selena's lips curled into each other and she stalked on, glad for the protective walls and the large expanse of grounds on which she could take out her fury without worrying about night falling.

What the hell am I going to do?

What she'd planned on being a calming, mind-clearing walk to smell the evening flowers and check on Frank's garden had turned into another dilemma. *Why? Why again!*

Just then, an unfamiliar noise caught her attention. Selena paused and looked around. She'd strode and stalked farther into the depths of the grounds than she had for months. Probably even years. Past Frank's massive vegetable and herb garden, and toward the clump of trees that mounded in the far western section. Frank had another garden toward the south, camouflaged by trees and debris carefully arranged to completely obstruct it from the bounty hunters when they came.

But back here, in the western section, where the trees grew tall and thick, she didn't remember there being anything but a collection of overgrown, rusted-out machinery.

The noise was coming from there and it sounded like a low rumble, followed by a long groaning-squeal. And . . . were those lights?

Through the trees?

The sun was low, but it wasn't even dusk yet. Then she saw it again . . . a flash of movement *above* the trees. And lights. And more odd sounds . . .

Selena moved closer, along a path that was overgrown and untended. The noises became louder and there was definitely movement, but as she got closer, the height of the trees blocked the lights.

Then she came through a clump of bushes and found herself in the clearing with all of the machinery.

She stopped, stunned and fascinated at the sight that greeted her. Much of the overgrowth had been cleared away from the center of the space, now stacked in large brush piles beneath the trees. A large upright wheel, taller than the house, taller than the trees, was randomly lit with small lights. And it was turning, slowly, with groaning protest . . . but it was moving. There were boxes hanging from it, like swings with sides . . . Selena had seen that before, in DVDs. A fairies' wheel.

Who in the— But she didn't even need to finish the thought. Of course it was Theo. She knew it had to be him. He'd fixed her DVD player and rewired a light that had been giving Frank trouble, and did something to the washing machine that made Vonnie weep with gratitude.

It wasn't long before she found him—near the base of the fairies' wheel, sitting on the ground, swearing at a metal box fixed on legs, filled with wires and levers. Tools cluttered the ground around him and his hair was standing up every which way. His dragonless arm was in view, taut and flexed deliciously as he struggled with something in the box.

For some reason, Selena's palms grew damp as she approached. Those damn butterflies started up in her stomach again.

How is he going to react when he sees me? Still angry?

Her mouth was going dry and her heart was pounding. She wasn't certain how to approach him, or whether he'd be annoyed if she interrupted. So she just walked over and stood there. Her feet would be in his peripheral vision and eventually he'd notice.

When he did, it was with a little jolt and a start, and then his gaze traveled slowly up from her rope sandals, over her long loose skirt, and higher to meet her eyes.

"I thought you were Frank," he said.

"I'm not," she replied, relieved that he hadn't ordered her to go away.

"There's definitely no mistaking you for Frank."

And there was definitely no mistaking the inflection in his voice. That made the butterflies a little more excited.

Theo pulled to his feet and she found herself looking up at him and stepping back a bit. His expression was reserved; just a bit warmer than merely polite. "Want to try it out?" he asked, gesturing toward the big wheel.

Selena couldn't hold back a gasp of surprise and delight. And terror. "I don't know . . . it's so high."

He chuckled a little, softening, and the low rumble sent a little frisson of warmth down her spine. "Don't tell me you're afraid of heights."

"I don't get very high very often," she said, and for

some reason that made him laugh again. She liked the sound of it, and realized she'd heard it quite often.

"Come on, Selena," he said. "What's another risk in your already dangerous life?" There might have been a warning edge to his voice. Or maybe it was sadness.

"Is it safe?" she asked, following him onto the little ramp that led to the lowermost seat.

"Of course. Well, at least this one is," he said, jiggling the seat a little. "I just rebolted it and double-checked its weight-bearing load. See those boulders over there? They were the first to take a ride."

The sight of the three massive boulders comforted her. How he even got them into the box was a mystery, but if they'd made it on the ride, then she and Theo should be okay. "All right," she said. She saw now that the wheels' "spokes" were covered with tiny lightbulbs. Only a few were lit—intermittent glows of red, blue, green and yellow.

He gave her a smile and opened the box with a flourish. "Beauty before age," he said, gesturing for her to climb in.

Selena laughed and gave him a *you're crazy* look as she stepped onto the little cradled seat. It swayed and wobbled and she froze with one foot on and one foot off. "It's rocking," she said.

"It's supposed to. Go ahead, pick a side."

She scooted over to one side of the box and then was nervous, waiting to see if he'd sit next to her or across from her. When he climbed on, she was more than a little disappointed that he chose the opposite seat.

"I want to make sure it's balanced," he said, mollifying her a bit. Then he bolted the little door to the cart and settled back in his seat. He lifted a small gadget that looked like a DVD remote control, but it had a stiff wire extending from it. "Normally, there's a guy down there running the machine. He throws the lever and it starts up, and he stops it when it's done. But that's not going to work in this situation—unless you want to go alone?"

"Not on your life!"

He grinned. "I didn't think so. So I have a remote control for the machine. Are you ready?"

"Yes. I think." Selena braced herself, sitting in the middle of her seat, arms extended so that her fingers could clutch each side of the box. She closed her eyes and braced her feet against the edge of Theo's seat.

She thought she heard the rumble of his chuckle again, but if so, it was lost in the long, low groan of the machinery beginning to turn and lift the seats.

Selena didn't know what she'd expected—probably some crazy-fast liftoff or some sort of sharply-upward-vaulting motion. But all she felt was a little delicious breeze and an odd, weightless sensation. The seat swayed gently, not violently as she'd expected it would.

When she opened her eyes, she found Theo watching her. There was a half-smile curving his lips, but the expression in his eyes was anything but amused. *Hot and heavy.*

Her stomach's butterflies shot into full flight, and it wasn't, Selena realized, just because the wheel had reached the top and was now falling in its full descent. She swallowed and shifted her gaze, feeling the breeze rush gently over her face.

Wow, she thought.

"You like it?" Theo asked. He'd settled back into his side, arms extended casually over the back of the seat instead of bolt outright like hers were.

"Yes. It's marvelous. I've never experienced anything like this." Selena relaxed her grip and even released one side of the box. She shifted as if to drop her feet to the floor, but he moved suddenly and stopped her.

Closing his fingers around her ankle, Theo said, "You don't have to move your feet." He didn't release her foot, and before she could protest, he'd removed her frayed rope sandal and dropped it to the floor of their swing. His fingers shifted on her ankle, and the next thing she knew, he'd shifted *her* so that her foot was positioned between his knees and he was using both hands to massage her sole.

Oh, heaven. Absolute . . . *heaven!—Those strong fingers.*

He was kneading the ball of her foot with just the right pressure, then moved along the delicate arch more gently, so as not to tickle her—and pressed with a firm thumb and forefinger at the back of her ankle. *Ohhh.*

"You have really sexy feet," he said, glancing up at her as the trees scrolled down behind him and the breeze teased her hair.

"Thank you," Selena managed to say. Her knees were turning into soup and she couldn't draw her attention away from the sight of his elegant hands and the long dark fingers cupping her lighter, honey-colored foot.

"I mean, *really* sexy feet. That was one of the first things I noticed about you."

She couldn't swallow. And then her scattered mind remembered his question from the other day. "The red paint on my toenails? It's made from clay and honey and some other things. Dandelion root for the color."

"I like it." He bent forward suddenly and captured

her other foot, which had slid to the floor between them as she relaxed.

Selena didn't resist as he began to give it the same treatment as the other. She closed her eyes and settled back against the seat, let the breeze and the pleasure wash over her. If only she could make this moment last forever.

"How long have you been working on this project?" she asked, opening her eyes after a minute.

He didn't release her feet. Now he was stroking the top of one, up to her ankle and easing to her calf. Selena couldn't help but wonder where this might lead . . . and she wasn't altogether uninterested.

In fact, if the spreading warmth in her body and the tingling down low were any indication, she was more than a little interested. But she wasn't impatient, nor did she feel any pressure.

"For a few days," he replied to her question. "I decided I would make myself scarce for a while—and there were a few things I thought I might do while I'm here, and this was one of them."

While I'm here. She ignored the pang of disappointment she felt at that reminder, and forced herself to nod and look interested.

"I thought I might coax you out here for a surprise when it was finished . . . but you beat me to it. I'm surprised you found me. The only person who comes out here is Frank, and that's only because I asked him to show me. What were you doing all the way out here, a mile from the house?"

Of course, his question had the effect of bringing the problem with Sam and Jennifer back to the forefront of her mind and wiping away most of her enjoyment of the ride. "I needed to walk off some anger," she finally answered, shifting in her seat and trying to return her feet to the floor.

He held firmly, but gently. "Anger? At who?"

Selena looked away, and realized with a start that she could see all of the grounds of the estate from the highest point of the fairies' wheel, and that the sun had dipped half below the horizon. The view was beautiful and intriguing—she'd never seen it thus. And now they were on their way back down again, a little tickle in her belly joining the uprush of breeze. With the lowering of the sun, the tiny lights seemed to glow brighter above and around them.

"Selena."

She turned back to him. "I just noticed the view."

He nodded. "You aren't going to tell me who you're angry with?"

She shifted. This wasn't really a conversation she wanted to have with him . . . yet. Maybe he'd have a different perspective, being in a similar situation himself. Sort of. But beside that, she *wanted* to talk to someone. She needed to.

Hadn't she just been thinking about how lonely she was?

"I came upon Sammy and Jennifer making out, just now over by the roses."

Theo's eyebrows rose very high and he stopped rubbing her foot for a minute. "Oh." Then he shifted and began to press his powerful thumb just below the ball of her foot, strong and circular and so heavenly that she wanted to groan and slip into a coma. "That must have been awkward."

"I heard your conversation with Jennifer the other day. The day you—uh—helped me move my bookshelf."

Theo grinned briefly. "That's a new euphemism: 'move your bookshelf.' But it doesn't really do justice to the activity, in my opinion." Then the grin slipped away. "I know—you told me you heard us."

"Oh, yeah. Well . . . I think she's trying to make a point. And I don't want Sammy to get hurt."

Theo considered her foot for a moment, his thumb now stroking gently over the top just where it met her ankle. Slowly and tenderly. "You think she's jealous? Or you think she's trying to compare her relationship with Sam to . . . us?"

"The way she looked at me . . . it was smug and sort of like *Ha! See how you like it?* I just don't want her to use him to get back at me. To make a point. He's had an Orange Crush on her for a long time."

"An Orange Crush?" He looked at her with such affection that, despite the fact that she was the elder here, she felt like he was the older one. "I like it."

Suddenly, he moved. The next thing she knew, he was up and over to her side of the box, wedging in next to her and leaving the car swaying with too much gusto for her taste. Selena stifled a little squeak of surprise, but when his solid body had settled next to her, large and warm, she felt better.

"And," she said quickly, to fill the moment, "what if she gets pregnant?"

"Don't want to be a granny just yet?" he asked, turning to smile at her.

He was so close. Right there. But, they were hardly touching—just the brush from his arm's hair against hers. "It's not that," she said. "I don't think he's ready to be a father, and I know Jennifer's not ready to be settling down with a seventeen-year-old boy."

"You know this the same way you know that I

couldn't be at all interested in hanging around a woman who seems to be twice my age. Right?"

Selena rolled her eyes. "The situation is a lot different. He's hardly a grown man yet, first of all. She can't really be interested in him. She never even looked at him before. And I'm sure if you were to give her any attention at all or show any interest in her, she'd drop him like a rock. You know?"

He looked at her steadily. "I hope you're not suggesting that I give her some attention in order to distract her from Sam."

She bit her lip and looked at him hopefully. "You could."

His brows drew together. "And how would that make me look? I've already had the pleasure of being lectured by your son in regards to my intentions. He wasn't pleased."

"What?" Selena felt a mixed wave of shock and delight. Theo was smiling at her. "He wasn't pleased, but he was very polite. And very firm. And in regards to Jennifer—I'll tell you what I told him: there's no interest there on my part."

"Well . . . okay. But if you just gave her a little attention—just to see if I'm right? It would be for a good cause. The naive, tender heart of a seventeen-year-old boy."

"Not a chance. I don't hang around women I'm not interested in. I don't flirt with them, and I certainly don't make love with them." His voice bordered on annoyed but was laced with a dusky edge that made her mouth dry again. "And besides that, heartbreak is part of life. It sucks, but it makes you stronger. Helps you to see things more clearly . . . at least, after the pain goes away."

She wondered if he was talking about the woman named Sage. The one who seemed to have broken his heart. Selena swallowed hard and scrambled to redirect. "And what do you mean when you say 'a woman who *seems* to be twice your age'? So maybe that's an exaggeration, but I'm fifty, Theo. And you can't be more than thirty, maybe thirty-five at the outside."

"I've said to you before, I'm not as young as I look."

She settled back in her seat and puffed the air from her lips so that it joined the breeze in tousling her bangs. "Like *I* said . . ."

He shook his head slowly and kept looking at her. As if he wanted to say something. Finally, he spoke. "I have to ask you something. What happened when you brought me back to life? Exactly? How did you do it?"

"Well, I . . ." Selena said as she turned a little, arranging herself in the corner of the seat. And while she was adjusting, he reached for her calf and lifted her left leg to settle over his lap, where he once again held her foot.

She bit her lip. *How much should I tell him?* "That crystal that I was wearing . . . the other night."

"The one that burned? When you were out by the zombies?"

Selena nodded. "I touched that crystal to your . . . to the eye of the dragon on your back. It's . . . what is it, anyway? It was metal or something. You gave this big . . . jolt, and sort of shuddered. And then you opened your eyes."

"Well, that explains that," he muttered. "You just touched it to me?"

"Yes. It was like a spark or something. But what is that thing in you?"

"Yeah. See, Selena," he said, settling into his respective corner, too, his knees turned to face her, bumping her right one. "There are a few things you don't know about me either. I have my own secrets."

She waited, expecting him to continue. But he didn't. Instead, he massaged her big toe with great attention, as if it were the most important thing in the world. A precious jewel or piece of metal that he was rubbing and polishing.

Theo looked up all of a sudden with a sheepish smile. "I'm getting really turned on doing this," he said. And he looked at her with eyes that proved his statement.

"Rubbing my foot?" Selena managed a little chuckle, but it came out more like a husky breath. *Those butterflies again . . .*

He laughed a little too. "I know. It's a bit weird. But I think it stems from this photo spread I saw once, a long time ago, when I was just about Sam's age. Very impressionable. It was a series of pictures of a couple making love—nude, of course, in most of them. Really tasteful, though, as those sorts of pictures go. But the last photo was one with just her feet showing. Elegant and feminine, with the same sorts of smooth curves as the rest of her body. The nails painted bright red like yours, just sticking out from the white bedsheets. The sheets were all rumpled and messed up, and you knew what had just happened . . . and one foot was straight up, and the other one was cocked to the side. I don't know. It just . . . got me."

It 'got' her a little bit, too, listening to him talk that way.

Their car was just about to the top again, and she felt a sudden rush of breeze as they crested . . . then that flippy, dropping feeling as they started down again. A wonder that she'd been so nervous, when this was such an enjoyable, sensual ride. The sun was nearly gone, and a generous moon had appeared in the southeast. The world was turning from muted color to every shade of blue-gray and mottled with shadow.

"That little metal thing in my back is what's called an integrated circuit. Or IC," he said finally. "It was embedded in my body during . . . during a massive underground explosion."

Selena didn't speak. She just waited for him to continue.

"It healed in my skin, integrated into my body somehow . . . and it changed me." He'd stopped rubbing her foot and now simply held it in his warm hands, cupping her heel and the ball of her foot. "I don't know how or why, but the circuit gave me this ability to produce electrical power at will."

She blinked, staring at him. The sun had sunk low enough that she couldn't really see his features; she couldn't tell if he was serious, or making a joke. "And . . .?"

"And, all of a sudden, now that I've been resurrected, I seem to have lost the ability. Which, incidentally, I've found to be quite handy in the past."

She realized she'd pulled away from her corner, interested and tense. Now she settled back in her seat. *Ah. So he couldn't demonstrate this odd thing. Very convenient.*

But why would he lie about something like this? She knew from her own experience that there were inexplicable things in life, and beyond. "It doesn't seem to bother you that much," she commented. "Losing that ability."

He smiled briefly and gave her foot a little squeeze. "It's not like losing an arm or a leg," he replied. "I mean, I'm still fully functional," he added with a brief sidewise smile. "And it wasn't something I used all the time, or even every day. It took a lot of effort and energy to bring that power forth and use it . . . and afterward, I was always really weak. I couldn't hardly stand up. I'm thinking that maybe the charge that came from the crystal and jolted me back to life had the effect of blowing the circuits, so to speak. So the power is gone now   but I'm still alive. I'm thinking it was an even exchange."

She didn't really understand everything he was talking about in regards to blowing circuits, so she just nodded.

"Nothing I can do about it. I can ask why all I want, but I never seem to get an answer," he said.

Selena stared at him, something flowering inside her. "I know the feeling."

"I don't know why that happened, or why you were able to bring me back to life. I wish I did. It seems like there must be some reason. But so far, I haven't figured out what it is."

Selena let his words wash over her like the gentle breeze, taking them for their worth. She liked him. She didn't want to disbelieve him, or wonder if he was weird. He was different, and she wasn't certain what he was up to, but she liked him. A *lot*. And not just because of those broad, square shoulders. She felt comfortable with him. As if he understood things at a deeper level than most people. He was easy to talk to, and he listened. But she still wasn't ready to tell him everything. She'd *loved* Brandon; she'd had a child with him . . . and *he* hadn't been capable of fully understanding her.

"I don't think we ever get the real answer to *why* anything happens—good or bad," she said. "Easy or difficult. But we only seem to ask when we don't like it. When we need to know why someone died, or why this tragedy happened, or why something difficult is required of me."

Theo flashed another brief smile. "That's not completely true. Right now, I'm asking the universe why I got so lucky as to be sitting in a Ferris wheel with you."

He shifted in his little space, and the next thing she knew, he was leaning toward her. Releasing her foot so that it was free to drop to the floor, he moved in closer, the beam from a red light touching his forehead. She looked at him, their eyes meeting as he filled her vision and then covered her lips with his.

Warmth and heat blossomed through her as their mouths touched. Just perfectly. Lips aligning as if molded that way, soft and full and tender. He didn't touch her, except on a spot near where his hand, planted on the seat beside her for leverage, was resting.

And then, just as smoothly, he pulled back after that one, simple kiss. The quiet sound of breaking suction punctuated the constant low groan of the wheel's mechanism. Theo settled back into his corner and looked at her. His hooded eyes were narrow and dark, gleaming where they picked up the light of the moon.

Selena's heart was pounding and she wanted to surge back toward him and pick up that kiss . . . but something held her back. The light over him was dim and tinted green now, but she could see the way he held his body: reserved, restrained.

The wheel brought them down again, and as they rounded the bottom of the circle, it began to slow, the breeze gentling. The upswing, which she somehow understood was the last one, took its time . . . cresting, the lights on the wheel's spokes casting their multicolored circular glows, then almost sighing as it seemed to waft to a halt at the bottom.

"This was really nice," she said. "I enjoyed it. I enjoyed talking to you. I don't have anyone else . . . to talk to."

"It was my pleasure," he told her, reaching over to unlatch the door. His inked arm brushed hers, warm and solid, reminding her suddenly of the rest of his warm, solid body up against hers.

As Selena stood, she caught a different view of a patch of lights on the fairies' wheel and noticed that they were flickering wildly: red and green and yellow, with a couple blue ones. "Zombies don't like blinking lights like that," she said . . . and then wondered why she'd been so foolish as to bring up that touchy subject.

Theo climbed out after her. "I didn't know that," he said mildly, and she wondered if she'd be able to escape without going down that conversational path: Why she went out, what she was doing . . . "Are they afraid of it?"

Selena walked down the ramp, her knees a little wobbly. "It seems to confuse them. I'm going to go back now, Theo," she said to forestall any more questions. "Thank you."

"Selena," he said, halting her escape. She turned. "You aren't going to go out tonight, are you?"

She shook her head. She wasn't ready. Not yet. Not so soon. "No. I haven't been out since the other night."

"I know."

A little shiver tickled her. He'd been watching over her? She wasn't certain how she felt about that, but she wasn't really surprised. "You have my word," she said.

And then, instead of turning away and walking off as planned, she moved toward him. "Theo," she said.

He opened his arms, and she went into them, and

their mouths found each other with ease. This kiss was hot and furious, nothing like the little tender buss from on the fairies' wheel. His fingers plastered all over her back, pulling her up against him like bark on a tree . . . his hands sliding to cup her butt.

He smelled good and fresh, tasted a little salty on his cheek and jaw. His hair was soft silk beneath her fingers—and when he drew her mouth back to his, their tongues thrust and slid strong and deep. She had her hands on his shoulders, sliding over the bulge of his biceps and the warmth of his skin beneath the sleeves of his shirt. Her foot found his leg and slid up along the muscled calf, ruffling the hair growing there. *Yes.*

The world had become a dark, hot one that spun just the right amount. She'd awakened—swelling and dampening; her breasts tight and ready, pressed against his shirt.

Theo dragged his mouth away, his hands settling at her hips, holding her in place as he stepped back. The lights from the wheel above mottled his face yellow, blue, and red and she could see his lips parted, his eyes dark, and even his chest rising and falling.

"I'd like to do a lot more than that," he said in a low voice, his eyes dark and heavy on her. "But I don't think it's a good idea. For a while, anyway—or until I can't stand it anymore," he added on the gust of a breath, releasing her and stepping away even farther. "Because I think you need to see me as more than a young stud whose body you get to play with."

Selena gasped—partly in indignation, and partly because she was out of breath, trying to catch up to this moment. "That's not—"

"Really?" He laughed unsteadily. "Not that I mind

you playing with my body, or vice versa . . . but you've got this whole complex about me and how old I am—or how old I look—and I think you see this as a temporary thing. Maybe it is, but I'm not sure how temporary temporary is. So I decided I'd make myself scarce, do some things around here, maybe get to know you and Sam and Vonnie better so that whatever's between us isn't just physical. Because, Selena, I told you the other day . . . I can't stop thinking about you. And I don't just mean your body rolling around the sheets with mine. And those things you can do with it." His smile flashed in the multicolored world. "I have scratches on my back—and believe it or not, they aren't from the *gangas* the other night."

Now Selena's face burst hot and she was glad it was too dark for him to see. "I'm sorry."

His laugh sounded strained. "No apologies necessary, believe me. I can't wait to see what you can do after I really get to know you . . . and what you like."

Oh God. Her heart was slamming in her chest, and her whole body seemed to suddenly waken. *What you like.*

"Okay," she replied. Dazed. Confused. And absolutely shimmery-kneed. "If that's what you want."

"What I want," he said, suddenly very serious and very strong, "is for you to trust me enough to talk to me like you did tonight. To let me understand you. And then we can have all sorts of fun."

Right. She wasn't sure that was possible . . . but, she thought when she tripped as she turned away, she was getting closer to being willing to try.

CHAPTER 10

The problem with a cold shower was that the numbing effects only lasted as long as the shower itself did.

Once a guy got out and his mind went back to the place it had been that caused him to get in the cold shower in the first place, he was screwed. Figuratively, of course.

Which was why Theo, his hair still dripping chilly water down his bare shoulders, found himself trudging back up the dark flight of stairs to the arcade only an hour after the Ferris wheel ride. At least he could focus on something productive instead of rolling around sleepless in his hospice ward bed.

Back at the computer, his fingers in their familiar, comforting position on the keyboard, amid the hums of monitors and the whirrs of hard drives, Theo checked his messages.

Nothing from Lou, but that didn't surprise him. They'd had a few mind connections during the day.

Then he watched Brad's video again. This time, he concentrated on the environment, the setting behind him. It definitely wasn't here at Blizek Beach. It looked like a simple office space, or even a hotel room, with plain walls and no furniture.

He tried to listen for noises in the background, using a sound mixing software to isolate the hum of noise in the background. Although he wasn't completely sure what difference it would make if he figured out where Brad was. It wasn't here, and it had been fifty years ago.

And as he listened to the video one more time, he realized something else. Brad said, "I'm working with *truth* to collect data . . ."

Truth?

Was it possible he meant Remington Truth? One of the masterminds behind the Change?

If that was the case, then maybe Remington Truth had double-crossed the Cult and that was why they were looking for him. Or at least—

"Ruuuu-uuuthhhhhh. Ruuu-uuuthh."

He glanced outside, looking into the expanse of darkness, and saw the remnants of destruction that still existed fifty years later. Cratered ground, heaved-up earth now covered with grass and trees, and, most telling of all, the shadows and silhouettes of annihilated buildings.

And then he saw a glint of orange in the distance.

Instinctively, he looked down at the grounds below, behind the protective gates. And he saw a shadow moving quickly and purposefully from the house. Toward the gates.

There was no mistaking Selena, nor her intent.

She'd *lied*.

Selena was just approaching the small, side door that led beyond the protective walls when she heard the scuffle of foot on stone behind her. A long shadow fell across the rippling grass, mingling with her own and framed by the moonlight above. She turned, hoping it was Frank but knowing it wasn't.

"You said you weren't going out tonight."

"Theo," Selena replied, scrambling to pull her thoughts together. "What are you doing here?" A stupid question, like bad dialogue from a DVD, but she couldn't think of anything else to say. Maybe that was why those lines were used in the first place.

When he shifted around nearer and the light caught more of his face, she bit her lip. He was not happy.

"You said you weren't going out tonight," he said again. His voice was low and hard.

She swallowed and began to allow her own anger to replace nervousness and apprehension. "I changed my mind. I'm an adult. I'm allowed to do that."

He'd moved closer, one arm coming out and blocking her from going any further as he rested his palm against the door. That pissed her off even more, and she demanded, "What do you think you're doing?" She could have ducked under or gone around, but dammit, she wasn't going to give him that satisfaction.

"You can't go out there," he said. "Selena."

"I have to."

"You don't *have* to do anything." Then his voice changed, sounding a little broken as he continued, "Especially by yourself." He stood upright, his arm falling away. "Remember what happened last time?"

She snorted. "How could I forget. It's part of the chance I take. And so far, I've only come away with a few cuts and scratches."

"I hardly call this" —he reached out and shifted the neckline of her shirt aside— "a few scratches."

His fingers brushed gently against her skin and she became aware of how close he'd moved. Close enough that she felt his warmth in the cool night air. And that his bare foot touched her shoe. And that he wasn't wearing a shirt. That his skin and hair smelled clean and a bit damp.

Selena swallowed. She looked up at him and found his gaze fastened on hers, strong and steady.

"*Ruuuu-uuuthhh. Arrrleeyyyyyyy-aaaaaanee.*"

The horrible moaning sound wafted through the night, and she broke the stare, turning away and looking at the tall wall as if she could see through it.

She didn't want to go out there, but they drew her—called to her. The crystal around her neck felt heavy and hot. If she didn't save them, who would?

Give me a reason to stay.

"Not tonight," he murmured, reaching to brush away a strand of hair that had fallen from her ponytail.

Her heart pounded so violently, she thought it must reverberate through each of her limbs. Her belly churned with indecision, with need versus desire versus fear . . . versus guilt. She thrust it all away, focusing on the words Wayren had said to her long ago: *It is a gift, and a responsibility.* Then she reached with a heavy hand for the door's latch.

"No," Theo said, taking her fingers and pulling her toward him. He wasn't rough or even fast; it was almost as if it was in slow motion . . . and suddenly she was up against that bare, warm chest. "Not tonight. Stay with *me* tonight."

Without waiting for her to respond, he bent to kiss her and she lifted her mouth to meet his.

Give me a reason.

This was the reason, she told herself, sinking into the kiss. There will be other nights, she told herself. *I can't save them all.* And the cold shiver of duty turned to a swell of heat as his hands spread to cover her back, to hold her close. His fingers slid into her hair, loosening it from the tie, slipping along her shoulders and over the special, heavy shirt she wore for protection.

Beneath it, her taut nipples were rubbing against the heavy, soft plastic material, and the sensation was irritating and erotic at the same time.

"My place," he murmured, lifting her into his arms, "or yours?"

He curled her protectively against his bare chest and she closed out the sounds of the zombies beyond the walls, calling and moaning and searching, as she burrowed her face into his neck. "Whichever is closer," she murmured into warm skin.

He walked rapidly, the rhythm of his footsteps easy and soothing, and Selena rested against him—contented, awakened, and determined. "I thought," she said quietly against his ear as he slipped them into the house, "that you were going to stay away from me for a while." And she bit the edge of his earlobe.

His hold tightened around her as he walked quickly through the kitchen and, to her surprise, toward the back staircase that led to the arcade. "That was my intent," he said. "But you blew that all to hell earlier tonight. Do you know how long I spent in a freezing shower after that?"

He took the steps with ease, the rhythmic jolting of the climb lodging her against him as they ascended. She started to say *Are you going to hate me in the morning?* as a joke, but a pang of guilt slashed through her and she shoved the thought away.

She wanted *this*.

She didn't want to be out there.

Theo had first accosted Selena filled with anger and

fear, but it gradually subsided as he recognized the indecision in her expression and demeanor—and then the softness. He wanted to erase that worry, that hesitance from her face. She did too much.

Now, as he mounted the stairs to the arcade with her in his arms, those emotions gave way to the less virtuous ones of anticipation and pleasure.

As they came through the mocked-up boarded door, he let Selena's feet slide gently to the ground, enjoying the feel of her body moving along his. He was secure that he had her now, that she wouldn't be slipping away to go beyond the gates. At least for tonight.

And then he put all thoughts of zombies and Brad Blizek aside as drew her close, began to unbutton the heavy shirt she wore. It was stiff and slick, and he got the sense it was made from plastic or some other artificial material. Immediately, he found the long thin cord with the heavy crystal pendant still encased in its small pouch. Before she could be reminded of it, he slipped the cord over her head and flung it to the floor, then parted her shirt. Beneath, her breasts were free and their nipples tight and inviting. He made a low sound in the back of his throat when he looked at them, framed by moonlight and the glow from random computer monitors.

"What was I thinking?" he said, sliding his hands beneath to gently lift and cup them. The size of generous apples, each a perfect teardrop shape, maybe a bit longer than they'd been when she was younger, but just right to him. *Just right.* Her nipples were hard and dark and when he stroked a thumb over one of them, she arched closer to his palms.

"About what?" Her voice was unsteady and low, sending a ripple of desire shooting through him.

Selena didn't waste time; her hands were already tugging down the loose shorts he'd pulled on after his shower. He kicked them away when they slid down to his ankles, his body bumping against her jeans and naked, warm belly.

"Denying myself this," he replied, his hands smoothing up over the tops of her breasts and back down to her torso. "I don't know what I was thinking."

Her shirt fell next, and then her jeans—he gave a mental nod of relief in the back of his mind that she at least had dressed properly for her nocturnal excursion—and then stopped thinking about anything but the curvy, golden body he had in his hands.

There were many sofas and large armchairs in the arcade, but Theo tugged her toward the wheeled desk chair and sat down, pulling her to stand between his legs. The moonlight silvered her skin and shone behind the fullness of her hair, and he held her wrists to each side, positioning her in front of him so he could just look for a minute. Eat her with his eyes, and trace the curve of her hips, the swell of her breasts, and the delicate lines of collarbone, throat, shoulders.

"Theo," she said with an embarrassed little laugh, and moved toward him. All at once, she was sliding those sleek thighs over his legs, straddling his hips, settling herself right on his lap. He throbbed and strained when her heat bumped up against him, when she sidled her warm skin and fascinating curves against his torso, trapping his hard-on against her stomach.

"No hurry," he said, his voice thick even to his ears, burying his face into her heavy, sweet hair as he nibbled on her neck. But he jolted when she slipped her hand between their bodies and began to trickle her fingers through the wiry hair below, lifting and stroking his balls. He closed his eyes, letting her play as he lost himself in the scent of her skin and the texture of warm, soft woman. *Oh, yes.*

When he had enough, when he was getting too impatient to wait any longer, Theo shifted and brought her back to him for a strong, deep kiss. He moved his hand down between them, finding her beautifully swollen and slick. A stab of lust shot through him. Pulling himself back from the edge, he kissed her again, unable to keep from smiling into her mouth as he realized how *good* this was. And he teased her as she'd done to him, moving his hand between them where she straddled his hips, open and slick and ready.

She shifted back a bit, trying to catch her breath as he took his time, watching her face tighten and her mouth open in little panting gasps. His desire rose, driven there by the expression on her face, the little sounds of pleasure, the musky scent of woman. The light behind shadowed her, so he only caught glimpses of her heavy eyelids and the curve of her cheekbone, her face tilted to the ceiling as she arched back, held in place by one of his arms as he made her tremble and sigh in front of him.

Her torso was bare and in full view and he enjoyed it as her breasts shifted and her nipples were pointed and taut, outlined by the light from the monitor behind him. Bending forward, he licked one, sliding his tongue long and flat around it, around and around and around it. She sighed and shook, her fingers clamped onto his shoulders, the pain of her nails battling with his own pleasure.

He wanted to taste her, to touch her, to be inside her and to see her face blossom into ecstasy. And he was ready. Hard and turbulent and ready.

She seemed to sense that, and before he tipped her over the edge with his teasing fingers, Selena opened her eyes and gave him a look of readiness and demand. Without hesitation, she rose and then impaled herself, over and *down*.

Theo exhaled sharply as pleasure surged through him. *Oh . . . yessss . . .* She moved and he moved and the world started to turn red and spiraled and suddenly he felt her convulse around him, shuddering and making that soft little sound of pleasure that made him want to come right then too.

He closed his eyes, waiting for the intense moment to pass, willing his body not to move. And before he could change his mind, he shifted and quickly dislodged her. Selena's eyes opened and he answered her unspoken question with a quick, fast kiss as he stood, carrying her.

"We're going to do this my way this time," he managed to say, his arms filled with a naked bundle of satisfied woman.

Before she could react, he shoved a couple keyboards out of the way and sat her pretty ass right on the counter near his workstation. She squeaked at the temperature of the cold table, clutching at his shoulders.

That would be a good memory, he thought, as he settled in front of her, hard and slick and ready to finish this up.

Then he stopped cold. *Jesus.*

"What?" she said, her eyes opening when he started to release her.

"I have to get a condom," he said, thinking how much he *hated* this world after the Change, which in turn, helped pull him back from the precipice. The condoms they had now were little more than animal intestines:

bulky, thick, and loose. He had managed to acquire a couple of them from the guys in Yellow Mountain. And they were on the other side of the damned room, buried somewhere where Vonnie or Sam wouldn't see them.

"A condom? What the hell are you talking about? You've got everything you need *right here*," she said, wrapping her hand around him. And tugging.

Oh. Shit.

He staggered and she stroked him again, hard and without mercy, and the world started to turn red and spirally again, and he tried to think clearly, but she was pulling him closer, and wrapping her legs around his waist.

"Baby," he managed to say as she fit him into place. And he groaned in relief and pain as Selena lifted herself off the desk and slammed against him. Deep and thorough.

"I told . . . you," she sighed as she got him to moving with her. "I'm . . . too old . . . to . . . *oh!*"

His vision blazed bright red and he let himself go, holding her hips, ignoring the scores of her nails gouging his skin as she rocked against him, still shuddering and moaning as he gave one last thrust and shot home.

Theo sagged against her, resting his cheek on the top of her head, holding her close as his hands fit between her ass and the desk. Her legs still locked around him, they loosened their hold as she withdrew her nails from the imprints on his shoulders.

He realized dimly that he was going to be hiding more wounds over the next few days. No shirtless weeding in the hot sun.

Finally, he lifted his head and began to pull away. Their hot, damp skin stuck in places, and it was a relief to separate so that the little breeze from the open window could cool them.

"Wow," she said, still sitting there on the desk, propped up and back on her palms. Naked, curvy, gilt with moonlight, hair tumbled over her shoulders and rumpled around her face. His mouth dried at the sight.

Yes, would be a very nice memory when he was working.

"I agree," he said, leaning forward to kiss her again—an easy, sensual *thank you and yes there will be more of this* kiss—in gentle movements over her lips followed by a tender nibble.

"But next time," she said, sliding off the table with a fascinating jounce of breasts, "don't stop in the middle of it to talk about planning for a family."

He gave a short laugh. "I'm not irresponsible in that way, but geez, Selena, you make me forget what I'm doing."

"So do you," she said softly, glancing toward the window. Her expression changed, but it was too dark to see clearly how.

Was it regret? Remorse?

Theo pushed away his own niggle of guilt. She'd nearly died last time. If she'd gone out alone tonight . . . if she'd gone out even with him . . . anything could have happened. He'd seen the way those creatures fought and clawed to get to her . . . *Why?*

Why does she do it?

I don't want anything to happen to you—he couldn't say the words. Instead he pulled her close and tried to show her, aware that something great and fearsome was opening up inside him. After a moment, when he felt her shiver from the little breeze coming through the window, he stepped back and offered her one of his shirts. In the last week, he'd taken over the arcade as his living space, spending a lot of time there. Only problem was, it got really hot during the day unless he opened all the windows and let the breeze rush through. Now, in the middle of the night, it was almost chilly.

She pulled the shirt on and Theo gently tugged her over to the large, wide sofa he'd claimed as his bed and covered with sheets and blankets. "Come here," he said. "Stay with me?"

Selena smiled and patted the sheet. "I don't know. I thought you were keeping me at arm's length so I didn't wear you out." She tossed him a slanted grin.

"Let's see who wears who out," he said as his own insides gave a little jerk of interest. He reached for her and she fell onto the couch bed, dragging him with her.

But instead of diving into another long, hot embrace, Theo lay next to her, propped up on his elbow. He just wanted to look at her for a minute; and with a long forefinger, he gently traced a line down from the curve of her collarbone, down around her wrinkling areola, and along the curve of her torso. Settling his hand, palm flat on her thigh, he caught her gaze.

She was watching him; and in the dark he could see only that her gaze was fastened on him, that it was heavy and strong. He leaned forward and kissed her gently on the mouth.

"Tell me about Sage," she said.

Out of the fucking blue.

Theo gave a little laugh, feeling very light. He hadn't thought about Sage in ages. "Nothing like a mood killer," he joked.

"Is it? I wondered," she said. Her eyelids fluttered a bit, and he realized he'd better clarify.

"I don't mean—well, it's a mood killer because it

was just the two of us, and now there's someone else here. It wouldn't have mattered who. You know? I was enjoying being with you. Just you."

"Did she hurt you badly?"

He shifted a little. He had to think about it, he realized. "It sure as hell felt bad at the time—a lot of asking why—but it's clear she wasn't right for me any more than Jennifer is. Aside the fact that she never cared for me as more than a brother."

"I'm sorry," Selena said.

"Well, if it had worked out," Theo reminded her, "I wouldn't be here with you now. And there's nowhere else I'd rather be." He realized as he said it that, not only was it true, but that he didn't think it would ever change. That wanting to be with her, that level of comfort and connection. The intelligent conversations. Wanting to have his hands and mouth all over her rich, golden body.

She smiled and reached over to touch his cheek. "Thank you. You know, I don't know very much about you, Theo. You seem to have as many secrets as I do."

You have no idea.

He wondered about telling her more about what happened during the Change, but pride made him hesitate. Couldn't she accept him for who he was, regardless of what she assumed was his age?

"Have you ever been married, then?" she asked.

"No. Never." He'd always thought he'd have time—before the Change. And since then, he'd been trying too hard to figure out who the hell *he* was, why he was resurrected and altered, to think about sharing that life with someone else. And then there'd been the two or three years when the only woman in his mind was Sage, worshiped from afar, as she was.

"You must have children, though."

A wry smile shifted his mouth. "No, can't say that I do. Though it's not from lack of trying," he added with a full-fledged grin.

"What?" she exclaimed. She sounded truly horrified and actually shifted away.

"I'm kidding. Really, I'm kidding," he stressed, still grinning, cupping her shoulder to bring her back. "I've been careful not to let that happen."

"Some people would say that was morally wrong," Selena said a moment later, when she'd obviously decided to believe him. "Preventing pregnancy when we need to reestablish our race."

"What do you say?" he asked, moving a lock of hair from her face, brushing it over the top of her head.

"I say that parenting is hard enough when you're doing it with someone you love, when you're ready for it. But it's even harder when you aren't. So, I don't advocate for people to have babies just to populate the world. My view might not be the most popular, but that's it." She shrugged. "That's another thing I used to ask why about—why I only have Sammy."

"That wasn't your choice?"

Selena shook her head and that lock of hair fell back down. She pushed it away, then let her fingers slide gently against his chest. "I've had five pregnancies, possibly more."

"But . . . any ch—" he started, then stilled. *"Five?"*

Her mouth drew down a bit at the corners. "At least three miscarriages, one little girl that died as an infant, and of course, Sam."

"Oh . . . Selena," he said, his voice low. "I'm so sorry."

She nodded, her face sideways, her eyes holding his

in the low light. "Me too. But . . . it was a long time ago, the last one. And obviously . . . Well, for whatever reason, Sam is my only surviving child. I always wanted another baby, though. So . . ." Her voice trailed off. "If it happened again, even at my advanced age, I would be happy."

Theo's mind scattered into little pieces of shock, panic, curiosity, and warmth. And one big question: How did he feel about that?

But Selena, as she often appeared to do, seemed to understand his quandary. "As much of a stud as you are . . . and you definitely are," she added with a meaningful smile, "don't worry that I'm using you to father my child. I'm definitely not."

"I wasn't worried about that," he interrupted. "I just . . . well, becoming a father isn't something I'd take lightly. I'd want to be married first, to a woman I knew I'd want to be with for the rest of my life. Which is why I was angry when I wasn't prepared—even though I should have been."

Selena sighed. "I wish Sammy felt that way. I don't know if he and Jennifer are having sex, but— Well, what do you think? What are the chances?"

"Uh, pretty good. I'd assume they're moving bookshelves," he replied with a grin at the euphemism. "Seventeen-year-old boy and a girl who looks like Jennifer? Done deal. Sorry," he added when she looked at him with displeasure.

"Ugh," Selena replied. "That is not a thought I'd like stuck in my mind."

"Then let me take your mind off it," Theo said, reaching for her.

She slid close with an eagerness that heated him up again.

This time, everything was long and slow and easy. Body sliding against body, pausing to feel the way they fit, looking at the way the different shades of skin matched up in the faulty light, the texture of hair-roughened flesh against smooth, silky skin. He couldn't seem to get enough of tasting her, sliding his fingers through her heavy hair, of the little sounds she made when he did something pleasurable, of the now-gentle tracing of her nails on his shoulders.

When he lifted himself over to cover her, to fit into her, he made those strokes last, allowing the threads of pleasure to weave slowly, in soft little waves, until he felt the change in her breathing and the pumping of her heart beginning to match his own. And even then, they moved in that sensual rhythm, holding back as comfortable lovers do, knowing that the end would come and taking their time getting there.

And when they did, they matched that too. It was as if he slipped over the top of the Ferris wheel, arching and then sweeping down in a long, rush of pleasure that ended in a bubble of heat that burst through him just as she tensed and shuddered beneath on her own ride.

Wow, he thought as he uncurled his toes and rolled his eyes back into position some time later. His body slowly came back to earth.

Once again, shifting a bit, he gathered her against him and curled an arm around her shoulders. Tucked under his chin, she sighed and he felt her relax into slumber.

But Theo didn't sleep.

He didn't dare. He lay awake, holding Selena, wondering about all of the variety of emotions barreling through his otherwise exhausted body.

He'd succeeded in keeping her in tonight. Keeping her safe.

The very thought of her going out there into that wildness again was enough to thrust away all of the pleasure and satiation of the last hours. He was still angry that she'd lied to him, or changed her mind, or whatever. Whether he had the right to be or not, he couldn't dismiss the feeling—it was a fury driven by fear and confusion.

He had to find a way to stop her. To keep her safe.

To convince her that it wasn't worth the danger. That she was needed *here*, for her patients. For people who came to the Death Lady and needed her peace and guidance.

And that she had a responsibility to those who *lived*, those who loved her. Vonnie, Frank, Sam.

And, Theo considered, very likely himself.

He was a very different person since he'd awakened from this second resurrection. Or maybe he'd just reverted to who he was before.

Maybe that was *why*.

He realized as he felt her comforting presence next to him, as the sun just started to light the sky beyond the window, that he could do this every night. That he would.

So much for staying away from her until she got to know him.

CHAPTER 11

Theo awoke to the sun blasting with great force through the easterly window. Selena was gone, but the stab of worry that had him vaulting from his bed lessened when he remembered that he'd remained vigilant until the danger of night was past.

She couldn't have gone out after those zombies; she was safe somewhere.

Nevertheless, he dressed quickly and thought about going down to the kitchen to see what Vonnie was cooking . . . and to see how Selena was.

Now, in the light of day, did he feel uneasy about manipulating her into staying in?

No.

Mayyyybe.

He knew it was for her own good. But would she see it that way?

Hell, he'd seen and felt the resistance and apprehension in her as she approached the gate last night. Whatever it was she thought she was doing helping the zombies to die a humane death, it wasn't something she *wanted* to do. He hadn't had to work hard to convince her to spend the night in his arms.

Theo told himself all of those logical arguments, but he couldn't quite dismiss the fact that she was gone. That she'd left without waking him.

His thoughts, circular and greedy, were interrupted

by the sound of footsteps on the stairs and a dull rapping on the side of the door.

Theo pulled to his feet from the couch when he saw Sam. "Hey," he said, shaking off the last vestiges of worry.

The kid had a tray with food on it—*Bless Vonnie!*—and he set it on the table next to the monitor that was still lit up. So much for a screen saver, because the image of the Cult of Atlantis still glowed there. Was probably burned onto the screen forever.

"Brought this for you," Sam said, gesturing to the food. But he was looking at the monitors. "I want you to teach me about these. What you're doing. Hey"—he froze, and his eyes goggled as he looked at Theo; suspicion, and maybe a little fear, glowed there—"I've seen that before."

He was pointing to the labyrinthine symbol.

"You have?" Theo asked casually, taking a drink of sweetened tea for his dry mouth, and doing a quick glance around the room to make sure Selena hadn't left any signs of her presence. This sleeping with a mother had definite complications. "Where?"

"The Elite. When they come here, they have it sometimes on their list. I think I saw it once, inked on someone's arm."

"Do they come here often?" Theo asked, trying the thick hunk of bread. Slathered with butter, just a bit warm, it tasted like heaven. Zucchini bread. And scrambled eggs. Vonnie was a goddess. He could marry her.

"Yes. Once or twice a year. What are you doing?" Sam had moved forward and looked as if he wanted to touch the keyboard. Fascination warred with apprehension and he hesitated.

"Go ahead. Try it." Theo came over and shoved the keyboard from the second computer toward him. Right onto the spot the kid's mom's bare rump had been only a few hours ago. He nearly blushed at the memory, and had to pull his thoughts back to the present. Yep, he had it bad if he was fantasizing about the kid's mom while the kid was here.

"I don't know what to do with it," Sam said. But he sank onto the chair and tapped one of the keys.

"Why do the Elite—or the bounty hunters—come here?" Theo asked.

He had heard a variety of horror stories about the Elite—or Strangers—and their visits to settlements. Sometimes they were uneventful, but other times there were repercussions later. Only two months ago, he and Elliott Drake had been trying to save a group of teens about Sam's age from being taken off into slavery for the Elite. The Strangers had tricked the teens into becoming addicted to grit, the post-apocalyptic version of crystal meth, and had lured them away from Envy with the promise of more. "You should stay away from them."

"That's what Mom says," Sam replied. He was pecking at the keys, typing nonsense on the coding screen Theo let him get a feel for it.

"Listen to her. I've seen lots of bad things happen with them."

Sam paused and looked up at him, his eyes wary. "You seem a lot older than you are. I mean, than you look."

"I am," Theo replied. Not that the kid would believe him, but lying was never a good policy. "What do they do when they come?"

But Sam didn't get a chance to reply, because they

heard the sound of footsteps, followed by his mother's voice calling for him. The kid bolted from the chair faster than Theo had ever seen him move, and was across the room trying not to look at the pinball machines and video game consoles when Selena appeared.

"Vonnie said you were up here," she commented, looking at both of them, but speaking to Sam. Her glance over Theo had been impersonal, but she generally was all business in front of her son. It didn't necessarily mean anything. "Sammy, you and I are overdue for a chat, I think."

Theo tried not to ogle, but it was hard not to. She just looked so good, so casual and warm and feminine with her dark hair long and loose, and in a deep-vee pink shirt that buttoned down the front. Her legs were bare beneath dun-colored shorts, long and golden, and—*Oh boy*—she was wearing something around her ankle. A woven cord with little beads on it, low and sagging just slightly over the curve of her ankle. Just loose enough that he could slip his little finger beneath it, slide it around the tender skin of her foot.

Anything he might have said was interrupted when she gave Sam a firm look and gestured to the stairway door. Apparently, she wasn't about to be dissuaded from her chat with him.

"Later," Sam called, and trudged off.

Theo watched them go, trying to quell an uneasy feeling that bubbled up higher and larger than he liked. He couldn't talk to Selena now, but maybe in a little while they'd have a minute together.

Instead of worrying about something he couldn't do anything about for now, he snagged a spoonful of eggs and turned to the computer. Now that he knew the truth about Blizek, he had to dig into the system and find all of the data Brad had been hiding. He wondered if there were any other clues in his video message, along with the mention of Truth.

Lou. I could really use you!

His brother's response came back almost immediately, filled with hubris. *Knew you couldn't handle things without me. I'm close, brother.*

Theo smiled and sent back a *fuck you*. Then a *hurry your ass up*. He opened his mind and felt Lou's direction, and agreed that he was indeed close. Maybe tomorrow. *Sure you don't want me to come get you?*

The *fuck you* came back just as swiftly as Theo had sent his, and he chuckled, returning to the computer puzzle at hand. Definitely, two brains would be better than one. Theo might be the better hacker, in general, but Lou was smarter about other things . . . not that Theo would admit it to him.

He sat and worked some more at it, focusing on the problem of getting even deeper into the annals of the computer system, then decided to take a break and play some pinball. He'd rebooted the Star Trek game the other day, and it had worked fine, although the ball shooter had stuck a few times. Today, in deference to his dream, he plugged in Aragorn and Legolas and waited for the lights to start up after the reboot.

The lights.

Blinking, rapid lights.

A prickling started over him and Theo leaned closer, looking at the game and its bells and bumpers and *lights.*

What had Selena said? *Zombies don't like blinking lights like that. It seems to confuse them.*

And then he had an idea.

* * *

The minute she saw the circling hawks in the distance, Selena had a bad feeling.

She was still tense and upset from her conversation with Sam earlier today, which had not gone as well as she'd hoped. And now, with his angry words still ringing in her mind, she was bringing a basket of vegetables from Frank's garden to Yellow Mountain, as well as delivering Robert's swaddled corpse to Cath, who would cremate the man for his family.

Sam was supposed to be the one doing it but stormed off in the middle of hitching up Thelma and Louise when Selena tried to approach him again, just to smooth things over. He was still not talking to her, and Selena decided she could use a change of scenery. She also thought she might have the chance to speak to Jennifer, if she was in the settlement.

Along with all of that tumult, she was trying not to think about last night for a variety of reasons—the least of which was how good it had felt to waken next to a man who felt so solid and comforting.

Theo had found her later, not long after her conversation with Sam. Just before lunch. Selena had been angry still; angry with Sam for his stubbornness, for his blindness in the face of love, for his unwillingness to talk about consequences—and, if she had to be honest, angry with Theo for stopping her last night, for giving her an excuse to stay inside. And, most of all, she was angry with herself for being so weak. For giving in to momentary pleasure in the face of responsibility, just because it was easier.

So when Theo approached her, seeking her out in the guise of informing her that lunch was ready, she wasn't in the best frame of mind. But then he said nothing; he

merely gathered her into his arms in the storage room
and held her.

And the rush of warmth, of comfort, flooded her.
When she was in his arms, she felt so good. Home.
Safe. As if she had nothing to fear.

"I just want you to be safe," he said, reading her very
thoughts. "Selena. I don't understand it. I'm trying, but
I have to be honest with you—I'm having a hard time
comprehending why you put yourself in such danger."

"It's not some big deal what I do out there at night,"
she said in a rush, her face buried in his male shoulder.
Oh God, here I go. It was all going to come out. "It's
not that it's such a huge secret. I just don't tell people, I
don't want them to know—because they might misun-
derstand. People *have* misunderstood. And it's—well,
it's hard."

"I know," Theo said gently. "Vonnie told me a little
about Sivs. And Crossroads."

Selena nodded. She wasn't surprised. "Vonnie knows
more than anyone else, and she tries—but she doesn't
really understand either. No one does. They can't see
what I see, and really comprehend it, here." She pulled
away and touched her heart so he could see. "When I
help them die, when I touch the zombies and touch my
crystal, I feel like— no, I *know*—that I'm saving them.
They were human once, like you and me. And when
I touch them, somehow I know that they're released.
They can die in peace."

"They were human, a long time ago. But they aren't
any longer," Theo said. His voice was quiet but firm.
"I know that you don't want to see anyone or anything
hurt or tortured, and that you only want kind deaths
for them. I can't understand that viewpoint, because

I've seen enough of the damage they do. I've seen the bodies, the skin and bones and what's left after. There's nothing commendable or redeemable about a zombie, to me. But," he said firmly when she opened her mouth to speak, "I respect you and what you believe. And so I want to help you. Because I can't believe you want to risk your life like that, over and over."

"I don't want to, but I *have* to." Tears gathered at the corners of her eyes, and Selena tightened her fingers on his shoulders. "I can't not help them. Even if I can't save every single one of them, it's my responsibility to help as many as I can. Talk about asking *why*! I ask myself every day *why* I have to be the one. *Why* I was found with that damned crystal. *Why me?*"

"Ask yourself," Theo said, reaching up to touch her hand, "what would happen if you *didn't*. If you stayed inside, safe, and remained a mother to your son, a daughter to Vonnie, and a guiding angel to those who come to the Death Lady to help them die with dignity, and in peace. Would that be so bad?"

She was shaking her head, even as a soft flower of wondering opened inside her. Was he right? The tears burned her eyes and she blinked them away. *I don't know.*

"The zombies are already dead. Beyond help. They don't even know what they're doing. But what if something happened to *you*?"

I don't know.

I don't know.

She didn't come to lunch; she wasn't hungry. There was too much . . . too much to think about. His words, so compelling and his arguments so believable. His concern for her was so genuine.

Was he right? Was risking herself worse in the long run?

And shortly after ending their conversation, feeling brittle and confused, Selena had accepted the chance to run the errand to Yellow Mountain. It would be an opportunity for her to get away. To think.

To have some time to herself, away from the demands of mother, daughter, caregiver, lover.

But when she caught sight of the spiraling and diving hawks not far from the roadway, her insides began to churn.

She left Thelma and Louise tied to a large tree when it became clear that the path to whatever the birds were scavenging was through heavy trees and brush, and she walked the rest of the way.

Moments later, standing on a large patch of concrete overgrown with veins of grass, Selena looked down at two bodies. The stench was rancid, as zombie flesh always was.

And in the daylight, she could see the horrible green-gray tinge to their skin, the abnormal size of their pores, the way the bodies were rippled with stretch marks from being forced out of proportion. The hair on one was threadbare and gray-blond; on the other, it was just as thin, just as bland but with a darker tinge.

Their skulls were bashed in like eggshells, one from the back, one from the side, slick with dark red blood that still oozed but was beginning to dry. Their hugely knuckled hands, with nails grimy and sharp, curled into the ground like crab legs. Flies, ants, even maggots ran in and out and through the flesh and worn clothing, and the shadows of waiting hawks flashed on the ground in a similarly eerie pattern. Remorse and grief had her turning away; the rank smell and the disturbing sight had her stomach rebelling. She vomited into the bushes until her belly hurt and then returned to the scene, letting the guilt and the anger dig a little deeper into her belly.

It killed her to know that the souls of these two creatures—these people—were trapped forever in limbo.

Wounded with guilt—for if she'd gone out last night, she might have saved them—and yet resolved, she found some brush and brittle sticks and used them to burn the corpses. There was no sense in allowing them any further indignities.

And she went on to Yellow Mountain, heavy and bleak.

Theo didn't see Selena all the rest of the day. He learned that she'd gone to Yellow Mountain on an errand, and as the sun made its descent, he began to wonder if she would return before dark.

Or if she'd purposely stay away so that she could go out and do whatever she did without having to face him.

The lower the sun sank, the tighter his gut grew and the more certain he became that that was her plan.

He tried to focus on his other projects, and working on his idea with the pinball machines, but more often than not, he was standing at the eastern window of the arcade, watching for Selena to approach.

Lou popped into his consciousness again, felt around and obviously sensed Theo's unease and general pissed-offness, and left after a brief connection.

Dinner was meagerly attended by Sam, who scarfed down his food, and Vonnie, who was chatty but said nothing of import and seemed to only wish to fill the silence. Frank didn't join them, for he was apparently busy fixing something in the barn.

When the sun finally slipped below the horizon, and there was still no sign of Selena, Theo knew what he had to do.

It took him longer than he liked to pry Frank away from the rototiller he was trying to fix; and had to lend his sharper vision to assist Frank in fixing a loose wire before he would help him pick the right horse. They saddled a mustang and Theo slung a satchel over his torso. The elderly man's grumbling about being interrupted in his work followed him beyond the walls.

The clank of the gates closing behind Theo made a sound of finality.

The darkening world was still and silent but for the howl of a distant wolf and the rustle of leaves in the breeze. Zombies weren't the only danger, of course; wolves, feral cats, and even tigers and lions prowled the night.

But Theo had the advantage of agility, speed, and height on the horse, as well as a lit torch in one hand and supplies in his satchel. He had no concern for himself and his own safety. Generally, the wild animals would have no reason to attack, especially a much larger creature, unless they perceived a threat.

Theo's mouth tightened more and more as he rode swiftly along what passed for a road to Yellow Mountain. By now, the last bit of sunlight was gone and the world was lit by a profusion of stars and a healthy chunk of moon. But the trees brought thick shadows and blocked the light, making it harder for the horse to see his path.

Theo. Lou filtered in, breaking his twin's concentration.

You okay? Theo responded briefly. *Busy.*

Okay.

He listened for the telltale sounds of Selena's wagon, or the calls of the zombies. A twinge of smoke caught his nostrils; someone had recently been burning something nearby.

No more than two miles into the five-mile trip, Theo heard them. He paused for a moment to catch the direction of the sound, his fingers tightening on the torch. He had bottle bombs in his satchel, and the torch would of course work to beat them back, to smash a skull. Destroying the brain was the only way to kill a *ganga*.

The hair on the back of Theo's neck rose when he realized the groans were closer than he'd thought; the wind had carried them away. Now, in a lull, the sounds came through loud and clear and were just north of the pathway.

Where there were zombies, there might be Selena.

He made a quick decision and veered off the path, stomach tight and heavy. As the horse darted through the underbrush, he thought he heard something else in the distance. The cries were growing wilder, more desperate, and he recognized the sound.

They'd found someone. Selena was there.

He kicked the horse and urged him faster, leaning over the long, strong neck, his mane flying in Theo's face.

Selena! was all he could think. *I'm coming.* A dark horror stabbed him somewhere, filling his mind and heart. Something was wrong. Something was very wrong.

"Hurry, hurry!" he begged his mustang. *"Faster!"*

At that moment, the horse lost his footing and stumbled, then caught himself and reared back as something came darting out of the darkness. Theo tumbled off with the torch, and landed in a heap on the ground, barely managing to hold on to the flaming staff. As he scrambled to his feet, the spooked mustang ran off, leaving Theo on foot and out of breath.

But he still heard the sounds of insistent, desperate zombies and, ignoring the pain radiating from his body, ran toward them, bolting through bushes and around trees and rusty cars.

There were horrifying sounds and as he came closer, through the trees, he could see the flickering of orange lights and eyes. He ran, using his free hand to dig in his bag for a bottle bomb, ready to go. All he had to do was light the rag stuffed into it for a wick, and toss it into the mass.

Suddenly, he was there, coming upon the scene of a gathering of zombies. They were fighting to get to something, wailing and moaning and clawing.

"Selena!" he shouted, trying to spot her in the center of half a dozen of the monsters.

And then he tripped over something in the shadows, something soft and alive. He heard the body's groan as he flew through the air again, landing on his face and arms over a fallen tree trunk. The torch fell this time, and as Theo, trying to drag his breath back into his punched diaphragm, turned back to pick it up, he saw the gleam of silver in the light.

Silver hair.

Long silver hair.

It was an instant—the image in an instant—and the mental connection . . . and he knew it was Lou.

Theo hesitated for only a moment, somehow registering that faint groan, then he shouted his brother's name even as he dashed toward the huddle of desperate zombies. He swung the torch, calling for Lou, shouting for Selena, wild and berserk as he tried to fight his way into the group.

The torch frightened the monsters, and Theo used it to drive them away, smashing a skull with brute force propelled by fear; whirling and crushing another one's legs, then bringing the torch down on its head.

In the midst of the melee, he caught sight of jean-clad legs on the ground, limp and streaked with something dark, and he didn't allow himself to think about it. He just grabbed, and pulled with one hand as he whaled with the other. The monsters weren't moving back, and claws drove into his skin; the smell of the creatures filled his nostrils and he felt one of his arms laid open. Something wet and warm streamed from it, and one of the monsters turned its attention to him.

Theo slammed the torch down on its head with all of his force and stumbled back, pulling Selena's ankle with him, trying to extricate her from the mess.

All at once, the zombies changed. They shifted, their groans altered and became higher and tight, and two of them peeled off from the group, staggering away as if called. Theo slammed another one with his club and tugged on the ankle with a hand now slick with his— and someone else's—blood.

"Stop!" A shout reached his ears.

Theo spun to see Selena burst from the trees, a red-glowing orb bouncing on the cord around her neck.

The zombies lunged for her, staggering and swarming, all at once leaving the body Theo had been trying to save. He looked down and recognized the grimy, blood-streaked face.

Sam.

Selena braced herself as the zombies surged toward her. They left behind, released, whatever victim they'd been attacking, clawing for the crystal instead.

"Meeeeeeeeeee."

The glowing stone was hot in her hand, but she held it, waiting for the onslaught, tears of frustration and anger wet on her face. *"Nowwwwwmeeeeeeee."*

"No!" she screamed again as Theo whirled toward one of the creatures, slamming a large, flaming branch onto its head, crushing it like a melon. *"Stop!"*

He shouted something back at her, his face suddenly illuminated by the torch, stark and wide-eyed. A horrified mask. She couldn't hear him, and suddenly found herself swarmed by the zombies as they reached for her in familiar desperation.

"Noooowwwwwwww meeeeeeee nooowwwwww."

The sounds filled her ears like a horrible, deep wind drowning out everything but those desperate cries for salvation.

She touched one and looked into a young man's eyes, taking on the jolt of his life as the light of his soul died from the orange eyes, the impact battering her like a succession of stones. Tears burned her eyes. *Theo, Theo, he didn't understand.* She tried to catch her breath, hold herself steady as she drew in a foul-scented gasp of air, ready for another. *"'Ellllllpppp 'eeeeeeeeee."*

Another shout, more insistent, human, caught her ears, and suddenly the flaming torch was flailing into the cluster of zombies clamoring to her. One fell back, making an opening, and Selena turned toward Theo, rage in her face as he pushed his way through.

"Leave me!" she shouted, pushing at him even as she reached for another clammy, rotted-fleshed hand. "Get away!"

She couldn't understand what he said over the horrible cries that were growing more desperate—"I—

am!" she thought she heard—but he grabbed her hand and dragged her away, using his torch to drive the monsters back.

Selena fought him, hating him, slamming him with her fists and shouting at him with fury and fear, but he ignored her, pulling her away.

He shouted something over her head—*"Who!"*—and she saw, with a shock, another figure staggering to its feet in the shadows. Long light hair shone in the light as he—*she?*—came upright.

Theo held on to Selena, dragged her away from the monsters and shouted, *"NOW!"*

Even as she fought, the arc of something flaming cut through the night, flying from the long-haired person to the cluster of zombies held at bay by Theo's torch. *"Noooooo!"* she screamed as Theo shoved her away, falling on top of her as they crashed to the ground.

The explosion was a loud, shattering pop and the night flared golden. Debris rained down on them, on the ground and into the trees around them.

And then, there was silence but for their gasping breaths.

Selena lay on the ground beneath Theo, unmoving, frozen with despair and breathless with betrayal. The grass and dirt was cold and damp beneath her fingers, and she lay there, her face pressing into it, tears seeping into the soil even after he moved off her. He killed them. Killed them all. Left them trapped.

She could have saved them. And he *killed* them.

She hated him. Her insides were tearing apart.

"Selena." Theo's voice was urgent. His hand touched her shoulder, and she felt the sting of his betrayal.

She rolled over and gave him a look of loathing. "How could y—"

"*Selena,* please. Stop. It's Sam." He'd taken her shoulders and was looking into her eyes. That mask that had tightened his features had changed to something else.

"Sam?" The expression on Theo's face made her go cold. Her knees weakened. "What is it?"

It was a dream. Everything after that was a horrible nightmare.

She turned—*was* turned; and walked—was *led*—to an awful scene.

A man with long silver hair knelt, bent, next to an inert body. Sam.

Her Sammy. Illuminated by a generous moon that had somehow found the center of her world.

His torso and legs were a mass of slashing cuts, one arm was mere ribbons. His face, his handsome face had scratches on it, and dark, wet blood was everywhere.

From the zombies. The very zombies she'd tried to save.

Oh God. Her knees buckled, and someone caught her.

"He tried to save me," said the old man, looking up from where he crouched.

Sammy wasn't dead. He *wasn't* dead.

She half fell, half knelt next to him, touched her son, watched his mouth move and his eyes slowly open. Focus on her. Her heart leapt, her clammy hands closed around his bloody ones, and she pressed her lips together.

And then she saw the glittering gray cloud filtering in the moonlight, coiling and rising above him.

CHAPTER 12

Not my Sammy. Not my boy!

Selena repeated those words over and over in her mind all the way home. She didn't remember any part of the trip back, just Theo's solid presence next to her, carrying her boy—*her boy!*—in his arms. She battled the dark wave of hatred, of undulating fury that threatened to set her to screaming.

She kept a hand on Sam's arm, terrified at how cold it felt, watching the silvery gray cloud around him, trying to convince herself that it was dust lit by moonlight, or fireflies, or something else.

And the underlying anger fueled her powerful steps. The memories of the carnage, the scene in the clearing—Theo flailing and whaling, crushing skulls and pulling her away, shouting something in her face that she couldn't understand. The death, the blood, her *son.* Her *son.*

She was dully aware of the conversation around her between Theo and this other man, an older man with long hair who seemed to know Theo.

"He tried to save me," the older man, whose name appeared to be Lou, said. "They came from nowhere. No moaning. No warning."

"I knew something was wrong, but I didn't know it

was you," Theo said, his voice taut. "If I'd listened—I didn't get there in time."

"But what was Sam doing out?" Selena managed to ask, coming out of her darkness for a moment. "Why was he outside the walls?"

No one had an answer, but she wondered, deep in the pit of her stomach. She'd come from Yellow Mountain where she'd seen Jennifer. The girl had ignored her for the most part, except for one awkward moment when their eyes had caught. Selena had seen her talking and flirting with one of the other young men—one with whom she'd had an on-again, off-again relationship. She suspected Sam's nighttime excursion had something to do with that.

But she couldn't conjecture. She had to focus on now.

When they finally got Sammy into the bed that had belonged to Theo—Selena chose it for superstitious reasons, hoping for another miracle—she at last had the chance to examine him.

It was bad.

Behind her, when she drew away what was left of Sam's shirt, Theo breathed, "Jesus." He turned to the man named Lou. "We've got to get Elliott here."

Lou said something in return, but Selena didn't hear him because Sam had opened his eyes. "Mom," he whispered.

She touched his forehead, trying not to let him see the fear in her eyes, the knowledge. "Sammy. I'm here. We're going to get you fixed up. Frank's going to get Cath."

"Is he . . . all right?" Sam said in a low, ruptured voice. "The man."

Selena blinked back burning tears. This was her son. This was the man she'd raised.

"I'm here," said Lou, moving so that Sam could see him. "Thank you," he said. "Thank you for helping me."

"Good," Sam said. He closed his eyes and, terrified, Selena looked up and around to see if the cloud was there, and if it was changing.

Her heart plummeted when she saw the gray sparkles, though not yet turning blue, swirling so beautifully like silvery dust motes. *No. Go the fuck away. Leave my son.*

She didn't know how long she sat there with him; she knew that Cath came at some point and examined the deep gouges in Sam's abdomen, adding her own salves to the ones Vonnie had applied. Selena saw that Cath's face was taut and unyielding, that everyone seemed to speak in a hush, and that, in the corner, there were a man and a woman surrounded by a wavering blue glow. Waiting.

But the cloud stayed gray, and she prayed to keep it from blue. Because blue meant the end.

"Selena." The voice, accompanied by a gentle but firm hand on her shoulder, finally broke into her thoughts.

It was Theo, and he brought his face close to hers as if determined to get, and keep, her attention. His eyes were soft and brown, but determined. "You have to rest. Please."

"No," she said, turning back to Sam. "I can't leave him."

But as she gazed down at him, one of the blue-haloed figures came from the corner and stood beside the bed. Selena couldn't see her feet. It was a woman, with long dark hair; and when she looked at Selena, it was as if she were seeing herself in a murky mirror.

A shot of recognition zipped through her. *Mother?* she whispered.

"Selena," Theo's voice penetrated again. "You're dead on your feet. Come with me."

Go with him.

She allowed Theo to take her away then, assured that her mother would be with Sam until she returned.

Theo brought her outside where the sunshine warmed her dulled senses, and walked with his arm around her waist. Before she knew it, they were approaching the fairies' wheel, far from the house, far from the dark thoughts and the cloud of silver-gray reality.

He helped her on board one of the cars, and she didn't resist. Her numbness was beginning to thaw and a myriad of emotions battered her. Anger. Fear. Disbelief.

Hate.

But as the wheel began to lift, the gust of wind stirring her hair, she blinked and *felt*. The ground moved away, the trees shortened as their car rose easily and gently. He sat across from her, and she looked out over the wooded grounds. Riding in the fairies' wheel was a much different experience during the day. She almost smiled at the little tickle inside as they rounded the top and started down, still slowly and gently as if riding on a circular wave.

"Eat this," he said, forcing something into her hand as he looked at her from the seat across. "I don't know how long it's been since you ate. Yesterday? In Yellow Mountain? I know you haven't slept for a long time too."

At this, Selena seemed to come out of her exhausted trance, and Theo felt a wave of gratitude for the awareness that flickered in her eyes. He was still trying to put all of the pieces together of what had happened, and to deal with the variety of emotions that had erupted. Shock was only one of them.

And he knew that Lou was filled with guilt and remorse. "I should be the one," he'd said up in the arcade only a short while ago. "It should be me! I've lived *my* damn life. Why such a young one?"

Again, the why.

Theo looked over at Selena, who'd taken a bite of the sandwich he'd made for her. She was chewing, and her eyes were focusing again.

Suddenly, they lifted and leveled on him. "Thank you," she said. "I think I needed this. To get away."

He nodded. Her gratitude seemed genuine, but there was something else there, lurking beneath. "You could use some sleep, I think." He eased over to her side, the car lurching a bit, tipping with his added weight, and he slid an arm along the back behind her. "Rest with me for a little while."

She seemed stiff, but he attributed that to her shock and grief. He eased her close and was relieved when she settled into the crook beneath his shoulder. Maybe she would sleep.

He'd shown Lou the arcade, and any excitement his twin might have had about being introduced to Brad Blizek's private sanctuary was lost in the tragic moment. They'd logged in to the NAP, Theo on Blizek's computer, and Lou on the mini-laptop he'd brought with him.

The first order of business was to let Sage know that Lou was safely here with Theo, with only minor injuries from his scuffle with the zombies, and to get in touch with Elliott for advice on treatment.

If there was going to be a miracle and any chance for Sam to be healed, Elliott would have to get here soon.

"He's going to die," said Selena after a long while. The sun was much lower, completely behind the trees and distant house. She might have slept; Theo had felt her muscles relax and her body sag more heavily against him as the wheel rose and fell, their car rocking gently. Her breathing had regulated, and he was relieved that he'd been able to do that, at least, for her.

But now she was awake, pulling away from his shoulder.

"We don't know that," he replied, brushing hair from her face.

"I know it," she said flatly. Her golden brown eyes, though distant, weren't vacant any longer. "This is what I do, Theo. I know death. He's got the death cloud."

Theo prayed that Lou had made contact with Envy and that Elliott was on his way here. "The death cloud?"

"It starts off gray as the person's soul gets ready to move to another plane. Sometimes it takes a day, sometimes hours, sometimes weeks or months. When it turns blue, that means it's time. But the death cloud . . . there's no chance once that appears."

Theo curled his fingers around her hand and squeezed. This wasn't the time for empty placations, but he couldn't find the right words.

"His cloud is still gray. He's got time. I want to go back and see him," she said suddenly.

"All right," Theo said, adjusting the remote from where he'd wired it to the car.

As the Ferris wheel began to slow, rising on its last ascent, she gave a soft, bitter laugh. "Do you know how many people I've watched die? How many times I've comforted families? Helped someone in pain? Listened to them and held their hands? You'd think I'd be ready for this, accepting of this. I know death is natural, it's something we all do; and I know there's something beyond. But I . . . this . . ."

Her voice broke and Theo gathered her close. Her tears seeped through his shirt as he held her, feeling the little wrenches in her shoulders as she wept.

"He's your son. Of course it's harder," he said into her hair, and despite the horror of the moment, he felt a little rise of connection, of want and need. Of home.

Mine. This one is mine.

"I should be able to handle it better," she said.

"Why? Why should you be able to handle it? You love him; he's part of you. Yes, it's hard." He held her closer, wishing he had the words. Wishing he'd gotten to the clearing sooner last night; that he hadn't been thrown from his horse.

He might have saved Sam, then.

She sniffled and shifted away. "I think he was going to meet Jennifer. She hasn't been around for a couple days. I think that's why he was so angry with me yesterday when I tried to talk to him. As if he knew something was wrong, but he didn't want to admit it. And then he found that man. You know him?"

"Yes. His name is Lou." Theo held back telling her more; she didn't need anything else to deal with right now. "We're very close. He was coming here, looking for me."

"Sammy tried to save him. He put himself in danger to try and save him."

"He did save him," Theo told her. "Your son was brave and heroic. Just like his mom."

"He was." She sniffled again and rubbed the back of

her hand over her nose. She was blotchy-skinned and her eyes were bloodshot. She didn't look beautiful right then, with her ravaged face and red nose, but she was Selena. She was his. "And those monsters . . . they got him. They did that to him. Even though I tried to save them, they did that . . . they tore into him; they ripped him apart. He's going to die. I *hate* them."

Theo pulled her close again just as the wheel slid to a smooth halt, right in place at the bottom. *God, what do I say? . . .* "I know you do. I'm sorry, Selena. I'm so sorry."

"If you hadn't gotten there, if you hadn't killed them. . . ." Her voice trailed off, and she ground her wet face into his shoulder, muffling her voice. "I'm so confused. So full of anger. I don't understand why this had to happen. Why, after all I've done to try and save them? Why? Why would this happen to me?"

Tears pricked the corner of his eyes. The desperation and hopelessness in her voice dug deep inside him, prying into his belly and filling him with despair. He didn't have the answer, but he wondered if it was a sign her path needed to change.

"Elliott's not there," was the first thing Lou said when Theo returned to the arcade. "He and Jade are on a Running mission, and there's a woman ready to deliver a baby."

Theo felt a shiver of anger rush over him. "If they're in a place where there's an NAP, they can log in—"

"Already covered that. Sage is working on getting in contact with them. She's doing everything she can. How long do you think we have?"

Theo calmed himself. "I don't know. Selena says he's going to die. Things don't look good at all unless we can get Elliott here to heal him." He sat on one of the sofas and shoved a hand into his hair. His mind had pretty much not stopped since that little bit of slumber after making love to Selena all night the day before, and he was drained.

"Is it her?" Lou asked, turning on the chair to look at his brother.

"Yes."

"Then I'm even more sorry about what happened." Lou's aged face looked more ragged and elderly than Theo could ever remember seeing it. Or maybe it was just that they'd been apart for a long time. Or maybe it was that, since he'd been resurrected again, he looked at things more clearly now. Actually saw reality, rather than the way he wanted it to be. "Tell me about her."

Theo lay back on the sofa, staring up at the cracked, cobwebbed ceiling, and talked. He told Lou everything about being brought back to life, about Selena's zombie-hunter situation, about it all. There were no secrets between them. There never had been.

"I'm guessing you took advantage of the countertop here too," Lou said wryly, pointing to the table near where Selena's fine rear end had been sitting just a couple of days ago. "If I know you."

A smile cracked Theo's face. "Aw, you're just living vicariously through me, aren't you?"

A long silence settled there, and then a soft. "Yes."

Theo's eyes, which had begun to shutter, popped open. Something in his brother's tone—He sat up and looked at Lou, and saw the wateriness in his eyes the grief over tonight's events. His heart gave an awful *ker-thump*. "I was just kidding," he said quickly, but he knew it was too late. The damage—as innocent as it had been on his part—and on Lou's, on Sam's, had been done.

"I know," his brother replied. "But I was a damn fool for trying to be you. For leaving Envy and pretending I was fucking Indiana Jones or something, coming after you. Going on an adventure. Look what happened. Look what I've caused to happen."

"Don't be an idiot," Theo said. "Sam should never have been beyond the walls at night, alone. And I should have been listening more closely to you, asswipe. I was close enough to get to you. Don't fucking blame yourself for all this."

"Fuck you, Theo. You didn't know what was going on because I didn't tell you. Because I was too intent on being *you*, dammit."

"Okay, great, Louis Beally Waxnicki. Then let's all have a big damn pity party for you. Let's open a damned keg and get hammered and everyone can cry over the mistakes you've made, the stupid things you've done. Jesus, what an idiot!" Theo stood and stalked across the room, over to Ms. Pac-Man, and slammed his hand down next to the joystick. "At least everyone knows who you *are*. At least they all understand you. At least *you* know *who* you are and *what* you are."

"Yeah, life must have been pretty fucking awful for you, never growing old, always looking so young and prime, with your real-life superpowers too," Lou shot back, shoving the chair away so hard that it slammed into the wall and crashed to the floor.

"Well, they're gone now," Theo shouted, whirling back around from the video game console. "I'm just a normal sonofabitch like you, except I look like your fucking grandson. And I don't know if I'm going to live forever or stay like this for the rest of my life or what. I'm a damned, unnatural *freak*. And I don't know *why* I'm like this, and *what the hell* I'm supposed to do about it. And why everyone seems to keep dragging me back to life whenever I fucking *die*."

They stared at each other, anger spitting through the room—identical eyes glaring into each other from two very different faces.

"I'm outta here," Theo finally said, blinking hard, his mouth tight. "I need some damned space."

"Take your time, and don't let the door hit you in the ass on the way out," Lou snapped, turning back to the computer table. "I'm going to try and figure this thing out since you don't have the brains to do it yourself."

Theo slammed the door closed behind him as he ran down the stairs. His fury with Lou, with the whole situation, was already beginning to abate by the time he got to the bottom. Asshole.

"What was that all about?" Vonnie said, meeting him at the bottom of the steps. "Were you up there with that Lou person?"

"Just a little disagreement," Theo said briefly. "How's Sam?"

"The same. Hanging in there. Selena's with him."

"Has Jennifer been here?"

Vonnie's lips flattened. "No. Not for a few days. I'm sure she doesn't know—"

"I'll be back later," Theo said, his mind made up.

It wasn't difficult for him to find Jennifer in Yellow Mountain. Theo walked past the old McDonald's, which was where all the young, single men lived in a co-op sort of group, and behind it was the shaded patio where the young people had eaten and imbibed before Vonnie's storytelling the other night.

A cluster of chairs were gathered there, filled with many of the young people Theo had met that night two weeks ago. Although they were socializing, they were all working on something: sewing, carving, one of the women was even snipping green beans.

Jennifer was one of them, and when Theo appeared, she looked up right away. "Hi, Theo," she said in a casual voice, as if their last conversation about him and Selena had never happened. "What's up?"

"I came to see you," he said, purposely being vague. He'd managed to bank his raging anger to a dull fury, which was directed at a whole lot of the world right now.

Jennifer popped up out of her seat with enthusiasm. "Okay." She smiled, winked at one of the girls, and literally sashayed around the circle of her friends to his side.

Theo led her out of earshot of the others before he rounded on her. "Were you meeting Sam last night?" he asked.

Her eyes widened. "No," she said. "That's over and done with. He's too young for me, know what I mean?"

Theo nodded. "I certainly do. How did he take it when you told him it was over?"

Jennifer blinked and her eyes skittered away. "Uhm . . . well, I haven't had a chance to talk to him about it."

"I didn't think so." Theo drew in a deep breath that did little to contain his fury. "And how do I know this? Because he was coming to see you last night—probably because he hadn't heard from you in two days, and he was led to believe that there was something between the two of you—"

"That's not my fault," she wailed. "He's just not mature enough. He was crazy about me, talking about getting married and everything."

"But you did lead him to believe the feeling was

mutual, didn't you? You were playing a game with him to get back at Selena, weren't you?"

"Well, I—yes, but I was just having a little fun. I didn't expect—"

"And do you know what happened last night? He was coming to see you, and he was attacked by *gangas*."

"Oh!" Her eyes widened again. "Oh no. Is he . . . ?"

"He's not going to make it," Theo said, and now he took her arm as she gasped in horror at the news. He was gentle but firm. "And what you're going to do is come back to Selena's with me. And you're *not* going to let him know that you've already moved on, that it was some big game. You're going to make him happy his last few days. Got it?" He leaned into her face and let her see his disgust.

"Oh-okay," she said, her cheeks red. "But I didn't mean—"

"I'm sure that you didn't. But you're going to fix it as much as you can. Give him something. Make it convincing, too, Jennifer." He sent her a dark look.

"But . . . what if he doesn't die?"

"We'll all be very lucky and very grateful. And then," Theo said, "Selena might not want to kill you."

The look on her face would have been comical if the situation hadn't been so tragic and dark. As it was, Theo could hardly bear to look at the young woman as they went to find a horse for her to ride back. *Stupid girl.* No, it wasn't her fault that Sam had gone out at night, foolishly, but it could easily have been prevented if she hadn't been playing such an immature game.

They were just riding out from the gates when Theo heard the sound in the distance. The low, rumbling sound of an engine.

Jennifer, who was wrapped up in her own tragedy, didn't seem to notice, but he turned and looked.

He didn't have to shade his eyes, for the vehicles were approaching from the east. Theo was just able to make out the first one coming into view from behind tree-shaded and decrepit buildings. The westerly light gleamed on the black metal of the truck, and then skipped over the one behind it . . . and the one behind it . . . and to a fourth vehicle.

"Oh, bust," Jennifer whispered when Theo stopped and she saw them. "The snoot."

Theo knew it had to be either the Strangers or their bounty hunters. He hesitated, then turned the horse around. "Let's go back."

He wanted to see what was going to happen. And what he could learn from the bastards—whoever they were.

Back inside the walls, someone had already begun to ring the bell that announced the approaching of the vehicles, and Theo saw people coming out of their homes and workstations and moving about in preparation. Jennifer slipped away as soon as they brought the horses back to the stable, and Theo watched her go with mild irritation. It was just as well. He'd have a better chance of observing without that around.

Most of the flurry of preparation, he assumed, was moot: the bounty hunters weren't easily fooled. They were probably there for a particular reason. But since he had never been present during one of their visits, he wasn't certain how it would unfold.

The metalsmith, the plastics worker, the rubber smelter, the weaver and clothes menders all began to trail out of their shops, along with their assistants. The crowd that had been on the patio behind the

McDonald's scattered and looked as if they had things to attend to. The gardeners in the small plots of tomatoes and other vegetables put their baskets aside. When the snoot came, apparently everyone turned out to greet them.

Everyone except for Theo. He slipped between a well-maintained building and a tall tree and clambered up into the full, leafy branches. No one seemed to notice and he ended up with a good view of the entrance to the settlement while being well camouflaged by the leaves.

As he settled into the branches, Theo heard the sounds of trucks driving into the settlement. The gates would, of course, be opened for them without hesitation. The sound of tires grinding on the gravel-strewn center of the village was both ominous and familiar.

Theo saw about a dozen men climbing out of the Humvees, and watched as the residents of Yellow Mountain turned out to meet them, emerging from the buildings to gather in the very same area they'd sat for Vonnie's stories weeks before.

Then he recognized one of the men as he swung around to give direction to one of his companions, his long blond dreadlocks flying around his shoulders. *Sonofabitch.*

It was the bounty hunter named Seattle. The one who'd shot a bullet into Theo's chest—the bullet that had killed him.

Theo automatically ducked out of sight among the leaves. This definitely couldn't be good.

If Seattle were alone, Theo would have liked nothing better than to get his ass out there and shake the asswipe's hand. He could send a surge of his electrical power through his fingers and drop him like a fucking stone. *Oh fuck.* No he couldn't.

Not any more. *Sonofabitch.*

That anger he'd banked began to simmer and he gripped the tree tightly, breathing steadily. Not the time to do something reckless.

Were they here, looking for him? Or for some other reason?

By now, Seattle's companions had begun to pair off. They were holding guns and looked ready to use them. *Holy shit.*

Theo watched as the bounty hunters lined up the residents of Yellow Mountain in rows. Two of them seemed to be checking a list and the others were spreading out, heading toward the various homes and workshops.

What the *hell* was going on down there? Was it some sort of census count or were they identifying everyone, marking them off for a different reason? Theo pursed his lips, his heart pounding. It was no secret to him and the other members of the Resistance that the Strangers used mortal humans for everything from slaves to entertainment to whatever they wanted. Whether this was some sort of selection process or other authoritarian event wasn't yet clear. But either way, it smelled like shit.

Theo watched as Seattle and his companions continued to go through their list. At the same time, a group of Yellow Mountain residents began to carry out large vats. They set them on the ground in front of the visitors.

Seattle inspected the contents—clearly, he was in charge—and seemed satisfied. He barked more orders and gestured cockily with his rifle as he conferred with some of his companions. Others had emerged from one of the houses carrying what looked like another rifle and—*Oh, crap* . . . a computer. As Theo watched, the computer monitor—one of the big, boxy ones that had gone the way of the dinosaur even before the Change—was dropped onto the ground. Seattle stepped forward and used his rifle to smash the screen.

Niiiice, asswipe.

He continued to watch with rising fury as the invaders smashed what looked like some sort of car engine that they'd dragged from the back of some building. And another computer. Interestingly enough, there didn't seem to be an issue with televisions or DVD players—at least as far as Theo could tell.

So he guessed that the invaders had come searching not necessarily for people, but for contraband. Or, at least, what they considered to be contraband: Weapons. Vehicles. Computers.

Things that would connect people and communities and allow them to protect themselves.

"What's in the vats?" he wondered softly. The people of Yellow Mountain didn't seem to have any resistance to turning them over to Seattle and his comrades.

Just then, he noticed one of the bounty hunters just climbing out of his vehicle. Theo recognized him, too, and his apprehension grew. *Ian Marck.*

Theo had had more than one run-in with Ian and his father, Raul. If Seattle was a stupid, cocky, bullying sort of danger, Raul Marck was a greedy, malevolent son of a bitch—and he was smart.

Though not, Theo thought, quite as smart as his son Ian.

He frowned, watching the cluster of bounty hunters, wondering what Ian Marck would be doing with the likes of Seattle—who was clearly in charge. Ian wasn't the sort of guy to take orders from anyone. And yet it was clear from the body language of the other bounty hunters—including Seattle—that they not only respected but were wary of Marck.

And when Ian turned to speak to another of his companions, a slender, delicate-looking guy who tilted his head to look up at him, Theo froze.

He had a perfect view from his vantage point in the tree. That wasn't a guy at all. It was a woman, with startling blue eyes and inky hair.

Not two months ago, she'd been pointing a gun at him, Sage, Wyatt and Simon.

The daughter of the infamous Remington Truth.

The man the Strangers had been searching for for fifty years.

CHAPTER 13

Selena brushed the hair from Sam's face. He opened his eyes, curved his cracked lips into a little smile.

"Hi, Mom," he said. The whistle of death was in his voice and Selena tried to ignore it.

"How do you feel?" she asked. "Are you in pain?"

"A little."

"I'll have Vonnie get the bong," Selena told him. "Will you drink some of this tea?"

He nodded. "I'm thirsty."

She lifted the cup and he sipped with her help. The silver-gray cloud hovered, and would soon change to blue. The zombie attack had not only slashed his skin and muscle, but also well into his organs. He was bleeding internally and there was nothing that could be done except to keep him as comfortable as possible.

"Mom," he said, shifting his hand as if to touch hers. "I'm sorry. I shouldn't . . . have gone out."

Sudden tears burned her eyes. "Sammy . . . don't apologize to me. Please. I love you, and I just want you to get better." A blast of anger churned her belly. It could so easily be *her* lying there with *ganga* wounds. In fact, it was a miracle it wasn't. Or a tragedy. All the times she'd gone out, all these years, all of the danger she'd put herself into . . . The roles could so easily have been reversed.

And, God, she wished it had.

"I was . . . stupid. Just wanted . . . to see . . . Jennifer."

The anger flared hotter and Selena forced herself to hide it. It wasn't the girl's fault that her son had made a bad choice. Although she really didn't think she'd be able to look at the little bitch any time soon without wanting to strangle her. She'd definitely led him on.

"Love her . . ." Sam said, and gestured to the mug for another drink of tea. Selena helped him, working hard to keep her expression calm and composed. "Where is Jennifer? . . . I want to see her," he said. "Tell her . . ."

Selena swallowed and nodded. "I know, Sammy." She wasn't going to lie to him. She wasn't going to give him false hope.

"Before I die," he continued. "I'm dying, Mom . . . I know. They're waiting . . . for me."

"Sammy," she said, blinking hard against the tears.

"It's okay . . . Mom," he said. "You know . . . it's okay."

It's okay for you, but it's not *okay for* me!

But she didn't say that; she just nodded.

Then his eyes lit on something behind her, and they brightened. "Jennifer." He struggled to move, his mouth curving into a smile.

"Sam," the young woman said, moving quickly to the other side of his bed. "Oh, Sam, what did you do?"

Selena stared in shock, watching her son's face light up and his full attention move from her to Jennifer. Even the gray-silver cloud wavered and thinned for a moment. It wasn't until a gentle hand rested on her shoulder that she turned to see Theo standing there. He met her eyes briefly, and then his gaze moved to watch the young people.

Comprehension flooded her, followed by another prickle of tears. Gratitude and something else, something stronger than affection, compelled her to go into his arms—the need for comfort, for something solid to hold on to . . . but she didn't move. There were too many other emotions warring within her: shock, anger, disbelief, and something darker. *Hatred*.

She didn't think she could soften.

But when he came closer, his hand strayed along her arm and he gently curved his fingers around her biceps, coaxing her up. She did stand then; and before she knew it, he had his arm around her and was leading her away.

"Thank you," was the first thing she managed to say once they were out of earshot and sight of Sam and Jennifer. "Theo . . . thank you."

"It had to be done," he replied. His hand was gentle now, sliding over her hair. But there was something else in his face. Tension, a hardness that she hadn't noticed before. "It was the least she could do." He focused his dark brown eyes on her. They were concerned, but there was something else lurking there. "How are you doing?"

"A little better. Thank you for taking me away this afternoon too," she said. "I really needed that. I'm beginning to accept the inevitable," she admitted. Her mouth trembled and she told herself that now was not the time to cry. "I'm going to get through this. I'm grateful that I'll have time with him, but I pray that he won't be in pain for long."

"You're not going to have to go through this alone," he told her. "I'm going to be here."

"Thank you," she said, meaning it, wanting to cling to someone—to him—during this time. He gathered her against his chest and she just let the feel of his embrace soothe her. It was hard to believe that less than a month ago, she hadn't even known him. And now she was clinging to him for sanity during this awful time.

"The snoot came when I was in Yellow Mountain today," he said after a while. His voice rumbled deep in his chest next to her ear.

Selena pulled away and looked at him, suddenly glad to have something else to think about than her dying son. "How bad was it?"

He made a sharp, short gesture. "I don't know. How bad is it usually? They smashed up an engine, found some guns, took away something in big barrels, and searched every house from top to bottom. But no one was hurt or taken away." His voice dripped bitterness.

"That's good."

"That's *good*? Is this normal? How often does this sort of thing happen?"

Something about Theo had changed. He seemed to age before her—not literally, of course, but in his eyes. She replied, "It happens often enough. A few times a year. Those things they take—it's for our own protection; it's like a cleaning out—"

"You're fucking kidding me, right?" Theo said in a low, dangerous voice. "They come in and just take things? Search? Destroy things? And it's for your own *protection*?" His eyes flashed with fury and shock. "Explain to me how that's for your own damned protection!"

Selena didn't know what to say at first; her brain was still mushy from shock. "Well," she began, searching for the words to help him understand. "It's for the best. Guns are dangerous. They're left over from the Change—no one makes them now—and the world before it was filled with violence. Everyone used them back then and people were always being killed. They're unpredictable and deadly and we don't have any need for them now." The words tumbled out, words she'd heard over and over. Words she'd tried to make herself believe, and, more importantly, to impress upon Sam.

It was safer that way.

Theo was staring at her as if she'd grown three heads. "Is that what you believe, or what you've been told?" he whispered. His face looked raw and savaged. "I had no idea . . . " He shook his head, jamming a hand up into his hair and ruffling it into spikes. "Do they ever come here?"

"Sometimes. Not for a while. There's one of them who's spooked by me."

"What do you mean? Because you're the Death Lady, you mean? Or the other . . ."

"They came here once, a couple years ago. Four of them. One of them had a death cloud around him and it was turning blue—but there seemed to be nothing wrong with him. I was angry that they were here, disrupting things and searching, and I told them that the guy was going to die any time now. When the leader—his name is Seattle, and he's a— *What?* Do you know him?"

"Oh, yes. I know the asswipe. He's the one who put the damn bullet in my chest and nearly killed me."

"Well, actually, he did kill you," she reminded him.

"True." A bit of humor flashed through his eyes, but it was gone in an instant. "What happened to the guy with the blue cloud?"

"He died, of course. While they were here, in fact—though I hadn't expected that. It was just a coincidence. He had a heart attack or something, and just dropped. The snoot left shortly after that, and we haven't had the pleasure of a visit from them since. I think Seattle's afraid that I'll foretell his death," she added wryly.

"Even so, Frank's taken steps to make sure they don't find the things in the arcade with that fake door. And . . . What's he hiding in the back?"

Selena felt her eyes widen. "So you know about that?"

Theo nodded. "Yeah. If I had to guess, I'd think he was growing something back there he didn't want them to find."

"You'd be right," she said. "Those big barrels the snoot came for—it's cacao pods. The Yellow Mountaineers were given the task to grow cacao trees for the Elite, and that's the harvest. I guess it's for something—"

"Chocolate. That's where they get the chocolate," Theo said. "They use it for bribes sometimes, the Strangers. I've seen them do it. Where is it all? I haven't seen any chocolate here."

"We don't get any of it. The people in the settlement grow it and give it to the Elite. They're told it's poison; very dangerous. They have to use gloves when they harvest it."

Theo gave another one of his sharp, bitter laughs. "Cacao is used to make chocolate, which I'm sure Frank and probably even Vonnie remembers. It's not dangerous in the least. It's—"

"I know that," Selena interrupted. "That's what Frank's doing back there—trying to grow his own trees. He managed to sneak a few pods—as you can imagine, everything is very carefully protected—and has been nursing a few trees on his own. So far, they haven't produced much, but he babies them like they're the last ones on earth."

"Smart. Good for him."

Selena looked at Theo. "Maybe. It's dangerous, you know. If the snoot catches someone with anything they call dangerous . . . there are always consequences. People disappear, most often, if the snoot think they're in too deep—they take them away. Or they take the stuff away and destroy it. That's why I think you're taking a big risk, Theo, playing around with those things in the arcade."

"I'm not afraid of them," he said. "I know a lot more about them and what they stand for than they realize."

Selena was taken aback by the ferocity in his face. She would have asked more, but Vonnie appeared. "Sammy's asking for you," she said.

All other thoughts fled and Selena rushed off, terrified that the death cloud had changed and she had missed saying goodbye to him.

But when she got to Sam, she found him looking better than he had since he'd opened his eyes earlier. Jennifer was gone; and although the death cloud still lingered, he was animated and seemed more comfortable.

Selena turned back to thank Theo for his intervention, but he wasn't there.

Lou heard the footsteps on the threshold of the door and turned back to the computer screen.

It was either bad-ass Theo returning for another round, or that bossy woman with the curly hair who kept trying to feed him while giving him the hairy eyeball at the same time.

He had work to do, trying to figure out how to get into Blizek's deepest secrets. And his damned eyes were tired, because his glasses had been smashed in the rout with the *gangas* last night.

"Hey."

It was Theo. Lou turned from the computer to look at him. All of the last bit of anger he'd been holding on to evaporated when he saw his brother walking across the floor.

"Geez, that was a stupid argument," Lou said, at the same time as Theo spoke: "What the hell were we fighting about?"

He stood and met his brother halfway, and they hugged, clapping each other on the back the way they did when their emotions were high and they didn't want to get weepy. "I'm sorry," Lou said.

"I was out of line," Theo replied, shaking his head as he stepped away. "The things I said were stupid."

"Yeah, but I was even more whacked. I never realized you felt that way about being . . . the way you are." In fact, Lou had been beating himself up about it for the last few hours. How could he have missed that? How could he have been so dumb? Fifty years of being in his brother's head and he didn't get that he felt like a freak of nature. *Fucking idiot.*

Theo shrugged. "Whatever. It'd just be nice to know if I was going to die, or live forever. You know? And the way things are going, I'm starting to get the sense that someone up there doesn't want me to die."

"Well, I'm seeing a lot more stubble on you," Lou said. "And a few more gray hairs. So I wouldn't worry too much about living forever. Pretty soon, you're going to look like me." He swiped his hand over the ponytail that reached just past his shoulders.

"So you figure that out yet?" Theo asked, gesturing to the computer. "You had all afternoon."

Lou snorted. "No. Blizek's security's ridiculous. Whatever he had on them, he had to have buried it deeper than China. But did you see those prototypes and screencaps in there for Jolliah's Castle? That game would have been sweet."

"I know. I wonder if we could figure out how to build it," Theo said, pulling up an extra chair. "Maybe even improve on it."

"Improve on UniZek? That's blasphemous!"

Theo gave a gruntlike laugh. "You hear anything from Sage or Elliott?"

Lou sobered. "Not yet. She's trying. But I don't think there's much chance of getting him here in less than a week, even if she gets in touch with him. Jade knows how to log on to the network, but I'm not sure where she and Elliott are."

"I don't think he'll last that long," Theo replied, already tapping on the keyboard. His face was set, and Lou recognized worry and grief in his expression. "I've got some news." Theo paused in his work to look at Lou. "Ran into a couple of old friends just over that way, in Yellow Mountain—the settlement there—this afternoon."

"Who?"

"The guy who tried to kill me when I was with Fence and Quent—bounty hunter named Seattle. And guess who was with him?"

"Ian Marck."

"And that woman Remington Truth."

Lou's eyes widened. Remington Truth had been in Envy for all of a few hours before she ran off. She'd thrown a snake at Wyatt, in fact—a fact that still didn't fail to amuse Lou. No one understood exactly why she was running, and what she had to hide—but there was obviously something because she kept giving them the slip. "They were all together? What were they doing?"

The twins had automatically settled next to each other, each working a different angle, on a different computer, and Theo described what he'd seen in Yellow Mountain.

"Hmm," Lou said. "No one was hurt, though?"

"Interestingly enough, no. But there were a couple of guys who looked like they'd been trying to build a car. The snoot destroyed it." Theo sighed and settled back in his seat. "Damn, Lou. I want to go after those bastards and fucking kill them. Or something. Especially Seattle. And the fact that Remington Truth is hanging out with the bounty hunters doesn't bode well."

"Why don't we follow them? They can't be far. We might find out something. It's the first chance we've had to do something like that." He had taken one of the Resistance's three Humvees when he left Envy. Unfortunately, it had gone into a ditch about fifteen miles from here and he couldn't get it out alone—which was why he'd been on foot when the zombies attacked. But it would be easy for the two of them to remedy that.

Theo was nodding. "I'd be out of here in a minute if it weren't for Selena, and what she's going through. I don't want to leave her right now."

"So, she's definitely it," Lou said. "The one?" *Thank God.*

"Yes. She is."

There was silence except for the clickety-clack of the keyboards and a few punctuated curses for a time. Then suddenly, Theo started chuckling to himself.

Lou looked over. "What?"

"I don't know why, but I just remembered Beagle McAnus."

Lou smiled, then couldn't hold back a guffaw of laughter. "And Joe Schlong." He was cracking up, remembering the mischief making in high school. They'd hacked into the school email system and changed the names on the emails of the principal and one of the vice principals, so that when Betty McArdle sent an email, it appeared in the recipient's inbox as being from Beagle McAnus. And Don Schlueter's name was changed to Dick Schlong.

"And we never got caught," Theo chortled. "We were fucking good. Remember that time we changed the receipts at Wal-Mart?"

Lou laughed harder. It had been a summer job for both of them, each in different departments. But on their last day, as a parting joke, they managed to log into the operating system and changed the wording at the bottom of the company's receipt from "Have a Nice Day" to "Shit Happens." For hours, every single receipt from every single transaction at that store popped out, saying "Shit Happens"—with a big Wal-Mart smiley face after it—until one of the cashiers noticed and called it to the attention of the manager.

"If we're that good, then why the hell can't we get into Mr. Blizek's deep secrets?" Lou asked.

"I dunno, but some of those game prototypes are fucking sweet—and it looks like our boy Brad might have been gay, too, based on a couple of very explicit emails to one Tony Filletti. And here's a bunch of things— Hmm. I didn't know he was working on a geocaching thing. Looks like he was going to tie it into another game; make it a sort of online and real-world treasure hunt. That would have been sweet too."

"Tony could be a girl's name," Lou commented, trying yet another variation on yet another layer of security. "*Sonofabitch*. This guy was paranoid."

"Well, if I were in the Cult of Atlantis and planning to double-cross it, I'd be paranoid too," Theo replied wryly.

And then suddenly, it hit him. Lou stopped, resting

his hands on the keyboard. "Geocaching." He said it out loud. "That could be it. That's got to be it!"

"What? Are you in?" Theo rolled his chair over to look on his computer screen. "What?"

But Lou had already started to dig into his pack for the list of the strings of numbers he'd been trying to decode for weeks. "I'm so stupid. I've been a complete idiot. They're decimal degrees. Coordinates, on a map."

"You mean those numbers from the Strangers? From Remington Truth's old notes?"

Lou pulled out the handwritten information. "Yes. When you said geocaching, you made me think of it. I bet these numbers identify locations of—something. Something important to the Strangers. I have no idea what, but if I had to guess, I'd say either strongholds or locations of supplies or something like that."

Theo was nodding, his eyes excited. "Yes. That could make total sense. Yes. The only problem is," he said, "now that everything's all fucked up and the earth's axis is changed, how the *hell* are we going to interpret them?"

Selena wasn't sure if it was a blessing or not when Sam's cloud turned blue.

Pain had etched deep grooves into his face even in this short time, and his breathing was labored and rattling. He'd opened his eyes more than once and spoken to her quite lucidly. And the visit from Jennifer had been a godsend, eliminating his lingering hurt. Selena felt another wave of appreciation toward Theo. For whatever it was worth, Sammy would die with what he needed from the woman he loved.

But now, just over twenty-four hours after the zombie attack, the light was fading from his eyes.

Selena hadn't left his side since Vonnie called her back. And, in these last few hours of energy, so common in the dying, she and Sam had actually had a few laughs, remembering stories from when he was young.

"They're ready for me, Mom," he said finally. "They're waiting. It's your . . . mom and dad . . . you know."

She nodded, fighting to keep the tears from her eyes. With Sam gone, her life would be so empty. She wouldn't have anyone of her own. "I'm glad you'll be with them."

"I won't leave you . . . Mom," he said. He smiled, and for a moment, she saw the baby, and the toddler, then the years of the young boy flash through his face. "Not . . . really. Will . . ."—he drew in a staggering breath—" . . . always . . . be . . . with . . . you."

"It's okay, Sammy. You can go now," she said, knowing how important it was for him to hear these words. "I love you. I know you love me. There's nothing to forgive. Be at peace."

"Love . . . you . . ." he said, and he closed his eyes.

Selena now allowed the tears to trickle down her cheeks, to plop onto her hand, the one still holding his. It was so different, so awful to sit through this with someone she loved. Someone who'd come from her.

She felt as if her insides were being torn out.

The guides moved from the corner, where they'd been keeping their vigil, and the blue cloud sparkled and twinkled and whirled in a gentle vortex.

He breathed, in . . . and out . . . in . . . and out . . . in . . . and out . . .

And then, nothing.

Nothing.

Nothing.

CHAPTER 14

Theo arrived a moment too late . . . or perhaps it was the right time after all for her to have her privacy.

Selena was drawing the sheet over Sam's face, and all was silent. There was no one else about. It was the darkest part of night and, somehow, mercifully, there were no other patients in the ward that needed her attention.

"He's gone," she said, turning as Theo approached.

"I'm sorry," he said, and stood there, his arms spread open at his waist, waiting to see if she wanted him to hold her or to be left alone. "He was a great kid."

She came into his embrace and he folded his arms around her so that she could shake with silent sobs, wetting his shirt as she curved her face into his shoulder.

"He said he'd always be with me," she said after a long time, pulling her tear-streaked, swollen face from him. "And I saw my parents. They went with him."

He nodded. "That must have been comforting to you, knowing that he wouldn't be alone."

She nodded too. "And it was odd," she said, her voice surprisingly steady. "When he went, I didn't feel anything . . . like I normally do. When someone leaves. I usually feel a little jolt, and . . . it's strange, but I see their memories flash through my mind. It was different with him."

"Maybe that's a blessing," he said. "In a way."

Her head moved against him in affirmation. "I think so too."

"I wish I'd known him better."

"He wanted to learn about those computers," Selena told him. "I wouldn't let him, but he wanted you to teach him."

"I would have."

"I know."

He held her for as long as she let him, and then, when she pulled away, he resisted the need to kiss her, sensing that it wasn't the right time. Instead, he let her slip free and return to her son's side.

When he asked if she wanted anything, she shook her head and told him to get some sleep.

She was going to sit with Sam a little longer.

"Remington Truth is dead."

Remy froze, then continued raising the spoonful of stew to her mouth. She looked at Seattle, who'd been the one to make the pronouncement, because it was the obvious thing to do, and their other companions were doing the same. But her mouth went dry and all of a sudden, her stomach was no longer interested in food.

Damn it. She'd been itching for her and Ian to get away from this group of men now that they'd done the annual raids on Yellow Mountain and a few other settlements, collecting the harvests and checking on what was going on there. Policing them. Seattle made her uncomfortable, with his heavy gaze and the way it followed her all the time. But Ian had seemed to be in no hurry to ditch his companions now that they had come together, despite the fact that his distain for them was clearly evident.

"The old man, I mean. The one we've been search-ing for all these years," Seattle continued, chewing on a piece of bread.

"How do you know that?" asked one of the other bounty hunters, a guy name Rake.

"I have my sources," replied Seattle. "And they also tell me that although the old man is dead, his daughter or granddaughter or someone is alive."

"Sounds like we ought to be looking for a young woman, then, instead of an old man," Ian said. He rested his plate aside, the utensils clattering. He lifted a bottle of beer and drank, long and easy.

There was a woman, the wife of another bounty hunter named Jose, who got to her feet and took the dishes away to wash. Ian didn't spare her a glance as he lowered the bottle and leveled his cold blue gaze at Seattle.

"If you believe the rumor," Seattle replied. "Hey, Lisa, right here," he said, pointing to his own dishes. Jose's wife returned and scooped them up without comment.

Remy hadn't moved and now she reminded herself to start chewing. How the hell did they know this? Or was it just, as Seattle said, rumor. It meant nothing.

No one could connect her to Remington Truth . . . except for those men from Envy. But the one thing she knew about the men from Envy was that they weren't doing any favors for the Elite or their bounty hunters.

Still. She didn't trust them anymore than she trusted anyone, including her so-called partner. She felt Ian's gaze on her and she swallowed the bite of venison stew and scooped up another one in her spoon. It was time to get the hell out of here.

Between Seattle's contemplative looks and the fact

that if Ian knew who she was, or figured it out, she'd be turned over to the Strangers for whatever compensation he could get.

As she forced herself to eat, to listen to the conversation about the raids in Yellow Mountain and how they would be going back to "finish things up"—whatever that meant—Remy glanced toward the fringes of trees. The sun was just setting, and soon they'd all go inside the old house to the second floor, where they could sleep safely from the zombies. Dantès was in the shadows somewhere, beyond the circle of four vehicles that were parked in a small clearing.

He'd be ready to leave whenever she was, if he wasn't off hunting a rabbit or fox.

If she only knew how to drive one of those trucks, she'd be set. But Remy didn't, and she didn't dare try it now. She should have watched Ian more closely, maybe even asked him to teach her.

After all, she was his partner. Her lips moved in wry humor.

Instead of waiting for Lisa to take her plate as she'd done for the others, Remy pulled to her feet and brought it to the woman.

Then she took the opportunity to wander away from the others and their talk of the raids and their plans for Yellow Mountain and the two young men who had been found with "dangerous" equipment.

She had to get away from them, even just for a minute. The malevolence and ugliness of the group made her feel dirty. Yes, she'd participated with the raids because she had no choice, but to watch the destruction, to see the expressions on the faces of the people in the settlements made her ill.

Ian was the worst of them. The mere sight of his icy

blue eyes and harsh features was often enough for even the boldest of the people to step back. And when he smashed the windows of a house because the residents didn't come out quickly enough, there was such an underlying edge to his violence that Remy shivered and moved away.

Seattle had joy in his destruction; there was a haughty smile on his face when he smashed a computer monitor or set fire to something. He reveled in the work and the fear he generated. Power made him greedy for more.

Ian, on the other hand, did everything with such cold, emotionless intensity that his actions were that much more disturbing.

A noise behind her had Remy pausing near the edge of the wooded area. The back of her neck prickled and she turned to find Seattle standing there. His long blond dreadlocks hung free today; and although his face wasn't particularly unattractive, it was the expression in his eyes that made her stomach pitch.

"It's getting dark," he said. His voice was smooth, as if he was aware of her dislike for him and was trying to alleviate it. "I hope you aren't going into the woods alone."

Remy took comfort in the weight of the pistol stuck in the back of her jeans. Even Ian didn't know she still carried it, although, he might suspect—because it was the pistol that had convinced him to help her escape from those people who'd found her in Redlo. She'd shoved its barrel into his back to made him drive her away.

"Thanks for your concern," she replied coolly.

"If you want company—"

"I don't want company."

Seattle's eyes narrowed. "You know Ian Marck isn't

well liked by the Inner Circle. If you want to get the sort of information and respect I have from the Elite, you'd do best to stay clear of him. He'll taint your experience."

"I have my own ways of getting respect from the Inner Circle," Remy replied.

"I wonder what Lacey would say if she knew you were trying to trying to manipulate a new partner?" Ian's voice cut through the night. "I don't think she'd be very pleased."

Seattle didn't seem surprised by the approach of his rival. "Lacey can go fuck herself. Or you, which I know is a common occurrence." His voice had turned from cordial to cold.

"Sore point for you, hmm, Seattle?" Ian hadn't spared a glance for Remy, nor did he move near her. He simply stood there, watching them.

"Fuck you," the other man replied.

"I suspect you'd enjoy that," Ian said. "Stay the hell out of my business."

Remy started to slip away, having no desire to watch two alpha dogs square off, but Ian's hand reached out and grabbed her arm.

After a moment, Seattle turned and stalked off, thrashing through the bushes back toward the others.

Remy tried to pull away, but Ian didn't release her. "You've made an enemy," she commented dryly.

"Oh? Another one? How terrible." His reply was thick with sarcasm. He pulled her around to face him, and she inched her hand toward the pistol in her waistband. *Where's Dantès?*

"Don't bother," he said, moving smoothly and snatching up her gun before she could get it by stealth means. He shoved it in his own waistband. "You won't need that."

Her heart was in her throat but Remy kept her face passive. "I'm going back. Give it to me," she held out her hand for her gun.

"In a minute." He'd made no move closer to her, and in fact released her arm. "Seattle is under the impression that we're lovers."

"Sounds as if he wants Lacey to know that too—"

"It's time"— he spoke over her words—"we made it a reality."

Remy's stomach plummeted and she looked up at Ian. He still hadn't made any move toward her, but she read heat mixed with loathing in his eyes.

"It's the best way to keep him from bothering you," Ian told her. Still unmoving.

Her hands were shaking and her belly had dropped, but the very thought had other parts of her body heating up. She didn't trust him, didn't like him, was maybe even a little afraid of him . . . but there was something about Ian that made her want to slide her hands over his sleek, lanky body and let him have his way with hers.

He moved toward her, then, taking her chin firmly, he covered her mouth with his. It was a harsh kiss; not meant to hurt, but to get the job done. As when they kissed before, his mouth was incredible, molding to her lips with just the right amount of mobility—not sloppy, not dry. Remy's eyes closed when she really should have tried to keep them open . . . and she felt a rush of pleasure rumble through her as the bark of a tree edged into her back.

One hand moved down to cover one of her breasts as his fingers slid to hold her jaw steady, lifting it, holding

her there. The tree lined up more solidly behind her
and Remy shifted so that her shoulder blades propped
against it, and her hips slid forward to match up to his.
He was tall, but so was she, and they lined up nicely.
She fit her hands to his chest, at last touching the torso
she'd been watching for weeks.

Ian broke the kiss and, watching her with those angry
eyes, positioned her against the bark as both hands rose
beneath her shirt to cup her breasts, finding her tight
nipples, and then lifting her shirt so that he could see as
he lifted and caressed them. She watched his shadowy
hands on her lighter flesh, her breath growing unsteady
and desire billowing through her belly and beyond.

He yanked at her jeans so hard she jolted, opening
them so that the breath of night air cooled the skin of
her lower belly. Without delay, he shoved them down,
and her panties, and found the place between her legs.
To her surprise and a little shame, she was swollen and
wet, and she had to bite her lip to keep silent when he
touched her.

Ian held her in place as he unbuckled his own trou-
sers with the same sort of efficiency and lack of emotion. But his eyes had darkened and hooded, and his
breath shifted into something more ragged.

Remy dragged his face down for another kiss as
he lifted her and she wrapped her legs around him.
When he slid inside, she felt him tense and shudder. He
paused, resting his forehead against the bark next to her
temple, breathing. Then, he straightened and began to
move, his eyes closed, his face stony.

She watched him until the pleasure became too
great; saw the last bit of daylight illuminating the
strong blade of his nose and the sharp, high cheekbones

and forehead—and felt her body warming and swelling around him.

His hands shifted to push her more tightly against the tree, ignoring the sharp edges of bark on her bare skin. Remy let her head tilt back and closed her eyes as her world tightened and tightened; and then when he moved faster and harder, she opened her legs, shifting and lifting her hips, meeting him with the same urgent efficiency until she got what she needed.

A soft little *oh* was all she allowed herself as hot liquid shuttled through her and then exploded. She sagged in his arms, little crunchy pieces of bark rubbing and falling against her as he made one last thrust, then yanked away.

He was leaning against her, breathing heavily; his hands trembling at her hips as he finished with a low groan.

Remy realized what he'd done, and she was flushed with shame and gratitude. The last damn thing she needed was to get pregnant—especially by Ian Marck. *What the hell was I thinking?*

He released her with more gentleness than he'd shown thus far, steadying her until she had her balance. Her knees were weak and she just wanted to stand there and bask . . . but that wasn't going to happen.

"Why," she breathed as he yanked up his pants, "do you always look so angry when you're kissing me?"

Ian glanced at her, his mouth tight and eyes hot and dark. He gave a sharp shrug. "There's someone else I'd rather be kissing," he said. "If I had the choice."

Remy caught her breath. "Well, that's probably the first time you've told me the truth," she managed to say. *Bastard.*

He didn't smile as his belt clinked back into place. "Probably."

"Lacey?" she couldn't help but ask.

"Christ. Fuck, no."

He stepped away, reaching into his pocket. Then he handed her back the pistol. "Don't think about trying to slip off tonight. You'll be sleeping next to me. Tonight and for the foreseeable future."

She glared at him. *As if you could keep me here.*

He looked at her. "You don't think I'm about to let Remington Truth's granddaughter just walk away, do you?"

"I have something I'd like to talk to you about," Theo said to Selena.

It had been more than two weeks since Sam died, and he'd seen much less of Selena than he liked. A lot less.

For both of them living in the same house, it was amazing how she never seemed to be at the same meals he was at, and how their paths didn't cross very often. He'd begun to suspect, with a deep, unpleasant knowledge, that she was purposely avoiding him. He understood that she needed time to work through her loss, but there was a large part of him that wondered why he wasn't a part of it. Why she didn't share it with him.

Perhaps because Sam had been *hers* and not his. Maybe she didn't think he grieved for the boy. But he did.

Not that he and Selena each weren't busy with other things. The day after Sam died, three patients arrived for Selena. Theo had been angry about that, angry at the world or the universe or whoever for disrupting Selena's grief. But she had accepted it with grace and peace and attended to the dying with the same empathy he'd seen before.

Perhaps that, too, was a blessing—the distraction and a return to normalcy.

And Theo had been busy too. He and Lou had been working night and day on the Blizek security (it was a joke on him that he thought he'd made it through the first layer so quickly and easily so many weeks ago), as well as the number strings that seemed, as Lou theorized, to indicate geographic coordinates. But they had to figure out how to recalculate them, now that the earth's axis had shifted. And Theo had been thinking about what he could do with the pinball machines and game consoles, and their blinking, flashing lights.

Aside from that, now that Sam was gone, Frank had pressed the twins into helping him in a variety of other tasks—which they did willingly, even though Lou grumbled about the speed and strength of the ninety-three-year-old man.

"Forget about you. I think *he's* the damned superhero," Lou said once, after three hours of lugging stones to rebuild part of the wall when Frank hadn't taken more than a five-minute break.

But now, Theo had managed to catch Selena and suggest a walk after dinner. The sun was a brilliant orange ball sinking toward the horizon, bringing the night. Oddly enough, he didn't feel that same sort of apprehension he had in the past, worrying that she would go out there.

She hadn't, since Sam was attacked. He'd been watching.

Maybe she'd given it up, realized that her life here, serving the dying, was more important than out there nearly getting herself killed. Maybe Sam's death had opened her eyes to the dangers, and to the reality of the murderous zombies.

Or maybe she just wasn't ready to face them again.

Selena looked at him. "What is it?"

His breath caught for a moment, appreciating the serenity in her smooth face, the way the lowering sun cast an even deeper golden glow over her skin and dark hair. Despite the circles under her eyes, and the deeper grooves of grief radiating from her eyes and mouth, she was beautiful. He wanted to kiss her; he'd missed her company, her warmth, her quirky sense of humor that came up at the oddest times . . . but he held back.

He'd meant to talk to her about Lou and the fact that they were twins, but it didn't seem like the right time after all. Maybe it was the grief lingering in her face—it had only been two weeks. Maybe he wasn't ready to take the chance that she, too, might think he was unnatural. Maybe he worried that she held Lou responsible for what had happened to Sam and that she'd never accept that they were twins.

"I've missed spending time with you," he said, reaching for her hand. *Maybe instead, I ought to tell her how I feel.*

She smiled, and it seemed a little forlorn. She squeezed his fingers. "I have a lot to work through right now."

He looked down at her, reached to brush that heavy, dark hair from her shoulder. "I understand. I just want you to know that I miss being with you. And I miss this." He couldn't help himself. He leaned forward, his hand gently curving under her jaw, and fit his lips onto hers.

His eyes closed at the pleasure, the familiar comfort and desire that came with that mere brush of mouth to mouth. He shifted, felt her mouth move beneath his, her lips part—a bit and he slipped the tip of his tongue along that little opening. Soft, warm, slick . . . Desire and need began to open up inside him.

And then she turned away, her hand moving to settle on his chest. "I . . . ah, Theo, I don't think I can do this. Right now."

A black hole suddenly yawned in front of his mind—empty and mysterious. His heart thudding, the suspicion he'd tamped back now blossoming into something unpleasant, Theo tried to catch her downturned gaze. "Too soon?"

"Yes." She drew in a deep breath and looked at him. "I have a lot of things to work through. I'm confused and angry—so angry—and . . . oh, God, I *want* it to be okay, but every time I think of it, all I can see is you, that night. Flying into them, smashing those zombies, like some sort of berserker warrior. I can't get rid of the images, the carnage, the violence. I dream about them. They give me nightmares."

Stunned, Theo stepped back. What had been a little prickling of worry became a full-fledged roar of danger. His hands suddenly felt cold. "Selena. I wasn't going to stand back and let them tear you—I thought it was *you* in there at first—or *anyone* apart. There was no way I wasn't going to stop them. If I had the chance, I'd do it again. I've got to tell you, I respect your trying to help them, but I'm not going to let them take anyone's life if I can help it. Especially yours."

A tear overflowed from her eye and made a gleaming rivulet down her cheek. "I know it, Theo. I understand it. The problem is me. I see you doing that; I see you destroying them, and I'm so filled with hatred and fury—that I want to do it. *I* want to kill them. I want to destroy them all, those damned monsters, for what they've taken from me." Her voice held a tone that was somewhere between madness and despair. "I *want* to do that. I *want* to fucking annihilate them, as violently and horribly as I can. All of them. But . . . I can't. And I can't go out there and try to save them either. The very thought makes me ill. I can't do *anything*."

By now, the tears streamed from her eyes and her once-peaceful face had turned angry and hard. There was an ugliness he'd never seen in her features. "And so, I think it's best if I have some time to try and figure this out. Alone."

Theo got the message. Loud and clear. He managed to subdue the bark of bitter laughter at the realization that this was the second time he'd fallen hard for a woman, and the second time he'd been shoved aside for some inexplicable reason that had nothing to do with him.

His mouth began to move before he realized what he was saying, but his brain caught up quickly. "That's good, because that was what I wanted to talk to you about. Lou and I are going to be leaving. Probably tomorrow. We've got some things to check on. I'm not sure when we'll be back. I just wanted to tell you."

She met his eyes now, and he realized he was frightened by the *nothing* that was there. "Thank you for letting me know." She began to turn away, to head back to the house, but she paused. "You'll come back?"

He resisted the urge to snort in derision. The pain was just beginning to overtake the numbness. "Yes, I'm sure we'll stop back sometime. I'm not sure when, though." He did his best to keep his voice neutral and casual.

She stilled, as if surprised, then nodded. "Be safe, Theo."

CHAPTER 15

"Well, Lou, you've got your wish," Theo said as he stomped into the arcade. "We're going to hunt down some bounty hunters."

To his surprise, there was no answer. "Lou?" he said, walking across the space that they'd turned into their own. The computers were on, as usual, but the screensavers were running. Lou had them set to come on after twenty minutes, so obviously he'd been away for a while.

Where the hell could he be? It was after nine, and old guys like Lou needed their beauty sleep. Or at least, they should be working on their hacking project if they weren't sleeping. Beyond pissed-off and well into furious, Theo sat down at the nearest computer and woke up the screen to see what Lou had been working on.

Nothing. The idiot had been messing around with Brad Blizek's new video treasure-hunt video game that looked as if he were going to combine it with geocaching. Not a bad idea, at least back in 2010.

Annoyed, upset, distracted, he began to look through some of the files of screencaps and mock-ups of the game. One of them popped up and he looked a little closer at one of the screenshots of the prototype and froze. *Sonofabitch.*

It was right here.

The symbol for the Cult of Atlantis—with its

swastika, labyrinth, and the scrolling waves—was there, in the screenshot for the game. *Holy fucking shit.*

Theo's fingers lost their nimbleness as he tried to start clicking through to other details of the game. Maybe everything they needed to know was here, right here in this game called Wobble.

Holy shit. That's what he said. "The earth's going to wobble."

It was all here. Right here.

After a few minutes, on a hunch, he input one of the strings of numbers that they'd theorized were decimal coordinates and—*bingo!* It came up as one of the listings for the "real world" geocache list, embedded in the game.

Excited now, Theo delved deeper into all of the layers of files, notes, and mock-ups about the game. There were only fifteen "real world" geocache sites listed in Wobble, but twenty numbers listed in the information Lou and Theo had from the Strangers.

In the real world, back in 2010, where geocaching could be considered anything from family fun to an extreme sport, geographic coordinates were posted on websites for a sort of public treasure hunt in which the hunters used GPS to find the general location of a geocache, within a few square feet. When found, the caches—which were weatherproof, animal-proof boxes like ammo containers—could contain anything from a few bucks to small toys or trinkets, to merely a logbook. But in this game, the geocache locations were much more than that.

They were centers of power, well beneath the ground; and the point of the game was to neutralize each one, like stopping a bomb from detonating before a chain reaction set them off and made the world . . . *wobble.*

Holy wobbling earth axes. As Theo looked at the notes about the game, examining the files, his emotions ranged from fascination to chills to debilitating nausea when he realized what it meant. Were these geocaches somehow the locations through which the Cult of Atlantis had made the earth erupt, causing the Change?

He envisioned synchronized subterranean explosions of horrific magnitude that caused tectonic plates to shift and subduct, to implode or otherwise erupt . . . thus beginning the chain reaction that caused all of the cataclysmic earthquakes, tsunamis, fires . . . and everything else that combined to destroy the earth.

So this was how they did it.

And Brad Blizek had created a video game that was really a synthetic version of their plans.

Theo was still staring at the computer, trying to assimilate the truth of what had been done to his world and his race fifty years ago, when Lou arrived.

"Oh. You're here," he said, sounding surprised. "I thought you'd be gone longer. Maybe even overnight." He gave a nervous little chuckle. "I saw you and Selena go outside after dinner."

"Yeah. Well, that's not working out too well," Theo said from between stiff lips. "Lou, you gotta take a look at this. It's all here—how they did it. And, by the way, we're leaving tomorrow."

Theo and Lou started in Yellow Mountain, casually asking about the snoot, trying to get enough information to decide which direction to go after them.

While they were there, Theo received some unsettling news.

"Wayne and Buddy are gone," Patrick Dilecki, the guy who'd organized the search party on the night of

Vonnie's storytelling, told him. "Disappeared about three days ago."

"Zombie attack?" asked Lou, but Theo was shaking his head. He'd seen them from his perch in the tree during the snoot visit. They'd been the ones who had the old computer monitor and the vehicle engine that had been confiscated and destroyed by Seattle and his men.

"Nope. No bodies, no evidence of any animal attack either. Just disappeared. Wayne's momma is pretty upset. And Buddy's wife—she's going to have a baby in a few months." Patrick shook his head, his lips flattening. "They got themselves into something they shouldn't have been messing with. Dangerous stuff."

"It's not a coincidence that the snoot visited two weeks ago and now they're gone, is it?" Theo asked Patrick.

The man's face shuttered and he looked away, squinting out over the horizon. "Couldn't say."

But he didn't need to.

"So they took them," Lou said to Theo once they left Yellow Mountain. "They came back and took them. The bounty hunters."

"That's my best guess. At least we know Buddy and Wayne were here at least three days ago. Might make the trail easier to follow, if we can find it."

"You gonna tell me what happened with Selena?" Lou asked as they hiked through the woods to where he'd left that Humvee in the ditch.

"You gonna tell me where you were last night?"

Neither of them replied.

Selena stared out the window, an ugly, aching gnawing working at her belly.

Night had come, as it continued to do despite her impotent wish to keep it at bay. Because with night came questions and guilt and confusion.

And, still, that deep, burning hate.

She'd stopped wearing her crystal, keeping it locked in its wooden box so that she wouldn't have to feel it grow warm, beckoning to the zombies. They sensed it; she knew that. They came, they gathered, they cried—all beyond the safe walls.

She saw their orange eyes glowing in the distance. She heard their moans.

She hated them. And yet she was moved by their piteous cries, which only she understood.

Still, she did nothing.

Sammy. Sammy. I hope you're at peace. I'm so sorry.

Oh, God, I miss him. The house was so quiet. It was as if a part of her heart had been carved away. A piece of her life . . . gone.

Seventeen years old. He never got to manhood, never got to fulfill the promise she'd seen in him: the kindness, the sense of reverence for the world and all living things. He'd have been a great father. The raw hollowing inside her wouldn't go away. It gnawed and scraped.

Selena peered west out the window, wiping her eyes and wondered where Theo was. If he was safe. What he and that old man Lou were doing, and whether they would ever return.

He'd insinuated himself into the household, into her life, and she missed him too.

Why did I send him away again?

And yet, when she closed her eyes, she saw his dark face, tight with fury and intent, his eyes flashing violence. She saw the spraying of flesh and blood, felt the stirring of the air as he spun and clubbed and fought the monsters.

How could she ever get beyond that, when that same violence stirred inside her?

Selena turned from the window and the glowing orange eyes beyond the walls. She ignored her bed to go down the stairs and check on one of her patients.

Sleep was something rare and fitful now.

Reggie Blanchard's breathing was shallow and labored, and she sat with him, watching the gray fog swirl and mist gently above him. Even in the night, the silvery glint was evident, catching whatever bit of illumination was available. He was an old man, perhaps as old as Vonnie; and he was merely wearing down, easing from life into death. He'd been living in Yellow Mountain, working as a metalsmith for the last two years, since his wife died in Selena's care. Now she and his sister waited for him, hovering with the blue glow of the afterlife, in the corner, as the guides often did. Waiting.

Selena stared into nothing, enveloped by numbness and apathy, holding his large, gnarled hand.

And threading through the night was the sound of moans in the distance. *"Ruuu-uuuthhhh."*

Mom.

At first she thought she was dreaming, that she'd finally found sleep. The sound was in her head, buried in her mind, and yet she looked up, searching. And there he was. *Sammy.*

In the corner, hovering with Reggie's wife and sister. The two women smiled at Selena, but she barely noticed.

I told you I wouldn't really leave you.

"Hi, Sammy. I miss you." Tears stung her eyes and

she looked at him, hardly able to see any detail when she focused hard, except his eyes. Nevertheless, she knew it was him.

I miss you too. And I'm worried about you.

"I'll be all right. It takes time."

Reggie is going to go soon. We're here to help him, Mrs. Blanchard and me. He was always nice to me when I saw him in town.

"So is this your new job? Helping bring people over to the other side?" She felt a little smile waver at the corner of her mouth.

Like mother, like son. I'll be around to help sometimes. Like a conduit.

"Are you all right?"

Yes. You can't imagine what it's like here.

"Then that's all I can ask, hm?"

Mom. Try to start living again.

She frowned, tried to hold back the sting of tears. "I don't know if I know how."

They tell me you have to figure it out.

Easier said than done, she thought.

I have to go now. I'll be back later to help with Mr. Blanchard.

"Okay. I love you."

I love you too.

When Selena opened her eyes again, it was still dark. And the zombies still groaned beyond the walls. Her crystal still glowed upstairs in its box.

She stared at the corner where Sammy had been and her heart squeezed.

Try to start living again, Mom.

She visualized herself going up, getting her crystal, slinging it around her neck, and walking out of the grounds. She closed her eyes and felt the zombies surge toward her; she could almost smell their foul stench, and feel the desperate clawing of their hands grabbing for her.

And then she saw herself exploding into a vicious whirlwind, smashing and hitting and clubbing at them, over and over and over until they were all piles of bloody bones and flesh.

She saw the hopeful light die from their eyes, the orange glow disappear as they collapsed at her feet.

Her stomach churned and rebelled, and she staggered to her feet, using Reggie's bed for stability, and ran for the toilet. When she lifted her face, wiping her mouth, her cheeks were wet from tears of confusion, frustration, and fear.

And Vonnie was standing there, looking down at her with worry and grief.

"Selena," she said, helping her to her feet. "Are you all right?"

I don't know if I'll ever be all right again. "Thanks. I'm fine. Just . . . not feeling too well."

"Do you want to talk about it?" asked the only mother she'd ever known.

Selena shook her head, and at that moment, she realized the only person she wanted to talk to was Theo.

And he was gone.

CHAPTER 16

A week after they left Yellow Mountain, driving in the Humvee that they'd retrieved from the ditch and running it on solar-charged battery power, Theo and Lou finally got a break. They'd been spending the last few days making larger concentric circles around the settlement, looking for any signs of recent Humvee tracks or any other evidence of the bounty hunters or the two missing people from the settlement.

It was slow going, prompting Theo to compare it to the long, boring segment in a book that had been published to great fanfare in 2007.

"It's like looking for a horcrux in a forest," he said as Lou navigated the Humvee along a nonexistent road.

There was a reason the common use of mechanized vehicles had gone the way of iTunes, shopping malls, and highways after the Change: they were no longer necessary, and they were difficult to maintain. Not only were the roads no longer navigable, cracked and potholed as they were, but no one felt safe traveling far from an established settlement. And by even ten years after the Change, what cars hadn't been destroyed by the earthquakes, storms, and weather were in no working condition. The gas pumps at the stations no longer had electricity to run them, and people were more concerned with food and shelter and the basic necessities of living than to try and rehabilitate them.

Within thirty years, they became impossible to find or fuel. And there were other impediments as well.

Thus, today, the only people who had access to trucks and cars were Strangers, or their bounty hunters. And the Resistance, who'd managed to obtain three Humvees, took care that they were kept in secret and only used judiciously.

Because of this, the sight or sound of a mechanized vehicle generally indicated the presence of a bounty hunter or the Elite. So when, on that eighth night after they left the settlement and were about thirty miles north of Yellow Mountain, they saw the jouncing beam of headlights in the distance, Theo and Lou knew they'd finally caught their break.

Neither of them had ever been this far north of Envy before—well over a hundred and fifty miles—and they were unfamiliar with the terrain and geography. But that didn't stop them from starting up their own vehicle and driving toward the other truck.

They'd readjusted the headlights so they pointed nearly straight down, which, although it helped keep their location and presence hidden from anyone else, it also made it difficult to drive through the overgrown environment. Everything from old cars to massive potholes and unexpected bumps in the ground, along with trees and bushes, could suddenly appear in their path.

Thus, trying to balance speed, safety, and stealth was quite a feat, and there was much swearing and giving of directions—mostly unwanted. They had to stop often, too, for Theo to climb onto the roof of the truck, or even a tree or other high location, to see which direction to go. For a while, he rode on top of the Humvee, holding on à la James Bond (although at much slower speeds), and gave directional advice from there.

Despite the danger and need for surreptitiousness, they made good time and closed the distance between themselves and the other vehicle, staying far enough behind that they wouldn't be noticed. Their cause was helped when their quarry stopped for the night, giving them a chance to drive even closer.

"Better find a place to hide this," Lou said when they got close enough that discovery was possible. Theo had climbed back into the truck.

They found a spot to hide it and each of them sprawled out on a seat to sleep for the night.

As Theo lay there, trying to find relaxation, he found himself unable to dismiss thoughts of Selena from his mind. The last week of searching and driving, picking at Lou and discussing possible theories about Wobble and Brad Blizek's involvement in the Cult of Atlantis, had kept him busy. Not that she hadn't crossed his mind—she had.

Oh, she had. Continuously.

Lou had taught Frank how to use the computers in the arcade to communicate via messaging—after all, he'd been well versed in email and Google before the Change happened, and it hadn't been difficult to retrain him even fifty years later. Theo appreciated it because he at least got basic updates about Selena.

He knew that at least she hadn't gotten herself killed or injured saving zombies again.

He knew that she didn't sleep much. That she was busy with patients. That the harshness and grief was still etched on her face. That she'd been sick a week or so ago but seemed to be better now. At least physically.

He frowned in the dark. That was an awful lot of detail, coming from Frank. Maybe the guy was more verbose when he had a keyboard in front of him.

"If we find that woman, Remington Truth," Lou said, breaking into Theo's thoughts, "what are we going to do?"

"Try to talk to her. She must have some secret. Something to do with this whole mess. Otherwise why would she be hiding and running away all the time?"

"She's with the bounty hunters now, though. If she's aligned with them, and she has whatever it is they've been searching for for fifty years . . . that's not good for us."

"I know," Theo said. "But if she was going to ally herself with them, why wouldn't she have done so years ago? Seems like something's wacky." He stared at the ceiling of the Humvee, noticing that the fabric was coming undone near the windows, hanging like Spanish moss. "I'll tell you one thing. If we find Seattle, I'm going to kill the bastard."

"What about Ian Marck?" Lou asked from where he lay on the backseat. He'd claimed the more comfortable one, citing his advanced age.

"I don't know what to make of him. He kidnapped Jade and locked Elliott and me in the mall with a bunch of zombies, but he didn't kill either of us when he found us rescuing Jade. He could have—me at least."

Lou shifted, sounding sleepy. "He needed Elliott's doctor skills, but you're right. You could have been dead, even though Elliott bargained for your life. I don't trust him. Simon doesn't either."

"Simon should have killed him when he had the chance," Theo said flatly.

"Geezus, when did you get so bloodthirsty?" Lou mumbled. "Go to sleep."

Theo rolled his eyes. "You were the one who started talking."

But Lou's words stuck with him, as jesting as they were. *When did you get so bloodthirsty?*

Was that what Selena saw? A man fed by violence and who wanted to kill?

Ironically, the only time Theo had ever killed a man had been during an incident just after the Change, when there were looters and people crazed from PTSD. A man had attacked a group of people—no one really knew why; he was crazy and Theo had to shoot him.

Other than that, despite the fact that the ways of the world had become more like every man for himself, he'd never taken another life. Unless one counted those of the zombies.

But he still couldn't fathom not slaying the feral creatures. They were freaks of nature who had no mind of their own and were bent only on accomplishing their two goals—to feed and to find Remington Truth.

If they were left to run wild, humanity wouldn't have a chance to survive.

Ah, Selena.

He missed her.

The next morning, Theo woke just before the sun started to rise and slipped from the Humvee to see how close he could get to their quarry.

Not that he'd slept, but at least he'd closed his eyes for a bit. Thankfully, there'd been no sound or sign of *gangas*, so at least his downtime had been restful. He trekked through the woods and toward where they'd last seen the other vehicle, silently and swiftly. The smell of something delicious cooking led him to the building where the other truck had been parked, and he got close enough to see two people moving around inside an old party store.

Creeping closer, he used what was left of the fading darkness and some rusted cars as cover. Whatever they were cooking smelled really good. Theo and Lou had long gone through the food Vonnie had sent with them and had resorted to wild berries and carrots, as well as some dried venison and, two days ago, a couple of fish.

He thought about making a distraction so they'd come running out and he could go running in and snatch up their breakfast, but in the end decided that remaining unnoticed was a better option than a good breakfast. Still, his mouth watered and the closer he got to the building, the more his stomach rumbled.

Skirting a crushed Dumpster and a pile of rubble, Theo edged around the back of the building and finally could hear voices. Taking his time, he moved closer, using the broken windows to his advantage.

"We'll drop these two off and then meet up with Seattle. Should get 'em to Ballard by noon, and back to meet Seattle a few hours later." It was a man, and the voice wasn't familiar.

"He's going to get rid of Marck?" said another, feminine voice. "Lacey's not going to like that."

Theo edged closer, wondering if it was the female Remington Truth. He lifted his head, using a thick vine hanging over the window to peer through. No. This woman had much lighter hair.

The guy, whose face was in better light, was one of the bounty hunters who'd come to Yellow Mountain. And the more Theo looked, the more he thought the woman might have been there too.

"That's the plan—he's offing Marck. If anyone can do it, Seattle can. He's a fucking crazy bastard," the man replied. "And Lacey's part of the reason he wants to get rid of Marck, you know."

"What about that girl with Ian? She doesn't say much. What's he want with her?"

"I dunno, Lisa. What do you think? Ain't you seen the way Seattle's been looking at her?" The sarcasm in his voice was thick. "All's I know is Seattle wants to find whoever's left of Remington Truth's family, and he wants to do it first. Getting rid of Marck is part of the plan. He's scared ball-less that Marck'll find the Truth person first and get crystaled before him."

Well, that was interesting. If the female Remington Truth was with the bounty hunters, why didn't these guys know about it? Was it possible they didn't know who she was?

"What are you going to do with us?" came a third voice, which sounded thready and frightened.

The man replied, "Oh, you'll be all right. We're not going to kill you." He laughed, and even from where he was, Theo felt a chill.

"I'm hungry. Can't we have something to eat?" the scared voice said again, with a little more force.

The man laughed again. "You don't need to eat. You're gonna be all set in a few hours. Ballard'll take good care of you. Goddamn, Lisa. What's takin' so long? Want to get on our way now, okay?"

And that, Theo realized, was his cue to move his ass.

But he waited another minute. He wanted to see who the third person was, because he suspected it might be one of the guys missing from Yellow Mountain. He also wanted to search the Humvee and see if there was anything interesting there. Like guns.

Making a quick decision, Theo traced his path back around to where the truck was parked. Ears cocked to listen for approach, he opened the door on the far side of the truck and looked in. And smiled.

Just what he wanted. The automatic rifle was in his hands in a moment, along with a pouch of ammo. The sounds of approaching voices raised the hair on the back of his neck, but he took another moment to check around and see if there was anything else worth taking.

And then, when the heat got too close, he shut the door carefully and darted off into the woods, just as they came out of the store. Fifty yards in, he stopped and slung the rifle over his shoulder. Then he scrambled up a tree where he could see the male bounty hunter and his companion, Lisa, dragging out two people behind them.

Yes, definitely Wayne from Yellow Mountain. The red hair gave Wayne away. *Probably going to sell them into slavery. We'll have to put a stop to that.*

Theo pulled the gun from his shoulder and tried to get a bead on them, but they were too far away and there were too many trees for a good shot.

That's okay. We'll follow the bastards.

He clambered down the tree and took off back toward Lou.

"Let's go," he said, jumping into the truck. "They've got Wayne and Buddy. They're taking them somewhere a couple hours from here." And he filled his brother in on the rest.

In some ways it was more difficult to shadow the truck during the day, and in some ways it was easier. But using the same process as the night before, they managed to follow Lisa and her companion to their destination.

They knew they'd arrived at the destination when they caught a glimpse through the trees of a massive solid metal fence. Theo hopped out of the truck and climbed up the nearest, tallest tree to see what he could find.

Holy shit.

"It looks like the Black Gate of Mordor would have looked if they'd had electricity and our technology," Theo told his brother when he got back to the ground.

"Instead of magic, you mean?" Lou replied dryly.

Theo ignored him. "We can't do anything in the daylight, but I'm betting it'll be a piece of cake for two fucking computer geniuses like us to disarm whatever they have for security. I saw cameras and electric wiring across the top, but I doubt there's much more. Why would they need it? I haven't seen a sign of any settlements or people in the last three days. There's no one around."

"Could you see anything else behind the wall?"

"It's sheer metal; I can't see through it. There's a main door where the truck went through and a smaller one to the side. I'm betting that's the one we want."

"Okay, then. Let's see about taking out a couple of the cameras in the mean time." Lou hefted the rifle Theo had acquired.

After a short time, the truck left through the gate again. Lou and Theo looked at each other. "I could stay here and you could follow them," Theo suggested. "Wouldn't you like to know where they're meeting Seattle? And see what happens to Ian Marck?"

Lou nodded. He looked tempted. "Could you tell if Wayne and Buddy were in the truck?"

Theo shook his head. "Windows tinted. Couldn't tell. But my guess is no. They said they were dropping them off."

"Then let's stay here and wait for nightfall. I don't give a shit what happens to Marck. I want to get those kids back home," Lou said. "And in the meantime, I'm going to get a temporary NAP set up and get us into the network—pretty sure we're in range from here—and message back to, uh, Sage and let her know what's up."

They looked at each other and nodded in agreement.

Remy opened her eyes. For a moment, she didn't move.

Something felt wrong.

Ian was there behind her, his arm locked around her waist as he spooned her. That was the way they'd slept every night since he told her he knew who she was. They slept in their clothes, and tonight they happened to be on the roof of the truck because there weren't any secure buildings nearby.

"It's either this," he'd murmured in her ear the very first night as he settled behind her, "or I've got a pair of handcuffs. Your choice. But," he'd said, shifting his hips nearer to her, "I have the feeling you'll prefer this." His hand had moved to cover her breast and his mouth went to her neck, slowly and sensually along that tender line of skin and tendon.

Sometimes they made love first—not that she thought of it as making love. It was sex. Pure, hot, businesslike, but yet toe-curling, liquid-heat, sex. And every time, he seemed to be at war within himself even as he made her body come alive.

And now every time, he made sure he didn't finish inside her.

"The last thing I want is you pregnant," he said once, even though she hadn't asked.

Dantès had accepted the change in their relationship with unexpected ease. Maybe it was because Remy muffled any sounds of pleasure or release—purely out of spite to Ian, who hardly seemed to get out of breath himself. She didn't want him to know how much she enjoyed it.

But she knew he did. It was there in his eyes, amid the self-loathing and the banked violence.

He hadn't said anything to Remy about her grand-father, beyond the fact that he knew who she was. Nor had he told anyone else. He meant to keep it a secret, she supposed, until such time as he would act on it—however that would be. Selling her off. Exchanging her for something valuable. Giving her to the Elite.

If she didn't escape from him first.

And if he noticed the silver-wrapped crystal she wore at her navel, he didn't seem to realize its significance. He'd never even touched it, let alone commented on it.

Now, though, as she lay there, having just sunk into sleep on the thick blanket atop the metal roof, she real-ized something had awakened her in the early night.

Ian hadn't moved. His lean, strong body lined her from the top of her head to her feet, warming her from behind. His breathing hadn't changed. Not one lanky muscle had twitched.

Remy tried to relax. If there was something amiss, he would react before she even noticed it. He had an animalistic sense about that sort of thing; she ought to know, because he'd kept her from sneaking off to free-dom twice in the last week.

Her eyes were just sinking closed again, her breath-ing evening out, when an explosion splintered the night.

Ian was on his feet, rolling off the truck in an in-stant, swearing under his breath. Yanking her down with him, he had a gun in his hand before she was even sliding off. She landed on the ground with a terrific jolt. "Come on," he said, pulling her in his wake. Toward the explosion.

If Remy had thought this would be her chance for escape, she was disappointed. His grip was iron clad, and he towed her through the underbrush with no care for her lighter weight and shorter legs. She called for Dantès, and Ian whirled around and told her to shut up as he dragged her on.

The forest of trees and the random jut of brick foundations from long-lost houses made their trek rough and painful. Her legs banged into trunks and concrete, and branches whipped back into her face and arms.

He was ahead of her, and that was why, when four shadows leapt out of the dark, he caught the brunt of it. The next thing she knew, she was torn from his grip as three of the shadows pulled him away and bore him to the ground.

She didn't have any time to react before Seattle, who was the fourth shadow, lunged toward her and caught her around her torso. Fighting and kicking, she tried to scratch herself free as the sounds of fists pummeling flesh and the grunts of pain and effort came from the melee.

"Come on," shouted Seattle. "Throw him over! It's a forty-foot drop."

He began to drag Remy away, clamping a hand over her mouth when she tried to whistle for Dantès—who hadn't appeared since the explosion. She turned back and saw the other three lifting a limp figure, and then, before her eyes, they lifted him, heaved, and tossed him out into nothingness.

"There we go," Seattle said, his face close to hers. He smiled, his flattened teeth gleaming in the moonlight. "Now we don't have to worry about a mess, do we? How about showing me where you were camping. I'm sure Marck left behind at least something useful. Besides you, of course."

Everything had happened so quickly that Remy

could hardly believe that Ian was gone. Dead, or on his way to being so.

Dantès was missing; that hurt her heart too much, so she didn't think about that.

And she was now in the possession of Seattle.

Out of the frying pan and into the fire.

The only good thing was that the fire would be a lot easier to escape than the frying pan.

Chapter 17

Selena was just walking back to the house from Frank's garden when she heard it: the purring sort of mechanical rumble that had portended nothing good, ever, in her entire life.

Her belly tightened and she adjusted the basket of green beans and tomatoes against her hip, hurrying toward the house, heart pounding.

They hadn't come here in a long time. The snoot. Not since she'd foretold one of Seattle's companion's deaths. Had it given her a false sense of security?

Yes, of course.

She looked beyond the gate and saw a single black vehicle trundling along toward the wall. She'd heard about Wayne and Buddy going missing from Yellow Mountain and she thought of the arcade upstairs, with all of its mysterious computers and games that had gotten a lot of use in the last few months. *Foolish, foolish!*

The vehicle was close to the gates now, and Frank had appeared from nowhere, shading his eyes against the sun, watching silently as well.

Neither of them moved to open the gates.

The truck stopped and two doors opened. A man stepped out on each side, each of them tall and dark and too far away for her to clearly read their expressions.

Frank scrubbed a hand over his short bristling hair and shuffled toward the gates, moving at about a quarter of the speed he normally did. He had a rather long conversation with one of the men, who'd moved close enough that Selena could better see his face. He was good-looking enough to make her look twice, maybe in his thirties, and she didn't recognize him as any bounty hunter she'd ever seen. He didn't seem threatening, although he moved with confidence and certainty.

Frank nodded and opened the gate, and moments later the truck rolled through.

The two men got out again and she walked forward, looking at the second man. She guessed he was a little older, maybe closer to forty. More rugged than handsome, he had an air of barely restrained . . . something . . . And there was an aura of competence and power about him.

Selena moved closer, partly to give Frank support and partly out of curiosity.

"I'm Elliott," said the first man, moving directly to Selena. "A friend of Theo's. And Lou's." His blue eyes were gentle and concerned. She immediately felt comfortable with him. "I'm so sorry to hear about your son. I had hoped to get here in time to help."

Selena swallowed the big lump that had suddenly formed in her throat and managed to keep her eyes dry. "Thank you. I don't think there was anything that could have been done. But thank you. Did you come from far?"

"We came from Envy," said the other man. She turned her attention to him and immediately recognized deeply submerged grief beneath his hard eyes and a stony face. "We've been traveling for more than ten days, trying to find you. Name's Wyatt."

There was a sharp barking sound from the truck at that moment, causing Wyatt to turn back. His face softened slightly and he went over to the vehicle, opening the door to allow a huge, ferocious-looking dog to jump out. He landed and stumbled on an obviously weak leg, causing Wyatt to crouch next to him and give the animal an embrace and a good petting.

"This is Dantès," Wyatt said, that hard expression settling back on his face as he stood. "We found him in the basement of an old house the other day, not too far from here. Looked like he'd been there awhile, trapped down there. He . . . He belongs to someone we know. Is she here?"

Selena shook her head. "Not unless her name is Gloria and she's dying of cancer."

"No, her name is Remy. She's got dark hair and the most amazing blue eyes you've ever seen," Elliott replied. "Maybe early thirties? Very striking."

Selena paused and looked at him. She'd known someone named Remy. A girl, from a long time ago—maybe almost twenty years. Her grandfather had been dying, and Selena had come upon them quite by accident in a small house far away from any other settlement. She'd never forgotten that incident.

The man had been aged in appearance, and also in years. He seemed dry as an old stick, ready to blow away in the breeze, shriveled into himself in misery. His blue eyes were empty and filled with grief, and he spoke very little, but mostly not at all. His hair was white, with only a bit of gray threading through it. He clutched something in his hand and would not release it, even when the pain made his eyes roll back into his head and discomfort shuddered his body.

He was disturbing and yet pathetic in his desperation. Selena felt great weariness and angst in the man, and threading through his every breath was fear, deep-seeded fear. It was as if more than physical pain tortured him.

He was one who fought death, who held back as long as he could, fighting, fighting, crying and moaning against the inevitable. He was terrified of what was to come. And yet, she realized, he was terrified of living too.

She spent two days with him, trying to ease his way. No guides came to help him. No one gathered in the corner to draw him through. At last, he opened his cloudy eyes and asked for the girl. The silvery cloud had turned pale blue.

The teenaged girl came and sat, holding the elderly man's hand.

"It's time for me to go," he'd whispered.

"I know that, Grandfather. I love you."

"I love . . . you too." He seemed to gather up his strength and his voice became sturdier. "Take this," he said, opening his hand over hers, pressing something into it. "Keep it safe. With your life."

"What is it?"

He closed his eyes. "It's the key. You'll know what to do with it . . . when it's time."

The girl opened her hand, but Selena couldn't see what she held. "A key? I don't understand."

"Remember everything I've told you," he said. A great shudder wracked his body. It was a long moment before he spoke again. "I've done such a great wrong. So many lives. . . ." A tear trickled from his cheek and he choked, trying to catch his breath.

Selena rushed to his side as the cloud swirled faster. She covered his hand with hers, and felt the chill beneath his skin. It was time.

But he was looking at the girl, and she, with the most brilliant blue eyes Selena had ever seen, was looking back at him.

"You're . . . the only hope . . . of changing it," he whispered. "Hide yourself, Remy. Don't let them find you. Don't . . . let . . . them . . . find you."

Selena had felt his last shuddering breath as the life left his body—abruptly, harshly, shuttling dark, wrenching memories through her mind. When she looked back at the girl, determination and grief blazed in her sapphire eyes.

"Have you seen her?" the man named Wyatt asked again, yanking Selena back to the present. He was asking about Remy.

She shook her head. "No."

"Where's Theo? And Lou?" Elliott said.

An empty feeling churned in her belly. *I wish I knew.* "They went on a trip a few days ago. I'm not sure when they'll be back. But Vonnie would probably love to feed you something. You're welcome to stay here a bit."

"Right," grunted Frank, sliding into the conversation for the first time. "I've got some holes in the goddamn roof that needs mending. You two'd be better climbing up there than a damn old man like me."

"I'm going in," Theo said to Lou. "You stay here and warn me if anyone comes."

The sun had set and the last bit of light lingered in the overgrowth behind them. The bounty hunters had left hours ago and the twins had spent the last few hours systematically taking down the security system:

breaking lights, redirecting cameras, checking out how the locking system worked.

"Fuck that," Lou replied. And walked through the door they'd just opened in the Black Gate of Mordor, post-Change style.

Having no choice, Theo followed him through to the interior.

His first impression was that the inside reminded him of a high security prison. The wall enclosed a large expanse of grounds, empty of foliage and the overgrowth that was so prevalent elsewhere. In the center was a curious structure that looked like a massive pool with glass walls. A sort of aquarium type of thing with transparent sides that rose twenty feet high and had a heavy roof.

In front of it was a small building, spare and windowless, not much larger than a garage. A single Humvee was parked in front of it and there were few lights on the exterior. There was a sense of desertion about the place.

"What the hell is that?" Lou muttered, looking up at the giant aquarium as Theo came up behind him.

The light was faulty, but they could make out the gentle slosh of water near the top of the enclosed tank. And as they drew closer, Theo recognized shadows floating inside the water. Dozens, perhaps hundreds of large shadows suspended, unmoving, packed into the pool.

They'd hacked into the security system by cutting into an external wire and integrating their computer into the network. Then they'd reset the interior cameras to show old footage of the grounds, the video looping over and over—which gave them the freedom to move about outside. The windowless building added to their boldness, as well as the single Humvee. There couldn't be that many people in there; and based on the simplicity of the security system, Theo didn't have any great fear of other barriers.

"Let's take a look," Theo said, moving closer to the tank, eyes focused on the walls rearing above him.

But just then, they heard a noise and ducked into the shadows—the only shadow, which was from the tank itself. As they watched, a door opened at the rear of the garagelike building and a man came out.

"I'm guessing that's Ballard," Theo whispered. "But don't quote me on it."

They watched as he approached the tank, and for the first time Theo noticed a door at the ground. No, that wasn't a door. It was an elevator.

Ballard went into the elevator and it rose alongside the tank to the very top. He came out and stood on a platform near the roof and knelt to look down into the water. Using a long pole to stir up the shadows as large as he was, the man spent a long time looking down into the tank.

"Should we go inside?" Lou whispered, gesturing to the building, which could very well be empty at this time.

Theo nodded, but he was still watching Ballard, who'd stood and was moving toward the wall of his catwalk. He remained there, looking out over the tank. A low rumbling sound broke the silence—and as Theo watched, a large cranelike arm appeared, rising over the top of the tank.

Something inside him began to feel very uncomfortable as he saw the arm plunge into the water as Ballard, who seemed to be controlling it from the side, waited. The crane went into the tank, not unlike those claw games from fifty years ago, where you tried to pull a stuffed animal out and drop it into a chute.

And that was exactly what happened. The mechanized arm dove, grasped one of the shadowy figures, and pulled it up and out of the substance, which wasn't water because it oozed and plopped off in globs. Theo went cold as he at last saw what it carried. Then the crane dropped its burden into a hole in the corner of the tank. A chute.

"Holy fucking shit," Lou said, before Theo could catch his breath and assimilate what he'd seen. "Was that a *body*?"

"Yes," Theo whispered, staring at the tank. "My God, it's all people in there!"

"There could be a thousand bodies in there. Are they dead?"

"I can't tell," Theo replied, trying to unfreeze his brain. He had an awful, deep-down feeling that he knew what was going on here. His stomach tightened into a horrible knot. *I hope they're dead.* But he'd seen the jerky wave of an arm as the body was moved, and he was afraid his hope was in vain.

The crane was moving again, and as they watched in stunned silence, it plucked another body from the translucent muck and dropped it down the chute. And another. And another.

"That's ten," Lou said unnecessarily as the crane at last returned to its original position.

"Let's go," Theo said, grabbing his brother's slender arm and tugging him toward the building. "Before he comes back down."

Skirting the bottom of the tank, they moved silently over to the back of the building. Theo eyed the top of the elevator shaft to see when Ballard was starting his return trip. When the elevator started down, he dashed from the tank to the building's door, knowing that the angle of Ballard's descent would hide their flight.

The door opened easily, and he ducked inside, Lou on his heels.

They found themselves in a large, sterile room, lit with bright white lights. A single door loomed on the opposite wall, but other than that, the room was open and sparse. *Nowhere to hide* was his first thought as Theo closed the door.

Operating tables with open restraints lined the space and Theo found himself growing more numb by the minute. Smaller tables, just as cold and metallic, stood near one of the walls. They were lined with large hypodermic-style needles and a dish containing a substance that looked like clear jelly. Next to it was a padded tray that held tiny orange gems.

They were just bigger than coarse-ground salt—tiny crystals that glittered in the bright lights.

"Theo," Lou whispered from across the room, drawing his attention.

He went over and saw what had put the hushed horror in his brother's voice. A long four-foot-walled channel ran along the edge of the room and through the wall. Inside it floated human bodies.

"Good God," he said.

Lou was just about to reach into the gelatinous substance when Theo snatched his hand back.

"We don't know what that is. Better not fucking touch it," Theo told him, staring down at the bodies.

They were clothed in what appeared to be normal attire. Hair floated like seaweed around them, the hems of their shirts drifted. From what Theo could see, the skin of the victims was pale, not necessarily gray. Only one of the three who'd come through the opening in the wall faced upward, and her—it was definitely a woman—eyes were open.

As Theo looked down at her, she blinked and her mouth moved.

"Holy God," he whispered, realizing she was *looking at him*. "She's alive."

Just then, the sound of a clank alerted them to Ballard's return. With one mind, Theo and Lou dashed across the room toward the other door. Like the other, the door opened easily—there seemed to be no cause for extra security once inside the main walls—and Theo slipped through, dragging the slower Lou with him.

They barely had time to look around the new space and determine there was no immediate threat, then close the door, before the opposite one opened.

Now they were in a short corridor lined with three doors—one at the opposite end, and one on each side of the hall. No need to speak; they read each other's minds and each of them approached a door on one side of the hall, first listening and then cracking it open in an effort to find a place to hide in case Ballard came through.

"Hell, Theo, get over here," Lou hissed as Theo peered around the door he'd chosen. It appeared to be a bedroom with a small kitchenette; obviously Ballard's living quarters.

Aware of the noise of human movement coming from the operating room, Theo closed the bedroom door and joined Lou on the other side of the hall. His brother shoved him through and followed him in.

"Holy shit," Theo breathed staring at the man-sized tubes that hung on the wall. There were a dozen of them, and they looked like massive test tubes. Inside three of them were bodies, suspended in a bluish-tinged liquid.

He recognized two of them: Wayne and Buddy.

"What the hell are we going to do now?" Lou asked, approaching one of the tubes.

"Are they still alive?" Theo asked, walking up to the one holding Wayne and saw that at the top of the tube was a little pipe that extended into the liquid.

Wayne's eyes were open, and his face and hands moved sluggishly as he seemed to notice Theo. Terror blazed in his eyes and he jerked once in the small space, like a fish trying to escape a net. "God, they're alive."

"What do you think is in the tube? They seem to be able to breathe whatever it is," Lou was saying. Now he was moving a stool over to climb up and look into the top of the container.

"I don't know. How're we going to get them out of there?"

Lou shook his head. "We could break the tubes, but with what? And whatever that stuff is could be toxic or dangerous, spilling all over the floor."

"We've got to—"

Theo snapped his mouth shut and they stilled. Another sound had caught their attention, coming closer. The slam of a door. The ringing of footsteps, drawing near.

Again, they thought as one, each darting behind an empty tube in the shadowiest corner. Wedged between the tube and the wall, Theo looked over at his brother. For being seventy-eight years old, the guy was moving as well as he was. But that didn't mean he could keep it up.

Which was why Theo wasn't going to do anything reckless. Lou's safety was of paramount importance. They had to get out of there without being seen.

So he watched through the tube, his vision warped

by the blue liquid, as Ballard entered the room. This was the first time he'd seen the man close enough to observe the details of his face. The man wore a white lab coat in the biggest cliché ever, and he had dark, white-streaked hair. Approximately fifty years old, he looked vaguely familiar to Theo. Ballard walked up to Wayne's bottle and looked in, tapping the glass as if to measure the man's response.

"Good for you," he said, speaking to him, then going over to Buddy, whose movements were more lethargic than his redheaded companion. "You're looking a little upset there, sir, but we'll soon remedy that," Ballard said with a little chuckle. And then he shifted to the third and final tube. "Very well," he said to himself— or the room at large—as he turned away.

Theo held his breath, hoping that Ballard wouldn't look closely enough at the other tubes that he must know were empty to notice him and Lou. The man walked over to the wall where he paused at a panel of buttons on a low counter. *Click, click, click* . . . He pushed three of them.

And then, as bubbles began to rise in the three occupied tubes, he turned and walked out of the room. Whistling the *Jeopardy* song.

Theo waited until the door shut behind him before emerging from his hiding place, then he dashed over to Wayne. The bubbles were coming fast and thick and Wayne's eyes had widened, his mouth open in a silent scream.

The liquid in the tubes churned and swirled angrily and Theo ran over to the panel . . . but before he could determine which buttons to push, a loud *swoosh*—like the sound of a toilet flush—filled the room.

He spun just in time to see Wayne disappear down

in a vortex of bubbles, and then another *swoosh!* And then a third one.

"Holy shit," he moaned, running to the tubes as Buddy and the other person dropped through the bottom and were sucked into the ether.

"What do you want to bet they're on their way to that big tank," Lou said, standing next to him.

"Fuck," Theo groaned softly, slapping his hand against the tube in defeat. He tried to look down into it, but there was nothing to see.

"We've got to do something about Ballard," Lou said, pulling his brother away. "I don't know what he's going to do in that operating room, but we've got to stop him."

"He's making fucking *gangas*," Theo said, putting into words what he'd suspected from the very beginning, when he saw the bodies suspended in the pool. "The guy is a zombie Frankenstein."

"Did you recognize him?" Lou asked as they started toward the door.

Theo stopped. "What? Ballard, you mean?"

Lou nodded. "Yeah. You didn't recognize him?"

"No."

"Lester Ballard," Lou said, his hand on the doorknob.

"Holy fucking crap," he said for about the tenth time that day. "Dr. Lester Ballard?"

"Yep. He's got to be wearing a crystal under that white lab coat, because he looks the same as he did fifty years ago. I recognized him from the picture on the cover of *Time* magazine."

"The guy who used stem cells to cure MS in ten different people. Sonofadamnedbitch." Another member of the Cult of Atlantis. Which meant that he was going to be an extra pain in the ass to kill, because the only way to do it was to cut out the immortalizing crystal that kept an Elite alive.

"Let's go," Theo said grimly, noting that the rifle Lou had been carrying wasn't going to do shit for them against Ballard. "Let's get out of here and figure out what to do."

Lou shook his head, looking at him through his square glasses. "No way, Theo. I know what you're thinking—you're not going to take any risks with your old grandpa here. Well, that's bullshit. The longer we delay, the more damage this quack is going to do."

"Don't be stupid," Theo began, but Lou's arm shot out and shoved him in the chest, slamming him into the wall before he realized what had happened.

"If you don't make a plan with me right now, I'm going to walk out of here and walk my ass plain as day into that room and do what needs to be done. I'm tired of being relegated to the computers and the safe room. If anyone is going to risk their life, it should be me—I'm practically in the grave myself."

"Jesus, Lou—" Theo began, shoving his brother's hand away.

"I'm going." Lou started to open the door.

"Actually, I was going to say," Theo began, catching the door but resisting the urge to slam it shut, "that might not be a bad idea, much as I hate it. You walk in there, honestly, he's not going to find you much of a threat. Maybe you can distract him and I'll come in through the outside door behind him. I'm guessing I can get there through that door." He gestured to the one at the end of the hall.

Lou's face relaxed. "I like it. I'll do my best to get him talking and keep him facing away from the door. You come in behind and we'll go from there."

"But you have to do something to make him think you're alone. Otherwise—"

"Christ, Theo, do you think I've lost my brains with my ripped muscles? I've got it," Lou said. "Get going. Give me ten minutes."

Theo hesitated, then nodded. "All right. It's your funeral, bro," he said lightly, even though his stomach was still in knots. "Ten minutes, and I'm in. And by the way," he added as he started toward the door, "what ripped muscles?"

Adrenaline spiked through Lou as he approached the door to the operating room. He had the rifle Theo had taken from the bounty hunters' truck slung over his shoulder, and little else to protect himself—except his wits.

He decided on the bold approach; and after giving Theo a few minutes to get outside, Lou opened the door and walked into the operating room.

Ballard didn't seem to notice him at first because he was using a pulley and sling to drag the woman in the channel out of the goop. She hung there for a moment, her legs and arms moving sluggishly at first, and then with greater agitation as the slick matter fell from her skin.

"Now, now," Ballard told her. "You're going to be just fine. Take it easy, my dear. Take it easy." He shifted the pulley and maneuvered the woman over to one of the tables. Dropping her onto it, he moved quickly and attached one of her legs before he slid the sling from her body.

"Tell me," he said conversationally, "would you like to know how long you've been under suspension? That state of . . . being in limbo."

She didn't seem to have enough strength to fight him, and Lou watched in horrified fascination as Ballard restricted her other leg and torso on the long table.

"How long I've . . ." she said.

"According to my records," Ballard replied, his back still to Lou, "you've been suspended—my term, you know—since June fifteenth, two thousand ten. That's more than fifty years. Can you believe it? And not one gray hair." He gave a gentle laugh. "If only you didn't have to swim in that horrible gel."

"What?" the woman gasped. "What are you talking about?" She started coughing, hard, and Ballard looked up from where he was affixing her wrist, concern on his face.

"Oh dear, already?" He made a facetious *tsking* sound. "That was quick. Well, we'd best work quickly. I don't fancy having to dig another of your companions out tonight."

The woman managed to get her coughing spell under control, and she asked, "What are you—" Her voice broke and she started coughing again, racking and arching under her restraints as she tried to catch her breath.

"My dear," Ballard said, sounding annoyed, "this is not going well. You're going to need to stop that if you want me to continue. Perhaps if you calmed down a bit, we could chat, you could tell me about what you used to do . . . and then we can—"

"You're a long way from stem cell research, aren't you, Ballard?" Lou said, unable to wait any longer.

The doctor spun and paused when he saw the old man standing there. "Who the hell are you?" He had a pistol in his hand before Lou could blink.

"I remember your picture from when it was on

Time," Lou said casually. "But I never thought I'd meet you in real life. I figured you'd died with everyone else back during the hell of two thousand ten."

"Who are you?" Ballard asked again, and he cocked the gun.

"It's not important. But I'm quite curious about what you're doing here. It doesn't look like you're taking the Hippocratic oath very seriously, Lester."

"Put your gun over there, and move slowly and carefully to that wall." Ballard didn't seem to be interested in conversation—at least with Lou. "You're interrupting a very important process and I don't have time to waste."

Lou moved slowly to place the gun where directed, relieved that the position Ballard pointed him to was on the wall opposite where Theo would appear. If he could keep him distracted, Theo would have the opportunity to slip in behind.

Gun. He thought the message hard and sharp to his twin as he took his place near the wall. The gun still aimed at him with a steady hand, Ballard approached and clipped a wrist restraint over Lou. Meanwhile, the woman had been coughing and choking more violently, causing Ballard to keep looking over at her.

"I'll deal with you in a minute," he told Lou, hurrying back to the woman. "This is not going well."

"What are you doing?" Lou asked. "Reviving her?"

Ballard had moved over to the table with the utensils on it and rested his pistol there, well on the other side and out of Lou's reach. "In a manner of speaking. They don't usually react this strongly so quickly after being retrieved. She must be of weak constitution. But . . ." His voice trailed off as he became engrossed in selecting a huge hypodermic needle from the line-up on the end of the table near Lou.

Theo. Hurry up!

"Now, my dear," Ballard said, projecting his voice toward the woman, "if you would just calm yourself—perhaps answer a few questions—then you wouldn't be in such distress. Can you remember what it was you used to do before this all happened?"

Lou watched as the doctor moved with spare efficiency: testing the needle, priming it with the liquid in the small dish, and then carefully selecting one of the orange crystals and inserting it into the needle's cannula, where it floated in the liquid inside. *Oh, that can't be good.*

The crystal glowed and the doctor turned back to his patient, who seemed to have begun to wither and wrinkle as time went on. The whole process reminded Lou of a sea creature being removed from the ocean and shrinking and drying up . . . trying to breathe, gasping for air.

"What are you doing?" he asked again, at the same time as he thought *Theo!*

The fact that neither of them answered gave Lou a bad, bad feeling.

The woman seemed to have tried to respond to the doctor's last question, but her answer came out more like a gasp or sigh than anything else.

"What was that?" the physician leaned closer in an attempt to hear. "A teacher? Is that— No? An officer? Oh, a *police* officer. I see." He moved toward the top of the woman's head and palpated the crown of her skull with his thumb as she tried to shift and struggle in the restraints. "That's too bad," he murmured, holding the

needle up and eyeing it, and then with a studied movement, as Lou watched in silent horror, he shoved the
four-inch needle into the woman's skull and pushed the
plunger home.

She screamed and writhed, coughing and choking,
her eyes wide with torture. Lou flew into action, struggling at his own binding, trying to find a way to unlatch
the cuff around his wrist.

"My God, what are you doing to her?" he demanded
as Ballard removed the needle, smiling in approval.

"Watch," the doctor replied.

As if Lou could turn his eyes away.

Just then, the door behind Ballard cracked open.
Thank God. What the hell took you so long?

You said ten minutes.

*That was the longest fucking ten minutes I've ever
lived through.* Lou kept his eyes away from the door.

Theo slipped through the opening, silent as a cat,
and Lou saw his attention go to the woman on the table.
He shifted, purposely clanking his restraint, so that his
brother would see that he was limited in range and mobility. But . . . his eyes lit on the table next to him. He
might be able to reach one or two of the needles.

They didn't need to meet eyes; the mental bond was
there. Lou knew when Theo was ready to move, and he
prepared himself.

They both went into action at the same time: Theo
leaping from behind, something long and flexible in his
hands, and Lou kicking out with his foot toward the
table. He hooked it and yanked it toward him as Theo
lunged toward the doctor, slipping the hose around his
neck from behind.

Taken completely by surprise, as he'd been engrossed
in watching his patient, Ballard dropped the needle and

reached up to grab at the tube cutting into his throat. Lou scrambled, trying to reach for something on the rocking table as it spilled needles and crystals all over the floor.

Ballard was shrieking silently and ineffectively, and Theo was doing his best to swing him around by the neck and keep him off balance. The Elite were super-humanly strong, as well as being immortal, and Lou knew his brother was going to have to rely on momentum and surprise to best him.

He managed to snag two needles, bending to scoop them up. *My God, these are fucking huge.* It was like shoving a straw into someone's brain. Lou glanced at the victim on the table and saw that her skin had begun to turn gray . . . and she seemed to be changing. Stretching, growing, elongating.

God in heaven.

Theo looked at Lou and swung the doctor hard to the side, crashing his head into the wall, and then using the momentum to whip around and do it again. They were working their way toward Lou and he knew what he'd have to do.

Scalpel. He looked at the instruments all over the floor and spotted one of the surgical knives. It was . . . just . . . in . . . reach . . .

He knelt, aware of the flailing, kicking feet of his brother and the man he was trying to subdue, managed to avoid a shoe in the face but got one in the arm, and grabbed the scalpel.

"'Bout time," Theo grunted, and shoved the man toward Lou.

With his free hand, Lou grabbed the white lab coat, trying to determine which side the crystal was on.

Ballard had slowed, his struggles getting weaker, his

breath wheezing. *Too bad being strangled won't kill him*—A leg whipped out and caught at Lou, who nearly dropped the knife.

"Fuck," Theo muttered between clenched teeth. "Hurry the fuck . . . up!"

Lou grasped the scalpel and yanked again at the lab coat as Theo swung the guy around once more. The flash of a glow caught his eye and he knew where to go.

With a cry of effort, he sliced down with the scalpel, dragging it through fabric and skin.

Theo felt Ballard jerk as Lou's knife finally sliced into him. He held on to the tubing around the doctor's throat, trying not to be distracted by the woman on the table, who seemed to be writhing and fighting off some sort of demon.

Three more times he had to swing the doctor around in front of Lou, who stabbed at each go around. His arms screamed with tension and effort, fighting against the strong, agile man. Finally, the physician's knees gave out and he slumped to the floor. Theo followed him, tearing away the cut-up coat and shirt and finding the crystal embedded in his skin, just below the collarbone.

It was hanging by a thread, like a fucking loose tooth, and he yanked it free.

Ballard screamed as the tube around his neck came undone and the crystal was pulled from where it was rooted in his muscles, skin, throughout. Long tentacles came with the pale blue gem, and Theo stumbled back, holding it in his hand, collapsing on the floor in exhaustion.

His arms trembled, aching from holding the bastard for so long. The crystal felt warm, and it was slick with blood and mucus; long tendrils that looked like delicate fiber-optic cables trailed from it.

Ballard gave one last heave, and his eyes went blank. And then, as Lou and Theo watched, he began to shrivel into himself, as if drying under the sun like a grape into a raisin. Soon, there was nothing left but skin and bones—dry, brittle, brown, and old.

Theo scrambled to his feet, remembering the woman on the table, and gave her his attention for the first time.

He stared down at the creature—no longer a woman—strapped to the table. Her eyes glowed orange, her mouth was open with rotted teeth, and flesh sagged everywhere as if her body had swollen and grown, stretching and splitting her skin.

"God," he murmured, reaching for the first time to touch the flesh of a *ganga. This isn't Mordor. This is Isengard, where the monsters are created.*

The monster—no, she was a woman—jolted and arched and began to groan and sigh. And as Theo looked down, their eyes met. A jolt of recognition flashed through him, for, deep inside them, beyond the orange light, he saw her. He saw the woman; he saw comprehension. He saw fear and confusion and desperation.

He saw life.

And all at once, his knees felt weak and both darkness and light swarmed through him—and comprehension and realization awakened.

Now I understand.

He looked over at Lou, who was still holding the bloody scalpel, staring at the woman with the same stricken expression Theo knew he had.

Ah, Selena. Theo closed his eyes. *I need you.*

CHAPTER 18

Selena was just closing Gloria's eyes after the last vestiges of bluish-gray cloud disappeared when she heard voices coming from the kitchen.

One voice in particular.

Her heart skipped a beat and she forced herself not to leap up, not to whirl around, in case she was wrong. But inside, her stomach was filled with fluttering wings and now her heart was slamming in her chest like a young girl hearing her first boyfriend's voice.

Theo.

She busied herself, doing what needed to be done for Gloria: covering her with a plain linen cloth after arranging her hands, saying a short prayer over her body, and standing as she drew the curtains of the carrel around her.

And only then did she allow herself to walk, slow . . . slower, back to the kitchen.

They were all there, filling up the space with the presence of their powerful bodies: Wyatt, Elliott, Lou, and Theo. Three heads of varying shades of dark, and one silvery one. Vonnie, too, of course, bustling around as if she'd just been given the greatest gift ever. Her cheeks were pink and her eyes bright.

But Selena only had eyes for Theo.

He looked good. *So good.* Young—especially in the company of the other men—and *really* good. Her mouth wanted to water, but it was too nervously dry. The shine of his jet-black hair, all tufted as it tended to do, and the smooth curve of his biceps beneath the rolled-up sleeve of his shirt made the rest of her just as warm and tingly from a distance as it had up close.

His eyes met hers as she came into view, and it was like a shock of awareness shuttling through her. *Oh God, I've missed you.*

But she kept her face passive, especially in light of the sober expressions on the faces of the men, who were talking as they stood around and ate. "Hi," she said, feeling awkward walking into her own kitchen. "You're back." *Gee, what an observation.* She felt her cheeks flush.

How was it that he was able to make her forget herself so easily?

"Selena," Theo said, his dark hooded eyes searching her face. "I—we—need your help." His expression . . . there was something reserved there, lurking in his eyes. Something hesitant and empty.

As if something terrible had happened.

"What is it?" she asked, tensing. *Was someone dying?*

"We need your crystal. Will you come?"

"Yes," she said, and the prickling on her shoulders told her that this wasn't merely as simple an agreement as it sounded. She realized she didn't know where or what or why, but she had no hesitation about going with him. Even if it meant bringing her crystal and facing the zombies again.

She was just so glad he was here. And he'd asked.

"Thank you," he said. Then he looked at the others. "The sooner the better."

"But you just got here," Vonnie replied, her gaze

casting over everyone as if terrified that she'd lose her diners so soon after their serendipitous arrival.

"I could stay," Lou offered. "I already saved Theo's life once yesterday. I figure it's Wyatt's turn this time."

Theo snorted and a brief smile quirked his lips. "What was it you were saying about ripped muscles, bro?"

"In the immortal words of Buffy: Bite me. All I'm saying is, that was the longest fucking ten minutes I've ever lived through," Lou shot back, leaning against the counter as he adjusted his glasses. "I think your watch was slow and it was more like twenty."

"That settles it," Wyatt said suddenly, standing straight up, clearly taking charge. "Lou stays—sorry, Vonnie—and we're heading back to— What did you call it?"

"Isengard. Didn't you ever see *Lord of the Rings*?" Theo said. "Isengard's where they birthed the Orcs— pulled them right out of the muddy bowels of the earth. That's what this place is: where they make zombies."

Selena stilled and met Theo's eyes around Wyatt's shoulder. That's why they needed her crystal. A little fear seized her deep inside. *What do they need me to do? Will I be able to do it?*

She didn't know; really didn't know.

"Can you be ready in five minutes?" Wyatt asked.

"Five minutes?" Selena gulped. "Yes, I guess." She turned to rush out of the room, realizing she had no idea how long she was going to be gone.

Selena hadn't taken the crystal out of its box since Sam died, and now she found herself running through the house to get it. She passed through the ward where only one patient lingered, and stopped—wondered if she was doing the right thing. She could be gone for a week, even longer . . . and who would be here for Sally? She was nearly ready to pass.

"I'll take care of her," Vonnie said from behind her. "You need to go with Theo."

Selena turned and saw worry in Vonnie's eyes. "I'll be all right; he'll take care of me."

"Come back safely. All of you. All three of you," Vonnie murmured, drawing Selena close for an embrace.

And Selena realized at that moment that she'd never been separated from Vonnie for more than a day or two . . . ever.

"Go on. I'll be fine, we'll take care of Sally, Frank and me. And that Lou guy. Theo needs your help, and I think you need him too."

Selena nodded. *I think so too.*

In retrospect, Theo wasn't certain that it had been the best idea for all four of them, plus Dantès, to ride in the same Humvee—but it made sense to leave one for Lou in case he had to get somewhere fast.

At least if he and Selena had been riding alone, they might have been able to talk.

Not that he knew what he'd say.

He could have insisted on driving, instead of Wyatt, who'd claimed the privilege simply because he'd been in Iraq in the marines, and commandeered a fire truck on a regular basis—or at least, he had before the Change.

Theo glanced at Selena as they jounced along in the backseat, noted her pert nose, the full thrust of her lips, and the long golden length of her arm. Not to mention the curves of that nicely proportioned, insomnia-inducing body.

Did she still see a berserker warrior, a bloodthirsty

killer, a man who thrived on violence when she looked at him? Was that why, although she met his gaze, there seemed to be a reserve there?

There was nothing in her expression or demeanor to indicate that she'd forgotten her revulsion for him and his actions—and the tension between them rose and fell, as choppy as the primitive terrain.

He tried to make conversation with her in between giving Wyatt directions—and he succeeded. He learned that she only had one patient now, and that Frank's cacao trees seemed to be surviving. The brittleness he'd noted before he and Lou had left seemed to have eased.

But she didn't smile as much as she used to. And the peacefulness and serenity that had so attracted him from the first seemed dull and diluted from what he remembered.

She'd changed.

Or maybe he had.

Yes, I definitely have.

So when they at last approached the looming walls in the truck, he felt a wave of apprehension chill him. He glanced at a tight-faced Selena, hoping everything would be all right when this was all done.

Selena looked down at the struggling figure linked to a long table in a very brightly lit room.

The creature's gray skin sagged and tore, and her orange eyes glowed with desperation and hunger. The face was long and rubbery and empty, with jowls that had sagged beneath her eyes, sunk deeply into her cheeks, and were hanging down around the chin and jaw. Holes and wrinkles in the foul-smelling skin exposed the white of bone, and the black muscle and tendon beneath the flesh. What might have once been thick glossy hair was now thin and brittle and gray. Lips were nonexistent. Clothing hung in shreds from a body that bulged around the ankle and the wrist cuffs that held her—it was a woman—to the table.

Oh my God, was all Selena could think. Despite her experience with zombies, she'd never seen one in this capacity: closely, and in the light where all of the details were clear. She had to blink to keep back tears. *How does this happen?*

"We didn't know what to do with it—her," Theo said, standing next to Selena. "I thought you could help."

At that moment, she wasn't thinking about the horrifying creatures of night, the ones who'd dragged her son into pieces. Those monsters were far removed from this pitiful being, strapped and confined, and desperate.

Her crystal glowed hot against her skin and she pulled it from behind her shirt, heart racing. This was easy, simple. There was no threat to her, no danger. No night.

"Let her up," Selena said to Theo, moving closer. She reached for the woman's rotting hand as soon as he'd freed the wrist and the hulking body shifted and moved, lurching as it tried to rise into a sitting position.

He refused to release the creature's legs, but it was enough. Selena touched the woman's hand and felt the grainy, flaky skin against hers, and closed her own fingers around the crystal. As she looked into the woman's eyes, seeking that last bit of humanity beyond the guttural moans that sounded like nothing, they connected for a moment. She saw deep into the burning orange, into the fear and angst buried inside.

Then a jolt of energy slugged through her, and Selena took in the memories from the woman as the last bit of energy died from those orange eyes. The horrible creature slumped and sagged, and then fell back onto the table with a heavy jolt.

Selena turned to Theo. "She's gone."

He nodded, and reached for her hand. "Thank you."

And that was when it truly hit her: that he'd waited for her to help the creature. Instead of killing her himself. Instead of doing the sort of blind, violent execution she'd witnessed.

Shaking a little, she looked around the room. Wyatt and Elliott had done nothing but stand there, watching in silent horror.

"Theo," Wyatt said now, pointing to a long channel behind him. "What's this?"

Theo glanced at Selena and brought her over to it. She gasped when she saw two people floating in some liquid that looked like thick, sluggish water.

"Ballard took her"—he gestured to the dead zombie—"from here. She was just like them until he took her out and injected something into her brain. A crystal and some other fluid . . . Over there, Elliott." He pointed toward a table with a finger that shook. "And then she turned into that. Right before our eyes."

The other three gaped, revulsion and horror branding their faces. "Just like that?" Selena asked.

Theo nodded. "The most horrible part about it was that he was talking to her all through it, after he took her out of that . . . stuff. She was still alive, still aware of what was happening. She even answered—or tried to—questions from him. And from what he said"—Theo swallowed audibly, his handsome face twisting into something old and haggard—"she'd been kept that way, in that stuff, for fifty years."

Selena clapped her hand over her mouth as she stared

at the two figures, but she wasn't able to keep her belly from tightening and purging. She barely found a can before she lost the contents of her stomach. When she looked up, she saw that the others were just as horrified. "My God," she whispered.

"I know," Theo said, holding her gaze. "It's completely changed how I feel about them."

"Why did you leave them in there?" Elliott asked, a note of tension and judgment in his voice as he gestured to the bodies in the channel.

Theo shook his head, his lips pressed together. "We took one of them out. They can't breathe; they can't move. They just sort of start to gasp and cough, like a fish out of water. Lou and I tried to save them, but didn't know what to do. It's like they're alive . . . but they aren't. So we put him back in until . . . until we figured out what to do."

Then Theo straightened and drew in a deep breath. "And that's not all. That big tank outside—you saw it when we came in—it's filled . . . *filled*" —his voice cracked— "with more of them. Including," he glanced at Selena, "Wayne and Buddy."

"Jesus Christ," Wyatt said, the words tight and low. His hard face had set even more, and he turned away.

"Those poor people. What the hell are we going to do about them?" Elliott asked, staring down into the channel.

Theo looked at Selena, his face weary, the silent question in his eyes.

She nodded, her mouth dry. "I'll do what I can."

CHAPTER 19

Remy opened her eyes slowly.

One of them was swollen half shut, but the other worked fine. The rest of her *hurt*. Everywhere.

The ground beneath her was cold and damp, and the only light was the smoldering fire beyond. She was under the vehicle, where Seattle had rolled her aching, limp body after he'd finished with her.

Remy shoved away the memory of his hands on her, yanking her clothing aside, spreading her legs, shoving himself inside. She'd emptied what little had been in her belly earlier, to his disgust, and all she had left was an ugly, empty scraping.

And the determination to get the hell away from him.

She couldn't move far; one hand was attached to some metallic thing by a handcuff. The *gangas* couldn't get to her there as long as she stayed under the truck, so she kept herself in the center, out of their reach. They weren't smart enough, she didn't think, to try and move the truck.

She just hoped Seattle meant to unlock the restraint before he drove off in the morning. She could live through another beating and rape, but not being dragged along beneath those huge wheels.

Things hadn't started off this badly when he'd killed Ian and took her off with him in the truck a week ago. That was how she'd lost Dantès, too. He couldn't have followed a truck, but he'd already gone missing when they drove off. Remy tried not to worry too much because Dantès *always* found her. No matter what.

And at first, Seattle had been what he must have considered to be charming and friendly. Remy had been plotting her escape from the beginning, taking care to keep her pistol hidden in the small pack she had, or in the back of her jeans. She should have left sooner, but they were with other bounty hunters and didn't want to raise suspicion. Plus, she needed time to plan.

But after three nights of her resisting his physical advances, Seattle had obviously had enough. He'd slipped over to her while she was sleeping there, in the same room as the other bounty hunters, and she'd awakened to his hand over her mouth and his leg shoving between hers. His long ringleted hair brushed her face.

"You gave it up for Marck, you'll give it up for me," he growled into her face when her eyes bolted open.

But Remy didn't sleep without her pistol, and when she reached behind her head to grab it in a pretend stretch, Seattle got the unpleasant surprise of the barrel jamming against the side of his head.

"Get off me," she hissed when he froze and she shoved his hand away. "And don't touch me again."

Seattle rolled away, but not before he fixed her with a look of loathing evident even in the dim light of night. She knew then she'd made an enemy, so she'd gotten more serious about escaping.

But the next day, as they were driving in the trucks, Seattle made a detour while the others went back to Yellow Mountain. And he took her with him, using a handcuff to keep her in the truck, and then with him later.

That was the first time he'd raped her.

The next day, she'd tried to escape by hitting him in the head with a rock when he was taking a piss near a river, her wrist cuffed to his.

He'd held her face under water long enough that the darkness came and took her away. When she came to, he hit her in the face, then yanked down her pants again.

Tonight had been the worst, which was why she'd been relegated to under the truck—to a night of discomfort and the fear of being dragged out and devoured by zombies. She preferred not to relive the other details that had led to being here. Instead, she tried not to cry, tried not to give in to the despair and fear and pain.

I have to find a way out of here. I will *find a way out of here.*

Her grandfather's voice came back to her. *You're the one. You're the only one who can change it.*

She'd never known what he meant, but she'd taken to heart his warning: *Hide yourself. Don't let them find you.* She'd lived her whole life by that mantra, never understanding why.

The irony of her predicament was that they hadn't found her—whoever "they" was. Seattle had no idea who she was. If he did . . .

Oh God.

What if I told him? And he realizes I'm the one they've been searching for?

Would that save my life?

Optimism stirred deep inside her. It might even protect her from further abuse.

But if she told him, then her secret would be over. They'd all know and they'd never stop hunting her.

Unless I killed him first.

Not that she hadn't been trying to for the last three days.

A little sob tried to work its way up from her lungs, but she didn't even have the energy for that. Her ribs hurt where Seattle had kicked her.

She shifted her handcuffed wrist under the truck, trying to get comfortable. It was dark and shadowy, but a slice of moon cast on the ground outside and gave a little illumination. Was there anything under here that she could use as a weapon? It was all metal, some of it was rusty . . .

Hope renewed, she began to feel around beneath the truck, wondering if she could break off a sharp piece of metal.

Damned if I'm going to let him win.

"You're *done*," Theo said. "Selena. You have to stop now."

The exhaustion and despair dragging her face frightened him. He'd exposed her to this; and now he had to watch her drain away, able to provide little but physical support. Talk about creating monsters . . .

"One more," she said, her voice thin, her eyes empty, dark pits. "I can't stop now." She turned to the channel, where yet another body waited to be revived and released.

Wyatt and Elliott had taken the elevator to the top of the tank and figured out how to work the machinery that slid the bodies down the chute—for there seemed to be no other more humane way to retrieve them; and Theo stayed with Selena—as she touched and released numb person after person after person from, literally, a *living* hell.

More than fifty of them in the last few hours, and he could see the toll it was taking on her.

Concern and anger spiked, and he grabbed Selena's shoulders, turning her to get her to focus on him. "I'm sorry I asked you to do this," he said. "It's too much, Selena. I don't want anything to happen to you."

"Nothing's going to happen to me," she said firmly, her eyes lighting briefly with determination, despite the whiteness of her face, the grooves near her mouth. "I'm the only one who can do this. The only one."

He nodded. "I know. But you need a rest."

"No," she said. "I have to—"

"Selena. You need a rest. It's too much." He'd seen her body shake and jolt with each person she touched, as she took on their pain or life or whatever it was she did. And he knew, clearly, that if they didn't leave this place, she'd insist on working nonstop until it was done.

Until all the people were saved.

Because that was his Selena.

"We're going back to Vonnie and Lou," he said. She opened her mouth to protest, but he overrode her. "Selena . . . these people have been here for a long time, some of them for decades . . . another week or so won't make a difference to them. But if you keep this up, it could hurt you. *Please*. We'll come back and do it little by little." He squeezed her shoulders, wanting to fold her into his arms, but not quite ready to chance that yet. "Besides that, don't you think we should rescue Vonnie and Lou from each other?"

She reluctantly agreed, and they all left the building.

As he and Lou had done previously, Theo left the security system armed and tweaked it so that it was secure from any other arrival. No one would be able to get in through the massive metal walls—which were five feet thick and topped with electrical wiring—without disarming the code.

"And since I'm a computer god," he reminded Elliott modestly, "no one's going to be able to hack through the changes I've made."

Wyatt rolled his eyes and ordered Dantès back into the vehicle, where they'd left him during their work inside the wall. Then he climbed into the driver seat next to Elliott, and Theo crawled in the back with Selena, who'd remained silent and white-faced. As they passed through the gate and drove away in the Humvee, Theo couldn't stop the niggling guilt. But he knew it was the best he could do. Selena simply didn't have the energy to work through the hundreds of bodies there without a rest.

He wasn't going to let her try. He glanced at her, and eased his fingers over to close them over her ice-cold hand. "Vonnie will be glad to see us," he said, trying to draw Selena out of her silence.

"If she and Lou haven't killed each other." Her lips formed the words softly and he could see her trying to stir herself awake.

So instead of trying to get her to talk, he slid to the seat's center and moved his arm around her, nudging her against him. She came easily, and he let her sag against his chest, the delicious, comforting smell of her hair filling his nose. He closed his eyes for a minute, breathing deeply, trying to calm the leaping in his veins.

When he opened them again, Theo happened to catch Wyatt's eyes in the rearview mirror. They were cool and emotionless, and then they slid away as Wyatt returned his attention to driving.

They went on for some time. The sun had begun

to set, and night fell—illuminated only by the faulty, downcast headlights. Suddenly, Wyatt snarled out a curse, jerking the wheel. The truck jolted and jounced into what felt like a crater from hell, and then nothing. Dantès whined, sniffing at the air.

"Fuck," Wyatt said, out of the vehicle before anyone else had recovered. "Sonofabitch," came his voice from outside. "Tire's gone."

Theo extricated himself from Selena, who'd awakened and was blinking the sleep from her eyes, and climbed out to check out the situation.

"I'll change the tire," Wyatt said grimly. "We could eat too. I could use one of those sandwiches anyway. I think we've still got at least twenty miles, maybe more."

"I'll give you a hand, Earp," Elliott said, and gave Theo a meaningful look that said, *Do what you have to do.*

"Do you need to . . . uh . . . go into the woods?" Theo asked Selena when he noticed she was looking around as she drank from a jug Vonnie had packed them.

She gave a little smile for the first time since he'd returned. "Yes, please."

That smile, weak as it was, went a long way in making him feel optimistic about things.

"I'll go with you." He grabbed a large stick and lit the end of it. "I hear a creek or stream that way. I don't know about you, but I could use a wash up too."

He followed her into the woods and washed up downstream while she did what she had to do. He heard her splash into the creek; and when she came back toward him on shore, he saw that her face was damp and shiny.

And beautiful. So beautiful and serene.

She stumbled over a root or something, brushing against him, and he caught her arm. He would never know if she'd done it on purpose, but it was enough of an excuse. This was the first bit of privacy they'd had. *Thank you, Elliott.*

"Selena," he said, turning to face her. He still held the torch and drew it closer so that she could see. "I'm sorry."

"Sorry for what?" She made no move to pull away and return to the camp, and he was grateful for that.

"For just showing up and expecting you to come and . . . do what you did. Especially knowing how you felt about me." He tried to find her gaze in the flickering torchlight, but it was difficult, for the shadows. He swallowed, feeling a heavy ache in the pit of his stomach.

"Oh, Theo . . . I've been so confused. I haven't been able to figure out very much of anything in the last few weeks. What to do, what my calling is—and, why, *why* all this had to happen." Her words roughened, but she pressed on. "But when I heard your voice . . . from the kitchen . . . I was *so glad* you were back. It felt like everything inside me started to move again. But at the same time, I was frightened that you'd just come to . . . to get your things and leave."

Warmth and relief blossomed. That explained the removed look on her face. "I've missed you. *So much.*" At last, he reached to touch her cheek, dying to feel the weight of that thick, heavy hair. "And it's only been a bit more than a week." He managed to find her gaze then, and held it in the flickering light. "I don't ever want to leave. Again."

"I don't want you to."

Thank God. "I was afraid that you'd never let me near you again, after . . . what happened with the zombies. That you'd be disgusted by me."

He shook his head, then dropped his hand away. "Selena . . . you were right. You *are* right," he said. "They're alive. And I'm sorry that it had to take me that horrible experience at Ballard's lab to believe you. To accept what you've been trying to tell me."

A little shiny trail had started down her cheek and she hooked a finger into his belt loop, her thumb rubbing against his belly. "It took me that experience today to truly understand it, in my heart too." She closed her eyes briefly. "I questioned it, even though I'd believed for so long. And after what they did to Sammy . . ."

Theo nodded. "Selena. Any mother would feel the same way."

"But they didn't know what they were doing, and I *knew* that. But I couldn't let my anger go. I had to keep it and stew on it, and let it churn around inside me. And it nearly drove you away."

"You would have needed to try a lot harder to really drive me away, Selena. I'm in love with you, if you haven't figured that out by now. I'm not ever going to leave you."

Her face brightened into a glorious smile. "Theo . . ."

He wanted to drag her up against him and fill his senses with her, but there were still other things to be said. He looked around for a place to put the torch, then shoved its end into the ground so he could have two hands free.

But before he could speak, she looked at him, focusing her gaze on his. "Are you finally going to kiss me?"

Well, maybe those other things could wait. "If you'll let me." He felt his lips move in a crooked smile.

"Give it a shot, kiddo." She gave him a bigger smile and he moved in.

It was like the heat of summer after a long, chilly winter, gathering her into his arms, covering her lips with his. Warm and familiar, tasting of the sweetness of Vonnie's tea and of Selena herself. Theo couldn't hold back a sigh of pleasure. *Mine.*

Things were just getting interesting—his hands were finding the swells of smooth, warm skin and his jeans were overly tight in the crotch—when they heard a shout, followed by a scream, terrified and desperate. Definitely human.

They sprang apart and Theo started off, dragging Selena after him, toward the sound which could be as far as a mile away. Heading back toward their camp, he rushed through the night, gripping her hand tightly.

The scream muffled and choked, and suddenly, Theo heard the sound of a dog barking. It was a whining sort of horrified bark and then there was the crazy thrashing through the underbrush, through the ruins and the forest as the dog—presumably Dantès—bolted off into the night.

The dog cut in front of Theo and Selena, and then moments behind him were Wyatt and Elliott tearing into the dark, trying to keep up with him.

Theo tore after them, Selena stumbling along behind. He heard the sound of a vehicle engine and the frantic barking from Dantès. Shouts and a scream, and suddenly they came upon the scene.

He didn't waste time saying or thinking *What the hell?*—he just took it all in at once and, releasing Selena's arm, ran over to help. By the time he got there, Wyatt was whipping a man from the front seat of a Humvee and Dantès was barking and whining and scrambling at something beneath it.

* * *

Remy thought she was dreaming when she heard Dantès' barking.

The truck roared to life above her, and she frantically, weakly, tried to grab something to hold on to, to pull herself up from the ground.

Seattle had come back out from wherever he had gone, and when he tried to drag her from beneath, she'd greeted him with the sharp, rusted edge of a slice of metal. Stabbing at him from under the truck, unwilling to suffer at his hands again—or to be left out in full view for the zombies.

He'd managed a few solid kicks at her, and she'd gotten him in the arm or maybe even the face with the metal . . . but that was the end of that. He stumbled back and climbed into the truck above her just as something burst from the darkness.

The engine roared to life just as a dog—it was Dantès—barreled up and launched himself toward the truck. She felt the vehicle jolt from the force of the dog's body slamming into the door. Weak and terrified, and beneath the vehicle, Remy didn't see exactly what was happening, but suddenly she heard footsteps running. The engine revved and she braced herself as it lurched forward, dragging her across several feet of ground. Agony scraped down her back and thighs, bare from loose, shifting clothing, from the sharp, hard rocks and rubble beneath. Her battered body screamed and ached as she fought to keep away from the massive wheels rolling so close to her.

There was a shout and a loud thump, and she wasn't sure what happened next, but the truck jolted to a stop. The door opened, feet were there next to her and there was a grunt and a strangled shout. The next thing she knew, Seattle was tumbling to the ground far beyond the truck.

Dantès was on him before the man stopped rolling, and Seattle's high-pitched, terrorized scream was cut off as the dog lunged for his throat. And then there was ugly silence filled only by the crunch of bone and gurgling beneath Dantès's fangs.

Remy tried to call out—*can anyone see me under here?*—but her voice was rough and weak and it came out only as a little wavering thing. She could hardly move.

Suddenly, a dark figure crouched next to her legs, which angled partway out from beneath the truck.

"Mother-*fuck*," he said, and began to pull her ankles gently out from beneath.

Remy was dimly aware of other figures coming into view, but she couldn't see much other than pairs of legs and feet. The man helping her had to bend down half beneath the truck to reach the metal thing to which she was cuffed, and the sucked-in, sharp intake of breath bespoke his disgust and fury for her predicament.

At last, the cuff was freed, though still around her wrist, and he was helping her to her feet. Remy's knees wouldn't hold her, and she sagged, lightheaded and trembling, as he pulled her out and helped her upright. Her vision darkened and spun, and she couldn't focus. She felt cool air on her skin where it shouldn't be, and dampness and pain. . . . everywhere.

"Jesus Christ," he said, his voice tense and urgent. "Elliott!"

Remy tried to stand, but she found herself clutching her rescuer and the metal edge of the truck door as another figure separated from the wavering shadows and approached quickly. Her back ached from being dragged only that short bit across the ground, scraped and cut and battered from the other assaults. Her jeans sagged from where Seattle had left them loose, and left her hips bare and scraped. Her stomach rebelled and she grabbed at someone's warm arm as she puked nothing but bile, retching painfully from the depths of her belly.

When she opened her eyes and raised her head, she found herself looking at a familiar face—the man she'd thrown a snake at in order to escape him. *"You,"* she gasped, her knees all weak again. "Dick . . ." She tried to form coherent thoughts, but everything fled except the man with the stony face who kept her from falling.

"Good God, it's *you*," he said, his lips flat and his face blank as he focused on her face. "Christ, Elliott," he said, "look at her." She faded in and out, still clutching the solid arm of the man she'd dubbed Dick Head.

The night spun and she could hardly move her mouth; her lips were cracked and busted and she felt damp spreading from somewhere on her back. Gentle hands touched her, and she tried not to flinch, tried to relax as they eased her onto a softish surface inside the truck.

She heard things like "shock" and "assault" and realized they were referring to her. There was a lot of short, sharp cursing, and firm, capable hands as they examined her without making her feel violated or frightened.

"Dan . . . tès," she whispered.

"He's here," said Dick, who was near her head, looming large in the closeness of the truck. "He took care of Seattle."

Seattle. She tensed, a wave of nausea flooding her as the memories came like the pounding of fists. She realized she was trembling and shuddering, and then someone—*his name is Elliott?*—was leaning over her to look into her eyes.

"Listen to me. Listen. Seattle is dead. He can't hurt you anymore. He's dead," he said.

Remy tried to smile, tried to believe him. She shifted, attempting to nod her head, but the world wavered and the next thing she knew, she slid into wobbly darkness.

By the time Selena caught up to the rest of her companions, everything was over. Theo met her as she approached and said, "Don't look over there."

Of course, she tried to, and he firmly turned her away. "Don't you ever listen? There's a dead man over there, and it's not pretty."

"Zombies?" she asked, still trying to look.

Theo shook his head, lips tight. "No, dog. It's—*was*—Seattle. Dantès got him. Turns out he took exception to the guy beating the shit out of his mistress."

All at once, something clicked in her mind. "Where is she?" But she already knew, and started toward the truck where Elliott stood.

Despite her grimy, busted-up face and the fact that she was almost twenty years older, Selena was sure the woman was the same girl she remembered. A flash of something whipped through her mind, and she paused, trying to catch it . . . but she couldn't.

She just knew it was ugly and dark, and it had to do with the girl's grandfather. And perhaps she didn't want to remember anyway.

"Is she going to be all right?" she asked, looking at Elliott.

He nodded soberly. "Yes. But she'll need time to heal."

"We'll drive her back to Vonnie and Lou now," Wyatt said. "We can fix the other truck later." He glanced over at the heap of bloody skin and bones that was, apparently, Seattle. "Where the hell's a zombie when you fucking need one?"

CHAPTER 20

"So," Theo said as he helped Selena climb onto the Ferris wheel. "I need to talk to you about something. It's about Lou."

They'd returned with the woman named Remington Truth late last night, and much of today had been spent seeing to her comfort and filling Lou in on the events of the day. Theo had been in the arcade, working on his idea with the pinball machines and helping his brother update Sage via electronic messaging. Theo hadn't had a chance to talk to Selena alone—or to do anything else—since returning.

But after dinner tonight, Selena had suggested a walk. The night was perfect for an amusement park ride: the moon was showing a large chunk of herself, the stars—as they always were now, fifty years after the factory and vehicular emissions were eliminated—sparkled bright and plentiful.

Yet, despite the romantic atmosphere, and the hot-eyed looks Selena had been giving him at dinner, Theo wondered how this conversation would go, on many levels. After all, if Lou hadn't come looking for Theo and been surprised by the zombies, would Sam have been safe? It wouldn't surprise him if Lou's very presence represented nothing more than a dark, terrible time to Selena.

"He seems like a really nice guy. I don't think Vonnie

likes him too much," she said with a little laugh, patting the seat next to her. "But I like him."

That made Theo feel a little better, and he slid in next to her.

"I'm not sure what happened between the two of them," he said. "All of a sudden, he started calling her 'that Vonnie lady' and she started practically slamming his plate down in front of him at dinner."

"I suspect it has to do with her role as matriarch being challenged," Selena said. "She's always been the motherly sort, and everyone lets her. Even Frank. He allows her to mother him, then he does whatever he wants anyway. But Lou doesn't let her fuss over him; and, in fact, I heard him telling her how to cook something a while ago, before you left. She didn't take too kindly to that."

Theo chuckled. "No, the kitchen is her domain. They must just rub each other the wrong way." He reached over and caught Selena's hand, smoothing his thumb over her knuckles as he started up the ride. How was he going to explain this?

"So how do you know Lou? How did he find you here, anyway?"

Theo felt the little lift as the wheel shifted into motion. "So, well, that's what I needed to tell you. I've been saying all along that I'm older than I look, right? And I told you about the little metal circuit that got embedded in my skin, and changed me. Well, the thing is," he said, then paused, trying to remember when or if he'd ever told anyone this before.

In fifty years, he didn't think he ever had.

"The thing is, that underground explosion happened during the Change." The last words came out in a rush.

He waited a beat, waited for her comprehension to dawn. "So . . ." she said uncertainly.

"So, the thing is . . . Lou is my brother. My *twin* brother."

Her face went through a series of expressions: disbelief, shock, confusion, and back around again. "So you're saying you're . . ." She shook her head.

"I was born in nineteen eighty-four. I'm actually seventy-eight years old. And something happened that severely slowed my aging process down—practically stopped it for decades, in fact." He waited.

She nodded, slowly, very slowly. "That's crazy."

"Tell me about it."

"But that would explain a lot of things," she said.

"I hoped it would."

"So I've been sleeping with a man who's thirty years *older* than I am?"

Theo nodded.

She was gaping at him. "So you're saying that, all that time I thought you were pity kissing me because you felt sorry for this old lady, *I* was really doing the pity kissing? Making an old man feel young again?"

"Um, yeah. I guess you could look at it that way." He wasn't certain if she was dead serious or if a little bit of humor had crept into her voice. He was pretty sure it was the latter . . . "But I have to say, those pity kisses of yours . . . they were the best any kind of kisses I've ever had. You're pretty good at it, for a youngster."

She was eyeballing him from her corner on the Ferris wheel car, the gentle breeze of descent lifting delicate wisps of her hair . . . and tickling the inside of his belly.

"You let me worry about that for all that time and you never told me?"

He lifted her foot and settled it on his lap, sliding his hands over the smooth—*such smooth*—soft skin. "I told you I was older than I looked. More than once."

She let her head tilt back as he began to use the pad of his thumb to make firm circles on the bottom of her foot. The soft little moan of pleasure had all sorts of interest spiking through him, but he kept his hands on that silky skin over the top, massaging and stroking gently.

"I knew there was something different about you," she said, lifting her head so she could look at him. "But, wow."

He'd need to tell her about the Resistance, and the role he and Lou played with the plans to build a network—both electronic as well as of people—to stand up against the Elite . . .

. . . But there'd be time for that later. Right now, he had other thoughts on his mind.

And, from the way she was looking at him, so did she. "I think I'm getting the better end of the deal," she said contemplatively, sliding her foot from his grip and letting it slip along the hair of his bare leg to rest on the floor. "You've got a bang body and stamina like you're thirty, but you've got the experience and patience of a seventy-year-old man. That can only be good for me." Her smile was wicked and sly.

He shifted closer, his hands finding their way beneath her shirt. "I certainly intend for it to be the case." He covered her mouth with a kiss, long and sleek and hungry. *Finally.*

"I love you," Selena said, moments later as his feet settled on the pile of clothes on the floor of the Ferris wheel car. "You're such a perfect fit for me, Theo."

The waft of night breeze brushed his bare skin, and he took a moment to admire the way the light from that chunk of moon silvered her golden body, outlining pert, tight nipples and perfect teardrop breasts. She stood boldly in front of him there in the small box, and he skimmed his hands along from breast to waist to hips, then tugged her forward and down.

Settling her on his lap, straddling her onto his hips, Theo eased her down to join with him. The car tipped a little, rocking and adding to the pleasure as he directed her up and down with those long, patient strokes that she tended to like. The car around them swung harder, too, echoing the rhythm of their movements.

"Well," she said a little while later, when their warm, damp bodies separated and the rhythmic rocking had eased. The ride slowed back into the slow, easy sway of the rise and fall, and she continued, "That's one thing I'm not going to ask *why* about. You and how you came to be here, and how you came to be just who you are . . . and why I got so damned lucky."

He shrugged and smoothed back the hair that had plastered to her face. "I could ask the same question. It's taken me almost eighty years to find a woman who can understand that things are not always what they seem. That all the layers of life aren't simple or neat." The breeze brushed over their naked skin and he gently cupped her bare breast, just because he could.

Right here, on a damned Ferris wheel. Under the moon.

"I guess," she said, coming closer to his mouth again, "there's never any answer to why. No matter how often or how desperately you ask, there's no answer—there's only what you do with it." And she reached her hand between them to curl around his already refilling erection, smiling against his lips. "And I know exactly what I'm going to do with this."

EPILOGUE

"I think we should be able to try out our idea tonight," Lou said, settling at the counter in the kitchen. It was the morning after the fairies' wheel ride when Theo had told Selena about their relationship.

She found herself searching for resemblance in the wildly different countenances of the twin brothers, separated by decades of aging. Nevertheless, it was definitely there: in the hooded, Asian eyes, and the mannerisms, and even the way they cocked their heads when they were thinking. Not to mention the way they seemed to read each other's mind.

Selena winced as Vonnie slammed a plate down in front of Lou with a little more force than necessary. Scrambled eggs bounced off onto the counter. She caught Theo's eye and raised her brows, then returned to the conversation. "Which idea is that?"

"Damn, that looks good," said Wyatt, greedily eyeing the plate of scrambled eggs and sliced tomatoes that Vonnie rested gently in front of him.

"Needs more salt," Lou announced.

Selena bolted up to get the jar of sea salt before Vonnie could throw it at him. *What the hell is wrong with them?*

"We've been working on reprogramming some of those pinball machines and video games so that the lights will hypnotize the zombies . . . sort of slow them down and confuse them so we can manage them better," Theo said, also trying to keep the peace. "Make things easier for you. We'll be moving them down to a corner of the grounds tonight to give it a try."

"I want to know who's going to tell Zoë that she can't hunt zombies anymore," Elliott said, buttering toast. "Or at least, not the way she's been doing it."

Lou chuckled. "Quent's going to put the kibosh on that for a different reason as soon as he finds out she's pregnant."

The physician's eyes widened. "Well, that's going to be interesting."

Selena didn't understand why everyone laughed, but she figured Theo would fill her in later. In the meantime, she said, "And how's Remy?"

"She's going to be all right. That bastard—" Elliott shook his head, his voice low and tight. "If Dantès hadn't taken care of him, I would have done the honors."

"If she's to be believed, Ian Marck's also dead," Wyatt added.

"Why wouldn't you believe her?" Selena asked, cutting herself a slice of pineapple.

"After a gal's shot at you, you tend to take everything she says with a grain of salt," Wyatt said flatly.

"Not to mention tossed you a snake," Theo commented.

"Yeah, that too. Christ, don't piss her off, Elliott, whatever you do. Who knows what she'll do next."

Selena watched them, following their conversation with interest. A fascinating group, to say the least.

The back door slammed and in stalked Frank. "Goddammit, what the hell is taking so long? I've been up for hours, waiting for you all to get your asses moving out there. The roof's gotta be patched, and it's better off to have your damned asses up there than my old white one. Rainy season's coming and we don't want those goddamn computers of yours getting wet."

He muttered and stomped, and Wyatt, who seemed to have thawed a bit in the old man's presence, stood and swallowed the last bit of his tea. "Let's go," he said to Elliott and Theo. "The sooner we get this done, the sooner Elliott and I can get back to Envy."

"I'll bring some breakfast to Remy," Selena said, grabbing a piece of cheese. "And then I'll be sitting with Sally for a little bit. She's hung on longer than I thought."

"I'm going to work in the arcade," Lou said. Then he looked over at Vonnie and said, much too casually, "Did you say something about moving a bookshelf?"

Next month, don't miss these exciting new love stories only from Avon Books

Hunger Untamed   by Pamela Palmer
For a thousand years, Kougar, a Feral Warrior, believed his lover, Ariana, Queen of the Ilinas, to be dead. So when Kougar discovers Ariana's betrayal, he must overcome his rage in order to save them from approaching evil. But the biggest danger of all could be the love they once shared.

What I Did For a Duke   by Julie Anne Long
Reeling with rage after Ian Eversea crosses him, Alexander Moncrieffe, the Duke of Falconbridge, decides to avenge the wrong-doing by seducing Eversea's sister, Genevieve. Will his plan be sweet revenge or will lust have something else in store?

One Night Is Never Enough   by Anne Mallory
In order to quench his thirst for Charlotte Chatsworth, the object of his infatuation, Roman Merrick engages the girl's father in a wager for one night with his daughter. Though Charlotte is devastated by the bet, the result of their tryst will leave them both gambling for their hearts.

Seducing the Governess   by Margo Maguire
Hoping for a fresh start from her cold and sheltered upbringing, Mercy Franklin takes a governess position in a far-off manor. But when a passionate kiss with her employer, Nash Farris, melts both of their hearts, they are torn between what's right…and what feels even better.

At Avon Books, we know your passion for romance—once you finish one of our novels, you find yourself wanting more.

May we tempt you with . . .

- **Excerpts** from our upcoming releases.
- Entertaining **extras**, including authors' personal photo albums and book lists.
- Behind-the-scenes **scoop** on your favorite characters and series.
- **Sweepstakes** for the chance to win free books, romantic getaways, and other fun prizes.
- Writing **tips** from our authors and editors.
- **Blog** with our authors and find out why they love to write romance.
- **Exclusive content** that's not contained within the pages of our novels.

Join us at
www.avonbooks.com

AVON

3 2953 01095629 2

An Imprint of HarperCollins*Publishers*
www.avonromance.com

Available wherever books are sold or please call 1-800-331-3761 to order.

FTH 0708